FIGHTING Solitude

ON THE ROPES
BOOK THREE

ALY MARTINEZ

FIGHTING SOLITUDE
Copyright © 2016 Aly Martinez

Cover by Ashbee Designs
Editor: Mickey Reed.
Photography by FuriousFotog
Cover Model: Alex InkFit
Formatting: Champagne Formats

ISBN-13: 978-1523635184
ISBN-10: 1523635185

DEDICATION

Daddy,
Thank you for forcing me to watch Rocky at least once a week for most of my childhood. The Page brothers wouldn't be here without you.
I love you.
P.S. Rocky IV will always be my favorite.

FIGHTING
Solitude

PROLOGUE

"MIA!" I SHOUTED.

It was worthless. She'd been deaf since the day I'd met her.

She'd never once heard my voice.

She'd never heard the deep rumble of my laugh when she was excited, signing so fast I could barely keep up.

She'd never heard my content sigh when she barged into the locker room after a fight—just her presence soothed the lingering madness brewing within me.

She'd never heard me whispering my deepest fears into her ear as she fell asleep on top of me.

She'd never heard the reverence in which I cried her name each and every time I took her body.

And she'd never once heard the ease in which the words *I love you* tumbled from my lips as I stared into her deep, jade-green eyes.

But, as I screamed her name while watching her petite body seizing in the passenger's seat beside me, I'd never needed her to *hear* me more.

"Mia. Oh God. I've got you, baby."

She was still thrashing violently as I made my way around to her door and yanked it open while pleading with whichever god was willing to help.

When she stilled, a whole new level of silence filled the air around us. It wasn't the absence of sound.

It was the absence of *life*.

"Mia, breathe!" I roared as her chest remained agonizingly still. "Help me!" I screamed at the closed emergency room doors, but no medical savior rushed out with the miracle I so desperately needed.

My hands shook wildly as I released her lifeless body from the seat belt.

"I've got you. Just hang on. Please just hang on, baby," I whispered, lifting her into my arms and sprinting through the sliding doors. "I need a doctor! She's not breathing!"

Nurses rushed toward me in slow motion as the seconds without air in her lungs passed at a terrifying speed.

Breathe.

A doctor appeared with a gurney and quickly took her from my arms.

The immediate loss was staggering.

Hope became my only solace.

She needed help I wasn't capable of giving her, but that didn't stop me from following close behind as they rolled her away. I was on the verge of self-destructing; letting her out of my sight wasn't an option.

I stood motionless in the doorway while doctors and nurses swarmed around her. Their mouths moved frantically, but without my hearing aids, I was worthless, unable to make out the words their faint voices carried.

I never wore my hearing aids when I was with Mia. There was no point. She rarely spoke with her voice.

We'd spent four years building a relationship with our hands.

Those hands had told me animated stories that had made me laugh until my face hurt from smiling.

They'd fought with me relentlessly, but they'd always ended the night raking down my back in silent ecstasy.

Her fingers had fluidly signed *I love you* more times than I could ever count—or forget.

But, as I felt the nurse attempting to physically remove me from the room, my eyes became fixated on her limp hand dangling off the side of the bed. It was the only sight more frightening than watching her flail mid-seizure.

It ripped the heart straight from my chest.

That hand was supposed to be full of life.

It was the very essence of Mia.

Pale.

White.

Still.

Oh, God.

After sucking in a deep breath, I held it until the room began to spin.

It provided me no relief even as it forced me to my knees.

There would be no distraction from this.

I was going to lose her.

Yet another woman I couldn't save.

CHAPTER
One

Liv

I MET QUARRY PAGE IN the back alley behind On The Ropes boxing gym. He saved my life. Well, more accurately, he saved me from a life sentence in prison for killing two twelve-year-old boys who thought picking on me was a good idea.

"Let me go!" the boy shouted, only seconds away from tears.

I squeezed my arm even tighter around his neck. "Take it back!"

"Dude… Get…her off me," he grunted to his friend.

His buddy wasn't about to jump in though. I'd already dropped him to the ground with a kick to the crotch. So, like a good little wimp, he watched with huge eyes, justly terrified as I clung to his friend's back and threatened to choke the life out of him.

All of this could have been avoided if they hadn't acted like idiots. I had been minding my own business, reading a book on my iPad with my headphones blaring, when they'd stumbled upon me.

I was sure I'd looked like an easy target for them to unleash some childhood cruelty on.

They couldn't have been more wrong.

Sure, I was a little girl who loved all things purple, makeup, and high heels, but that didn't mean I wasn't tough as nails. When you grow up with a druggie birth mother, you quickly realize that the world doesn't owe you anything. The random guys parading in and out of my house sure as hell didn't. If I was lucky, they left me the hell alone. If I wasn't... Well, anyway.

It wasn't until my mother overdosed on heroin a few years earlier that my father entered the picture, allowing me to breathe easy for the first time in my young life. He had money. A nice house. A warm bed. A stocked fridge. And, because he was the owner of Guardian Protection Agency, our security system was unrivaled. We were always surrounded by his men. They were part of my family too—and the reason I knew how to defend myself in the first place. Insecurity and fear should have been a thing of the past for me. But experiences like mine didn't leave a person easily, no matter how old they were. So, when those two boys snatched my iPad and began throwing rocks at me as I scrambled to get it back, I lost my mind.

And then they lost their pride at the hands of a nine-year-old girl.

"Take it back!" I screamed again as he painfully banged me against the brick wall.

My grip faltered, which allowed him enough time to flip my small body over his shoulder and fling me to the hard ground. At the last second, I caught him and dragged him down with me.

"What the hell is wrong with you?" the boy heaved as I attempted to regain my hold on his neck.

It was worthless. While I'd caught him off guard the first time, he was way bigger than I was and used that to his advantage. His body quickly covered mine as I fought underneath him.

"Get your hands off me, butt face!" I shouted.

Suddenly, he was gone, and I don't mean he let me go. I mean, one second, he was on top of me and, the next, he was flying away from me as if I had finally been able to harness The Force.

"Who the hell are you?" the boy, still cupping his balls, shouted.

Before I even had a chance to see who the question was aimed at, a pair of unforgettable hazel eyes leaned over me.

"Are you okay?"

I was nine. Boys were disgusting. They were even worse than snips and snails and puppy-dog tails.

But not this one.

This one was beautiful, and my normal sass evaded me as my mouth dried out.

I stared up at him from the ground for entirely too long.

With a wicked dimple denting his cheek, he tilted his head in question, causing his straight, black hair to hang in his eyes. "Did you swallow your tongue? I just heard you screaming, so I know you can talk. Are you okay?"

I nodded, still unable to find my voice. After pushing myself off the ground, I dusted dirt off the back of my purple dress, which I'd paired with adorable, sparkly leggings.

"You bitch!" the punk I'd almost killed yelled, rubbing his neck.

The hazel eyes I couldn't stop staring at never left mine, even as his jaw twitched from the boy's curse.

"Are you a bitch?" he asked calmly.

I shook my head and the most spectacular lopsided grin formed on his lips.

"I didn't think so." Spinning, he grabbed the boy's throat and swept his leg out from under him. Hazel Eyes crashed to the ground, pinning him. "What the fuck did you call her, dickhead?" He mercilessly grabbed his throat as the boy fought under his grip.

I wasn't sure how old my hero was, but I figured he had to have been at least fourteen. He was a giant compared to both of the wusses who had been picking on me.

Blue Balls made a tight circle around them, unsure whether to jump in and help his pal or not.

I made his decision for him when I shook my head and leveled him with a pointed glare.

His eyes nervously flashed between his friend and me. "She attacked *us*!" he yelled, slowly backing toward the door.

"I did not! You threw a rock at me first."

"You kicked me in the balls!" he returned.

"Yep. Want another go?" I took a giant step toward him.

"Judging by the fact that you're scared of a girl half your size, I'm not sure you had any balls to begin with," my nameless hero sniped.

I smiled proudly, turning to him. My stomach fluttered when my gaze met his. His murderous expression softened as he blinked at me with thick, black lashes.

We both awkwardly looked away.

"Apologize," he growled at the boy still pinned to the ground.

Hazel Eyes released his neck long enough for the boy to cough a, "Sorry," in my direction.

I crossed my arms over my chest. "Make him apologize for calling me a girl, too."

He swung his head to face me. "Um. You *are* a girl," he stated incredulously.

I let out a frustrated huff and looked away to cover the heat that rushed to my cheeks.

I was completely okay with being a girl in his eyes. Those two idiots though? No way.

"Just do it!" I ordered.

Shrugging, he shook his head and then barked, "Fucking apologize."

"This is bull crap. I'm telling Slate," the boy said.

"Telling him what? That you got your ass handed to you by a"—his gaze flicked to mine—"girl you were throwing rocks at? Let me know how that works out for you."

7

"No, I'm telling on *you*. There's no fighting allowed outside the ring. He'll kick you out of the youth program if he finds out you put your hands on me."

I swear I saw the proverbial light bulb flash on above my hero's head.

"Well, seeing as this is my first day and I don't want to be here anyway, that would be awesome." He moved to the back door of the gym before yanking it open. "My name's Quarry Page. Make sure you add that so there's no confusion."

"Ugh," one of them mumbled. "You're Till's little brother."

"Yeah. But don't let that stop you. Come on. Get moving. The sooner you get in there and rat me out, the sooner I can get the hell out of here."

"I heard you were only ten," the other piped up.

"And?" Quarry asked rudely.

Ten? Holy crap!

He was huge. He definitely didn't look like any of the boys I went to school with. However, he didn't exactly act like them, either. I'd known this kid for less than five minutes and I had already heard him say at least ten cuss words. I might have dropped a "damn" or "hell" under my breath every now and again, but Quarry cussed like the words had been custom-made for his tongue.

"Now, go on. Get the hell out of here." He took a menacing step toward them, which made them both flinch.

Quarry might have wanted to get kicked out of the youth program, but that was the very last thing I wanted.

If I planned on seeing this mysterious foul-mouthed kid again— and I definitely wanted to see him again—the gym was our only connection.

After dramatically clearing my throat, I announced, "My dad is Leo James. You might want to keep your mouth shut. If I tell him you messed with me, I'm not sure either of you would survive." I shrugged as if I hadn't threatened their lives.

I absolutely had.

They let out suffering groans, knowing they were in deep trouble. Of course they knew who my dad was. As the head of security for Slate Andrews, celebrity boxer and owner of On The Ropes boxing gym, my dad was a fixture at the gym. And, judging by their ghostly faces, they also knew he would have strung them up by their fingernails if he caught wind of what they had done. The best part was that he'd never believe what I'd done to them in return.

I was an angel in his eyes. I worked hard to keep that appearance up as much as possible; it was the only way to get away with all the stuff I really did. His wife, my adoptive mother, was the only one who knew the real me. And I adored her for keeping it our little secret.

"Okay. Leave her out of it, but get in there and tattle on me. Make sure you make it sound good when you tell them how I choked you out for no reason. Toss in that you think I'm crazy! I'm counting on you two dumbasses to really sell this shit."

I cut my eyes back to the boys. "You say a single word about him and I'll tell my dad that you hurt my back on the wall."

They both grumbled.

Offended, Quarry shot back at me, "Hey! What the hell did I do to you? I'm trying to get kicked out of here."

I smiled. "I know, but then we wouldn't be able to hang out again."

"Slow down there. You're pretty and all, but if hanging out with you means cleaning the toilets as part of my required chores for being in the program? Thanks, but no fucking thanks."

My heart sped. He thought I was pretty! Well, I mean, I knew I was, but I'd never cared if a boy thought I was before.

However, suddenly, I didn't care about anything else.

I tapped on my chin, trying to figure out how to fix this. Cleaning the toilets did sound like it would suck.

"Okay. How about this…" I looked back at the losers watching our exchange. "I won't tell my dad, but you two have to take Quarry's bathroom shifts for the next six months."

"No way!" they shouted in unison.

Fisting my hands on my hips, I screamed at the top of my lungs, "Daddy!"

"Wait!" They jumped in my direction, halting when Quarry protectively stepped in front of me.

"Six months or I swear I'll tell him." I stepped around Quarry.

"This is so not fair. You were the one who got all crazy."

The boy stomped his foot just as my father's massive frame appeared in the doorway.

"Liv? ¿*Todo bien*?" (Everything okay?) he asked as his eyes flashed accusingly around the group.

"Well…" I started, holding the boy's gaze in question.

"Deal," he mumbled under his breath.

Quarry barked out a laugh, and I smiled at my victory, innocently batting my eyelashes.

"¿*Me preguntaba si mis amigos podrían ir helado con nosotros?*" (I was wondering if my new friends could come get ice cream with us?)

"Oh, baby. The boys have work to do." He arched an eyebrow. "Isn't that right, guys?"

"Yes sir," was echoed by everyone but Quarry—he was staring down at the ground, kicking rocks. One dimple revealed his hidden smile.

My dad collected my iPad and my earphones off the ground then extended his hand toward me. "See? Now, come on. You can read in Slate's office while I finish up."

I skipped over, intertwining my tiny fingers with his. "Okay. Maybe next time?"

"I'm not sure that's a good idea." His eyes once again lifted to the boys. "We need to find you some girls to hang out with."

He guided me inside the gym, but just before the door closed, I peeked over my shoulder.

"Later, Quarry."

His eyes lifted, and a wide grin covered his gorgeous face. "Later, Liv."

For the following months, I used every possible excuse to travel with my father from where we lived in Chicago to On The Ropes in Indianapolis.

Much to my surprise, Quarry never did find a way to quit the youth program. It didn't escape me that his name was never once on the board for bathroom duty. I also noted the way his eyes lit up every time I would walk into a room. I pretended to play it cool when he was around. The last thing I needed was for him to know how much I liked him.

I suspected that it was a wasted effort.

Because I knew for certain exactly how much he liked me.

CHAPTER
Two

Quarry

I HAD BEEN A FIGHTER from the day I'd taken my first breath on Earth.

Literally.

Born six weeks early to absolute losers for parents, I wasn't even guaranteed survival. Luckily, my lungs and my heart didn't need love or affection to thrive. Lord knows I never would have made it home from the hospital if that had been the case.

My childhood had gone much like my birth. I'd grown up, kicking and screaming, in a world I was much too young for. My older brothers, Till and Flint, were the only reasons I'd thrived at all. Flint was only five years older than I was, and Till six years older than he was, but they had done everything in their meager powers to keep me fed, clothed, and out of the care of Social Services.

Back then, the concept of stability had felt about as realistic as wizards and mythical beasts.

Insecurity was what I knew.

It wasn't something to fear.

It just…was.

I was the ripe old age of ten when my mom took off with her piece-of-shit boyfriend. I wished I could have been surprised that she abandoned us like that, but I'd never known Debbie Page to be anything but worthless. If possible, my dad, Clay Page, was actually worse. He was serving time in prison when she left, so the responsibility of caring for Flint and me fell entirely on Till's shoulders. Already working his ass off at three jobs to make ends meet, he also spent countless hours at the gym to fulfill his dream of becoming a professional boxer. But, Till being Till, he didn't bat an eye about taking us in.

The excitement I felt knowing that he and his now-wife, Eliza, would be taking care of us permanently was unexplainable. He gave me a comfy bed with clean sheets and more ramen noodles than I would ever be able to choke down. But, honestly, I wouldn't have given a single damn if I'd had to fall asleep hungry on a cardboard box every night. The only part I could focus on was that I finally belonged somewhere. And, even though we didn't have a dime in our pockets, each night, as the four of us sat around the dinner table laughing and relentlessly making fun of each other, it felt like the first time I actually had *something*.

It was a scary realization.

Because, for the first time in my life, I found myself with something to lose.

Cue Liv James.

Liv rocked my entire world the moment I met her. There was something about the mischievous glint in her big, brown doe eyes that spoke to me on a level a ten-year-old couldn't even begin to understand.

But, somehow, I did.

Or, at least, I desperately wanted to.

She entered my life during a brief period when all the stars had momentarily aligned.

It wasn't until it all exploded, throwing my entire world out of orbit, that I realized she was the greatest gift I'd ever been given.

After we'd met in that back alley, Liv and I became close—or as close as a fourth-grader and a fifth-grader who lived three hours apart could be. I saw her once every few weeks, and those were the best days of my life.

On the outside, we were the most unlikely of friends, but on the inside, she and I had been cut from the same cloth. Everyone knew I was trouble. I had a good heart, but I kept it buried under layers of attitude and a million curse words. I'd learned years earlier that no one could damage what they didn't know you had.

My heart became my best-kept secret.

Liv was the exact opposite. She wore her heart on her sleeve and exuded innocence. With straight, brown hair and olive-toned skin, she looked like a tiny Hispanic angel. I knew her better than that though. Liv didn't have an innocent bone in her body. That girl made my brand of trouble look amateur. And, because of that, she quickly became my best friend and partner in crime.

Together, we pulled off countless pranks at the gym. They were harmless for the most part. Normal kid-type stuff. We both found it utterly fascinating, the havoc we could wreak with a single tube of crazy glue. At the end of the day, it never failed. I always got caught and she always giggled while watching me run punishment laps around the track. I swear my cardio was on point back in those days.

Six months after I'd met Liv, my newfound happiness took a huge hit.

It was easily the worst day of my life…at that point.

"You're going deaf. Just like me," Till blurted out.

I froze with my spoon halfway to my mouth.

Tears welled in his eyes, and that alone was scary as fuck. Till was the rock in our family; he didn't break down.

Ever.

Flint immediately pushed to his feet and began pacing the room. "Oh, God."

"What?" I asked, thoroughly confused as my eyes bounced between my two older brothers, who were obviously freaking the fuck out.

I wasn't sure what to think. Those two screwed with me on a daily basis. I was the youngest of three boys—being the butt of their jokes was a way of life. I was far from gullible, but either they had stepped their game up or it wasn't a joke at all.

My heart pounded in my chest. "Wait. You're serious?"

"It's genetic, Q. You and me both have it. Flint, you tested negative," Till said, but his eyes stayed glued to me.

This little announcement had come completely out of left field. We were supposed to be sitting down for a normal family dinner, and now, all of a sudden, I was deaf?

What the fuck is going on?

I'm a man. I'm a man. I'm a man.

Men don't cry.

Except the bullshit pooling in my eyes said differently.

"Are you fucking with me?" I asked around the overwhelming emotion lodged in my throat.

Till shook his head, and he didn't even yell at me for cursing.

He wasn't fucking with me.

"It's gonna be okay. I swear to God. I'm going to make this okay," he said as if it were supposed to be reassuring.

It wasn't. Not while the word *deaf* still rang in my soon-to-be useless ears.

"When?" I choked out, fighting down any and every possible emotion. "When am I going...deaf?"

"I don't know. It's supposedly degenerative. That means it will happen over time."

Blinking, I sucked in a deep breath. "You're full of shit."

He wasn't, but I clung to whatever hope I could grasp. I had no real concept of what *deaf* meant. I knew that it meant you couldn't hear, but I couldn't wrap my young mind around the depths of that reality.

And the unknown was the scariest of all.

More insecurity I just couldn't handle.

I was beyond terrified but refused to show any weakness in front of the two men to whom I owed my life. My feet attempted to flee from the problem, even though it followed me with every step. I didn't allow Till or Flint a single glance at my devastation as I sprinted from our apartment. I didn't know where I was going, but I couldn't stop until I got there.

I raced down the stairs, and I'd barely made it to the edge of the sidewalk when I came to a screeching halt. Reality came crashing down on my shoulders.

There was nowhere else to go.

No one else who cared about me.

My entire life was in that crappy two-bedroom apartment behind me.

My lungs burned as I held my breath for an impossibly long time. I knew that, when I released it, I wouldn't be able to hold the tears back anymore. That one breath was the only thing that kept me bound together.

I dropped to my knees as my head began to spin.

Don't breathe. Don't breathe. Don't breathe.

Passing out was better than losing my shit in front of Till and Flint.

Suddenly, Eliza's voice echoed off the building. "Quarry!" Her feet pounded against the pavement as she rushed from her apartment below ours. "What's going on? Are you okay?" she asked, squatting in front of me.

I wanted to be a man, but I was failing epically.

At least it was only Eliza. I hated when she babied me. But, right then, as my vision began to tunnel and the inferno spread from my lungs to my chest, I was all too willing to put my pride aside for a single second of comfort.

With a loud exhale, I dove into her open arms. Warm streams of useless tears poured from my eyes.

"What's going on?" she whispered, holding me tight.

I wrenched my eyes shut.

Till would have to fill her in because I wasn't anywhere near ready to admit my future sentence to anyone yet.

And that included myself.

It was funny. The world didn't shut down just because I was going deaf. In some ways, I think I would have felt marginally better if it had. Instead, I woke up the next morning and went to school, to the gym, and then home. I had dinner with my brothers, and Eliza dropped off a pan of my favorite twice-baked cheese potatoes. No one discussed my breakdown from the night before, not even to make fun of me for it. But there was definitely a blanket of anxiety dampening all of our spirits. Till had attempted to cover his own nerves with jokes, but forced laughter was all he got in return. Eventually, he disappeared, presumably down to Eliza's apartment like he usually did when he thought we were asleep.

The next day went much like the first—until that afternoon when I was finally alone in the On The Ropes locker room, getting ready to spar with one of the fourteen-year-old boys who fought in my weight class. I was so lost in my own misery that I never even heard the door open. Suddenly, two small arms wrapped around my waist from behind.

"What the hell!" I jumped, but the small body clinging to me followed me forward.

Thankfully, before I threw an elbow, I glanced back and recognized Liv's long, brown hair. Her face was crushed, nose first, against my back and her hands were knotted painfully tight at my stomach.

I was crazy about Liv, but we were young. Touching was still super weird. Our relationship, up until that point, had consisted of cracking jokes and getting in trouble together. With the exception of when we were huddled together in a dark corner, waiting for Derrick Bailey to pick his super-glued jock strap up, I wasn't sure we had ever touched at all.

"Uh…Liv," I said, contorting my body to see her.

"I'm so sorry," she whispered into my back.

"For what?"

"That you're going to lose your hearing."

"What?!" I yelled jumping forward, but once again, she followed. "Who told you that?"

"I overheard my mom and dad talking. He made me swear not to mention it. So, of course, I came straight to you."

Fan-fucking-tastic.

I dropped my chin in defeat. "Would you let me go?" I bit out roughly, attempting to pry her hands away.

She was miniscule; I shouldn't have had any trouble getting her off me. But this was Liv. Even wearing a hot-pink, frilly dress and glittery boots, she still could have taken half the guys in the gym—or, at least, she wouldn't have hesitated in trying.

"No," she murmured into my back.

I groaned, dropping my hands to my sides, giving up on trying to shake her off. "I need to be in the ring. And this is the boy's locker room. You're gonna get in trouble if Slate catches you in here."

She continued to talk into my back. "Whatever. I'll just tell them you forced me in here."

"Awesome," I deadpanned.

"Are you scared?" she asked.

"Nah. I've gotten used to running laps whenever you're around."

"No. I mean…about going…deaf." She squeezed me tighter as she finished on a whisper.

"Nah. I'm fine," I lied. God, did I fucking lie. I hadn't been able to breathe properly for two full days.

Deep breath in.

Hold it until the room spins, forcing me to concentrate on any-thing but the uncertainty that consumes me.

Fast exhale out, crushing me in its wake.

"Well, I'm scared enough for both of us," she said softly.

I barked a laugh. "What the hell are you scared of? I'm the one going deaf."

"The silence."

I tried to step out of her hold again, but I made no more prog-ress than I had the first time. "What?"

Keeping her face buried in my back, she whispered, "You're my best friend, Quarry."

She was more than that for me.

I just didn't know it yet.

"What the hell are you rambling about, Liv?"

"I was stuck in the apartment after my mom died for a whole day before the cops showed up. I don't remember a lot. But it was so quiet, Q." Her body began to tremble.

I wasn't sure what to do, but instinctively, I shifted back a step, pressing her even closer to me.

"That's why I wear my headphones all the time. I can't even sleep without them." Her voice broke as she nuzzled her face against the back of my T-shirt.

Blink. Blink. Blink.

I opened my mouth to respond three different times, but not a single sound came out. What the hell was I supposed to say to that? *Sorry your life is even shittier than mine?*

After a sniffle that revealed her tears, she spared me from having to figure it out. "I don't want you to have to live like that. It's gonna be so scary, Q."

I had no response.

I didn't want to live like that, either.

But I'd survive.

What I wouldn't do was allow her to worry about me. Don't get me wrong. I fucking loved that she cared enough about me to be scared. A small part of me was actually reborn with that knowledge, but I didn't need her sympathy.

No one had ever coddled me before. *No need to start now.*

"I kinda like when it's quiet," I admitted.

"I hate it."

"News flash, Liv. You don't have to deal with it. I do. You're in the clear," I smarted and immediately felt guilty when her body stiffened behind me.

"If it happens to you, then I have to deal with it too. You watch my back, and I watch yours. It's the most important rule of being best friends."

A warmth I'd never felt before washed over me.

I was important to her.

I swallowed around the newly formed lump in my throat. "Okay, what if I promise to be really, really loud when I go deaf? Then you won't ever have to worry about it again."

"What if you just promise not to go deaf?"

Fuck, I wished I could do that. For both of us.

"I'll try."

"Okay, and while you work on that, I'll learn sign language. That way, we can still hang out if it happens. I bought a book about it on my iPad last night."

Another blast of warmth filled my chest.

I had brothers—warmth wasn't exactly their specialty.

I liked Liv. It was no secret.

But, with an overwhelming rush, I suddenly more than liked

her.

In that moment, with her arms wrapped around me and her tears staining the back of my shirt, I never wanted her to let go.

And, for that reason alone, I folded my hand over hers and made a silent vow that, no matter what, I'd never let go, either.

If that meant protecting her from the silence, I was more than up for the fight. No matter how impossible it might be.

"You watch my back, and I watch yours."

I'd do whatever it took to keep her from being afraid.

Not for me.

Not from her past.

And definitely not because of anyone else.

Never.

Finally, she released her vise grip on my waist. An unwelcome chill slid over my skin in the absence of her warmth.

Suddenly, touching wasn't so weird anymore.

It was a necessity.

I took a step away and turned to face her. Reaching out, I caught her small hand in mine, giving it a reassuring squeeze.

"I'm good. I swear." And, for the first time since Till had dropped the bomb, it wasn't a lie.

I now had a purpose.

And her name was Liv James.

She craned her head back, and her big, brown eyes bored into my soul unlike anything I'd ever felt before. They were puffy and red from her crying, but they were still mesmerizing.

And comforting.

And exactly why I had to look away.

"What the hell!" Slate boomed.

I released her hand seconds before her fist landed on my chest.

"You jerk!" she yelled at me, but her eyes never turned angry. If anything, they softened.

My gaze flashed to Slate, who looked murderous.

"This is the boys' locker room, Liv!" he barked, clearly mad to have found her in there. But probably angrier that she was in there alone—with *me*.

A devilish grin formed on her pink-glossed lips before she spun to face him. "Sorry, Uncle Slate. Quarry pushed me in the hall. I couldn't let him get away with it. You taught me better than to let a boy hurt me."

Son of a bitch!

I couldn't see her face, but I was positive she was batting her lashes. And, as she sniffled and wiped her hands under her tear-stained eyes, I knew she was milking it.

Dropping my head back, I cursed at the ceiling.

"Quarry!" he snapped, but I didn't need him to finish.

I walked toward the door. "Yeah. I got it. Six laps. I'll meet you in the ring when I'm done."

Just as I got to the door, her angelic voice called out, "Later, Q!"

Shaking my head, I responded, "Later, Liv!"

CHAPTER
Three

Liv

AS TIME PASSED, QUARRY AND I only became closer. We were best friends. And, even though we didn't get to see each other every day, it was unforgettable each time we were together.

Over the next year, Till's dream came true as he started boxing professionally. Uncle Slate was his trainer, which meant, as the head of his security, my father was on the road with the Page family more often than not. It also meant that I got to see Quarry almost every weekend. Those visits were the highlights of my week. I spent Monday through Friday at my private school in Chicago, counting down the days until I got to see those hazel eyes and that boyish smirk again.

Quarry followed through on his promise to me and tried really hard not to go deaf, and I followed through on my promise to him and learned sign language just in case. I had to quit soccer in order to make the nightly classes at the local community center, but I was okay with that. Quarry was more important, and to be honest, shin guards and grass stains clashed with everything.

When I was ten, Quarry beat the snot out of some kid at one of Till's professional boxing matches for having called me a nerd. I hadn't even heard the comment because I'd been wearing my headphones and engrossed in a book. But that didn't mean I didn't take great pleasure in watching Quarry teach that jerk a lesson. He was always there for me, even when I didn't even know I needed him to be. It was yet another layer of security my timid soul so badly needed.

A fragility only Quarry knew existed within me.

And one he protected regardless of the punishment that usually followed.

When I was eleven, I broke my arm after he'd finally given in to my constant begging and agreed to teach me how to skateboard. He'd tried to catch me as I'd fallen, but the skateboard had clocked him pretty nicely in the head when it shot out from under my feet. He never left my side as I lay crying on the sidewalk. After ordering a kid to get my mom, he rubbed a soothing hand up and down my back while whispering profuse apologies intertwined with a million curse words. Just before we left for the hospital, he brazenly climbed into the backseat beside me even after my dad had told him that he couldn't go. Quarry didn't budge though.

Burying his hands in his lap, he boldly returned my dad's stare in the review mirror and said, "No disrespect, Leo, but this is my fault. I'm going."

We all knew that it wasn't his fault, but after a quick glance at me, and at my mother's urging, my dad gave up and slowly pulled out of the parking lot.

With a black-and-blue knot on his forehead, Quarry spent four hours painting my cast to look like a zombie hand. My dad laughed and patted Quarry's shoulder as I proudly showed it off around the gym. It was badass—especially after my mom had added a purple bow around the wrist.

Later that same year, Quarry's life got even harder when his oldest brother suddenly went deaf. The whole On The Ropes family pitched in to help the boys during the initial adjustment. And that family included my mom and dad. We spent a week in Indianapolis. I hated the reason why we were there, but spending a whole week with Quarry was the equivalent of a Disney vacation for me.

Unfortunately, it didn't feel like one. During that time, I saw something in Quarry Page I'd never be able to forget: fear. Of course, he'd never admit it, but the broken innocence hidden behind those hazel eyes was devastating even to a young girl like me. My heart shattered for him.

For the present in which he was forced to watch his brother fumbling through his new life in silence.

But mostly for the future in which he'd share the same fate.

He leaned on me. Or, more accurately, he let me sit beside him while he repeatedly held his breath and pretended the world didn't exist. Quarry wasn't lying; he did like the quiet. He also liked the dark. So, with my headphones blaring in my ears and my iPad illuminated in my lap, I spent countless hours in a secluded corner, pretending tears weren't dripping off his chin. We were at least six inches apart and we never spoke a single word. But we were together all the same. My company was the only comfort Quarry would allow me to offer him.

One thing I'd learned was that Quarry hated hugs. He dodged my arms every chance he got. I, on the other hand, loved them, so I snuck them as often as I could—usually by ambushing him from behind. He'd always curse and complain, but his body would relax almost instantly, and when I would bury my face between his shoulder blades, I could feel his heart pounding in his chest. He'd stand there motionlessly until I was done and then walk away as if it hadn't happened.

But it happened.

And I had a sneaking suspicion that he gave it to me because he thought I needed it.

Which I absolutely did.

But so did he.

It's funny how much a person can grow and change in only three hundred and sixty five days. On the flip side, sometimes there aren't enough days to ever change some things.

When I was twelve, I fell in love with Quarry Page. And not the kind of love that had me doodling his name in hearts on every notebook I owned. I'm talking the kind of love that seeps into the marrow of your bones and becomes part of your very being. I didn't have daydreams of wearing a white dress and meeting him at an altar. I did, however, want to sleep every single night for the rest of my life at his side.

I discovered that magical feeling on one of my numerous trips to Indianapolis.

It was Aunt Erica's birthday, and we were in town so my parents could go to the surprise party Uncle Slate and my mom had been planning for months. Minutes before they were supposed to leave, their usual nanny called out sick. Erica was ready to cancel the whole thing and stay home, but Slate scrambled, and luckily for me, newly turned eighteen-year-old Flint Page was first on his list of replacements.

I liked Flint. He was nice enough. Boring, but still nice.

But he wasn't why I was lucky.

My night took an exciting turn when Quarry came strutting in behind his brother. His dark hair was swept to the side but still hanging in his eyes as his gaze found mine. That dimple dented his cheek as a crooked grin formed on his lips.

"Sup." He lifted his chin in my direction, acting every bit as cool as he looked in a pair of purposely tattered jeans and a T-shirt that was hopeless to hide the muscles that made him appear far older than thirteen.

I, however, wasn't cool at all.

"Q!" I squealed, bouncing on my toes.

He laughed only to quiet suddenly when my dad caught him by the back of the shirt and said, "I'm watching you, boy." It was a threat, but he said it with a smile.

Everyone knew that Q and I were close. They also knew we were only friends. My parents loved the Page boys and trusted them implicitly. Sure, Quarry got into his fair share of trouble—usually my trouble he took the wrap for. But they always knew he'd never let anything happen to me. My dad actually adored how protective he was over me. It was probably the only reason he allowed his little princess to spend so much time with a rough-around-the-edges boy.

"Yes, sir," Quarry quickly responded.

"Okay, Flint. I put a list of emergency numbers on the fridge. Ty and Adam are both asleep in Adam's room, but if they wake up, turn on the sound machine and leave the door cracked. They'll fall right back to sleep," Aunt Erica said to Flint as my mom huddled beside her.

"Oh, don't worry about Ty. He sleeps like a rock," my mom added.

"I put a sippy cup in the fridge for Riley. It's the pink one. *Not* the blue one. Just remember: She's the girl. Pink."

"I think I can handle that," he replied, flashing his eyes to Uncle Slate in a plea for backup.

"Erica, leave the boy alone. This isn't exactly his first time with the kids!" Slate shouted.

"It is with Ty and Liv too! Four kids is a lot different," she called back, never dragging her eyes off Flint. "Are you sure you can handle this? I mean, it's not too late to say no." She nervously toyed with the ends of her long, blond hair.

"It'll be no problem." He laughed. "Riley and Adam are easy, and if Ty wakes up, Liv can help me with him."

Erica smiled, but her hesitance was still obvious. Turning to my mother, she asked, "Are you sure you're okay with this, Sarah? We could always go out another night."

"She's fine with it!" my dad confirmed. "Good lord, can we please go? I'm starving."

Slate made his way over to Erica, draping his arm around her hips. "Beautiful, he's got it."

"Fine," she huffed. "Give him some money for pizza and let's go."

Slate passed Flint a fifty-dollar bill from his wallet then ushered Erica toward the door. My mom waited as the adults filed from the house. No sooner had the door clicked than she laid into us.

"You two," she said, waving a finger between Quarry and me. "*Do not* give Flint any trouble tonight. No pranks. No games. Nothing. Eat pizza, watch a movie, hang out, whatever. Just stay out of trouble."

"Yes, ma'am," Quarry answered hastily.

I nodded, but when I opened my mouth to reply, she got there first.

"I'm serious, Liv. I'm not your father. Don't think you can just bat your eyelashes at me. You get in any trouble tonight, you won't be pinning it on Quarry."

Quarry attempted to interject, but she once again got there first.

"Don't you even try to cover for her."

He promptly closed his mouth and became engrossed with his shoes.

"Jeez, Mom. Chill out. We'll be good." I smiled.

Her shoulders sagged in relief. "Okay. You have your iPad, right?"

I nodded.

"Q?" she called.

His gaze lifted to hers.

"Keep her in line."

"I always do." He smirked.

She narrowed her eyes.

"I mean…yes, ma'am."

She didn't look any more convinced, but she relented and headed out the door.

Finally alone, I turned to Quarry and punched his shoulder. "I didn't know you were coming tonight."

He shrugged. "Yeah. Flint asked me if I'd come help. Of course—"

Flint immediately cut him off. "You're so full of it. He paid me twenty bucks to bring him."

Quarry's eyes flared wide. "Dude! What the hell?"

Flint laughed as he walked away.

I grinned, because well…Quarry was there. "Best twenty bucks you ever spent," I said, bumping my shoulder against his.

"We'll see about that," he mumbled under his breath as he glared at his brother.

He was wrong. There was nothing *to see* about. We had a whole night to hang out without anyone bothering us. I'd have sledgehammered my piggy bank months earlier if I'd thought it would have bought me more time with him.

A large pepperoni pizza and a two-liter of pop later, we sat on the large leather sectional in Slate's rec room, arguing over which movie to rent. I loved a good comedy, but Quarry wanted an action flick. And, regardless of how hard I tried, I couldn't sweet-talk him into letting me have my way.

It was infuriating.

And more fun than I'd had…since the last time I had seen him.

"Give me the remote." I dove toward him, but he quickly jumped to his feet, holding it high above his head.

He was at least eight inches taller than I was, but that didn't stop me from trying to snatch it from his hand. I was jumping when my sequined flip-flop wedged under the edge of the rug, tripping me. I would have fallen completely on my face if his hand hadn't snaked out and caught me at the last second.

"See? That's what you get for wearing such girlie shoes," he teased, settling back on the couch and flipping to the action movies on Netflix.

"Well, seeing as I'm a girl, it's my God-given right to wear girlie shoes."

He laughed. "Oh, please. You're not a girl."

"Excuse me?" I gasped, clearly offended.

It wasn't lost on me that I was, in fact, a girl. I was actually a very girlie girl in some ways. But it was the way boys used the term *girl* as if it were an insult that pissed me off. But, before that moment, I had no idea that someone—especially Quarry—telling me that I *wasn't* a girl could be equally as insulting.

He must have heard the hurt in my voice, because suddenly, the remote had been discarded on the coffee table and his attention was focused solely on me. His hazel eyes looked confused as he explained, "I just mean that you aren't like other girls. You're tough and funny. They're all wimpy and helpless. I've seen you hold your own against boys double your size. *Real girls* cry when their pencils break."

Wow. A compliment *and* an insult. How does a *girl* even attempt to respond to something like that?

I punched him hard on his arm. "You're an idiot."

"See!" He smirked as he rubbed his shoulder. "What girl punches a guy like that? Like you're freaking Rocky Balboa, raised on the streets. Not in a cushy Chicago mansion. None of the girls at my school—that's for sure."

And that was the first time Quarry Page broke my heart.

There were two parts of that statement that wounded me so deeply. The first being that I'd thought Quarry liked that I was tough. I hadn't always been raised in a cushy mansion. I'd had five years of struggle under my belt, even if I did only remember a few *silent* nights of those years. That was enough. I didn't need the rest of those memories. Not when only one nearly incapacitated me on a nightly basis.

The second way was that, for the very first time ever, I felt a dose of jealousy. I wasn't stupid. I had known that Quarry had girls at his school. I'd just never thought they were any competition for me. Or, better yet, that I would ever consider someone else competition when it came to him. Quarry wasn't my boyfriend or anything. That's not how our relationship worked. However, in that moment, I kinda wished it had been like that. Maybe he'd want to hold my hand while we watched a movie. He could get a ride up to Chicago and go to my middle school formal with me. We would have had so much fun together. I didn't want him to bring me roses and mushy cards, but even thinking of him doing that with someone else suddenly burned.

I'd never thought of Quarry like that before, so as I blankly stared at him, I couldn't figure out why my mind was trudging into such uncharted waters when, honestly, I didn't even like to swim.

Yet my mind wanted an answer and went directly to my mouth to get it, bypassing my self-restraint altogether.

"Do you have a girlfriend?"

His eyebrows popped high in surprise. "Not really."

"Not really" was *not* an answer. It was an evasion.

And it made it clear that he probably did.

It also burned so badly that I was afraid the blisters would be visible on my skin.

I focused on the TV, hoping the pain didn't show on my face.

"Why? Do you have a boyfriend?"

Nope.

Not even close.

"Kinda," I replied instead.

"Seriously?"

I didn't turn to look at him. I pulled my feet under me and settled into the corner of the couch. "So, what movie are we watching?"

"Liv—"

"I'm fine with action. But it better be good. None of that sci-fi crap."

I could feel his eyes locked on me for several beats, but I refused to look at him. He was allowed to have whatever girlfriend he wanted. We were still best friends. Nothing had changed.

Though it didn't feel like that as I curled into the corner of the couch, fighting back irrational tears and feeling more like *a girl* than I ever had before.

I didn't even make it halfway through the movie before I was lulled to sleep by the loud noises of car chases and explosions.

My body shot upright as I was awoken by the most terrifying sound in the world.

Silence.

Panic built in my chest as my eyes struggled to take in my surroundings.

The room was pitch-black—not even the light from the moon peeked in. I definitely wasn't in my bedroom at home, and my groggy mind was too overwhelmed to remember where I'd fallen asleep. I just knew I needed to get the hell out of there. Tears built in my eyes as I pushed to my feet and darted to where I hoped there was a door. I hadn't made it far when my leg slammed into something, and I tumbled forward in a fight to stay on my feet. I crashed into something else just before a heavy weight fell on top of me and knocked the air from my lungs. A whole new level of fear spiraled out of control within me.

My eyes had adjusted enough for me to see the large frame of a man rushing toward me. It wasn't large enough to be my dad, but it was menacing nonetheless.

"Daddy!" I shrieked, flailing my arms and legs, frantically trying to escape whatever or whoever was restraining me in my own personal version of hell. "Stop! Don't touch me!" I screamed at the shadow of a man when he lifted me off the ground.

"It's just me, Liv. I've got you."

"Quarry?" I squeaked, relief flooding my system.

"You're okay. I won't let anything hurt you. I swear."

I immediately burst into tears, and he wrapped me tight in his arms. Front to front, he hugged me as if he were the one losing his shit—not me.

Just then, the door swung open and a flashlight illuminated the room as a symphony of children's cries filtered in. The welcome chaos was music to my ears.

"Jesus Christ, what the hell is going on? You two woke up all the kids," Flint growled.

"Hey, shut the fuck up, dickhead. She was scared."

"Oh," he replied in understanding. "You okay, Liv?"

My body shook as I dangled in Quarry's arms. I couldn't even form a coherent thought, much less an answer.

"What the fuck happened to the TV?" Quarry barked, holding me even tighter.

"The power went out," Flint replied. "I'm gonna call Slate. You two good?"

"She's fine. I've got her. You go take care of the kids."

The lights suddenly flickered on only long enough to taunt me before plunging us back into darkness. Another round of sobs overtook me. I wasn't scared of the dark. Well, not exactly. It was just that silence tended to linger in the darkness.

"I...I...n-n-n-need my headphones," I cried into Quarry's chest.

"Flint?"

"Yeah. Give me a second. I need to grab Riley first," Flint answered before disappearing along with the flashlight.

Darkness once again cloaked the room, and I scooted impossibly closer to Quarry's chest, finding the immediate relief I desperately needed.

I'm safe with him. Always.

The power flashed one last time before staying on for good.

"Holy shit," Quarry breathed as we both took in the room.

The DVD player, the Xbox, and the cable box were all knocked to the floor, and the entertainment center that had once housed them lay on its side with one door completely broken off.

"Are you hurt?" He quickly stepped away and raked his eyes over my body, searching for any sign of injury.

I wasn't, but it was then that I realized what a mess I probably looked like.

"Don't look at me." I quickly ducked behind him and buried my tear-stained face in his back.

He chuckled and pulled my arms around his waist, resting his hands on top of mine. "She's okay," he said to himself.

"I'm not okay. I look like one of those girls at your school right now." I sniffled.

"Nah. They aren't cool enough to be like my Rocky."

Suddenly, *my Rocky* didn't sound so bad.

I rubbed my face in the cotton of his tee to dry my eyes. "Thanks. Ya…know. For that," I told his back.

He didn't even have a chance to reply before I heard Flint's voice heading in our direction.

"Yeah. Everyone's fine, Slate. The kids are back in bed, and I'm just about to give Liv her iPad. We're all good." He paused, "I'm not sure I can say the same about your entertainment center, but all of the homo sapiens under the roof are alive and well. Okay, I'll ask. Hang on. Hey, Liv? You want your parents to come back?"

"Um." I seriously considered it until Quarry's hand folded securely over mine, allowing me to answer honestly. "No. I'm good."

"She says she's good. Okay. See you later." He must have hung up the phone, because he let out a loud huff. "Christ, that was pandemonium."

"Sorry," I squeaked.

Quarry's body stiffened before he corrected, "She's not sorry.

You're *not* sorry. There's nothing to be sorry about."

"Right. Well, whatever. Here's your iPad, Liv. I'm going back downstairs. I'll leave the flashlight up here in case the lights go out again."

"Thanks," Quarry replied.

Flint's voice grew distant as he shouted, "And clean up that crap before Slate gets back? Yeah?"

Quarry didn't reply. Nor did he attempt to step out of my grasp. He actually didn't move at all as I clung to his back, still trying to get myself under control. My pulse slowly returned to a non-marathon pace, but my mind wasn't nearly as fast to recover.

"You gonna let me go any time soon?" he asked.

"Not if I don't have to," I retorted.

"Then you don't have to. You want to at least put on your head-phones. Just in case?" He lifted the earbuds attached to my iPad over his shoulder.

I removed a hand from his waist only long enough to shove them in my ears. Quarry pressed play on my music and my whole body slacked as the familiar sounds washed through me.

We must have stood there for fifteen minutes before he us back toward the couch. He was amazing and handled me with absolute caution. Not prying my hands away, he patiently waited for me to take the cue and lie down. Once I'd settled, he climbed on the couch in front of me. His large body teetered on the edge, but he turned and gave me his back again. Then he snagged my arm and draped it over his waist. I could only assume it was the teenage-boy version of holding me tenderly.

But it was Quarry doing it, so it didn't take but a second for me to realize that it was the best version of all.

And it absolutely ruined me at only twelve years old.

But, then again, Quarry had ruined me long before that.

Even if I hadn't known it yet.

It should have been difficult to find sleep with as scared as I'd been when I'd woken up. But, with my headphones blaring in my ears and Quarry guarding my front, there was little to fear. He'd rescued me from the deepest, darkest demon hiding in the shadows of my mind.

With him, I was invincible.

We slept tangled together until my father yanked him off the couch, pissed as hell to have found us sleeping together. Quarry didn't cower or offer any excuses as to what we had been doing. He looked my father squarely in eyes and told him, "She was afraid. I laid down with her and she wasn't anymore. Sorry. Not sorry."

It was one hundred percent Quarry Page. Breathtakingly unapologetic.

Emphasis on the breathtaking part.

As he sauntered out the door that night, I called out, "Later, Q."

And, for the very first time, his response changed.

I only caught the side of his face as he glanced over his shoulder, but that was more than enough to make my cheeks heat. The corner of his mouth lifted in a heart-stopping smile.

"Later, Rocky."

CHAPTER
Four

Quarry

SOMEHOW, OVER THE NEXT SIX months, I magically found myself in the world's good graces again.

Till had worked his way up the ladder in the professional boxing world, earning his very first title shot. Win or lose, it was a dream come true.

Eliza was pregnant and expecting their first child—a girl. Thank God! We didn't need any more Page boys.

Flint had recently graduated high school and was gearing up for college. He was ridiculously smart and could have gone anywhere he wanted. He bitched out, though, and decided to go to the local university in order to stay close to the family. Eliza was ecstatic. I guessed that'd had a big role in his decision. He was weird about her in those days.

I was kicking ass on the amateur boxing circuit, well on my way to following in Till's footsteps like I'd always dreamed since I'd first climbed through the ropes.

The Page family was happy, and life was simple again.

I should have known it would be short-lived.

We were all in Vegas for two full weeks for Till's big title shot—and the best part was that *we* included Liv.

Little did I know that the trip would end up being the biggest nightmare of my entire life…at that point.

In a desperate attempt to settle a gambling debt, my father, Clay Page, crawled out of the woodwork for the first time in years in order to convince Till to throw the fight. His bookie, Frankie, had other ideas. He showed up at our room with a gun and kidnapped Eliza.

I'd fought, but in the end, I was left bleeding and unconscious on the floor as he dragged her from the room.

That was the first time I felt the paralyzing anguish of failing a woman I loved.

I should have been the first line of defense in protecting what was ours. Eliza might have been married to only Till, but she belonged to all of us. I failed my entire family that day.

I could have prevented it all if only I'd been stronger.

Tougher.

Patient.

Careful.

Smarter.

In other words, not Quarry Page.

And I had to live with that knowledge while the police searched for Eliza, not knowing if she was alive or dead.

Flint got to be the hero that day, and his reward was a bullet he took in the back to protect Eliza and her unborn daughter.

It gutted me.

I should have been man enough to do that the moment Frankie had stormed in, waving a gun around. I hadn't though. After everything they had given me—*sacrificed* for me—I'd failed them *all*.

An insurmountable guilt devoured me the day the doctors told us that Flint might never walk again. I would have rather sat in a wheelchair for my entire life than watch the painful reality crumble my brother's face, knowing that it was all my fault.

It broke me in ways that could never be healed.

I wasn't a man.

And, for that reason alone, I lost it in the middle of Flint's hospital room with Eliza, Till, Erica, and Slate all watching on.

"Hey, Q," Flint called from his bed.

I didn't turn to face him as I answered, "Yeah."

"You crying over there?"

I deserved that for what I had done. And especially for what I hadn't done—protect them.

"Fuck you," I barked at my reflection in the window.

"Hey, you can't be a man and a baby. Either cuss or cry."

He was right. And it was exactly why I was crying like the little bitch I really was.

"Leave him alone," Erica urged.

There was nothing to leave alone though. I'd earned that when I'd allowed an armed man to take Eliza—the only mother I'd ever known. Till would have burned the entire world down before allowing anyone to ever lay a finger on her. And Flint... Well, he'd more than shown the lengths to which he would go to make her safe.

And I'd proved exactly how worthless I truly was.

In an exaggerated baby voice, Flint mocked, "Q, you want me to ask the nurse if she has a lollipop?"

I couldn't take it anymore.

Pushing to my feet, I stormed past his bed, mumbling, "I hate you."

I didn't hate him at all though.

I hated myself.

After sprinting from the room, I came face-to-face with a hall full of familiar faces and one pair of innocent, brown eyes I could feel even before they came into view.

"Quarry, wait!" Liv yelled, chasing after me as I rushed down the hall, desperately seeking an escape from my entire fucking life.

When I was sure I'd lost her, I quickly ducked into a supply closet and flipped the lights off.

This is not happening. None of it.

After sucking in a deep breath, I held it until my chest began to burn. Tears continued to roll down my cheeks, and I didn't even bother wiping them away.

The handle of the door twisted, and light from the hall filled the small space. I didn't need to turn to know who it was.

"Go away, Liv."

The door shut almost immediately. My body sagged in relief as the darkness once again cloaked the room.

"Son of a bitch!" I shouted as two arms folded around my waist from behind. "Get out!" I roared as her body came flush with my back.

"No," she murmured, resting her head between my shoulder blades.

"Leave me the hell alone. I don't want you here!"

"I don't care if you want me here or not. If it happens to you, it happens to me too, remember?"

But it hadn't happened to her; it'd happened to *me*. And nothing she could say or do would change that. It didn't matter one bit that I instantly felt better from knowing she was there. Not even Liv could fix this.

"Leave me alone. It's dark and quiet in here. God knows I can't deal with you freaking the fuck out right now."

"I'll be fine. I'm safe with you, Quarry."

That one sentence was the absolute worst thing she could have possibly said. It lit me on fire, because not only had I convinced her of that bullshit over the years, but I'd even convinced myself.

It was the biggest lie I had ever told.

"I can't protect you!" I roared, roughly removing her arms from around my hips. Spinning to face her, I continued to yell. "I can't fucking protect anyone! Not you. Not Eliza. Not Flint. Not even my fucking self."

"Then I'll protect you," she whispered.

And that damn warmth Liv seemed to magically transfer spread over me. My dependency on those brief moments of comfort was another one of my weaknesses. No more. Never again.

I grabbed her shoulders and shook her roughly. "I can't keep you safe. Look around us. It's still dark. And, in a minute, it's going to be really fucking quiet. You have to get over your shit before I have the chance to fail you too."

She attempted to once again close her arms around my waist, but I stepped out of her reach.

"Stop saying that. You didn't fail anyone," she said.

And that was the exact moment I lost her.

Rage and self-loathing boiled in my veins. She was so fucking wrong. And the sooner she realized it, the safer she would be.

Stomping past her, I did the unforgivable.

I showed Liv James exactly how unsafe she was with me.

After yanking the closet door open, I stepped out. I caught a glimpse of fear in her wide eyes just before I secured my spot in Hell by slamming the door behind me.

"Quarry!" she shrieked, frantically rattling the handle.

But I refused to release it.

She *needed* to know.

"Quarry!" Her fists beat on the wood as I sank to the ground, blocking the door with my body.

She had to understand that the world was a scary place, where people you love got kidnapped, shot, and paralyzed. The silence was the easy part.

"Quarry, please!" Utter panic colored her voice, but I didn't budge.

The vibrations of her tiny, pounding fists slashed my soul, ensuring that I'd wear the scars of that moment for the rest of my life. And maybe even a lifetime after that.

"I'm sorry," I whispered. "I'm so fucking sorry."

"Quarry!" she cried, her voice cracking as she broke into loud sobs.

She needed to know that the silence wasn't the worst thing that could happen to her—trusting me was.

"Daddy!" she screamed, giving up on me altogether—just as she should have.

But it wrecked me all the same.

After pushing to my feet, I released the door. It flew open, but I didn't dare look at her. I couldn't. I no longer had that right.

She should have punched me. No. She should have beaten the absolute shit out of me.

I would have let her. I'd have stood there until I was black and blue if it would have made her feel better.

Instead, all I got was the squeak of her shoes on the tile as she sprinted away.

It was the single best decision she had ever made—regardless of how it gutted me.

Standing completely alone in that hall, I anxiously awaited the moment when Leo or Slate would come after me. I'd done the deed; I *wanted* to pay the price. They never showed up though. There were no laps to be run. No hard lesson from her angry father. Till didn't even ground me when we got home. I wasn't actually sure Liv had told anyone.

But the punishment I received was more devastating than I was prepared for—even if it was exactly what I deserved.

It was three long years before I saw Liv James again.

CHAPTER *Five*

Liv

I USED EVERY POSSIBLE EXCUSE to avoid Indianapolis, On The Ropes, and, more specifically, a pair of hazel eyes that had broken my heart. My parents were extremely suspicious as to why I broke into tears any time the Page brothers came up in conversation, but I never told them what had happened that day at the hospital. As much as I liked getting Quarry into minor trouble, I knew that this would have been major in my father's eyes, mainly because it was major in mine too.

Quarry no longer had my back—that much was clear. I, however, had told him that I'd protect him, and despite months of nightmares about being locked in that dark, silent closet, I kept my word.

But just because I didn't rat him out didn't mean I forgave him—or ever would. Besides my parents and my counselor, he was the only person who knew about my fears. And he'd used that knowledge like a weapon, slicing me to the core. As sad as it sounds, the worst of it wasn't the fact that he'd so grossly broken my trust. No, the worst was that I'd lost him in the process. A few months after it'd happened, my dad started bringing home notes any time he saw the boys. They were all addressed to Rocky, and they all landed in the trash can without being opened.

I didn't want an apology from Quarry Page.

I actually didn't want anything from him anymore.

He'd made the decision, and I was the one forced to live with the consequences.

It fucking sucked.

I'd lost my best friend that day. Sure, we were just kids, but the bond Quarry and I shared was something that only happened once in a lifetime. I knew I'd never find anyone like him again, so I didn't even bother trying.

Much to my father's excitement, I met a few girls at school. Most of them were nice, but they didn't make me laugh the way Quarry had. They also never locked me in a closet, so I decided to keep them.

Life moved on. I grew up, and judging by the amount of time my dad spent traveling to boxing matches with Slate, so did the Page brothers. I overheard my mom on the phone the day Quarry had won the Golden Gloves championship. I was happy for him. There was a part of me that ached because I would have killed to be at that fight. I could even imagine his lopsided grin as he caught my eye while I cheered his name from the front row. That thought stung worse than I could have ever imagined. I knew how much he loved boxing—just exactly the way he knew how terrified I was of the silence.

With that, the ache went away, and I once again set on about living the lie that had become my life.

And it worked really freaking well for three years. I was just a normal teenager, texting friends, flirting with boys, slaving over geometry homework, and religiously sleeping with headphones. So, maybe normal was a stretch. But I was happy-ish. I rarely even thought about my old childhood pal, Quarry Page. And, by rarely, I mean maybe once a week. Okay, so maybe *rarely* was a bit of a stretch too. It's not like I had a scrapbook of all the articles that were published about him in the sports section as he became the up-and-coming golden boy of boxing at only sixteen. Being that Till was a former world champion and his trainer, Uncle Slate, was too, boxing fans everywhere were watching Quarry destroy the amateur circuit. A scrapbook like that would have taken hours each week to keep up—hypothetically, of course.

I never hated Quarry for what he had done to me. I hated him for what he had done to *us*. It had been the ultimate betrayal, and it affected me far more than those sixty seconds in the closet. I had already been a bit of a loner, preferring to spend my time with a book and music rather than actual people. But, as the years passed, it became worse. If I didn't trust anyone else, they couldn't hurt me. It was a hard lesson learned but surprisingly easy to maintain. I had friends, but not a single confidant.

That is until I met Mia March, the only person who would ever be able to fill Quarry's shoes—complete with shredding me in betrayal.

It was a Friday, and I'd just gotten home from school. I was looking forward to a low-key weekend spent in my room with the radio blaring. Maybe doing a little online shoe shopping. But my entire life changed as I was going through the mail. My heart stopped, and panic rolled in my stomach. With shaking hands, I lifted my father's latest issue of USA Boxing Magazine. On the front was a picture of Till and Quarry standing back to back. I would have ripped it out and added it to my scrapbook—err, if I'd had one. But the headline stopped me in my tracks.

Find out how newly deaf Quarry Page plans to not only follow in his brother's footsteps, but also surpass The Silencer's reign in the ring.

"Mom!" I yelled, dropping the magazine and tearing from the room. "He's deaf?" I accused when I found her sitting in her office, probably working on something for my dad's security company.

Her eyes lifted to mine, and a tight smile formed on her lips. "Well—"

"Why didn't you tell me?"

"I didn't know you'd be interested in news about Quarry."

"Are you crazy? He's deaf! Of course I'm interested!"

"I am a little crazy, but so are you if you think you're going to continue yelling at me like that." She nonchalantly brushed her long, blond hair back and pushed out from behind the desk. "Okay, so you're interested. What now?"

"What do you mean? What now?" I stared at her, incredulous.

"Do you want me to tell you what's been going on with Quarry for the last three years, or do you want to ask him yourself? I bet he'd sign something to add to that shrine you keep tucked under your bed." She absently smoothed her fitted dress, which I promptly decided to order in my size.

"Just tell me," I huffed.

"Well, his hearing took a significant downslide about—"

She didn't even get all the words out of her mouth before my stomach dropped. I couldn't imagine how Q was handling it. He wasn't a boy anymore—that much was visible. But I'd witnessed firsthand how devastated he had been when Till had lost his hearing. Now, it was the future and he was the one adjusting to a new life—in silence. Just the thought terrified me.

"I want to go to Indy," I blurted.

Her knowing smile grew. "About time. I'll tell your dad I need to discuss some things with Erica."

"What? Dad wouldn't care if we—"

"Pack a bag, Liv. We don't want to get on the road too late." She breezed past me, leaving me alone in the quiet room.

But that wasn't why I started freaking out. What the hell was I doing?

Later, Q.

Later, Rocky.

It was officially later.

I needed to be there. If not for him, then for me.

It was time to let the past go.

Crap.

Three hours later, I was standing in the doorway of On The Ropes, watching a shirtless Quarry Page destroy a speed bag. It was late and the gym was mostly empty, but even if it had been packed, I wouldn't have been able to miss him.

I knew he'd changed from the pictures, but *God*, had he changed. Not quite seventeen yet, but he was well over six feet tall, and two black tattoos graced the traps at the base of his neck. His hair was probably the same length as the last time I'd seen him. However, it was no longer hanging in his eyes. The front was slicked back, most likely with a combination of gel and sweat, and the underneath was buzzed short. Not a hair fell out of place as he rhythmically pounded the swinging bag, switching hands with every punch. The sheen of sweat indicated he'd been at it for a while, but his arms remained steady, never slowing. My mouth dried as my eyes raked over his strong body—every inch rippled with muscles.

Quarry was a man. And a gorgeous one at that.

I stared for entirely too long before remembering why I was there in the first place.

He was going to think I was insane, showing up after all these years. But, if there was ever someone who would understand why I needed to be there, it was him.

Rushing forward, I slammed into his back and wrapped my arms around his waist, burying my face between his shoulder blades.

His hands stilled in midair, but his muscular body instantly relaxed. His heart pounded out a rhythm that matched my own. Though his was probably only from the exertion of his workout. I couldn't handle the idea that he might be excited to see me too. I was there to soothe my own fears. Not for him. Well, not completely.

"Hey, Rocky," he said in a deep baritone without even looking back.

Staying flush against his back, I lifted my hands in front of him and signed, *Hey, Q.*

"I was wondering if you were going to show up."

I continued to clumsily sign with my hands in front of him, using his body to make some of the gestures. *I just heard. I'm so sorry. Are you okay? How are you doing?*

His shoulder shook as he chuckled. "I'm okay. I see you kept up your end of the deal and learned sign." His voice was thick but unreadable. "I'm kinda failing on my end. Sorry."

Don't you dare apologize. You didn't fail anything. This was—

He gently pushed my hand down with his glove to interrupt me. "You can talk, Liv." Stepping away, he turned to face me. No sooner had he stilled than his eyes flared wide as he drank me in for the first time in over three years. He wasn't the only one who had grown up—and had grown up well. "Jesus," he breathed, dropping his gaze to the ground after it had lingered on my boobs for a beat too long.

I was used to the attention. When I was fourteen, I'd gone from an A cup to a D. I no longer looked like a little girl in any regard. While I wasn't the most popular girl in school, there wasn't exactly a shortage of boys asking me out. There was, however, a shortage of me being interested—a fact that thrilled my parents. But, with only a single glance, I was suddenly very, very interested in one boy in particular.

Thankfully, my mind was still focused on the reason for our little reunion. Snapping my fingers in his line of vision, I drew his attention back to my hands.

How are you handling all this?

"Stop with the sign language and talk."

I tipped my head to the side in confusion then once again started to sign.

He barked a laugh. "Liv, I can hear you. Just talk."

"What?!" I shrieked.

He tapped his ear with a gloved hand. "Hearing aids."

"What?!" I repeated.

His lips spread into a wide smile that only grew when my eyes became fixated on it.

"Jesus," I repeated and flashed my gaze away.

"I heard that."

"Wha...how?"

"Shit, Liv, did *you* go deaf? I said...hearing aids." After tucking a glove under his arm, he tugged it off and then repeated the process on the other side.

I glared at him. "Oh my God! Did you lie to that magazine? It said you were deaf! That's seriously messed up."

He laughed loudly while raking a hand through his hair. His abs flexed deliciously—not that I noticed or anything.

"I didn't lie. But I probably would have if I'd known it would bring you back from that cave you've been hiding in." He smirked.

A real-life, mouth-watering, manly smirk. It was infuriating—and gorgeous.

For a champion boxer, his reflexes were seriously slow. Thus, when I threw a punch, it landed squarely on his shoulder.

"I'm not back!"

That freaking smirk morphed into a megawatt grin as he rubbed the spot where I'd hopefully left a bruise. "She's back."

"I'm *not* back! But tell me why a magazine reported you were deaf when—"

He crossed his thick arms over his chest, regarding me humorously. "When what?"

"You can hear."

"I can." He bent at the waist and leaned in close. "With hearing aids."

I threw my hands out to the sides. "That's not deaf!"

He tipped his head to the side. "I wasn't aware you got your medical license over the last few years."

I crossed my arms over my chest, mirroring his posture, only I was sporting a scowl instead of a smile. "It's good to see you're still a liar."

His eyebrows shot up. "Liar? How exactly do you figure that?"

I was becoming more and more annoyed. Mainly because I wanted to be annoyed but couldn't manage it due to my overwhelming relief that he could still hear. But also because, with every word he spoke, I realized just how much I'd missed him over the years. Unfortunately, I also couldn't forget how much he'd hurt me.

And, just like a switch had been flipped, I was suddenly able to overcome the annoyance and longing. I replaced it with anger—irrational, juvenile, straight-up-bitch *anger*. I wasn't above a low blow.

Mocking a deep voice, I said, "I can't protect you, Liv. I'm a failure, Liv. Hey, let me get my kicks out of scaring the fucking piss out of you, *Rocky*." I spat his nickname for me like a curse. Dropping the voice and stepping toward him, I poked his chest with my finger. "Yes, Quarry. You're a liar. You're also a coward. And I hate you for it. And I hate myself because, even knowing all of this…I've still missed you."

The shit-eating grin disappeared from his handsome face, but it didn't make me feel better in the least. The remorse left behind was staggering.

I didn't cry, but as I stared into his haunted hazel eyes, I still wiped my face because I was sure the tears were on their way.

I wanted to go back for another verbal jab, just to make him hurt, but my voice broke. I couldn't do it. No matter how mad I was.

"I never should have come here. I'm glad to see you aren't deaf," I called over my shoulder as I headed for the gym door.

I didn't get but two steps away before his arm snaked around my waist and pulled my back against his chest. I didn't fight him. Sure, he was more than twice my size, so there was no use anyway. But, honestly, I just liked the way I felt in his arms.

"You're right," he gritted out. "I was a coward. I was also a thir-teen-year-old boy who had no idea how to deal with the fact that the woman I consider a mother had been kidnapped and my brother had been paralyzed. I was fucked up, Liv. Christ, I'm still fucked up. Thirteen, seventeen, eighty. That shit was enough to screw with any-one's head regardless of age."

"That's not an apology!"

"I see you didn't read my letters."

"I see you're a moron," I bit back. It didn't make much sense, but with him so close, it was all I could come up with.

"I apologized a million times in those letters."

"I didn't want your apology then."

"But you want it now?"

"Yes! I mean…no." I sucked in a deep breath and tried to cling to some semblance of composure. I wasn't there to make up with my best friend.

As far as I was concerned, those didn't exist.

I was only selfishly attempting to quell my own anxiety. "Look, I didn't come here to rehash this. It happened. I just came because I *thought* you were deaf."

"I am deaf."

"Oh my God! Quit lying! If you just heard me say that, you aren't deaf!"

His whole body stiffened behind me, and his arm flexed around my stomach. "You can sling whatever fucking insult you want at me, and I will happily take them all from you. I'm an asshole for locking you in that closet. I'm a dumbass who sent you a million goddamn letters in order to apologize. I'm also an idiot who even went so far as to tell your dad what happened, hoping for some kind of help in delivering those same damn letters."

Now that was a surprise. It also explained why my mom had lied about our little excursion.

"You told my dad?"

"Yep. And trust me—not my smartest decision. He. Was. Pissed."

A giggle slipped out when I tried to imagine how that conversation had gone down.

"What I am *not* is a liar. I won't even take that shit from you, Rocky. Yes, I can hear you now, but if I take these hearing aids out, I wouldn't be able to understand a damn word you said. I can still hear noises, but I'm useless with words. Five weeks ago, they vanished. And doctors are predicting even the noises will be gone soon enough."

"Oh." My cheeks heated with embarrassment.

"Yeah. Oh." His arm fell away as he took a step in front of me, fisting his wrapped hands on his hips. "You had three hours on the ride down here. I figured you'd have at least read the article."

Hmm. I *should* have read the article.

"I was worried," I snapped, holding his glare.

He arched an eyebrow. "You didn't ask your parents before driving all the way down here?"

Damn. I *really* should have let my mom finish.

"I was worried," I repeated, narrowing my eyes.

It only caused one side of his mouth to tip up. "Right. Well, I'm glad. I've missed the fuck out of you too. I seriously need the cardio. I haven't run a punishment lap in years." He poked my side.

I'll be damned if he didn't remember exactly the right spot to poke, too.

"Stop!" I laughed against my will, swatting his hand away.

When I looked back up, Quarry was watching me with a solemn

expression.

"I'm so fucking sorry, Liv."

"Yeah," I replied, becoming enthralled with my shoes.

It was easier to be mad than truly entertain an apology from him. I did miss him though. I just didn't trust him.

"We cool?" he asked.

I wasn't a liar, either. So, as much as I would have liked to let him off the hook, I couldn't. Instead, I answered, "I don't know, Q."

He twisted his lips in a grimace. "Okay, well, are we *coolish*?"

"How about this—we're *cooler*."

His eyes lit with hope. "I'll take it." He smiled wide, and my mouth was helpless not to follow suit. "How long are you in town for?"

I shrugged. "Um…probably just the night."

"Hey, Flint's picking me up in a few minutes. We're supposed to be meeting up with Till and Eliza for dinner. You think your mom would let you come with us?"

"She drove me three hours on a whim to see you, Q. I'm relatively sure she wouldn't have a problem with me having dinner with the Page family."

"Sweet. Wait until you see the van Flint drives. It's seriously pimp in that 'Hey, little girl, you want some candy?' way."

"So what you're saying is I should jump from the van screaming for help when we get to the restaurant?"

His eyes grew wide with excitement before he pulled me into a hug. "I'm so fucking glad you're back. I'm thinking I should go ahead and run, like, twelve miles to bank up some laps in advance."

I was frozen.

Quarry Page was hugging me.

Shirtless.

Front to front.

We were suddenly getting a lot more than coolish. Actually, with his firm body pressed against me, I was becoming *hotish*.

I laughed awkwardly. "Probably not a bad idea." *Neither is climbing into a cold shower, Liv.*

Releasing me, he stepped back as his mouth cracked into an epic smile. I had never known that something so beautiful existed. My heart raced, and I found myself unable to drag my eyes away. That is, until I realized that it wasn't aimed at me.

Hi, he signed with his gaze directed over my shoulder.

That was the third time Quarry Page broke my heart.

This time, he didn't actually do anything at all, but it still shattered all the same.

Glancing behind me, I saw a girl with a pixie cut and a bold stripe of pink through her sweeping bangs. She was pretty—there was no denying that. But, given her tattered skinny jeans, clingy vintage tee, and a pair of Chuck Taylors, I wouldn't have considered her any competition. The kind of guys who went for girls like her didn't go for my style of dresses and heels.

Which was exactly why my heart broke.

When she signed, *Who the fuck is she?* I realized she was the type of girl *Quarry* went for.

Looking back at Q, I caught him signing, *Chill.*

My head flipped back and forth as they carried on a conversation as if I were invisible—while part of me wished I were.

Not until you tell me why I just walked in and found you dry-humping some preppy bitch.

Clearly she'd noticed how different we were as well.

She's not a bitch, and we were hugging. That's hardly dry-humping, he shot back, completely immune to her death-stare.

I wasn't positive if the sign language was for her benefit or his, so I decided to both sign and speak as I stepped toward her. "*Hi. I'm Liv.*"

I extended a hand, but her eyes remained glued to Q.

"Maybe I should go," I said out loud to Quarry.

He too ignored me.

"*Mia, this is my old friend, Rocky. Rock, this is my insanely jealous, well…really just insane-in-general girlfriend, Mia.*" He smiled patronizingly. Without talking, he signed, *There. Now you gonna drop your attitude and get over here and kiss me?*

Her attention finally snapped to me. Raking her eyes over me, she signed, *I thought you two weren't friends anymore.*

She knew about me. *Interesting.*

Quarry sauntered in her direction, pulling her into his side and kissing the top of her head. "*Well, now, we are. She's going to dinner with us too, so be nice.*"

Suddenly, I wanted to go to that dinner about as much as I wanted to pay full retail for the Louboutins I was saving up for.

"You know, maybe I should take a rain check. I'd hate for my mom to eat dinner alone. She did just drive me here and everything."

"Bullshit. She'll be with Erica. You're going," Quarry said. "*And you'll need to sign because Mia's the real kind of deaf. Not the fake kind like me.*" He winked.

When he leaned down and caught her mouth in a kiss, I heard the actual crunch of the shards of my heart being stomped on.

I wasn't exactly sure why though. It had been years since we had seen each other, and even back then, we'd been just friends. I could only think of one reason for the searing pain that consumed me when his lips touched hers.

It was Quarry.

CHAPTER
Six

Liv

DINNER THAT NIGHT WAS...WEIRD.

Gouge-your-eyes-out-with-a-spoon, swear-you-will-never-do-it-again-for-as-long-as-you-live, push-delicious-food-around-a-plate-while-staring-at-the-clock-on-your-phone kind of weird.

It was great to see Till and Eliza again. They had their daughter, Blakely, with them, and Eliza had just found out the baby she was carrying was a boy—hence the reason for the celebratory family dinner.

It was also nice to see Flint again. He was out of the wheelchair, but he still needed forearm crutches to get around. He remained quiet and cranky most of the meal—only talking to Till and occasionally signing insults at Mia. He'd always grin, and she held her own with rude comebacks, so I guessed it was just part of their dynamic.

In between all of this, I chatted with Quarry while Mia glared at me. She didn't even attempt to hide her disdain, and Quarry's only acknowledgement of it was to swear to me that she would get over it. I wasn't sure I believed him. But, being that I was the random guest at their family dinner, I stayed quiet and tried not to make it as awkward for anyone else as it was for me.

After I'd received hugs from everyone—but Mia—my mom arrived to pick me up.

Even though Quarry had insisted that we switch phone numbers at dinner, I had absolutely zero intentions of using his. I didn't even have a chance to beg my dad to let me change my number before my phone pinged from a number I didn't recognize.

It seemed Quarry shared more than just saliva with Mia.

She texted me to see when I would be back in Indy.

Then she texted me the day after that to ask if I would be at Quarry's next fight.

I knew she didn't honestly care about seeing me again. She just wanted to know when I was going to be around Quarry. And then she was going to make sure her ass was parked on the other side of him.

She texted me again the following day to find out why I hadn't replied.

Then Quarry texted me to make sure I was okay because I wasn't replying to Mia's texts.

Shoot me.

I finally replied, hoping they'd just leave me the hell alone. It had the exact opposite effect though. That one text opened some kind of magical door to an alternate dimension. Mia started texting me all the time. Most of which had nothing to do with Quarry. It was strange at first, and I ignored just as many messages as I responded to, but God, that girl was persistent.

She was also pretty cool.

Before I knew it, I was the one texting her. Once the bitchiness had melted away, it was easy to see why Quarry was so crazy about

Mia.

She was hilarious.

And feisty.

And unbelievably witty.

She wasn't prissy, but she still loved shoes (flats), manicures (skulls designs), and makeup (her palette of choice: neon.)

We were just different enough to keep things interesting, but similar enough that we never ran out of things to talk about.

It wasn't long before I fell in love with Mia March too. We texted every single day and eventually started video-chatting almost nightly. I started going down to Indy to spend weekends with her, during most of which she'd ditch Quarry and we'd eat junk food and laugh until midnight. Her parents even let her catch rides up to Chicago with my dad so she could visit me too.

Sure, I saw Quarry a good bit, but it wasn't weird anymore. He and Mia were good for each other. Besides, I had met an amazing girl who I'd truly bonded with *and* I'd gotten Quarry back. That was enough for me.

The three of us were the true definition of best friends. They had my back and I had theirs. No matter what. We had no secrets from each other. Well, that's not true. I still checked Quarry's ass out every time he left a room, but that was one secret I'd take to the grave.

One night, as we shared a twelve-pack of beers Quarry had bought with his fake ID, I told them the few memories I had of my birth mother, including the night she'd died. Mia told us about how scared she had been when she'd lost her hearing to brain cancer as a kid. And Quarry told us about how screwed up he had been the first few months after Flint had been paralyzed. Mia and I ended up crying, and Quarry ended up cussing about how he needed to stop hanging out with chicks before he started his period. This was said only seconds before he threw his arms around our shoulders and pulled us in for a painful group hug.

Yeah. What I had with the two of them was more than enough

for me.

Or so I lied to myself. Daily.

Mia and I spent a lot of time at Quarry's fights. His already-successful boxing career soared to a new level over the years. There wasn't an amateur opponent he hadn't destroyed in the ring. Quarry "The Stone Fist" Page lived up to his name, with the majority of his wins coming by way of knockout. Mia and I, along with Eliza and eventually Flint's girlfriend, Ash, were in the front row at every fight. The four of us rushed into the ring each time his glove was lifted into the air.

The boxing world had been waiting on baited breath for Quarry to go pro. The media covered him closer with each passing year. But, despite the excitement from the boxing community, Till and Slate refused to allow him to make the transition to professional boxing when he turned eighteen.

He wasn't ready was what they told us.

Whether he was or not, I had no clue, but I knew for sure that he was pissed.

When Flint, Quarry's agent, made the announcement to the media, I thought there was going to be a riot, both on the TV screen and in the middle of Till's living room. Quarry erupted, and Till quickly told him to get the fuck out if he wanted to act like an asshole under his roof. Mia and I snuck out the back door while that one played out. I love the Page family, but God, did those brothers fight. And Quarry, being Quarry, was almost always in the middle of it.

Quarry actually moved out a week later, but it wasn't on bad terms. Till agreed to help Q get his own place since he was eighteen but not going off to college or starting the career he was so passionate about. Till also gave him five hundred bucks for his birthday to put toward the huge back tattoo he'd been planning since he had been fourteen. The excitement of those two things was enough to take the edge off him.

Mia spent a good bit of time at Quarry's apartment. I, however, wasn't allowed over there at all. My dad had gotten over his issues with Quarry about the same time I had. He knew we were only friends, but he did not approve of his high school daughter hanging out at a guy's apartment. He never said anything about Flint's house though. So, on the weekends I was in town, we'd all go over there. It worked because we all loved Ash and she somehow even managed to make grouchy Flint fun.

When it came time for me to go off to college, picking a school and a major was easy. My two best friends were deaf and living in Indianapolis. I didn't delay in enrolling in the local university there and declaring American Sign Language as my major. Picking a roommate was equally as easy. Mia and I got an apartment right next to the college, only about ten minutes from Quarry's.

Without the distance dividing us, Mia, Quarry, and I were inseparable.

We were living the dream of college kids everywhere.

Which only made Mia's deceit that much more unbearable.

When I was nineteen years old, I learned that dreams didn't exist.

Our happy lives were nothing more than the gentle melody that lulls you into a nightmare.

Mia March died three weeks before her twentieth birthday.

Parts of Quarry and me slowly died for years to come.

CHAPTER
Seven

Quarry

"MOVE!" I ROARED, PUSHING THROUGH the cameras all furiously snapping pictures around me.

"Just keep walking," Slate said, nudging my shoulder before pushing his palm into the chest of a waiting reporter.

I wasn't famous. Hell, I'd never even stepped foot inside the ropes of a professional ring. The only reason I'd been on the covers of magazines was because of my connections and my bloodline. But I guess when your girlfriend is put on life support the same day you're supposed to announce your professional boxing debut, the paparazzi makes their own definition of fame.

I'd spent years wishing for the attention Slate and Till got. However, right then, I wished I could push every one of those assholes into the giant pit and light that bitch on fire. Hell, given the way I was feeling, maybe I'd dive in myself.

I dipped my shoulder out of Slate's grip. "Get your fucking hands off me."

"Walk," he growled, pushing me toward my sports car.

Cameras continued to click.

After tugging on the knot, I ripped my tie off and threw it at the closest scumbag, wishing it were my fist instead.

"Quarry! Quarry! Quarry!" the reporters clamored as I pushed a pair of sunglasses up my nose to hide my red-rimmed eyes. "Is it true you were against Mia March being taken off life support?"

Ha! I hadn't just been against it. I had been fucking rabid about it. And it was exactly why I was being escorted out of her wake. I hadn't been able to sit there a minute longer and watch her piece-of-shit parents mourn the daughter they'd killed. They'd pulled the plug. They'd made that decision. I would have fought for the rest of my life to keep her alive. But they'd just fucking quit, throwing in the towel before Mia had even had the chance to prove she was stronger than everyone gave her credit for.

"No comment," Slate barked as flashes continued to fire off around us.

"Quarry! How long had you known about her brain tumor?"

About ten fucking minutes *after* I'd lost her. She had taken that fun fact to the grave—literally. Bile rose in my throat.

"No comment!" Slate once again pushed a reporter out of our path.

"Slate. Is it true that Quarry's first fight has been set for next month against Madden? How do you think Mia's death will affect him in the ring?"

In the ring?

In the fucking *ring?*

I froze as an angry chill spread over my skin.

Deep breath. Hold it…

Oh, fuck it.

Swinging a hand out, I sent that asshole's camera flying. I quickly twisted my fist into the front of his shirt, forcing him against a car.

"In the ring, you motherfucker? It's going to affect my entire goddamn life!"

Slate's arm wrapped around my shoulders as he desperately fought to drag me away. "Stop!"

I couldn't though.

She's gone.

I tightened my grip, staring murderously into his eyes. "You people show up at a funeral home? What the hell is wrong with you? Don't worry about how this is going to affect me in the ring. You should be more concerned with how it's affecting me right fucking now."

"Let him go!" Till ordered, appearing beside me. After looping an arm around my waist, he dragged me away.

Flint stepped in to run interference with the douchebag reporter.

"Jesus Christ, Quarry! Calm down. You're making it worse." Till pointed toward the building where the woman I loved lay dead in a coffin.

Oh, God.

My eyes, tunneled by rage, flashed around the mob of reporters before landing on the front steps of the funeral home, where an even bigger crowd of Mia's friends and family were watching me violently break down—again.

"I need to get out of here," I mumbled, straightening my shirt.

"Good idea," he replied, shoving me toward my car. "I'll drive."

"No. I want to be alone."

"You can't drive right now, Q."

"Watch me."

"You cannot be behind the wheel..." He carried on with some explanation, but I was more than done listening. The silence had never sounded so good.

Looking up at the sky, I sucked in a breath so deep that it caused my lungs to ache. I refused to release it though.

Don't exhale.

Ignoring Till's protests, I dug my keys from my pocket and folded into my car. Barely managing to squeeze around the relentless reporters, I started toward the exit.

This is not happening.

Don't breathe.

My lungs were on fire, but it felt a hell of a lot better than what was going on in my heart, so I bit my lip and let it blaze—praying that it would eventually engulf me.

Glancing in my review mirror, I saw the cops rolling into the parking lot, but that wasn't what made me stop. My breath left me on a rush as I slammed on the brakes the moment she came into view.

Liv was standing in the middle of the road, staring at my taillights.

Her big, brown eyes were as empty as I felt, and her face was painted with absolute anguish. Without out a single second of hesitation, I leaned over and pushed the passenger's side door open in invitation. In a pair of heels and a short, black dress, she sprinted forward, not slowing until her ass hit my leather seat. Her door hadn't even shut before I was off again.

After turning her cell phone off, she tossed it in the glove box. Mine quickly followed. She didn't ask any questions as I pulled onto the highway in the exact opposite direction of both of our apartments. She didn't want to go home any more than I did.

Our destination was unknown, and that alone made it infinitely better than the one we'd just left.

I drove.

And drove.

Then, when I was sick and tired of aimlessly driving, I drove some more.

With the exception of Liv flipping the radio on when the sun went down, we sat in absolute silence for over four hours.

Alone, yet still together.

Finally, around ten p.m., with an empty tank of gas and sleepy eyes, I slipped into a parking space in front of the apartment Liv and Mia shared. Liv didn't delay in pushing the door open, but that's the only effort she put into getting out.

Dropping her head against the headrest, she whispered at the windshield, "Her parents told me she left letters for us. We can pick them up whenever we're ready."

"I don't want a fucking letter. She lied. She's sorry. I got it. Nothing left to say."

"Maybe it will explain stuff though. It might help."

My angry gaze jumped to her, but she was still staring out the window.

"Will it bring her back?" I asked. "No? Then I don't need a goddamn letter. Fuck that. Fuck her parents too. I don't want shit from them."

"They didn't kill her, Quarry."

"How can you say that?"

Her eyes finally met mine. "It was what Mia wanted. She signed the Do Not Resuscitate order, not them."

"What the fuck are you doing here? Please, God, tell me you are not actually siding with them? Because, if I recall correctly, we *both* begged them not to give up on her. They didn't give a shit about anyone. Liv, they didn't even get a second opinion."

"I'm not siding with anyone but Mia. She made a choice. We have to respect it." Her expression was emotionless, even though her voice trembled.

"Respect it? Fuck her shitty choice. She should have respected me enough to let me have a say."

She laughed without humor. "You never would have let her go, Q."

I slammed the heel of my palm against the steering wheel. "You're goddamn right I wouldn't have!"

"She had brain cancer. It was going to happen one way or another. She knew it. And she made a decision. We don't get to be mad about that."

"Get the fuck out of my car."

"No. Listen to me—"

"I'll start listening the moment you stop spouting the bullshit her parents shoved down your throat tonight."

She raised her voice for the first time all day. "It's the truth!"

"It's bullshit! All of it. How am I supposed to respect the fact that she lied to me for six months? Six fucking months that I could have used to prepare for this."

"Oh my God, Quarry!" she yelled, exasperated. "Do you seriously think six months could have ever prepared you for this? I could have known since the day I met her and I still wouldn't have been ready to lose her."

"I could have tried! I could have spent that time devoted to being with her instead of traveling to fights. Jesus Christ, Liv, last weekend, I went out with the guys from the gym to play pool. The last fucking Saturday night of her life on this Earth and I was shooting pool with a bunch of assholes I can barely stand. Six months she kept the fact that she was dying a secret. Six. Fucking. Months. You're right. I wouldn't have been ready to let her go, but at least I could have figured out how to say goodbye. Instead, all I got was to squeeze her hand, say, 'I love you,' and then be escorted out of the hospital by security. Fuck!"

"That's because you were acting like a fool and threatening her family! That was *your choice*!"

"Get the fuck out of my car. Now!"

"And it's also the reason you got thrown out of the visitation tonight. Get your shit together or you won't be allowed at the funeral tomorrow."

"I don't want to go to the funeral!" I shouted at the top of my lungs, making her flinch. "I don't want there to be a funeral at all.

Now, I'm serious. Get. The fuck. Out. Of my car."

Through gritted teeth, she seethed, "You know what I'll never understand? How you claim to be so in love with her, but in this entire conversation, I haven't heard you say a single word that wasn't about *you*. How this affects *you*. How this hurt *you*. Last time I checked, you aren't the one being buried tomorrow."

"I wish I were!"

"Fuck you! The world doesn't revolve around Quarry Page!" With that, she jumped out and slammed the door.

I didn't even wait for her to make it to the sidewalk before I was peeling out of the parking lot.

Fuck her.

Who the fuck is she to say that shit to me?

Had she forgotten that Mia had lied to her too?

What about how many times she'd begged Mia's parents to give it a few more days before taking her off life support? No. That must have somehow magically slipped her goddamn mind.

None of it was about me. It was all about Mia and the absolute hell she'd *chosen* to put us through.

How dare Liv try to act like I was the one being selfish? God forbid I'd wanted to know that my girlfriend was dying. Or, better yet, have a chance to fight to keep her alive.

That doesn't make me selfish.

It makes me a man.

I could barely contain my anger as I whipped my car around and headed back toward her apartment. I had every intention of stomping up those stairs and telling her just what I thought about the bullshit she'd been spewing, but the moment I slammed my car into park, my temper disappeared.

Liv was crumpled over at the foot of the stairwell. Her arms were looped around her legs, her face buried in her knees. As I opened the car door, her loud cries sliced through me.

No. Liv hadn't forgotten anything.

She was just doing a better job at masking it than I was.

After jogging over, I lifted her off the ground and cradled her in my arms.

"I c-can't go in there," she stuttered through sobs. "She's supposed to be in there."

"Shh," I whispered into her hair. "I know."

"I can't do this. Please just tell me she'll be here when I wake up tomorrow. Please," she cried into my neck.

My heart sank. "I'd give anything to make that happen."

"I...I...can't stay in that apartment without her."

"Okay. Okay. I've got you, Rocky. Let's go home."

She didn't offer the first complaint as I settled her in the front seat or when I carried her up to my apartment after we arrived.

She didn't actually say anything at all.

Lost in my own grief, I didn't have much compassion to offer anyone.

But it was Liv.

I dredged up what little I could muster, knowing she'd have done the same for me—more, actually.

After snagging a blanket and a pillow off my couch, I placed her on the futon in my messy spare bedroom that doubled as a computer-slash-weight room. Then, using my laptop, I clicked on one of the playlists Mia had made, setting it to repeat before turning sleep mode off so the screen would stay lit all night. Once all of that had been set, I made a beeline out, ready to lock myself away in my own room and break down in private.

Just as I made it to the door, she called my name to catch my attention.

She stammered several times before giving up on her voice. Lifting her hands in the air, she signed, *I'm mad at her too. Really fucking mad. I don't want to read her letter, either. At least, not yet. But I swear I understand how you feel. I loved her too. You can't forget that we're both struggling here. You don't get to be mad at me for how I'm han-*

68

dling this. And I shouldn't have gotten mad at you, either. I'm sorry.

Locking my fingers together, I rested them on the top of my head and sighed. "Don't be sorry. You're right. I'm a fucking mess right now. I just don't know any other way to deal with all of this. I'll get my shit together before the funeral tomorrow. I promise, okay?"

"Okay," she squeaked back.

"Get some sleep."

"Later, Q."

The corner of my mouth tipped up a fraction of an inch as I stepped out, shutting the door. "Later, Rocky."

CHAPTER
Eight

Quarry

One Year Later...

LIV NEVER WENT BACK TO her apartment. A few days after the funeral, her parents showed up at my place to get her. She all but lost her mind when her dad said that she wasn't allowed to stay with me anymore. Liv didn't bat her eyelashes at her father that day. Nor did she plaster on the sweet and cry crocodile tears until he caved to her demands. No. That night, she squared her shoulders, looked him directly in the eyes, and showed him the real Liv James.

My Rocky.

Her mom and I watched with gaping mouths as Liv boldly stood her ground and informed Leo that she was moving in with me. I think Sarah was in awe to see Liv talking to him like that. However, I was shocked because never once had we discussed her moving in.

Though, as I watched that crazy woman go toe-to-toe with her even crazier dad, I wasn't about to wade into the middle.

I could stand the company.

Two days later, Leo and his army of bodyguards moved all of Liv's stuff into my guest room. After attempting to intimidate me for most of the afternoon, each one of her father's grunts pulled me aside for a lecture on watching out for her and keeping my hands and my eyes to myself. The latter wasn't going to be a problem. However, failing women I cared about seemed to be a skill of mine, so I made no promises on the former.

After we'd lost Mia, Liv and I grew even closer. Everyone around us was affected by her death, but no one truly understood the vacancy she'd left behind in our everyday lives.

I'd heard of phantom pains when a person loses a limb. That's the only way I could describe the first few months without Mia. I'd wake up each morning with a smile on my face only for the jagged edge of reality to demolish it. I couldn't count how many times I picked up my phone to text her something funny only to hurl it across the room when I remembered the cold, hard truth. And, each time my glove was lifted in the air, my eyes would automatically scan the crowd, searching for Mia's beaming face. It was a knockout blow when my mind reminded me that I'd never experience that again.

Liv was always there though, smiling proudly from the front row—the hollowness in her eyes matching my own.

Despite the turmoil in my personal life, my career couldn't have been going better. The transition to professional boxing was easy for me. The opponents were bigger, stronger, and more talented than ever before, but I was a vortex in the ring. On the outside, I was a whirling force to be reckoned with, unable to slow down. But, on the inside, I was completely empty. I funneled the anger and debilitating pain of having lost her into every punch I threw. With a never-ending supply of anguish fueling me, I became unstoppable.

I was in the ring, sparring with Slate, when Liv came stomping through the ropes. Panic built in my chest when I saw the tears streaming down her cheeks and the storm brewing in her eyes.

Dropping my hands, I started toward her, but Slate's glove caught me on the chin, sending me stumbling back against the ropes.

"Fuck!" I gritted before spitting my mouthpiece out and tearing my headgear off. Being clipped by the former heavyweight champion was no small blow—headgear or not.

My head was still spinning as he stepped into my face and barked words I couldn't make out without my hearing aids. Focused on the woman charging toward me, I didn't even entertain the idea of reading his lips. Rolling my eyes, I waved him off as Liv close the distance between us.

"You!" She accusingly pointed her finger at me.

"Me?" I replied, tugging my gloves off.

Her mouth was moving a million miles a minute with obviously angry words, but I had no clue what they were or why they were aimed at me.

"Sign," I said, interrupting her.

In mid-thought, her hands lifted, forming the words even as her mouth kept going. "*It was about you! Just fucking you!*"

"What the hell are you talking about?"

"*Mia's letter!*"

The air between us suddenly became toxic to my lungs. My eyes grew wide as I took a menacing step forward. Liv held her ground, but out of the corner of my eye, I noticed Slate inching closer.

"You read her letter?"

"*Yes. And I don't give a damn what you have to say about it. You're still pissed. Fantastic. But I woke up this morning needing her more than ever before. So yeah. I called her mom and went and got my letter.*"

A war raged inside me. I didn't want to give one single fuck about what Mia had written as her goodbye to Liv, but despite my best efforts, I was dying to know exactly what it said.

Word for word.

Thought for thought.

Every single noun, verb, and adjective.

Hell, I was even desperate for the inkblots her pen might have left behind.

I'd never considered actually getting my letter from her parents, partly because I knew they hated me for the way I'd acted when she'd died. Another part of me didn't want it because I'd spent the last year holding on to my bitterness against her ghost. But, deep down, I knew the main reason was those words were the only remaining bit of Mia left. As soon as I read whatever message she'd left me, she'd really be gone.

Forever.

In the words on those pages, she was alive. Just knowing they existed made waking up each morning slightly less agonizing.

However, judging by Liv's face and attitude, I'm not sure she felt the same.

"What'd it say?" I finally asked.

She shook her head. "*I'll tell you what it didn't say. It didn't say, 'I'm sorry.' It didn't say, 'I love you.' It didn't say, 'You were the best friend I ever had.' It didn't even say, 'I'll miss you.'*" Her chest shook as I watched a silent sob ravage her. "*One sentence is all I fucking got. One sentence from my best friend in the entire world. And you know what? It wasn't even about me.*"

I didn't move a muscle as her angry fists flew toward me, slamming into my chest while she screamed, "It was all about you!"

I had no need for my hearing aids or even sign language to know what she'd said. I'd read every excruciating word as she'd forced them through her lips.

Slate stepped forward, looping an arm around her waist and pulling her into a hug, but she fought ravenously, attempting to claw her way back at me.

"You! Quarry! You!"

I was dazed, watching her unravel, unable to process what the hell she was talking about. What was about me? It wasn't until the fight had left her and she'd sagged in Slate's arms that I became unstuck. Taking two giant steps forward, I was ready to pry her from his grasp if I had to. That was rendered unnecessary when she dove into my arms.

Till caught my attention from the ropes, signing, *Take her to my office. She doesn't need the whole gym watching this.*

I nodded and moved through the opening he'd created by stepping on the bottom rope.

Liv dangled in my arms as I carried her. She wasn't crying anymore, but her hands had begun to tremble as if the emotions were attempting to find a breach.

Once in Till's office, I sat her in his chair then squatted in front of her.

"Tell me what's going on," I demanded.

"*Why did Mia start texting me after we first met?*" she spoke and signed with shaky hands.

"Uh...I don't know." I scratched the back of my head, confused.

Her sad eyes lifted to mine. "*She didn't say a single word to me at dinner that night we all went out, but when I left, she wouldn't stop texting me until I finally gave in and responded. Why? She obviously thought I was after you. Why would she want to be my friend? I've never understood that.*"

I laughed without humor. "I don't know why Mia did half the shit she did. She was insane, Liv. Hell, the first time I met her, she walked up to me and declared that she was my new girlfriend. I laughed, but she only stood there confidently smiling. It was my first day at that private school for the hearing impaired Till forced me to attend. I didn't want to even be there, much less date some girl who may or may not have a few screws loose. But she was so fucking funny and wouldn't let up until she got her way. Needless to say, our first date was that Friday night." I shrugged. "I don't know why she wanted to be your friend, but I didn't question it because it made her smile and it meant I got you back."

"*I don't have a lot of girlfriends, Quarry. All the gossip and pretending to be someone you're not is exhausting. I can't handle the drama of it all.*"

Using my thumbs, I wiped away the black makeup smudges under her eyes. "I can tell."

"*I'm serious.*" She swatted my hands away. "*But Mia wasn't like that.*" Swallowing hard, she looked back to the door. "*I asked her a few years ago what had made her reach out to me and she had no real answer. She avoided the question by saying that she could just tell I was cool. I suddenly have this sick feeling that our friendship was formed on nothing more than the theory of 'keep your friends close and your enemies closer.'*"

I barked a laugh, but her gaze stayed locked on the door.

"Jesus Christ, women are weird," I mumbled at the ceiling before refocusing on Liv. "You seriously think she spent over three years being your friend because she was jealous? Liv, she liked you more than she did me half the time! Once, we got into a huge fight because I'd taken her to a nice restaurant for our anniversary and she spent the whole dinner texting you about your prom dress. She loved you!"

I was still chuckling when her tortured eyes met mine.

"'*Take care of Quarry.*'"

"Huh?"

"*That's what my letter said. 'Take care of Quarry.' That's it.*"

My stomach fell.

Shit. Shit. Shit.

What the hell had Mia been thinking?

Then my stomach dipped even lower.

What if mine only said '*Take care of Liv*'?

I'd spent over a year obsessing over all the words I hoped she'd written. Just because I wasn't man enough to actually read them didn't mean I hadn't envisioned what they would say a million different times. I'd drafted that letter in my head more often than I'd ever admit, but never once had it been about Liv.

The disappointment must have shown on my face, because she immediately said, *"I'm sure yours is better."*

I wasn't.

But, suddenly, I had every intention of finding out.

Had Mia been capable of being friends with Liv just to keep an eye on her? Yup. She had even been crazy enough to pull it off. I was already going to be livid if that were the case. But, if I found out that her final words to me had been written out of jealousy, I was going to lose my fucking mind.

There was only one way to truly know.

After the world's quickest shower, I donned my hearing aids and headed out in search of the only remaining pieces of Mia March.

Twenty minutes later, Liv and I stood on the front porch of a familiar, brick, two-story house in the middle of the suburbs. Liv had called when we'd left the gym and said that Mrs. March seemed excited that I was finally coming by. I was so damn nervous about what I was going to find in my letter that I couldn't even bring myself to worry about what I was going to say to Mia's parents.

That all changed when Mrs. March opened the door.

Mia had gotten her mom's deep, green eyes, and the sight of them smiling up at me caused my heart to wrench.

"Hey there," she said cheerfully, pushing to her toes to give me a hug.

It wasn't quite the greeting I had been expecting, but I wouldn't complain.

Mr. March was standing behind her, and no sooner had his wife released me than he extended a hand in my direction.

"Good to see you again, son."

"You too, sir."

"I saw your last fight on HBO. You should be proud." He smiled as if I hadn't threatened his life the last time he'd seen me.

"Thank you," I said, following him into the large family room I'd spent numerous nights in with Mia.

I'd never been so thankful for the distraction of that letter until I was in that room. It would have been easy to get lost in the memories, and I had a feeling I wouldn't have been left in one piece on the other end of that journey back in time.

Mrs. March stepped in front of me and offered a hot-pink envelope in my direction. "As much as we'd love to catch up, I'm sure you're eager to read this."

I stared at the envelope for several seconds before gathering the nerve to take it from her hands. You would have thought it was filled with anthrax for the way my pulse spiked when my fingers made contact.

"We'll give you a minute," Liv said, squeezing my forearm. The quiver in her voice was obvious to everyone—but especially me.

I never tore my eyes away from my name written in Mia's handwriting as I caught her elbow. "Stay."

"Are you sure?"

My words might have been firm, but my eyes were pleading as I looked up at her. "If this goes downhill, I'm going to need someone to keep me from losing it."

She released a loud sigh of relief. "Okay. I'll stay."

Walking from the room, Mrs. March called out, "Well, if you two need anything, just holler. Oh, and, Quarry, my wedding china is in that cabinet." She pointed across the room. "Please leave it standing."

It was a joke, but I still felt like a dick that she'd felt the need to make it.

"Look, I'm really sorry about…well, everything."

She smiled warmly. "We may have known about the tumor, but we got letters from Mia, too. The second paragraph of mine was devoted to apologizing for whatever hell you caused after finding out she was gone. She threatened to haunt me if I had you arrested for any of it." She giggled, but her eyes filled with tears, revealing her true emotions. "I miss her so much. I wouldn't even mind a ghost right about now. So don't tempt me, okay?"

I chuckled around the lump in my throat. "I'll steer clear of the china."

"That'd be nice."

With one last grin, they left me and Liv alone—together.

Less than five seconds after that, I slid a stack of folded, white notebook paper from the envelope.

Quarry,

Surprise! I'm dead!

I'd worry that it was too soon for that joke, but I'm assuming you aren't reading this thirty seconds after I took my last breath. You've been known to hold a mean grudge. I'm also going to assume that Liv caved first and it took her rushing to your house, screaming that I didn't love her, to drag your ass here today.

Am I right?

You should probably put her out of her misery and give her the last two pages. That's her real letter. And tell her I love her. TONS. And TONS. And like fourteen more than that.

Don't question it. Just do it!

A laugh bubbled from my throat. I shouldn't have been surprised that Mia had manipulated us from the grave. She was a nut.

Liv tipped her head in question as she studied me warily. "You okay?"

"Um…she says she loves you tons. And tons. And like fourteen more than that."

Her chin began to quiver as I peeled the back two pages off and handed them her way.

"That's your letter."

Snatching them from my hands, she yelled, "Turn around!"

"What? Why?"

"Turn around!" she screeched so loud that I decided right then and there that even going deaf had its perks.

As I turned away, she didn't delay in burying her forehead between my shoulder blades. She didn't wrap her arms around my stomach, but I suspected that was only because they were holding Mia's final words in front of her eyes.

Good words.

Happy words.

Not jealous at all.

I blew out a relieved breath, and as Liv start giggling behind me, I decided to go back to reading.

First off, I need to apologize.

I'm sure you had to put on a suit and sit through some dreadfully boring funeral. My bad. I really wanted something a little more "lively," but Mom nixed it, complaining that a DJ would be tacky. Whatever. Besides, I figure, if I let her plan my funeral, it will at least give her a distraction for a few days. It's the least I could do since I croaked and all. Anyway, I hope it didn't suck too much.

Now, on to the hard stuff. I'm guessing that you're still mad at me for not telling you about Tommy the tumor. (Yes, I named him. Zip it.) But, if you're here expecting an apology, I don't have one for you.

Wait! Wait! Wait! Don't start shredding shit yet. I do have an explanation. It's best if I start at the beginning.

(Imagine I'm dramatically clearing my throat right now.)

The day the doctors found that asshole Tommy in my brain was the most surreal day of my life.

I went from happy and healthy to dying in just one visit to the doctor.

My mom cried as he rattled off statistics about the typical life expectancy for someone like me, but with every number, I only got more and more pissed.

I didn't want to know that shit. Months. Weeks. Days. Why? So I could waste the rest of my life marking days off the calendar?

That's not living, Quarry.

That's waiting to die.

I typed out no less than seventy-five texts to you on my way home that day, but in the end, the only one I actually sent said "I love you." You know what you replied? "Love you too. Whatcha cooking me for dinner? I'm starved."

I was dying...and you wanted me to cook dinner. I laughed until I couldn't see the words through my tears. It was the first time I'd smiled since I had been given my life sentence—and the exact moment when I decided not to tell you or Liv the truth.

Fine. I have a brain tumor. But why does that get to dictate how my life ends? Why did I have to spend an entire afternoon holding my grief-stricken parents' hands when we could have been making jokes over a greasy burger that I no longer had to worry would make me fat? I mean, who wants to live like that? Where everyone around you cries all the time and treats you like you're made of glass. Definitely not me. I wanted to live the fun life I'd made with the people I loved while I still had it.

You might remember the feast of lasagna, salad, cheesy, garlic bread, and banana pudding I made you that night. But what I remember is the peace I felt while you sat on the counter trying to throw lettuce into my hair when you thought I wasn't looking. I remember the rush of excitement that morphed into a fit of laughter when you threw me over your shoulder and spun around *after you got caught mid-toss. And I remember the overwhelming sense of contentment that washed over me right before I fell asleep securely tucked into your side on the couch.*

That night, and however many nights I got after it, I wasn't waiting to die, Quarry. I won't apologize for that.

I am sorry I couldn't stay with you forever though.

I love you, Quarry Page. And I know you loved me too. But, if you're reading this, I'm past tense. You can't be afraid to move on.

Live, Q!

Love.

In the present!

Go!

Like, right now!

Put this letter down.

And live.

I know I did.

Thank you for an amazing life,

Mia

P.S. It's safe to exhale now.

My breath left my burning lungs on the rush of a laugh. *God, Mia.* In all the times I'd imagined the words on those pages, I'd never once considered how I'd feel after having read them. The relief was just as surprising as it was exhilarating. Her note didn't really say anything I didn't know, but it still freed me. The last memory I had of Mia alive was her connected to a slew of wires and machines at the hospital. And the one before that, she was seizing in the front seat of my car. But, in that letter, she wasn't broken and helpless. She was laughing and cracking jokes. Which was exactly how I wanted to remember her.

Two arms folded around my waist. "You still okay?"

"Yeah, Rocky, I'm good. You feeling any better?" I asked, tilting my head to wipe a stray tear away with my shoulder.

"Much," she replied, squeezing me tight. "I'm getting a tattoo!" she announced. "Right now. Tonight."

I dropped my chin to my chest and sighed. *Fucking, Mia.* Somehow, in only two pages, she'd convinced our little Miss Preppy to get inked.

"I wouldn't mind starting on my sleeves," I said, glancing over my shoulder.

Moisture was flowing from her eyes, but a wide smile split her mouth. "Thank you. I know you didn't exactly want to be here, but I needed that."

I grinned because, deep down, I knew I'd needed it more. Instead of admitting that, I said, "Come on. Let's get that virgin skin some ink." I paused, shoving my letter into my back pocket. Quirking an eyebrow, I said, "You tell your dad I took you to get a tattoo, I'm kicking you out."

She hiccoughed a laugh, drying her eyes on the back of her sleeve. "I'll blame it on Mia. He can't be mad at her, now can he?"

"I'm sure she'd be willing to accept the blame even if he could." I laughed.

With quick goodbyes and promises of returning for dinner, Liv and I left.

Three hours later, we headed home newly inked.

Alone—together.

CHAPTER
Nine

$\mathcal{L}iv$

Three years later...

"LIV!" GWEN YELLED AS I exited my classroom at the community center.

I made my way toward her desk. "Would you stop yelling? You're making the sign language students wish they were deaf. No one wants to hear you shouting all the time."

"It's not *all* the time! Only when I need you. If you have such a problem with it, maybe you could talk to that rich boss of yours and see if he'll fund getting the intercoms fixed."

I rolled my eyes. She wasn't talking about Melvin, the man who ran the local community center where I ran the American Sign Language program. She was talking about my *other* boss. The one who more than likely wouldn't bat an eye at buying a new intercom system. I, however, refused to ask him for anything else after he'd paid for all new desks and books not even six weeks ago.

"Nope. No way," I replied.

"Fine. Then learn to deal with me yelling." She shrugged. "Anyway, the new volunteer is waiting up front."

Folding my hands together in a prayer, I pleaded, "Tell me he's better than the last fifteen people I've seen."

"Can he really be any worse than the lady who brought her parrot to the interview?"

"God, I hope not. Who would have thought it would be this difficult to find some decent help?"

"Uh…" she drawled. "It's a free assistant position. Who would have thought anyone would want that job?"

"Well, let's just pray this guy does. He's my absolute last chance of hiring someone and getting them trained before I leave next week."

"Okay. I'll have a chat with the big guy upstairs. And you hurry up before he gets sick of waiting and decides to find a real job."

Smoothing my dress down, I sent up my own prayer. *Please, please, please let this guy work.* "Give me a minute. I need to grab my phone so I can give him some dates."

"I'll put him in the after-school room." She closed her eyes, dramatically craned her head back, and began loudly praying to the ceiling.

"Thanks," I laughed, snagging the papers from my inbox on the corner of her desk.

While flipping through the various announcements and memos, I wandered back to my classroom just in time to hear my phone chirping in my purse.

When I picked it up and saw the two names I'd been added into a group message with, I knew it wasn't going to be good. It chirped repeatedly as message after message popped up on my screen.

Quarry: Fuck face?

Quarry: Limp dick?

Flint: How old are you again?

Quarry: Old enough to know that if I can wipe my ass with a hundred dollar bill, I can damn sure dress myself too.

Flint: As your agent, you'd have to pay me 30% before you even found a shitter.

Quarry: Good point. You're fired.

Flint: Oh please, I'm not that lucky.

Me: What the hell are you two blowing up my phone for now?

Flint: Thank God! The voice of reason! Tell him he has to wear a tux tonight.

Quarry: She's not telling me shit. She's gonna tell you that I can wear whatever the hell I want.

Flint: Liv?

Me: Please hold. I need to catch up on all 78 messages I missed while I was...ya know...WORKING!

I quickly scrolled up to find that this argument had started when Quarry had asked if Flint or I would drop off the red Chucks he'd left in his locker at the gym. He wanted to wear them to the On The Ropes Youth Boxing Fundraising Gala we were attending that night. This had resulted in Flint's telling him that he had to wear a tux. Which had led to Quarry's refusal. Which had led to Flint's insulting him for his lack of professionalism. Which had led to Quarry's rattling off his vast knowledge of curse words in search of just the right one to accurately describe his brother. It had apparently been going on for over an hour. I hadn't heard Quarry refer to anyone as a unicorn dildo in a while, so I was almost sad to have missed all the action.

But not really.

Me: Okay. All caught up.

Quarry: So tell him.

Me: You don't have to wear a tux.

Quarry: BOOM! Forget about bringing my Chucks. I'm about to drive over to your house just to rub this shit in your face.

Me: Not so fast. You don't have to wear a tux, but you do have to wear a suit. I hung a new Armani in your closet this morning.

Quarry: Fuck. That.

Flint: Oh look! The great and powerful Oz agrees with me. How'd that go again, Q? Boom? LOL!

Quarry replied with a picture of Flint taking a hard right to the chin back in his boxing days.

Me: You two need to grow up. Q, wear the damn suit. No tie and with your black Chucks. You can take the jacket off after we get there. BOOM! I win. Now, leave me alone. I have to finish up here so I can go get my hair done.

Flint: Thanks, Liv.

Me: No prob. Later.

Quarry: I just cut you out of my will.

Me: I'll survive off the money I've been swindling out of your bank account.

Quarry: Ha. Ha. Ha. So funny.

Me: Who's kidding? My heels aren't cheap, and you pay shit.

Quarry: And here we go again. You aren't getting a raise!

Flint: He can't afford a raise. I went up 2% last month.

Me: 2% for Flint is my entire salary! What the hell?

Quarry: *No hablo Inglés.*

Me: *No seas un cabrón tacaño y dame el maldito aumento*!

Flint: Runs to Google Translate.

Quarry: Waste of time. They don't do all the cuss words. I tried.

Me: Fine. No raise. But you should know, it's your month to pay our water bill. I will be taking approximately 427 baths, washing 333 loads of laundry, and flushing the toilet 8422 times. I have a weak bladder. Sucks for you!

Flint: You're going to bathe over twenty three times a day?

Me: If I have to!

Flint: While doing eleven loads of laundry?

Me: Hey, don't doubt my commitment. I'm all about sticking it to The Man.

Quarry: Good to know we at least have transparency in the workplace. But, as The Man, I'm curious how you're going to manage to pee 280 times a day.

Me: Oh, I forgot to mention I'll also be drinking 1298 oz of water. Cha-ching! You sure you don't want to just give me the money and save us all the trouble?

Quarry: Nah. This sounds like more fun. See you tonight.

Me: Later, Q

Quarry: Later, Rocky.

Shaking my head, I hurried toward the after-school room, continuously praying that this guy had actually read the help wanted ad all the other people I'd interviewed had seemed to struggle with.

"Sorry I'm late!" I said as I entered the room.

A tall, older man with salt-and-pepper hair and blue eyes greeted me with a warm smile. "Don't worry about it," he said, pushing to his feet and extending his hand in my direction. "I'm Don Blake. I'm here about the assistant position."

After returning his shake, I lifted my hands and signed, *Nice to meet you too. I'm Liv James.*

His smile grew as his hands fluidly replied, *Nice to meet you too. I believe we spoke on the phone earlier.*

"Oh thank God!" I rushed a relieved breath. "You actually know how to sign."

He tipped his head in amusement. "I figured that would be a requirement to assist the director of the ASL program."

"You would be amazed! I had a guy come in earlier and the only sign language he knew was a song he learned at church when he was eight."

He narrowed his eyes in question as he settled back into the chair, signing, *Jesus loves me. This I know. For the Bible tells me so?*

"*Yes! That one!*"

He let out a deep laugh then signed as he spoke. "*Wow. I didn't know my competition would be so steep. Should I just leave now?*"

And he was fluent! Maybe that first guy hadn't been wrong. Jesus really did love me.

"You're hired!" I yelled. "And, when I say hired, I mean, I'll be working you to the bone for free. I do, however, bring Starbucks every day. Oh, and baked goods on the days my roommate doesn't demolish them. So there will be perks."

"Now there's no way I could turn down an offer like that," he teased with a grin.

"You have no idea how excited I am right now. I've spent weeks trying to find an assistant who could help out on the nights I can't be here. I adore teaching, but with my other job, I just can't keep up with all the tutoring and grading. Plus, I travel a lot, so I need someone who could cover some group exercises on the nights I'm away."

"I should be able to handle that without a problem. What do you do for your other job?"

I swayed my head from side to side in consideration. "I'm an assistant."

He chuckled. "So you need an assistant so you can be an assistant to someone else?"

"Pretty much." I shrugged. "My best friend is a hearing-impaired professional boxer. What started out as translating for him during post-fight interviews as a favor quickly turned into a full-time job. Now, I'm his translator, personal assistant, chef, maid, stylist, and, most recently, acting referee when he gets into arguments with his brothers. That alone could be a full-time job."

"Wow. You sound busy."

"You could definitely say that, but I love it. I've been doing most of those things for the last four years anyway. At least, now, he pays me. It's fun too. Quarry and I have been friends forever, so it's more like just hanging out than really working."

He leaned in close. "Wait. Quarry Page?"

"That would be him. Are you a boxing fan?"

"Absolutely! I've lived in Indy all my life. I remember seeing his older brother fight back in the day."

"Oh cool. Yeah, Till's retired now. He still trains Quarry and some of the other kids at the gym now."

"This is incredible. I can't wait to tell the friends I'm the volunteer assistant to Quarry Page's paid assistant." He smiled teasingly, but I could see the genuine excitement sparkling in his eyes.

It always made me laugh when people thought of Quarry as famous. I mean, I knew he technically was, but to me, he'd always be that boy I'd met in a back alley all those years earlier. Sure, he was loaded now, but our lives hadn't changed all that much since his career had taken off.

Thanks to fights and a few big endorsement deals, Quarry was worth millions, but it's not like he was out blowing money all over town. Yes, he had a mild obsession with expensive sports cars, but that was about the extent of his frivolousness. We still lived in the same apartment we had since I'd first moved in.

There was a brief period about two years earlier when he started house shopping. We must have looked at over a hundred.

Big houses.

Small houses.

Expensive houses.

Starter homes.

Mansions.

Condos.

And everything in between.

Quarry was too picky though. I had fallen in love with one, but no matter how nice the place, he'd managed to find something wrong with it. Till had even set him up with the architect who'd designed his and Eliza's house, but Quarry had hated everything she had come up with.

Eventually, he had given up and decided to buy a huge TV and new furniture for our apartment.

I hadn't complained because...well, I hadn't wanted him to move out. I loved living together. He'd also let me pick the furniture out. Win-win.

Leaning across the table that divided us, Don prodded, "So tell me about Davenport. That fight finally gonna happen or what?

I gasped and plugged my ears with my fingers. "No! Don't say that name! It's like Beetlejuice or that guy from Harry Potter. We *never* say that name!"

Garrett Davenport, while he sounded like a pretentious dick, was actually a badass boxer. Not as badass as Quarry, but then again, I couldn't guarantee that since they hadn't actually fought yet. Davenport was the four-time reigning world heavyweight champion, and he loathed Quarry Page something fierce.

Over a year earlier, Quarry had been given his long-awaited, highly anticipated title fight. He'd busted his ass in the gym day and night in preparation. However, three days before the match, Davenport sprained his ankle. Quarry was disappointed, but shit happens. However, two weeks later, when Garrett was photographed skiing in Vail with his girlfriend, his injury seemed a little too convenient (read: fake). Over the three months, he was "recovering," Davenport spewed more shit than a sewage line that had sprung a leak. But he didn't just talk about Quarry's boxing. He attacked him personally. It was like a political campaign and he was determined to slay Quarry in the public eye. He cast slanderous shadows on Quarry's role in Eliza's kidnapping and, ultimately, Flint's injury. He even went so far as to bring up Mia's death, making outlandish accusations that suggested Quarry hadn't acted quickly enough to save her.

That was when Quarry lost his mind. And not just like he was pissed. I mean we all thought there was a good chance Garrett was going to be found dead with Quarry standing over his bloody carcass.

When it finally came time for their fight, Quarry was still fuming. Thus, when Davenport whispered a sweet nothing in his ear during the weigh-in, he blew up. Punches weren't just thrown—they were weaponized. By the time the men were pulled apart, Davenport was unrecognizable and Quarry's right hand was broken. Needless to say, the fight was canceled—again. As the champion, Davenport was assigned a new opponent a few weeks later, while Quarry sucked it up and nursed his injury.

The boxing association stiffly fined them both because of the widely televised brawl at the weigh-in, but that was one check Quarry didn't mind writing.

It pissed me off though.

I got it. He was hurt and angry. But beating the shit out of a man was no punishment when he still walked away with the belt slung over his shoulder. Quarry deserved that title; he'd more than proved that. But Davenport knew that the only way he could win that fight was if it never happened. So he weaseled into Quarry's brain, lit the fuse, and then sat back and watched the fireworks.

That's when "Golden" Garrett Davenport became *my* opponent.

Fuck with Quarry physically all day long—he could handle it. But no one screwed with his head. I didn't care if he was six feet three and over two hundred and fifty pounds of solid muscle. I was protective.

So yeah, after the shit we'd been through, no one got to utter Garrett Davenport's name. Not even clueless Don Blake.

"Okay. Okay." He chuckled as I shook my head and pretended to shiver. "I'll never utter *his* name again."

"Good call. We should probably change the subject immediately before Quarry senses this conversation and feels the need to destroy my apartment."

He chuckled again. "Okay. So, any other names or words I should know that are off-limits?"

"Nope. Just that one." I returned his smile. "Tell me a little about yourself, Don?"

He reclined in the chair and regarded me humorously. "It's an exciting story, so brace yourself."

Clutching my chest, I exaggerated a deep breath. "I'm ready."

"I sell cars at a dealership downtown. Relatively flexible schedule. I'm single. My wife and I divorced over a decade ago. I have a couple of kids, but they're all grown and married now. Figure it's as good a time as any to get out and do something in my spare time."

"Wow. That was riveting," I deadpanned.

"I know. I get that a lot."

We both laughed.

"So, where'd you learn sign?" I asked.

"I was never formally taught or anything. I was raised by my grandparents, and my grandfather lost his hearing when he was eighteen. It was a necessity to communicate with him. He passed away when I was a teenager, but some things just stick with you."

Hmmm. He looked a long way from a teenager.

I decided to test him one last time. Only signing, I asked, *How have you maintained your competency all these years? You don't seem rusty at all.*

He shrugged and his eyes momentarily flashed to the ground uncomfortably. "*Honestly?*"

"*I'd appreciate it if you were.*"

He nodded absently. "*I was extremely rusty a few years ago. Then I met someone, and let's just say, I found a reason to brush up on my skills.*" His smile dimmed as he dropped his hands into his lap. "So here I am now, just hoping I can use this position to keep myself polished up in case I ever get the chance to talk to her again." He paused and released a sad sigh. "A man can dream, right?"

I offered him a sympathetic smile. "You came to the right place. I have more than enough tasks to keep you at the top of your game."

He clapped his hands together and painted on another grin. "So, when do I start, boss?"

Me: OMG OMG OMG I finally found an assistant!!!! He's grading papers for me tomorrow, so I'll have the whole day off.

Quarry: Does this mean you're good to go with me next week?

Me: Yep. I'm celebrating by getting drunk tonight!

Quarry: Thank God…but no.

Me: No what?

Quarry: You aren't drinking. Last time you did, I ended up almost fighting an angry circus clown after you made his girlfriend cry by complimenting her Oompa Loompa costume.

Me: That was NOT the last time I drank. That was my 21st birthday. And I won't say it again. She looked like an Oompa Loompa and you know it!

Quarry: She wasn't in costume!

Me: Then why was she orange?!

Quarry: Who the hell knows? The better question would be why the hell her boyfriend was dressed like a clown? And why exactly he thought picking a fight with me would end well for him?

Me: Oh my God! Do you remember when Ash started begging him to make her balloon animals because she thought Flint hired him for my birthday?

Quarry: I thought someone was going to have to bail Flint out of jail when Bozo snapped at her.

Me: Ya know, for a man whose face was painted in a big, red smile, he really was a grouchy clown.

Quarry: Come on. Give the guy a break. It was probably the first time he realized he was in a relationship with a dangerous escapee from Willie Wonka's Chocolate Factory.

Me: Lol! That was such a fun night.

Quarry: No.

Me: No. What?

Quarry: No, we aren't going out after this charity thing tonight.

Me: Oh, Grandpa Page, I would never dream of dragging you out. I'm well aware how much you love hiding out at home. I'll just celebrate by drinking wine and making you watch me reenact Grease 2 again.

Quarry: Dear. God. Why?

Me: You want me to grab you some beer on my way home?

Quarry: Yes and a bottle of chloroform.

Me: Hi-larious!

Quarry: Where are you anyway? Isn't it gonna take you four days to get dressed? We have to leave in an hour.

Me: I had my hair and makeup done. I just need to put on my dress and shoes. The most time-consuming part will be yelling at you to change until you finally relent and put on the damn suit instead of whatever jeans you have on right now.

Quarry: Promise me no Grease 2 and I'll be in the suit when you get here.

Me: Deal. See you in ten.

Quarry: Cool.

Me: Actually, make that twenty. I'm gonna stop at a Redbox and see if they have The Sound of Music.

Quarry: Fuck!

CHAPTER
Ten

Quarry

WHEN I WAS EIGHT YEARS old, my mom's latest loser boyfriend found a way to steal cable from the neighbors. It was short-lived, seeing as everyone in our apartment complex had figured it out months earlier, but for that weekend, Flint and I thought we had hit the jackpot. We huddled around the TV every waking minute. The picture was shit, constantly breaking into static, but we didn't dare give up or turn it off for fear it would disappear for good. It was only a matter of time before we were rewarded for our dedication when the screen unscrambled. And, like the dumb kids we were, we gasped with excitement, hoping those minutes of clarity would last forever.

They didn't.

The snow once again clouded our view, leaving us longing to reclaim those stolen flashes of clarity.

Over the years, my life began to resemble those days spent staring at a half-assed TV. There were bits of entertainment breaking up the otherwise monotonous drone of static, but for the most part, my life was nothing more than a black-and-white, jumbled mess. The world around me functioned as nothing more than a noisy distraction to keep my mind occupied while I desperately waited for the bigger picture to come into focus.

The only problem was, after Mia died, I wasn't even sure what the picture of my life looked like anymore.

My only clarity came inside the boxing ring or in the solitude of my apartment—with Liv.

It took a long time, but the wound Mia had left behind eventually scabbed over. But nothing filled the hollowness inside me. I couldn't exactly pinpoint what was missing. I just knew that it was gone.

Every single day, I smiled.

Every single day, I lived.

Every single day, I laughed.

And, every single night, I stared at my ceiling, trying to figure out why none of those things left me feeling even an ounce of contentment.

Those feelings usually led me to pace our small apartment until I gave in, donned my hearing aids, and sat in the hall, listening to the music blaring from under the crack of Liv's door. For a while, I thought she was on to something with the whole sleeping-with-music thing. But, after several failed attempts at sleeping while sitting up in order to keep my hearing aids in, I gave up and found myself leaning against her door again.

Nightly.

For years.

Occasionally, I'd doze off.

More often, I'd go back to my room and wait for sleep to overpower the lingering chaos consuming my mind.

But, sometimes, if I got really lucky, I'd think of an excuse to wake her up.

Those hours spent in her dimly lit room, discussing whatever random topic I could find to keep her talking, were enough to temporarily extinguish the static. And, if I hadn't felt so fucking guilty each morning as she left for work with dark circles under her eyes, it would have become my nightly routine.

Liv never said a word about my late-night appearances in her room—not even to give me shit about them. That wasn't who she was. She knew I needed it and she gave it freely.

That was Liv James.

It was who we were together.

On the flip side, I gave it to her too.

I never once said a word about the nights I'd wake up to find her in my bed. I wasn't sure why she was there because she never woke me up to talk or cuddled into my back for comfort. She was just there. Headphones on. iPod on the nightstand. Long hair fanned out behind her. Black lashes fluttering in REM. There.

The next morning, she was always gone when I woke up.

But she'd been there. I knew because those were the nights I basked in the silence.

Every single time, I'd smile as I tugged the blanket over her.

Every single time, I felt alive while watching her lost in peaceful slumber.

Every single time, I'd laugh as her chest shuddered with what I assumed was a soft snore.

And, every single time, I'd stare at the ceiling as contentment washed over me, lulling me into the most amazing sleep of my life.

Those nights weren't just the clarity—they were the blinding colors that made me wake up the next morning, put one foot in front of the other, and take on another day.

It didn't happen frequently, but at least once a month, I'd find her at my side.

But guilt overwhelmed me.

Because, nightly, I'd selfishly wish that whatever demon had her sneaking into my room would find her and allow me a few hours with her at my side to escape my own.

I can honestly say without a single doubt that Liv James was the only reason I didn't self-destruct over the years. I could have easily gone off the deep end, losing myself in anger at the fucking universe that seemed so hell-bent on ruining me.

Liv wouldn't let go though. She fought for me even when I desperately wanted to throw in the towel.

We were friends—best friends. But that wasn't where our relationship ended.

She was the little sister I never had but would've killed to protect. No matter the price.

She was the roommate who threatened to move out on a daily basis because I left my shoes all over the place. Half the time, I did it on purpose because I loved watching her rant in Spanish as she furiously swirled around the room, picking them up, only seconds before throwing them at me. Plus, she was fair to a fault. Despite the fact that I made more in a single fight than she would in ten years, she still insisted on paying half the bills and alternating the utilities each month.

Liv was also my chef, not because I'd asked her to be, but rather because she knew I needed a healthy diet despite being worthless in the kitchen. I was a professional heavyweight boxer; my metabolism was insane. I consumed thousands of calories when I was training up for a fight. Every morning, I'd wake up with a tote bag full of food to take to the gym with me. Good food. Healthy food. Shit no one but professional athletes would ever want to eat. And she made it *for me.*

Most recently, she had become my assistant. She knew me so well that it was as if she could read my mind. Liv could predict what I needed without my ever asking. And then she made sure I had it. I wasn't exactly easy to deal with—I knew that much. But Liv was tough and didn't pull any punches when I got out of line. Not even when I needed her to. I'd never in a million years be able to replace her.

Liv James was absolutely everything to me.

Well, almost.

She wasn't mine.

Yet.

See, when a man is in love with a woman, he doesn't allow himself to see the perfections in anyone else. I had been so blinded by my devotion to Mia that, while I'd seen Liv daily, I hadn't truly recognized the insanely sexy and desirable woman she was. That is, until one night, when the scars covering my heart were finally able to close the gaping wound Mia March had left behind.

It was a Friday when it happened.

A Friday when everything I'd missed over the years came slamming into my head at a million miles an hour, rocking me back and forcing me to take notice.

A Friday I'd never forget no matter how desperately I tried to block it from my memory.

A Friday when I realized I was probably going to lose my best friend.

A Friday when I knew I was in for the biggest fight of my life to keep her.

It was a Friday when the picture of my life finally came into focus and I saw Liv James for what felt like the very first time.

"Oh my gah!" she shouted as she slammed the door and dropped her purse on the floor.

"That good, huh?" I asked, sprawled out on the chocolate-brown leather sectional Liv had picked out.

Fisting her hands on her hips, she tilted her head. "Can you please tell me what is wrong with your generation of men?"

My eyebrows popped in humor. "My generation of men?"

"Yes! Why are you all assholes?"

Sitting up, I replied, "Present company excluded?"

After pulling her heels off, she carried them to her room, calling over her shoulder, "I'm not sure. The jury is still out on that."

"Hey!" I started to follow her when she returned to continue her rant.

After making a brief stop at the fridge to pour a glass of wine, she cozied into her spot in the bend of the couch. "So, get this... He took me to The Roads for dinner."

Snagging two bananas and a jar of peanut butter, I headed to the couch to join her. "What's wrong with The Roads? Their steaks are fucking insane and definitely not cheap."

She curled her legs underneath her. "Nothing's wrong with it... unless your ex-girlfriend is a waitress there and you specifically ask to be seated in her section...while on a date...with someone else." She curled her lip.

"No shit?"

"No. Shit," she confirmed.

"What'd you do?"

She scoffed. "What I did was order a hundred-dollar bottle of wine I barely got to touch because he kept trying to hold my hand over the table, and then I ordered another hundred dollars in food, which I scarfed down in record time. Because, well...you aren't wrong about those steaks, but he was a self-absorbed snob who made me wish his steak had bones just so he could choke on one. But *then!* I told him to go fuck himself and caught a cab home. I seriously don't understand what's wrong with men."

Swallowing another bite of banana, I propped my feet on the ottoman and reclined into the couch. "It's not them. There's something wrong with *you.*"

"Excuse me?" she said just seconds before her fist landed hard on my thigh.

"Ow. Shit. Stop punching me. I didn't get to finish."

"Then by all means continue, oh wise one." Rolling her eyes, she tipped the wine to her lips.

"You have shit taste in guys. I can't believe you even went out with him after he showed to pick you up wearing boat shoes."

"Hey! I like boat shoes."

Coating the tip of my banana with peanut butter, I replied, "No. You like douchebags." Holding her eyes, I dared her to challenge me as I took a bite.

She didn't hesitate. "I do not!"

Since I was chewing, my only response was to quirk my eyebrow in a silent *Really?*

"I'm serious! I don't." She glared.

"See, your problem is you're pretty and not stupid. You wear tight dresses and those fucking heels, so guys think you won't notice when they parade you around town all while they count down the minutes until they can get you home to remove the dress…but keep the heels on." I winked.

Her mouth gaped open in a mixture of disbelief and disgust.

"But what they don't expect is for you to be smart. Given the fact that your dress and shoes cost a fucking mint, they sure as fuck don't expect that the fancy car they borrowed from their rich daddy and the expensive meal they feed you will not help get that dress off. Since I know you so well, I'm pretty sure it might get the shoes off."

Her eyes turned murderous, but I chuckled, shaking my head.

"But only because, when he finally got the balls to make a play, you'd throw them at him. So yeah, Rocky. You have a problem. You keep going for douchebags, they're gonna keep treating you like douchebags. End the cycle. Stop going for douchebags." I shrugged.

"Wow. How enlightening from a man who hasn't been on a real date in over four years. And don't even say it! Hooking up with a girl after a fight doesn't count."

Mid-bite, I swung my gaze to hers. "What the hell are you talking about?"

Unfortunately, I knew exactly what she was talking about. I just didn't know how she knew what she was talking about.

Did I sometimes pick up a girl after a fight? Yes. Did I ever once let on to anyone that it happened? Fuck no. Not Till. Not Flint. And sure as fuck not Liv. It didn't happen very often, and the women always knew the score. But fuck...as much as my mind would rather be in the peace and quiet of my own apartment, my body was twenty-four years old. Back when it had started, I'd been struggling, and while I had known that those empty orgasms weren't helping anything, they definitely hadn't hurt anything, either. If nothing else, they at least relaxed me so I wasn't a pent-up, miserable bastard all the time. Well, maybe they just helped with the pent-up part of that equation.

It was either screw girls after fights, jack my dick until it fell off, or find someone I actually wanted to date. And no fucking way were the last two options happening.

So yeah, on occasion, I wrapped my cock in a condom and found a warm body to essentially jerk off inside.

Fuck. I was a douchebag of a completely different variety.

"I have eyes, Quarry. Just because you don't tell me doesn't mean I haven't seen you carting some skank back to your hotel room."

I huffed, unimpressed. Though, secretly, I was seriously impressed that she'd actually noticed. I'd thought I'd done a damn fine job of keeping that part of my life hidden.

"Your eyes didn't see shit. All of those kinky books you read are fucking with your head." I stood, twisting the top on the peanut butter then snapping my fingers for her empty wine glass. "Another?" I didn't bother waiting for her answer before taking the glass and walking to the kitchen.

"It doesn't make you a bad person, Quarry," she called after me.

"Drop it," I growled.

"You don't have to hide the fact that you might actually be moving on. Honestly, I'm just hoping one of them figures out how to pack a twenty-pound lunch box and relieves me of my duties. You know I won't always be here to feed you."

I should have shut the conversation down right then and there, but for some reason, I snapped back entirely too roughly, "Oh, yeah. You want to be relieved of your duties? Consider it done. But I'm not getting a girlfriend just to cook for me."

As I rounded the corner carrying her second glass of wine, her soft, brown eyes met mine.

"It's been four years, Q," she said. "It's time to move—"

"What are you doing?" I asked. "Hosting an intervention for my cock? Till and Flint gonna bust up in here any minute with condoms and lube?"

Her eyes turned hard, and her lip curled. "Lube? Ew! I did not need to know that."

And, just because I felt the need to be a dick and make her just as uncomfortable as I already was, I popped a shoulder in a half shrug and grabbed my dick, giving a firm shake as I said, "This big, Liv, lube becomes a necessity."

As her eyes grew wide, I realized my attempt at making her uncomfortable had backfired.

Monumentally.

Taking the glass from my hand, she asked, "Noted. Should I start adding lube to your travel bags for the girls after the fights, then?"

It was a snarky comment that proved she wasn't buying my story, but that wasn't why my plan went haywire.

No. That question was only the beginning of the biggest mind-fuck I would ever experience.

Her heated gaze dropped to the hand cupping my cock. Then, within seconds, her nipples very noticeably peaked beneath the fabric of her clingy dress.

What. The. Fuck.

But that wasn't even the worst of it.

The head of my cock responded by swelling while I drank her in…drinking me in.

"Uh, no," I mumbled, twisting away before she could spot the bulge growing in my sweats.

Shocked, I stared down at my cock as if it could somehow tell me why it was standing at attention after I'd checked Liv James out. *Christ.* How hard up did I have to be to sprout wood over my best friend?

Apparently, it was time to find one of those girls I had been lying about. ASAP.

Wait. I wasn't the only one who'd been turned on by our awkward exchange. How hard up was she?

"When was the last time you got laid?" I blurted, my back still facing her—not wanting to display the flagpole currently tenting my pants.

"A while, but you can't blame me. Douchebags suck in bed."

Not this one.

Oh, God!

I jumped in surprise when her arms suddenly folded around my waist from behind.

Goddamn it!

"Don't be mad," she whispered into my T-shirt.

My heart raced as her front came flush with my back. Liv hugged me all the time, but never—not once—had I noticed how firm her tits were as they pressed against me. Right then, in the middle of what was clearly some kind of sexual psychotic episode, it was all I could think of. Every breath I took ground her large breasts into me. And, with the rate in which my lungs sped at that realization, it left us only one step away from dry-humping.

Her grip shifted lower as she squeezed me tight.

She was only inches away from my straining erection, and I prayed that she didn't notice it, all the while hoping that her hand accidentally brushed against it—repeatedly.

With just the thought, my cock twitched.

Fuck.

Prying her hands away, I took a giant step forward in effort to gain some space and, hopefully, sense. "I'm…uh…I'm not feeling good. I'm gonna take a shower and head to bed."

Long strides carried me toward my room.

What the fucking fuck just happened?

Liv called out behind me, "I'm sorry, okay? I shouldn't have said anything. I'll stop dating douchebags and you screw whoever you want."

Well, that would be you right about now.

Son of a bitch.

I need serious mental help.

I waved her apology off. Just before closing my door on the most confusing interaction of my entire life, I replied, "See you in the morning."

It was a lie.

Five minutes later, I saw her on the backs of my eyelids as I stroked my cock in the shower.

Then I saw her again thirty minutes after that as I tried to flood her out of my mind with Internet porn. I was going to Hell, but the two of us starred in every one of those videos. Hence the reason my night ended with me coming on my stomach before finally falling asleep.

It had been a Friday three months ago when that had happened, and every single day since had been pure and utter hell.

Apparently, I was the only one who ate the freaky, ecstasy-laced bananas that night, because while I was pounding my dick like a thirteen-year-old who'd just discovered it any time she so much as walked out of her room in yoga pants, Liv seemed completely unaffected.

Just friends. Same as always.

I couldn't have her. I knew that much. But that didn't stop my mind from spinning in that direction every time I laid eyes on her.

And, considering that it was now the night of the On The Ropes Youth Boxing Fundraiser Gala, I knew I was in for an evening of torture.

She'd dress up. Something tight and sexy yet unbelievably classy. She'd put on a pair of heels I'd spend weeks dreaming about fucking her in. She'd have her hair and makeup done sleek, sultry, and agonizing—for me, anyway. The real pain was that, even though she would be on my arm when we walked through the doors, she would be fair game for every single man in the room.

No. Liv James definitely wasn't mine.

Yet.

CHAPTER
Eleven

$\mathcal{L}iv$

"HOW LONG DO I HAVE to wait before I can take the jacket off?" Quarry asked, offering an arm for me as we exited the black SUV and stepped onto the red carpet.

We were at a charity gala to raise money for the On The Ropes youth boxing program. Slate had been funding it on his own for years, and when Till had won the championship and bought half the gym, he'd done the same. It was quickly becoming too expensive for either of them to carry on their own.

The program was specifically geared toward underprivileged kids and keeping them off the streets. Since the Page brothers were the shining example of what the gym could accomplish, On The Ropes had gained a good bit of national attention. With a rising demand to expand into different locations across the country, Erica and Eliza decided to organize a yearly fundraiser to help pay the mounting expenses.

Professional boxers, new and old, graciously donated not only money, but also their time to attend the event. With Slate Andrews, Till Page, Quarry Page, and a slew of other celebrities in attendance, tickets were coveted—and expensive as hell. Wealthy businessmen and rich boxing fans flew from all over the country in order to rub elbows and hopefully sign donations checks. Last year's gala had raised over three point nine million dollars, which had all been funneled into the newest On The Ropes location in Brooklyn, opening later that year.

Eliza and Erica had done an amazing job putting that night together. Ash and I pitched in a good bit too. It was exhausting work, but the payoff was so huge that none of us could complain. As much as we loved doing it, we all looked forward to the planning being over so we could cut loose and celebrate by eating amazing food and drinking expensive champagne.

With that in mind, I didn't even have it in me to snap at Quarry for his continuous complaining about the suit.

"I'm going to sew you into that thing permanently if you don't stop bitching about it."

Okay, so maybe I did have it in me.

"And rob the world of my body? There would be riots," he said, looking down at me with a wide smile. Camera flashes sparkled the humor in his beautiful, hazel eyes.

"I'm willing to chance it. Besides, it could be nice not to find you half naked every time I exited my bedroom. I'm not sure what kind of breakup you had with shirts, but you might want to consider a reconciliation before your pants follow suit and I'm forced to move out."

His smile grew, but something pained passed over his face. I'd seen that look a lot over the last few months, and while I hadn't been able to figure it out, I knew that it didn't bode well for the rest of my evening.

"Right," he said shortly. Dropping my arm, he shoved his hands in his pockets and aimed a smoldering smirk—complete with one mouth-watering dimple—toward the cameras.

"Good lord. If you're going to pout, just take the jacket off now." I sighed, wondering if this was how my parents had felt when I'd first started my period. He was so damn moody.

"I'm good," he replied absently, tipping his chin toward a sexy, blond reporter desperately trying to catch his attention—and, judging by the way she thrust her boobs forward, she wanted more than just an interview. "I'll be right back." He sauntered in her direction, but at the last minute, her plastic smile faded when he veered to the clamoring fans holding magazines and other memorabilia out for him to sign.

I swept my eyes down his muscular back to his ass, which was pulling deliciously against the black fabric of his suit pants. I wasn't blind. It didn't mean anything though. He was hot. Checking him out was a perk of keeping him as my best friend. I'd recently given up even trying to stop my wandering eyes.

"Liv! Over here!" reporters shouted at me.

I'd also given up explaining to the press that I wasn't his girl-friend. The public didn't believe us. We lived together. I was his "date" to every social function he ever attended. I was in the front row at all of his fights. And I was the first one in the ring to hug him when he won.

No one understood us, but it didn't matter. They didn't need to. We got it.

As hard as it was for people to grasp, platonic friendships *could* work. Given the history Quarry and I had, it was no surprise we had so successfully done it for years. Either you had feelings for someone or you didn't.

Nothing could change that.

Not even checking out the other person's ass.

Or at least that's what I told myself as I tipped my head to ad-mire it from a different angle.

I jumped in surprise when my gaze flashed back up and I found I'd been busted.

His stare was aimed over his shoulder. He was sporting the same sexy smolder that popped that heart-stopping dimple, but his dark, heated gaze was locked on me.

Uhh…what the hell is that look for?

Under his scrutiny, my shoulders instinctively rolled back, doing great things for my boobs and causing his eyes to flicker down to my chest.

The hairs on the back of my neck prickled when he twisted my way.

Both hands in his pockets, his jacket pushed back, showing the wide expanse of his chest straining against the buttons of his shirt, his collar open, and the hint of one of his tattoos peeking over the swell of his trap. He was standing at least ten feet away, regarding me with the most beautifully bizarre expression.

Bizarre because it blasted an unexpected chill over my skin. And beautiful because, well, it was Quarry.

He didn't head in my direction. He just stood there, staring at me, for several beats.

I narrowed my eyes in question, but that only made his smolder morph into an equally confusing—and dazzling—smirk.

"*What?*" I signed, knowing he couldn't hear my voice amongst the chaos.

Removing his hands from his pockets, he signed without speaking, *You look gorgeous.*

Okay, something was *definitely* going on with him. As my roommate, Quarry had been subjected to countless hours of me trying on clothes before dates or interviews or really any time I'd been able to go shopping. I'd heard him tell me, "You look fine," or "You look nice," or "You look good." Once, on Halloween, after I'd had my makeup professionally done to be a zombie at the community center's haunted house, he'd even told me, "You look great."

Never once had I been "gorgeous."

Glancing over my shoulder, I checked to see if the busty, blond reporter had somehow snuck behind me. When I found nothing more than the On The Ropes logo on the red carpet backdrop, I turned back in his direction to find he was no longer there.

My whole body stiffened as callused fingers brushed the hair off my neck.

"I need a drink." His voice was gravelly in my ear.

"I feel like you might already be drunk. There's something wrong with your face," I replied breathlessly even as I insulted him.

He chuckled. "I tell you you're gorgeous and you tell me there's something wrong with my face?"

I craned my head back and peered into his eyes, "Okay, there's something wrong with your face *and* your hands. You're creeping me out."

His expression shifted, and his face was once again painted with something pained.

I smiled warmly, wishing I could figure out what the hell was going on with him. "Talk to me?"

Shaking his head, he pinched the bridge of his nose. "Sorry. I'm tired. That's all. Let's get that drink."

He was lying, but whatever had been bothering him vanished as he tossed me a wicked lopsided grin.

So I let it go.

I could give him that.

For now.

Looping my arm through his, I replied, "I wouldn't turn down champagne."

"Did you see Flint in that tux?" Ash asked for the twentieth time that evening. "I mean, I knew he was sexy in a suit, but God! That vest and bow tie are doing dirty things to me."

I laughed as she continued to ogle her husband from across the room.

"If you want, the boys can spend the night at my house tonight," Eliza offered before sipping on a glass of champagne.

Ash choked on her drink, and her eyes grew comically wide.

Pounding on Ash's back, I told Eliza, "I think she'd like that."

Eliza giggled.

Ash and Flint had two boys, Cole and Chase, whose birthdays weren't even a full year apart. Cole had been a planned pregnancy not long after Mia had passed away. But, when he was less than two months old, Chase had been created the old-fashioned *accidental* way. Flint and Ash loved those boys more than anything in the world, but there was no denying that they could use some time away. Ash was frothing at the mouth just standing in the same room as Flint, so they probably needed more like an entire week away. I made a mental note to talk to Quarry about us watching the hellions so they could do just that. Flint was crazy weird about leaving their kids with babysitters, and if it wasn't for Eliza and Till's long-time nanny having agreed to keep the boys for the gala, I wasn't sure Flint would have come at all.

"Are you sure?" Ash asked through a cough.

"Of course! There is no point in you guys picking them up tonight anyway. They'll already be asleep by the time we get home. But *you're* gonna have to tell Flint. I know how he is with those kids."

"Oh, I can handle Flint. Don't you worry about that." She pushed to her feet and smoothed her long, strawberry-blond hair down. Leaning into my face, she pointed under her eyes. "Makeup?"

"Perfect. You want some gloss?"

She smiled so wide that I thought her face might split. "Nah. It's too hard to clean it off his zipper. There's a strong possibility I may need to do some convincing. A little preview in the bathroom should do the job." She exaggerated a wink.

I groaned, not needing that mental picture.

Eliza pelted her with a balled-up napkin. "Gross!"

Ash crossed her arms over her chest. "Don't even pretend like we don't know why you came strutting out of the limo all disheveled tonight."

Eliza slapped a hand over her mouth, and her cheeks turned bright red. "Oh, God. Was it that obvious?"

Ash high-fived me as we both burst into laughter.

"Not at all. I actually just took a guess. He sprang for the limo. I figured he wanted a little more than just the extra leg room." She winked again then took off on her task to "convince" Flint to leave the kids with their aunt and uncle for the evening.

"Ten bucks she goes for the wallet first," I bet Eliza, sliding down to fill Ash's vacant seat.

"No. You watch. She'll bat her eyelashes, kiss him, and then slide a hand down the back of his pants. *Then!*" She lifted a single finger in the air. "After he at least agrees to meet her in the bathroom, she'll swipe his wallet. Only it won't be in his back pocket. Flint replaced it with the key to the hotel room he booked for them tonight."

"Seriously?!" I squealed, glancing back at Ash as she prowled away.

Eliza nodded, equally as excited.

"Oh my God! She's going to flip. We should say a prayer for the poor souls who get the room next to them tonight." I nabbed two more champagne flutes from a waiter's tray.

We watched as Ash made her move.

Eliza was right. She went for the wallet last.

I was right too though. She. Flipped.

"Ew. Ew. Ew," we said in unison as Ash practically mounted Flint.

"I should probably rescue my husband." She pointed to Till, who was one blink away from dozing off in mid-conversation with a group of gray-haired men.

"You do that and I'm going to find Q. Want to meet at the back bar for a drink in ten minutes? Shots?" I waggled my eyebrows.

Eliza wasn't much of a drinker, but after almost a year of hard work, she always made an exception at the gala.

"Sounds like a plan. I'll make Till get up with the kids in the morning." She laughed. "Want to come over and nurse our hangovers together?"

"You supply the coffee and Netflix. I'll bring the greasy fast food."

"Deal."

We split in different directions.

I made my way to the back of the room where I'd last seen Q at least an hour earlier when he'd been cornered by a group of guests.

When I didn't see him there, I headed toward the exit, thinking he might have snuck into the alley for a breather—a.k.a. hiding so he didn't have to be social. However, as I rounded the corner, I froze when I saw none other than "Golden" Garrett Davenport strutting past the security guard at the back door.

Shit. Shit. Shit.

CHAPTER
Twelve

Quarry

SHOOT ME.

No, seriously.

Shoot me.

I was in a suit.

Chatting with old men who wanted to tell me all about their glory days in junior league boxing. They were dropping names like I should know who the fuck amateur "Tornado" Timmy Turner was four decades before I was born.

Plus, I was stuck chugging nasty-ass champagne off the waiters' trays. Ducking to the bar for a beer would have taken valuable time away from the riveting stories of the youth in the Dark Ages.

And the cherry on top of this shit-sundae was that I hadn't seen Liv in ten hours. Okay, maybe it was only, like, one hour. But she was wearing that little black dress that left virtually nothing to the imagination, so even ten hours felt like an understatement.

She looked every bit as sexy as I had feared.

Her long, sculpted legs taunted me with every step. Urging me to drop to my knees and bury my face between them.

Those tall, black heels whispered promises to score my back with every click.

That silky, brown hair begged to be wrapped around my fist as I fucked her from behind.

Her bold, red lipstick pleaded to stain the root of my cock.

Fuck. Fuck. Fuck.

This is Liv! What the hell is wrong with me?

Never going to happen, buddy.

However, for a brief minute on the red carpet as I caught her eye-fucking my ass, I had hoped that it might.

It was ridiculous though.

Nothing good would ever come of me fucking Liv James.

She was my best friend. Slipping my dick into her was not an option. My fingers though…

Shit!

I loved her—like family. Unfortunately, my body had gotten a few wires crossed and now thought I should love her in that hey-let-me-make-you-come-until-you-forget-the-English-language kind of way.

I desperately needed to find a way to unscramble those thoughts so I could get over this bullshit and get back to where we should be.

Just friends.

Best friends.

Maybe friends who get off together?

Damn it!

With that, I decided it was time to throw etiquette out the window and make my escape.

"Excuse me, gentlemen. I need to check on my date."

Then check myself into a sexual rehabilitation facility.

Several handshakes later, I was free. While scanning the large ballroom for Liv, I caught sight of Eliza dragging Till out of another circle of loaded fogies.

No sign of Liv.

A sudden pain in my ear made me wince. God, I wanted to go home. My new hearing aids had been calibrated for the noisy environment of the fundraiser, but they were uncomfortable as fuck. I headed to the bathroom to check them out or, hell, maybe save myself from being caught in another Circle of Bengay and take them off altogether.

Ignoring a different group of guests trying to catch my attention, I hurried toward the bathroom.

All thoughts of my discomfort disappeared when I heard the sharp cry of Liv's voice. I couldn't make out what she was saying, but only the tone of her voice soured my gut. I sprinted in her direction, not slowing until her long, brown hair came into view.

Then my vision turned red as it zeroed in on a man holding her around the waist as she kicked and screamed in his arms.

"Get him out of here!" Liv shouted. "You don't get to do this! Not again!"

A small crowd blocked my view of who she was screaming at. Liv was definitely spunky—and slightly crazy. But she wasn't hot-tempered. If she was mad about something, chances were I was going to be livid.

"Hey!" I shouted, jogging over to the man restraining her. "Get your fucking hands off her." I possessively claimed her from his arms and then breathed a sigh of relief when I noticed the Guardian Protection Agency pin on his lapel.

That's when the proverbial record stopped.

Liv froze.

Dozens of eyes swung my way.

The crowd parted.

And Garrett fucking Davenport stepped in my direction.

Son.

Of.

A.

Motherfucking.

Whore.

"Quarry 'The Stone Fist' Page, ladies and gentlemen," he announced with a slow clap that grated down my spine.

As much as my fist ached to greet his face, I didn't respond. Not this time.

"Can someone go get Till? Or Slate? Or Flint? Or hell…anyone else? Please," Liv begged as she stepped in front of me. "Walk away, Q. He's only here to get a rise and you know it. Do not give that to him. Lock it down."

I gritted my teeth but remained silent—my eyes trained on the coward in the fitted, black tux looking every bit as pompous and arrogant as I knew him to be.

"I heard there was a fundraiser going on to benefit youth boxing." Davenport puffed his chest and then grinned. "Coincidence. I have funds and love boxing. What are the odds?" He laughed.

"We don't want your fucking money," Liv spat without ever turning to face him. "Walk away, Q."

My jaw clenched as my hands flexed opened and closed at my sides. His appearance had absolutely nothing to do with the fundraiser and everything to do with the fact that the boxing commissioner had emailed over the contracts on his next title fight. I hadn't shared with Liv yet, but I'd found out that morning that my name was finally back on the bottom line. His reign in the ring had been over the minute those contracts had landed on his agent's desk. I knew it. And it gave me great pleasure that he knew it too. This whole confrontation was nothing more than attempt to get in my head. Little did he know that my head had been fucked years earlier. He was only adding fuel to my fire.

That title belonged to me.

I wouldn't let him take this opportunity from me. Not again.

"Are you here to beg me to take it easy on you?" I asked stoically.

He barked a humorless laugh.

Liv squeezed my bicep. "Let's go home."

I ignored her and continued talking to Davenport. "No? Then what? You need my belt size? Routing number for my bank account?"

He took a threatening step forward, but I held my ground.

Liv blew out a loud breath of relief when Slate's meaty paw landed on my shoulder.

"That's enough," Slate said. "Not here, Garrett. This is neither the time nor the place for you to stir up something. You want to make a donation? Mail it to the gym. The kids would be appreciative of your generosity. Besides that, you have no business here."

Fucking Slate. All PC and shit.

"With all due respect, Slate." He paused and smiled condescendingly. "Fuck. You."

"You're not really my type, son," Slate replied with a chuckle, but his hand clenched painfully tight on my shoulder—his fist no doubt aching as well.

Flint's voice came from somewhere behind me. "Get Leo's ass over here. This is over, Garrett. Either you leave now or security will be escorting you out."

Till stepped to my side. Bumping his shoulder with mine, he gritted out, "Do not react. Hold on to this moment for when you have him in the ring. You have your shot. Do not blow it by giving in to this prick."

Shit, he was right.

"What's wrong, Page? Nothing to say?" Davenport goaded. "You just gonna stand there and let your washed-up trainer and has-been brother take care of your shit?"

I sucked in a deep breath.

Don't breathe. Don't breathe. Don't breathe.

Adrenaline surged in my veins, but it found no way out as I

forced it down.

Liv wasn't as successful.

"Who the hell do you think you are?" she erupted.

I hooked a fast arm around her waist and yanked her back to my chest. She continued hurling insults.

Davenport laughed loudly. With an evil smirk, he lifted his eyes to mine.

Three words.

Three *fucking* words secured his fate.

I'd already wanted his belt.

But, with three fucking works, I wanted his blood.

"Control your bitch."

The room exploded. Slate, Till, and even Flint jumped to restrain me.

I didn't move.

Liv was a button of mine he'd never pushed before. It was the only one left that could send me nuclear. Clearly, everyone around us knew that, but I wouldn't give him that knowledge.

That was mine. The last thing I needed was him launching a full-out attack on her just to set me off-kilter.

Every muscle in my body strained, but I didn't budge.

Not forward to kill him.

And definitely not backward in retreat.

I was rooted in place.

Eyes locked.

Plotting his murder.

Electricity charged the air.

I. Did. Not. Move.

I refused to give him what he'd so cowardly come for.

My breath escaped on a loud roar of laughter that stunned everyone, including the senior citizens club that had congregated around us.

Davenport's eyes narrowed in confusion, but my laughter only grew louder.

I repeated his words, shaking my head in humor. "Control your bitch."

"Uhh…" Liv said as I finally dragged my eyes away from Davenport.

Smiling, I said, "He's right, you know."

Her mouth got tight.

"Let him stay. I'm out of here." Chuckling to myself, I repeated under my breath, "Control your bitch."

Three words had never been truer.

As my body relaxed, Slate and Till cautiously released me.

"Show's over!" Leo announced and then started barking orders to at least five of his men, who went to work clearing the disappointed crowd. "Time to leave," Leo ordered, pressing a heavy hand into Davenport's chest. "And, next time you call someone a bitch, the Page brothers are going to be the least of your worries. Got it?" He shoved hard, causing Davenport to stumble back a step, his gaze still locked on me.

"That's it, Page? You just gonna walk away? I should have known you'd be a fucking pussy!" he prodded.

I laughed again as I draped my arm around Liv's waist. "You ready to go?"

"What the hell was that?" she asked, regarding me warily.

My expression turned hard as I looked down at her. "You stay out of shit like that from now on," I scolded her loudly. "I don't need you making things worse."

Her mouth fell open. "Are you kidding me?"

"I'm serious. That shit happens again, you stay the fuck out of it. Do not step between me and another man. Ever."

"You were about to lose it!" she snarled—even that was sexy.

I leaned into her face and lowered my voice. "I cannot worry about you jumping in on something and possibly getting caught in the middle. Now, keep your mouth closed. And back away."

Her eyes flickered with understanding. "Quarry," she warned, but she did it taking two giant steps away.

"Good girl," I whispered, knowing I'd pay for it later.

Spinning on a foot, I charged forward ready to give Davenport exactly what I wanted him to take from our little pow-wow.

Till and Slate were off to the side, chatting with Flint. Leo was still struggling to get Davenport out the back door.

"Yo, Leo!" I called as all the eyes in the room lifted to mine.

It was too late.

My adrenaline finally found a way out.

With a hard right Leo barely dodged, my fist landed on Garrett Davenport's chin, snapping his head to the side and sending him stumbling to the ground.

I dove for another punch, but Till caught my arms before I made contact.

"Only bitch that needs controlling is you!" I roared.

He jumped to his feet and lunged in my direction as security scrambled between us.

"Grow a sack and sign the fucking contracts! You want me? Make it happen." I pounded my chest as he fought the herd of men dividing us.

He'd come wanting to fight. He'd left with yet another sample.

The rest would be delivered in the ring.

My body slacked in Till's grasp.

I calmly watched as Leo's men dragged him, kicking and swinging, out of the back door.

"Jesus Christ," Slate growled, raking a frustrated hand through his hair.

"Dumb fuck," I mumbled as the door slammed shut.

Till let me go, but not before slapping me hard on the back of the head. "Him? What is wrong with *you*? This shit is gonna be all over the news tomorrow."

I shook my hand out, inspecting it to make sure I hadn't injured anything. "Maybe. But I bet Flint receives those signed contracts first thing in the morning."

Cutting my eyes across the room, I found Liv standing right where I'd left her. Her expression was unreadable, but her stiff posture looked positively pissed. *Great.* A lecture about keeping my shit together was on the horizon.

"I think it's best for everyone if I take off. Text me if a shitstorm starts to brew over this."

Till's eyes swung to Liv. "Christ. You're in trouble."

I chuckled. "Yep."

"Well, at least she can't withhold sex." He cupped me on the shoulder then shoved me in her direction. "Give him hell!" he yelled to her, but her hard stare never left mine.

Shit.

When I reached her, I shoved my hands in my pockets and rocked onto my toes. "You know this is all because you made me wear the suit."

She narrowed her eyes.

"My body was being suffocated. Eventually, it cut off the blood flow to my brain." I shrugged, and her nostrils flared. "I can't be held responsible for any of that. If anything, I deserve an apology from you." I quirked a teasing smile.

When she didn't reply, I sighed.

"Can you at least bitch at me in the car?"

Liv fumed while we waited just inside the building for our driver to pull around our car.

Whatever. She'd get over it. I was freaking stoked.

The title match was *on.*

Assuming Davenport had a sack at all, which was seriously in question, he'd be signing the contracts in the morning. The announcement to the press would quickly follow, and then I'd have had the legal right and obligation to beat the fucking shit out of him.

Flexing my hand out, I basked in the sweet ache of my knuckles.

"You could have broken it again," Liv said without looking at me.

"I didn't."

"You would have been out for months. No fights. And whatever hopes we had of getting another title shot would be gone. Do you have any idea of how bad that could have been in there?"

My lips tipped up in a smirk. "We? You getting a title shot too?"

"Yes. *We.* What part of this have you missed over the last fourteen years? I'm in this *with* you. Every match. Every opponent. I'm there. Just because I'm not in the ring doesn't mean your choices don't affect me."

I shook my head. "Don't worry, Liv. Your paycheck is safe."

The words had barely cleared my mouth when a fucking bee stung me.

I started to swat it away when Liv shrieked, "Shit!" Shaking her hand out, she continued to curse in Spanish as she danced a tight circle around me.

"Did you just punch me?" I questioned in all seriousness.

"I think I broke my hand," she yelled. "Why were you flexed?"

"Christ, Rocky. I just leveled Davenport. I'm a little amped. Are you okay?" I snagged her hand to inspect it.

"Oh God, is it broken? It really fucking hurts," she whined, and her face scrunched adorably.

"Maybe you should learn to control your shit. What the hell were you punching me for?"

Taking my time, massaging up and down her forearm, I continued to check her hand. It was fine, but I didn't release it. I hated that she was in pain, but I loved the way she peered up at me as if I could take it all away.

"Don't start with me, Quarry. I'm the one who gets to be mad here."

"Why? Because that prick decided to show up talking shit the day he found out we'd been scheduled for a rematch?"

Her eyes grew wide. "They scheduled a rematch?" she breathed.

I'd spent the night lusting over her as she'd pranced around the ballroom. Thoughts of taking her on every horizontal surface had filled my mind for the majority of the evening. But right then, as she stared up at me with a mixture of surprise and elation, all because I was going to get something I truly wanted in life, a warmth I hadn't felt in years washed over me.

"No, Rocky. *We're* getting a rematch."

Her eyes flashed between mine as she silently held my gaze. Pride and affirmation filled my chest from her unspoken praise.

God. This woman.

She was so fucking beautiful.

Guiding her injured hand to my chest, I fought the urge to kiss her.

She was close. It wouldn't have taken much.

I could have gripped her neck and tilted her head back. Leaning down, I could have brushed my lips against hers. She would have gasped, unsure of what to make of it. But, even in her confusion, her nipples would have swelled. Her breathing would have sped in what she would claim was nerves, but we'd both know that it was pure and erotic desire. Her feet would shuffle forward until those round breasts were compressed against my abs. Her hands would immediately snake around my waist for balance just before her eyes fluttered shut in invitation.

I wouldn't kiss her yet. No. I'd simply watch her face soften and her lips part in anticipation. Sliding my free hand up her side, I'd whisper my breath across her mouth, denying us both the contact we so desperately needed. Goose bumps would pebble her otherwise smooth skin as I made my way up to cup her jaw. Then I'd graze my thumb over her plump bottom lip until her tongue peeked out to dampen it. With a deep breath, I'd fill my lungs with the intoxicating mixture of champagne and Liv James—holding it impossibly long for no other reason than it had once been *hers*. I'd continue to ghost my lips over hers, torturing us both, until her eyes finally opened, dark with need. She would whisper my name as a question, and then and only then, when I was positive she was drenched, primed, and ablaze, would I crush my mouth over hers for the first time.

Deep.

Languid.

Hard.

Reverent.

Liv.

"Oh my God!" she yelled, snapping me back to reality. Throwing her arms around my neck, she pulled me in for a tight celebratory hug.

Meanwhile, the warmth in my chest disappeared as I mourned the loss of a moment that had never truly been mine to claim.

I had to get over this bullshit with her.

Or…figure out a way to get her on the same page as me.

Both seemed equally as impossible.

But, then again, she had been checking out my ass tonight, so maybe…

God, what am I doing? Am I seriously thinking about seducing my best friend? Then what? We fuck? We date? We go back to being friends? Shit, we get married?

Yes. I was insanely attracted to her, and I cared about her more than I could ever put into words. But what else? What if that was it? What if we had sex and nothing more came of it?

Liv didn't pour her soul out to me about dudes or anything—it was safer for everyone involved that way. She'd had boyfriends. I'd actually liked a few of them. But I had an inkling that she wasn't the casual let's-experiment-naked-and-see-if-we-have-any-feelings-for-each-other kind of girl.

I knew right then that I had to shut that shit down. She deserved someone better than me. If I knew some guy was having these wishy-washy thoughts about her, I would have beaten the absolute fuck out of him before I ever let him come near her.

The only problem was that this was one fight I couldn't walk away from.

Quarry Page versus Quarry Page.

The man who suddenly and desperately wanted to claim her versus the man who would protect her at all costs—even from myself.

Clearing my throat, I briefly returned her hug then set her away from me. "We need to get some ice on that." I nodded to her hand.

She ignored me. "So, when's the fight? How much money are we talking this time?"

I chuckled. "We'll talk when we get home. I have a copy of my contract in my room."

"I can't believe you hid this from me!" She crossed her arms over her chest in what I assumed was supposed to be an attitude, but a wide grin gave her away.

"I just found out this morning. I was gonna tell you tonight," I replied as our car finally pulled up. I was pushing the door open when she grabbed my arm.

"Wait. What time is it?"

I glanced at my Rolex. "Nine."

"Come on. Let's do something fun. I have a new assistant. You have a huge multimillion-dollar fight, which is surely going to net me a raise. Let's celebrate! What do you say? Chili dogs, cheese fries, a soda big enough to drown us both? Then we'll chase it with a million beers at the house."

"Shit." I curled my lip in disgust. "That sounds like the recipe for puke."

"So, you're in?"

My lip curled even higher. "I have the chance of a lifetime... for the third time...to win the boxing heavyweight championship of the world in a few months. Just because Davenport is a viper cunt doesn't mean he isn't a beast in the ring. It's going to be grueling, Liv. You remember how hard I worked out the last two times. Spending entire days in the gym, eating cod six meals a day, chugging protein shakes like they're an elixir from the gods. Training, conditioning, and a strict diet starts *immediately*."

She tipped her head to the side and repeated, "So, you're in?"

I blew out a hard breath. "Fuck yeah."

With that, I shoved the door wide and hooked my arm with hers. We laughed as we hurried to the SUV. Cameras flashed around us and people called our names, but as far as I was concerned, the real excitement would happen when we got home.

Alone—together.

CHAPTER
Thirteen

Liv

"YOU NEED ANOTHER?" QUARRY ASKED as he made his way to the kitchen.

"Mmm." I hummed around the bottle tipped to my lips. "Yes, please," I slurred, wiping my mouth on the back of my hand.

Usually, I wasn't much of a beer girl, but after the excessive amount of junk food I'd just consumed, there was no way my stomach could handle wine. As my mind buzzed, it became clear the six-pack had more than done its job.

Hot dog wrappers, remnants of broken french fries, and at least a dozen beer bottles littered the coffee table. I'd long since shed my dress and my heels, having opted for a comfortable pair of pink sleep shorts and a white tank top. Quarry had barely even made it in the house before he'd peeled off his shirt in search of his house uniform: a pair of variously colored workout pants—tonight was black with a white stripe down the side—and a T-shirt that on anyone else would have been plain. However, the way it was forced to stretch around his biceps and his pecs made it anything but.

It was well past midnight, and we were still "celebrating."

Since it was now a dual celebration, he'd nixed every single one of my movie choices and decided to put on some stand-up comedian neither of us was paying any attention to.

"Has Till texted you back?" I asked when he returned from the kitchen.

"Nah. He's probably still trying to drag Eliza's drunk ass home. I'm sure everything's fine. Flint or Slate would've messaged if Davenport was stirring up more shit. I'm just hoping tonight pissed him off enough to get him to actually crawl through those ropes."

Taking the beer from his hand, I replied, "He's such an asshole. What happened to champions like Slate and Till? Hell…even 'The Brick Wall' Mathews was at least humble."

"Ha! Yeah, humility is one gene Davenport is missing. He thinks the sun rises and sets in his asshole. If he weren't such a fucking pussy, it wouldn't be so bad. He's a fucking disgrace to the belt." He reclined in the corner of the sectional.

His legs were propped up on the coffee table, while I was cozied into the bend of the L with mine stretched out on the cushion in front of me. It was the way we always lounged when hanging out at the apartment together. And, considering that that was basically every weekend, we had clearly established our assigned seating.

There was a lull in our conversation, and we both absently turned our attention to the TV. For several minutes, I watched a man parading around a stage and ranting. My drunken mind wouldn't allow me to focus on what he was saying. Eventually, I zoned out. It wasn't until I felt the tingling sensation of being watched that I glanced over at Quarry.

Oh, he was watching me, all right. But his eyes were trained on my legs. I assumed he had zoned out too until his eyes very slowly slid up to my breasts and back down again. That realization tingled somewhere else, and I quickly cleared my throat before he was able to notice my nipples, which were inevitably going to turn hard. Those traitors reacted each time he so much as walked through the room. And, since we lived together, I swear it happened so frequently that it was how I burned the majority of my calories.

His eyes jumped to mine, and I arched an incredulous eyebrow. "Were you just checking me out?"

"W-what?" he stuttered. "No."

"Bullshit!" I laughed, and then I casually pulled a sip off my beer.

His mouth twitched, suppressing a smile. "Well, I figured it was fair game after I caught you drooling over my ass tonight."

I choked before I had the chance to swallow. Beer stung my nose as I covered my mouth to keep it from spraying across the room. It was a wasted effort. It still managed to leak out.

He snagged a napkin off the table and threw it in my direction. "Shit, look at you. You're drooling now just thinking about it."

I choked again, and he chuffed loudly.

"Stop." I laughed, cleaning my mouth before wiping beer off the back of my hand.

His smile grew even wider. "I didn't figure you'd be an ass girl."

"Are you drunk?" I giggled, not even the slightest bit embarrassed.

"Well, I'm not sober." He winked. "But let's get back to you and asses." He moved his feet to the ground and leaned forward, propping his fist under his chin like the statue of *The Thinker*—but hotter.

Finally collecting myself, I shot him a grin. "Okay, yes. Let's get back to that. Asses are totally my thing. It is not my fault that you have a nice one. But what about you?" I lifted my legs in an exaggerated cross, giving it my best Sharon Stone from *Basic Instinct*. "A leg man? Really? Mia was, like, five feet tall."

His gaze jumped from my legs. "I'm just a man. Period. You show me nice tits, legs, ass, stomach, face, eyes, whatever... I'll appreciate it all." He chugged the rest of his beer.

"Really? You don't have a type?"

He shrugged. "Not really. I guess I have more of a personality type than I do looks."

"That's so funny. I always thought the short, little punk girls like Mia were your thing."

"Mia was…different. She made me laugh and didn't let me get away with anything. Even when I dumped my world of shit on her, she never once showed me pity. I didn't care what she looked like. I just loved *her*." His voice was thick with emotion. Standing, he collected a group of the bottles off the table and started to make his escape.

Mia was still a hard topic for us. Not the fun stuff we could tell stories about all night and still fall asleep with a smile on our faces. It was the serious stuff that hurt the most. Those reminders that she wasn't just gone from our lives, but rather gone from the world, killed. I wasn't sure I'd ever stop hurting.

"Yeah." I looked down and started picking at the label on my bottle.

It had been four years and I still missed her. In a lot of ways, Quarry did a better job than I did of not letting her memories bring him down. I, however, was drunk; I'd probably end the night crying. I always did. It was exactly why I didn't drink to excess very often.

"Flexed or relaxed?" Quarry asked, snapping my attention back to his.

"Huh?"

"My ass. Is it better flexed or relaxed?" He tossed an encouraging smile my way.

"Oh. Um, probably relaxed. Especially when you bend over."

The beer bottles clanged loudly as they purposely fell from his hands.

"Shit. My bad." After backing up in front of me, he slowly leaned over after them.

I laughed and whistled as he put on a show of picking them up one by one.

That.

Right there.

Was exactly why I loved Quarry Page.

And it had nothing to do with his ass.

But everything to do with *him*.

After trashing the empties, he returned with four fresh ones cradled against his chest. Passing me one, he set the extras on the table then sank into his spot on the couch. An unbelievably comfortable silence fell between us. Simply turning our attention to the TV, we drank beers and watched the comedian.

An hour later, when the video finally ended, I was sauced. We'd not only polished off the extra beers Quarry had put on the table, but also two I'd delivered from the fridge on my way back from my five millionth pee break.

"Stop," I told Quarry without dragging my gaze from the credits.

"Nope," he slurred, punctuating it with a loud hiccough

I burst into a fit of drunken laughter, rolling off the couch to continue on the floor.

"You're obstructing my view! No fair." He gave the table a quick shove to the side so he could see me again. "Better. Now, carry on." He grinned around the mouth of his beer.

Quarry had been overtly staring at me for the last half hour. He'd informed me that it was payback for the show he'd put on while picking up the bottles. He noted that I hadn't even tipped him. Since I'd refused to lotion my legs as he'd suggested as payback, he'd announced that an hour of gawking was my punishment. I knew he was screwing around because he'd occasionally use a napkin to wipe imaginary drool away. Had I not been too drunk to care, it would have been ridiculous. However, because I was too drunk to care, it was ridiculous *and* hilarious.

"If you only knew how many times I've ogled you. I'd owe you way more than an hour," I confessed.

"Oh. Really? I think you should fully inform me of what a little perv you've turned into."

I grabbed one of his shoes off the ground and chucked it at him.

He batted it away as if it were the Home Run Derby.

"Turned into? Ha! I've always done it. You've just never caught me before."

"Seriously?"

"Oh, God, yes. I had the biggest crush on you when we were kids. I mean, back then, I wasn't checking out your ass. But you definitely made my little prepubescent heart flutter." I clutched my chest and closed my eyes dreamily.

"Seriously?" he repeated a little quieter.

"Uh. Yeah." I flopped flat on the floor, closing my eyes when the room began to spin.

"Why didn't you ever say anything?"

"Well, probably because I was twelve and terrified that you'd reject me."

"Liv—"

"And there's also that fact that you locked me in a closet. You weren't all that attractive after that."

"Shit. Liv—"

Keeping my eyes closed seemed to keep the french fries I'd eaten earlier from making an encore. However, nothing could stop my drunken mouth from vomiting my secrets.

"I got over that pretty quickly. I just accepted that I can't trust anyone. After that, it didn't hurt so bad. That's when I really started perving on you." I cackled until my stomach churned. "Ugh! Why did you let me eat that shit?"

"What do you mean that's when you started perving on me?" he asked from somewhere surprisingly nearby, but I didn't chance another stomach churn to open my eyes.

Dramatically lifting one finger in the air, I got back on topic. "Oh, right. I used to have this scrapbook of you that I kept hidden under my bed. It's in my closet now. I'll have to show it to you. You were one hot fifteen-year old. There was this one picture that seriously did it for me. You were only in a pair of boxing trunks…all muscly and stuff. Shhhhhiiiit." I hissed at the memory. "That was the first time I ever touched myself—"

The front door creaked open before slamming shut.

I bolted upright, pried my eyes open, and found myself surprisingly alone.

"Quarry?" I called but got no response. *Weird.* I attempted to go after him, but with my baby giraffe legs in a spinning room, I fell right back onto the floor. "Oh well. He'll be back." I sprawled out spread-eagle and got lost in the stupid home screen music of the comedy DVD.

I needed space.

Air.

A cartoon-size brick of ice I could use to bash my head with before icing my balls.

My bedroom wasn't far enough away to escape. I needed a quiet place where she wasn't writhing on the floor in a tiny pair of shorts so I could convince myself that it was a bad idea to listen to her tell me how much she used to want me—all the while inching closer, hell-bent on showing her how much I *currently* wanted her.

That was exactly what I'd been doing not thirty seconds earlier.

Yeah. Bad. Fucking. Idea.

It was bad enough that I now knew she liked my ass, but I did not need the visual of her touching herself for the first time with me on her mind too.

God. She was so fucking drunk.

So was I though.

And, right then, Drunk Quarry was about to make decisions Sober Quarry was going to have to answer for. Most of which started with my mouth on her neck and all of which ended with me emptying inside her.

What the fucking fuck is going on?

She used to like me?

Why did the idea of *used to* hurt so fucking bad?

Oh, right. Because *used to* wasn't *now*.

Something truly odd had happened that night during our conversation. And not just the fact that she had been overtly flirty. While that had been new, it wasn't what had set me on edge long before her visit to the drunken confessional on the floor.

When Liv had brought up Mia, I'd experienced the stab of grief I'd come to expect from memories of her. However, it hadn't been anything compared to the searing pain that had come from watching anguish etch across Liv's face. That had killed. I would have walked through Hell to extinguish that for her. Luckily, it had only taken a joke.

Guilt had engulfed me as I'd come to grasp that reality.

The source of my heartache was no longer Mia.

It was Liv.

Had I been sober, that would have been the moment I went to bed. Maybe get my head straight. Go talk to Till in the morning about what the hell was going on, see if he had any grand advice— which would probably just end with him making fun of me.

I wasn't sober though, so I'd started flirting with her all over again.

And, now, I was standing in the breezeway, holding my breath, wishing I weren't such a fucking mental case.

I was sick and tired of feeling like I shouldn't want her.

There was nothing anyone could say to change my mind. I needed to man the fuck up and talk to her. Explain why I'd been so weird the last few months. Hell, maybe she'd be receptive of my new feelings.

Or, more than likely, she'd be freaked the fuck out.

I wouldn't lose her though. I was positive of that. Liv wouldn't let my misguided feelings ruin us.

No. Our demise would ultimately be because I couldn't let her go.

To me, my feelings weren't misguided. They weren't weird. And they definitely weren't wrong. I wasn't a fool for wanting her as my own.

I was finally realizing what I should have known fourteen years earlier when I'd first laid eyes on her.

Liv James had never been just my best friend.

No matter what I'd told myself.

With new resolve, I squared my shoulders and headed back to my door. I would listen to any story she wanted to tell me about the past—especially the ones where she'd touched herself with thoughts of me. Because, when things went south—and, in my life, things always went south—those stories would be all I got of Liv.

I had her friendship.

I wanted more.

And, in that moment, I realized I wanted it *all*.

Pushing the door to our apartment open, I made the decision that I was done waiting to get over my feelings.

I was acting on them.

Right.

Now.

At the sight of Liv passed out on the carpet, I amended my timeline.

Tomorrow. I'd act on my feelings *tomorrow*.

After scooping her into my arms, I carried her down the hall to her bedroom. She was out of it, but she still curled into me, nuzzling my neck with a moan.

Gently placing her on the bed, I took one last eyeful and then dragged the covers over her. Pressing play on the iPad she kept connected to a set of small speakers, I drove out the silence with her favorite '80s playlist.

"Quarry?" she called over the intro to Phil Collins's *In the Air Tonight*.

"Yeah."

She stretched before tucking into a ball. "You 'kay?"

"I will be tomorrow. Just get some sleep." *You'll need it.*

"Mmmhmm," she purred. "Later, Q."

I chuckled. "Later, Rocky."

CHAPTER
Fourteen

Quarry

"LIV," I BREATHED AS HER ass glided against my cock.

With a deep groan, I snaked my hand out to squeeze the delicate curve of her hip—partly to stop her tortuous rhythm, partly to urge her faster.

Rocking, she continued an unapologetic assault.

After teasing my way under her shirt, I kneaded her large breast. When my palm came in contact with her nipple, I switched my focus. Rolling the tight tip between my thumb and forefinger, I increased the pressure as her hips sped in response.

"Fuck," I cursed, releasing her tit. I glided my hand down her flat stomach and into her panties.

She shifted to her back, her legs falling open in invitation. A growl vibrated in my throat when I reached her slick, wet heat.

One stroke down and I dampened my fingers before sliding

back up in search of her clit. Rough circles followed by gentle taps, I worked her until her hips angled up, guiding me toward her opening.

This was where all the dreams had ended. The ones that kept me up night after night yet still managed to send me to bed praying for them to invade my mind. I supposed it was fitting. Some deep-seated but not-so-hidden feelings must have been screwing with my subconscious. Taunting me about having parts of Liv but not being able to have her all. I'd touched her body in my dreams a thousand times, but never once had I been inside her.

Tonight was different though.

With a hiss through gritted teeth, I sank my finger deep into her heat.

The tight sheath of her body was too much, and it drew me awake.

Battling against consciousness, I fought to remain in my dreamworld. But it was one opponent I was no match for. My eyes slowly opened.

The strain of my aching cock was nothing new to wake up to.

However, the woman I was knuckle deep inside was something else altogether.

"What the…." I whisper-yelled, yanking my hand away.

Oh, but it got worse.

Taking a quick inventory, I realized that I was in my bed, slightly hungover, and thirsty as hell.

Oh, fuck.

My pulse spiked as I glanced down at the woman at my side.

Pink sleep shorts.

White tank top, lifted, exposing one perfect breast complete with a dark, peaked nipple calling for my tongue to lave over it.

Her head was resting on my outstretched arm, and her chest was evenly rising and falling. Long, brown hair covered her face, but I knew without a shadow of a doubt who it was.

Oh. My. God.

Liv.

She must have crawled into my bed at some point in the night, and my horned-out brain had taken it as an open-for-business sign.

Fuck. Fuck. Fuck.

I attempted to slide my arm from under her head, but it only caused her to turn toward me. Her hair fell away, revealing her wireless earbuds secured in place and two peacefully closed eyes. Snuggling in close, she tossed a leg over mine and her hand splayed over my stomach.

Okay. So we were cuddling.

Nothing wrong with that.

Friends could do that.

Maybe it would be nice. I could just go back to sleep and tell her that I'd accidentally-on-purpose felt her up in the morning—after she'd enthusiastically agreed to move our relationship to the next level.

Oh, but it got worse. Again.

I watched in both horror and anticipation as her hand began to inch down my stomach.

My panicked gaze bounced between her closed eyes and her hand making its descent.

No way. This was not happening.

I'd died and gone straight to Hell—where I belonged.

"Jesus fuck!" I yelled when her palm made purchase on my cock.

She suddenly sat up as I shot from the bed.

"It's okay," I soothed, recognizing the confused panic on her face.

When she caught sight of the tent in the front of my pants, her eyes flashed wide, and then her mouth started moving, but I didn't have my hearing aids in.

"I don't know what you're saying," I told her while grabbing a pillow off the bed to cover my erection.

"*What happened?*" she signed and spoke.

"Um…well. Hmm, funny story. I woke up and you were there…

and well… I guess I'm not used to sleeping with anyone else." I couldn't do this. Not right then, with a set of balls so blue that they were registering on the purple scale and a throbbing dick hidden behind a fucking pillow.

I needed a safe subject. As least until I collected my thoughts—or got struck by lightning, putting me out of my misery once and for all.

"What were you doing in my bed? You scared the piss out of me."

Her face fell as she swallowed hard. "*I heard a noise, and then I couldn't…*" She shrugged and shook her head, not wanting to continue.

I immediately hated myself for pinning this on her. She'd been secretly coming to my bed for years. Never once had anything happened. It wasn't her fault.

"Look, I'm exhausted. Let's talk in the morning, okay? Sorry I… woke you up like that." *Shit.* "Not that it was bad. I just mean…because I jumped out of the bed like that." *Dear God, stop talking!* "You know…'cause it scared you."

"*I'm sorry.*"

My eyes were drawn down to her nipples showing through the thin cotton of her tank top, reminding me that she wasn't wearing a bra—and how perfectly her breasts had fit in my palm.

Dropping my head back, I diverted my gaze to the ceiling. "Just. Go," I snapped.

Strangely, Liv didn't argue as she darted from my room.

Slinging the pillow onto the bed, I raked a frustrated hand through my hair.

Why? The night before I'd sworn to make a move on her…I'd literally made a move on her.

In my sleep.

While she had been asleep too.

What could have I possibly done in my past life to deserve this shit?

Liv

"Ohmygod. Ohmygod," I whispered to myself as I sank down against my door, blocking it on the off chance that Quarry had decided to follow me.

Tears welled in my eyes as his horrified expression flashed behind my lids with every blink. My body shook as if I were still being jostled from his mad dash out of the bed—away from me.

"Oh, God." Pulling my legs to my chest, I dropped my head against my knees. "What did I do?"

CHAPTER
Fifteen

Liv

"JESUS, WOMAN. WHAT ARE YOU doing here so early?" Till asked, opening his front door with baby Chase on his hip.

Lifting a bag of sausage biscuits and hash browns, I replied, "I have a hangover date with Eliza."

He pushed the door wide for me to enter. "Ah. Gotcha. I'll start the coffee. She's still asleep. You want me to wake her up?"

"Nah, I got it. Just deliver the brew when it's ready." I tickled Chase's stomach before casually heading down the hall to Till and Eliza's bedroom.

I knocked once before entering.

"I'm up!" Eliza said, dragging herself out of the bed.

Her light-brown hair was in complete disarray, and black eye makeup was streaked down her face. Her dress and her shoes were haphazardly strewn across the room. The small trash can on the floor next to her bed was telling of how she'd ended her evening.

"That good of a night, huh?"

Shaking her fist in the air, she headed toward the bathroom. "I didn't puke. Victory!"

"Bravo." I lifted my hand in sign language applause.

"I'm quite proud, actually. It was touch-and-go there for a while." She smiled weakly. "Go ahead through the window. I'll meet you in there after I brush the fur coat off my teeth."

I laughed, following her directions.

Apparently, back in the day, Till had been a smidge obsessed with windows. When he and Eliza had built their house, he'd had a window, instead of a door, installed as the entrance to her private art studio.

The large room was filled with every art supply imaginable. Black-and-white family photos covered the stark, white walls. The furniture consisted of a red overstuffed sofa and a plush futon that was more *Lifestyles of the Rich and Famous* than broke frat boy. They sat adjacent to each other, facing a large TV mounted on the wall above Eliza's desk. The guys called the room "Chick Central," and I can't say they were wrong. It was where Ash, Eliza, and I always seemed to migrate any time we were together.

After setting the bag of food on a small side table, I found the remote and pulled up the latest season of *Project Runway*. It was our go-to show and one of the few programs Eliza and I agreed on. She loved the artistic aspect of it, while I was enthralled with the fashion.

Eliza and I had a funny relationship. She was twelve years older than I was, and for all intents and purposes, she was Quarry's mom. But she was also a lot of fun. When I was growing up, she had always been friendly with me, but it wasn't until Ash had entered the picture that we'd really become friends. Ash and I had clicked right away, and eventually, she'd pulled Eliza into our fold.

The three of us planned monthly girls' nights together, and in addition to weekly Page family dinners, we also did lunch once a week.

So, needless to say, I felt completely at home as I fluffed a pillow then dragged the blanket off the back of the futon as I waited for her to join me.

Tim Gunn was still giving the contestants their assignments when she made her way into the room.

"Why do I always think drinking is a good idea?" She grabbed the bag of biscuits and settled on the couch.

Catching the greasy sandwich she'd tossed my way, I replied, "No clue. However, I can promise you my drinking days are over after last night."

"We said that after the Gala last year, too." She nibbled on a hash brown, curled her lip, and then continued to eat. "Wait. You guys went home early. What happened after you left?"

My stomach rolled. Though it had nothing to do with my hangover and everything to do with the memories of the night before flooding my brain.

They were the same memories that had had me sneaking out of my own apartment at the crack of dawn in order to avoid Quarry.

The question should have been: What didn't happen last night?

Drink too many beers. Check.

Flirt with my best friend. Check.

More drinking and then more flirting. Check. Check.

Tell him that I used to obsess over him until he runs from the house just to shut me up. Check.

Crawl into his bed in the middle of the night. Check.

Wake him up by groping his dick. Check.

Get kicked out of his room like a fangirl who, well…snuck into his room and grabbed his junk. Check.

Needing a cold shower each time I thought about it. Mother. Fucking. Check.

I kept that parade of embarrassment to myself.

"Oh, we just had some beers at the apartment." I shrugged, turning my attention back to the TV, but my mind refused to budge from the whole Quarry thing.

"That sounds better than my night. I think I passed out on the limo ride home." Eliza picked an errant biscuit crumb off the blanket.

"Meh. Could have been worse."

"At the risk of skeeving you out, I think I was…um…on top of Till when it happened."

My eyes flared wide.

She closed her eyes and nodded, embarrassed.

I attempted to hide my laugh but failed. I mentally prepared a hey-no-big-deal-you-passed-out-in-the-middle-of-sex speech when Ash saved me the trouble as she came crawling through the window.

"You were on top of Till when what happened?" she asked.

"Shit," Eliza mumbled. "I, uh…may have passed out."

"Jeebus! On the way there and home? I'd say Till got his money's worth out of that limo," Ash teased, flopping down at the foot of the futon.

"So, how was your night?" I asked, grabbing the bag of food from Eliza and throwing it down to Ash.

"Really good. I managed to stay awake and everything." She winked at Eliza. "I'm so freaking tired though. Flint got me up after only two hours of sleep to come get the boys. I love my babies, but today is going to kill me. I need a night away to recover from my night away."

"We're having a hangover party. You can nap here if you want," Eliza said.

"Nah. Thanks though. We're gonna take the boys to that new park by the house."

Till poked his head through the window. "Okay, ladies. Bad news. We're out of coffee. But Quarry's on his way over. He said he'd pick up Starbucks."

Noooooo! my mind screamed.

When I felt all of their eyes land on me, I realized my mouth had screamed it too.

"Something against Starbucks?" Till asked.

"I'm just…not a fan."

I touched your brother's penis, and now, I'm scared he's going to want to talk about it.

"Seriously?" Eliza gasped.

Dear God, please don't let me have said that out loud too.

"You drink it all the time."

Thank you, baby Jesus. "Yeah. I'm just sick of it. That's all. It's fine though. Really. Q knows my order." I relaxed once they'd seemed to buy it.

"You got any soda? I need a barrel if I'm going to survive today," Ash said, discarding her biscuit and moving Till's way.

"I'm not sure about a barrel, but I have at least one in the outside fridge," he replied, helping her through the window.

Two of her fingers shot back through the opening. "Peace out, ladies."

We called after her.

"Bye."

"Later."

Then Eliza turned her attention my way. "Are you sure everything's okay? You seem…weirder than usual."

"Weirder than usual? That's exactly what I was going for this morning."

"I just mean…"

"I know, I know. I'm exhausted. That's all. I'm gonna nap until the coffee arrives. Then I'm going to drink it and then nap some more."

She gave me the side eye but let it go.

I *was* acting weirder than usual, but that was only the tip of the iceberg for what was going on inside me.

We watched *Project Runway* for about five minutes until Eliza dozed off. If I'd known that Quarry would be up so early, I would have stayed locked in my room, pretending to sleep, while I paced my room all day. I loved a lazy hangover party as much as the next girl, but the real reason I was there was to collect my thoughts before I had to face him.

My mind raced with explanations for the night before, but it was sleep that finally won out.

I was sound asleep when the futon disappeared from under me. "Shit." I flailed, trying to catch myself before hitting the ground.

"Shhh," Quarry whispered, holding me cradled in his arms.

"What are you doing?" I asked, my voice thick with sleep.

He tipped his head to the side and gave me an impatient glare. "Shh!" He jutted his chin toward Eliza, who was softly snoring on the couch.

"Put me down. I can walk."

He didn't listen. Instead, he carried me to the window and carefully guided me back into Till and Eliza's bedroom. After folding his large body through, he caught my hand and dragged me down the hall to his old bedroom.

He hadn't lived there in over six years, but it still looked like eighteen-year old Quarry would be coming back at any moment. Posters lined the walls, and boxing trophies and medals covered the rest. Two oak nightstands framed a queen-sized bed covered by a midnight-blue comforter. A single photo of Quarry, Mia, and me at Flint and Ash's wedding graced the dresser.

I was lost in nostalgia until I heard the door shut.

"I went to check on you this morning, but you were already gone. What the hell are you doing over here so early?" he asked roughly.

"Uhh, Eliza and I made a date last night for a hangover party."

His lips twisted in disbelief. "At six in the morning?"

"What? I had to stop and get breakfast."

"For two hours?" He arched an angry eyebrow. "Till told me you got here at eight."

Note to self: When trying to escape Quarry Page, do not run to his brother's house for refuge.

"I…I wasn't sure what I wanted to eat, so I drove around until something sounded good."

"Right." He thrust a hand into his hair but stared down at the floor. "Listen, we need to talk about last night."

Fantastic. He wasn't going to beat around the bush. I guessed now was as good a time as any.

I quickly started before I had to hear his explanation. "I'm really sorry. I guess I got a little handsy. I fell asleep listening to 'Pony.' I must have had Channing Tatum on the brain."

His gaze lifted to mine, and the strangest tinge of disappointment showed in his eyes.

"Channing Tatum, huh?" His hands fisted on his hips.

"I don't know. I don't really remember. It could have been Chris Hemsworth, I suppose. I mean, if I was willing to grab your junk, it might have been a kinky combination of the two." I shrugged.

Shaking his head, he began to pace the room. "Wow. Thanks." He pinched the bridge of his nose. "Is that all you remember?"

Funny enough, no. It was just all I was willing to acknowledge. The rest…

God. The rest.

Those callused fingers of his gliding deliciously between my legs.

Or maybe he was asking about the part where he so skillfully rolled my nipple that it felt as if he had found a direct line to my clit—a few minutes more and I could have come from that alone.

Or perhaps, just perhaps, he was asking about the way he'd pushed his long finger so deep inside me that I would have happily kicked any combination of men in the world out a window just to experience it with him again.

If that was what he meant, then my answer should have been: *I can't fucking forget it!*

Blinking in mock confusion, I said, "Why? Did something else happen?"

He laughed without humor. "Yeah. Liv. Something else happened."

After sucking in a deep breath, he held it as he sank down on the corner of the bed. With a fast exhale through his nose, he rushed out, "I guess I was dreaming about someone or whatever too."

Uh huh. Mia.

"Really?" I breathed in fake disbelief.

Dropping his head into his hands, he continued. "Fuck, I don't know what to say here. I just remember waking up—" He chewed on his bottom lip. "My hand…was in your pants and your shirt was pushed up. I'm sorry. I guess I'm not used to sleeping with anyone else."

Since Mia. Yeah. I got that last night when you kicked me out of your room.

I laughed loudly, spinning toward a group of trophies. My vision swam as I pretended to read the inscription on each one.

"Shit. I kinda wish I did remember that. Most action I've had in forever," I squeaked out around the lump in my throat.

"I'm serious, Rocky. It was seriously fucked up. I'm so sorry." His voice shook.

My chin quivered.

It *was* seriously fucked up.

But that wasn't his fault.

"It's no big deal, Q. Stop apologizing. I'll make sure I don't drunkenly find my way to your bed again. We should be good."

I felt him at my back, but I didn't dare turn to look at him.

In a thick, jagged voice, he said, "About that. We need to talk."

Actually, that was exactly what we did *not* need to do. I needed to get the hell out of that room. Sleep for a week. Maybe take a vacation…to Antarctica. Where I could figure out how to get my head straight on what exactly had happened in his bed.

And then figure out how to turn it off.

My Quarry Page switch had been in the off position since the day I'd met Mia. But one night with his hands on me and that switch hadn't just been flipped—it'd been uninstalled. I had successfully harbored over a decade of feelings for Quarry, and last night, that dam had been broken, emotionally flooding me to the point of insanity.

I was not built to feel that much. Not all at once.

Definitely not for *him*.

And especially not when he was dreaming I was her.

I moved backward as I spun. He didn't budge as I hid my face in his back and wrapped my arms around his waist. My heart sputtered at the contact and then shattered when it slowed.

"Stop freaking out. It's fine. It was just a little grab-ass. I should be the one apologizing for all the crap I said last night. Let's just say there's a reason the government will never trust me with national secrets. Two drinks and I'd spill it all."

"That was the fun part." He laughed.

Oh goodie. That had been the fun part.

Stepping away, I pasted on a million-dollar smile. "It's all good. So stop being weird and point me to my coffee. I'm dying!"

He sighed and reluctantly mumbled, "It's in the kitchen."

I slapped him on the shoulder as I hauled ass out of that room.

I didn't go to the kitchen.

I went to the bathroom.

I didn't cry.

I wept.

CHAPTER
Sixteen

Quarry

EVERY MORNING WHEN I'D WAKE up, I would swear to myself that it was going to be the day I finally talked to Liv about how I felt.

Three weeks later, I was still telling myself that lie.

My job was to fearlessly step into the ring with giants and dodge their merciless fists while attempting to level them with my own. But, somehow, talking to five-foot-seven, one-hundred-and-twenty-five-pound Liv seemed more terrifying.

Although it wasn't like I got many chances. Liv had started avoiding me. It was subtle at first. But, as the weeks passed, I saw her less and less. Her work nights had started running later. She hung out with Eliza and Ash more than ever before. And, when I had to fly to LA for a few nights, she suddenly couldn't make it, even though she had found an assistant to cover her. It was hard to tell if I was just being hypersensitive and reading into her every move or if she really was pulling away.

She still packed my lunch, answered my e-mails, and texted me occasionally throughout the day, but it was different. The levity that usually surrounded us had faded. Sitting in uncomfortable silence became our new norm on the nights she was home.

Together—completely alone.

We were all at Till's the night my fight against Davenport had been announced. Liv was usually the first person jumping up and down, hugging me, and then ranting at whichever ESPN sportscaster had predicted I might lose. But, that night, she sat in Till's recliner across the room and signed, *I'm so proud of you.*

My family was shouting and cheering in celebration as clips of me flashed across the screen. But I couldn't tear my eyes off her. I held my breath as I searched her big, brown doe eyes, knowing I was only one exhale away from a breakdown.

I wanted that woman more than I wanted any title in the world, but I was losing her.

And I didn't have a clue why.

I knew that the way I felt was going to change things between us. But she didn't even know yet. I couldn't take it back or swear to her that we could go back to being friends.

I couldn't do anything at all to fix us.

Several times since that night in my bed, I'd attempted to talk to her about it. She would make jokes and dismiss it as no big deal. I often replayed those moments with her writhing under my touch, but I would have gladly erased them from both of our memories if we could have just gone back to the way things had been.

Eventually, things got so strained that I started avoiding her too. I didn't want to see her bright smile aimed at me when I got home, not when her eyes held such emptiness. I didn't want to sit on my couch night after night while she hid in her room, claiming she was tired—at six p.m. I didn't want to go to Till and Eliza's for dinner, where Liv would flitter around the room like the woman I so desperately missed only to have her mood shift so drastically when her attention would swing my way.

I couldn't swallow those moments anymore. They were acid to my soul, secretly devouring me from the inside out.

Unlike Liv, I wasn't doing such a stellar job at hiding my problems. With a title fight only months away, I was pushing my body to the limits. My mind just wouldn't follow. Till and Slate had both been riding my ass about my head not being in the ring, but I was falling apart. I'd taken punches that never should have touched me during training, and if Davenport had thrown them, I would have landed flat on the mat.

I couldn't stop thinking about her.

Nor could I figure out a way to get her back.

Without her, for the first time in my entire life, I was truly trapped in the solitude of my mind—alone.

It was past eleven as I shadow-boxed in the ring. The gym was empty. Till had left hours earlier instructing me to lock up when I left, but I didn't have anywhere to go. Alone was alone everywhere. At least, at the gym, I could distract myself from the flames in my chest.

Jab.

Duck.

Jab.

Duck.

Jab.

"Shit!" I yelled as Liv suddenly stepped in front of me.

"*What are you doing?*" Her mouth moved with her hands because she knew I didn't wear my hearing aids in the gym.

I dropped my hands. "Well, hello to you too. What are *you* doing here?"

"*I was driving home from work and saw your car. It's late.*"

I briefly swept my eyes over her. She must have taken her shoes off outside the ring to keep from damaging the mat, but she was still in the same short, turquoise dress she'd been wearing that morning. It was sexy as hell. Probably yet another reason I hadn't wanted to head home.

"Big fight. Long hours," I stated, unraveling the wraps on my hands.

"*Come on. Let's go home. Long hours mean you need more sleep.*"

"Nah. I'm good," I replied. "I'll see you in the morning." I ended the conversation by giving her my back.

Much to my surprise, and my disappointment, she left.

At least I thought she did.

Not even a full minute later, she crawled back into the ring.

Resting my arms on the top rope, I leaned against the corner padding. "What?"

She opened her hand to reveal the hearing aids she must have retrieved from my locker.

Great. "I don't feel like talking. Go home."

"*Put them in.*" she demanded.

With a sigh, I relented. It was a worthless fight. I'd listen to anything she had to say if it got her out of there any quicker—or made her stay forever.

When I got them situated, Liv started in.

"What the hell is going on with you?"

Stabbing a thumb into my chest, I argued, "Me? You've been avoiding me for weeks. And you show up here wanting to know what's wrong with me?"

"I haven't been avoiding you."

"Seriously? You're going to lie to my face?"

Her eyes narrowed. "Fine. I won't lie. Flint called. He was worried you were still here, and I told him I'd come get you and force you to get some rest."

"Tell Flint to drag his own ass down here if he's so worried next time. Babysitting is not part of your job description."

"Are you kidding me?" She threw her arms out to the sides in frustration. "Babysitting you is my only job description."

"Wow! The truth comes out."

"Oh, shut up. Quit whining and get your shit so we can go home," she snapped, crossing her arms over her chest.

A humorless laugh bellowed from my chest. "Tell Flint I wasn't here and fucking leave. I'm not doing this with you, Nanny James."

Unmoving, we defiantly stared at each other.

After several minutes, her mask finally slipped and I saw my Rocky for the first time since the Gala. A rush of relief filled my chest.

Her body didn't move an inch, but her face crumbled. "What's happening to us?"

It was a valid question, but one she had no right to ask. She held all the answers.

I erupted. "I have no fucking idea!" Storming forward, I cornered her against the ropes. "You've been avoiding me for *weeks*! Stop with the games and just tell me what the fuck I did wrong so I can fix it," I seethed through clenched teeth.

Never one to back down, she pushed up on her toes and got in my face. "You can't fix it!"

Her mouth was only inches from mine, but frustration overrode my desires.

"You don't know that! Let me try. I've apologized a million times for that bullshit—"

I stopped talking when she suddenly flinched. I don't even think she realized she had done it, but it was probably the most honest answer she was ever going to give me.

Lowering back down to her heels, she looked away. "You can stop beating yourself up about it. I'm not mad that you copped a feel."

"Don't do that. Don't make this a joke."

Her eyes lifted to mine. That fucking mask she'd been using to keep herself isolated from me fell right back into place. "What else would you consider this? I woke up to you asleep and tweaking my nipple. That's funny, Q!"

"It's not—wait. What?" Every muscle I possessed flexed as my body roared to life.

"What what?" she smarted, but her face paled.

Oh, she'd fucked up. Big time.

She knew it.

And, now, I knew it too.

A heady combination of anger and excitement swirled through my veins as her words filtered through me. I'd relived that night hundreds of times over the last three weeks, and as I stared into her dark-brown eyes, I finally figured out what was going on with her. It was an answer I hadn't even considered.

"You were awake," I accused.

Her eyes grew wide, but she covered it with a healthy dose of attitude. "I didn't exactly sleepwalk out of your room."

A wave of heat brewed in the air between us. Her side was laced with panic—mine with feral need.

Looping an arm around her waist, I tugged her against me. Her body stiffened as I slid my hand down to splay across the small of her back. Her palms landed on my pecs, but she didn't push me away.

"W-what are you doing?" she stammered.

She sucked in a fast breath as I leaned down and whispered, "Your nipples were first. That's when you woke up." I softly brushed my lips across her jaw.

I slipped my hand down to her firm ass, rocking her forward until her stomach made contact with my stiffening cock.

She squeaked in surprise but didn't back away.

"You were awake when I pushed into your shorts." I paused to capture her gaze. The corner of my mouth tipped up in a one-sided smirk. "You opened your legs for me, Liv."

She gasped through parted lips. Her eyes dipped to my mouth and back again, but she said not a single word.

I continued. "You grabbed my cock. If I'd known you were awake, we wouldn't be having this conversation right now."

She flinched again and swayed away.

Fisting a hand into the back of her hair, I stilled her retreat. "Because, if I had known any part of you wanted me, I would have been fucking you senseless for the last three weeks."

Her gaze shifted from heated to dark, and then I lost view of it altogether when I crushed my mouth over hers.

There was not one second of hesitation as her tongue snaked out, tangling with mine. Her moan vibrated in my mouth. I angled my head, taking it deeper, sealing our mouths so nothing—not even air—came between us.

Fucking finally.

Her hands roamed over my chest, exploring every inch, until sliding up the nape of my neck. Rolling her shoulders back, she pressed her breasts into me. A loud growl rumbled in my chest.

It wasn't enough.

It was *Liv.*

Palming her ass, I lifted her off the ground. Her legs immediately wrapped around my hips, and a hiss escaped my mouth as she landed directly on my cock.

My knees didn't buckle. Nor did I stumble. But we hit the mat all the same.

Breaking the kiss, I settled between her thighs. My lips drifted to the soft skin at the base of her neck. Her hips surged up, grinding a relentless rhythm over my cock. I was so fucking hard that it was almost painful, but as my name tumbled from her mouth, there was nothing I wouldn't have done to hear it again.

Pushing up on my hands, I glanced down between us to watch her writhing against me.

Liv.

Fucking *Liv.*

Fully clothed, riding my cock.

Not shy. Not timid. Not embarrassed.

Unapologetically taking, knowing there was nothing I wouldn't give her.

Not now. *Not ever.*

When I looked back up, her head was thrown back and her eyes were screwed shut. That shit did not fly with me. She could lose herself in ecstasy with me for the next eighty years.

But, this time, she was with *me.* I wanted her eyes opened until her tight pussy milked the cum from my cock. Some things were better seen than heard. And I wanted *her* to witness the moment I claimed her as my own.

Then *I* wanted to witness the moment when she realized she didn't need to claim me at all. I was already hers.

After a hard kiss, I bit her bottom lip as I pulled away. "Look at me."

She obeyed, fluttering her lids open but not stilling her hips.

The warmth hit me so hard it knocked the breath from my lungs. It also lit me ablaze.

Shoving her dress up to her stomach, I hooked a finger in her panties and pulled them aside. Finding her drenched, I didn't delay in filling her with two fingers.

Her back arched off the mat as a strangled cry escaped her throat. "Look at me," I ordered again, dropping my thumb to her clit. She didn't.

She sat straight up and crashed her mouth into mine. Our teeth clanked together as she rocked against my fingers. Her tongue swept my mouth, deeper each time.

Oh, fuck this.

Pulling out, I lowered her back to the mat. Her mouth was still attached to mine when I snatched my shorts down and freed my cock. Gripping the shaft, I glided the tip up to her clit then back down, poising myself at her entrance.

Releasing her mouth, I panted, "I don't have a condom."

I knew that Liv was on birth control. She had a stupid timer on her phone that went off every day at six p.m. to remind her to take it. Still, this was our first time together. She should be the one who made that decision.

"It's okay. Please, Qua—" Her plea morphed into a moan as I planted myself inside her. Her hands slammed down at her sides, fisting imaginary sheets.

I hadn't even moved yet and my balls were already drawing up with an impending orgasm.

That was going to wait though. No fucking way I was going to miss the sight of her coming on my cock.

Slowly drawing out, I tugged down the top of her dress until one breast popped free. Stroking her nipple with my thumb, I drove back in, stilling when I bottomed out. Her thighs sawed at my sides, urging me to give her more, but I couldn't move.

She was so fucking beautiful.

My cock inside her.

My hand teasing her breast.

Her eyes aimed at *me* taking her body.

Needy for *me*.

All fucking *mine*.

Liv.

Lowering myself to my elbows, I got my head together and gave her what she wanted.

I worked us both to the brink, backing off before repeating the process.

Our moans intertwined to form a harmony, guided by the melody of our bodies.

I wasn't rough. I definitely wasn't gentle.

Her core clenched, gripping me so tight that it almost sent me over the edge.

So close.

Angling my hips, I worked her even deeper.

Harder.

Faster.

Drawing in a deep breath, I pressed up so I could see her face.

My lungs burned for the exhale I refused them. I'd waited my entire life for this moment with Liv. Air could wait.

Finally, her arms flew up and folded over my back. "Quarry. Oh, God, Quarry," she cried, her nails scoring my back as she pulsed around me—ruining me in the best possible way.

Her body slacked, but she clung to my back. I pistoned in search of my own release.

Moments later, I buried my face in her neck and came on the life-altering exhale of her name.

CHAPTER
Seventeen

$\mathcal{L}iv$

HE HADN'T EVEN PULLED OUT before the guilt slashed through me. His lips were peppering kisses up my neck—each one so reverent that it felt as though it were being tattooed on my soul.

But hidden in my depths of soul would have to be where they stayed.

I wasn't giving them back.

But they weren't mine to keep, either.

My chest quaked with a silent sob.

"I need to get up," I rushed out so he hopefully couldn't hear the tremor in my voice.

"Mmmm," he purred into my neck without moving off me.

"Quarry, please."

"Do you understand how long I've wanted you?"

With a jolt, my entire body solidified.

The three weeks he was about to rattle off was going to hurt like hell. Especially since the time I'd wanted him was a lot closer to, oh....*my entire life.*

"Let me up." I shimmied up, and it regrettably caused his softening dick to slide out.

The loss severed our connection—and my heart.

He trailed kisses down my chest. "I couldn't stop thinking about you. For months, I've wanted you like this."

Months?

My breath caught in my throat.

"You." *Kiss.* "Naked." *Kiss.* "On top of me." *Kiss.* "On your knees." *Kiss.* "Under me." His tongue laved over my exposed nipple.

My chest defied my mind and arched into him as he sucked me into his mouth. Sparks rushed to my clit, awakening my sated body all over again.

No way could that happen again.

I gasped as his teeth raked across the sensitive flesh of my breast.

Well. Maybe. Just once more.

He kissed across my chest, scooping into the top of my dress in search of my other breast. "Want to take a shower?"

What the hell was he doing?

And why was I just lying there, letting him do it?

And why couldn't I breathe?

Or drag my eyes off him?

Or stop my heart from racing?

Or figure out why my hands were shaking?

It had to stop.

"Get off me!" I snapped.

His head popped up, confusion etched in his beautiful face.

"We can't do this," rushed from my mouth. The lie burned my throat.

I scrambled out from under him.

"Liv," he called in warning—one I did not heed.

I jumped to my feet, and he quickly followed, not even pulling up his shorts before grabbing my arm to stop my getaway.

Although I wasn't really going anywhere. We lived together. We worked together. He was my best friend. Our lives were braided together in every possible way. Where else would I go when the only place I ever wanted to be was with him?

"Talk," Quarry gritted out.

I snatched my arm from his grip and then righted my dress. "We shouldn't have done that."

Straightening his shorts, he barked a laugh. "Bullshit. We should have done that months ago."

That stung.

Months ago. What a joke.

I kept that to myself.

"Whatever the hell this is…it has to stop."

He closed in on me, gripping my hips and lighting my betraying body. His lips dipped to mine, where he whispered, "Stop freaking out. We're not stopping anything. This is the beginning of me and you."

I wanted to believe him. The idea of a me and Quarry was almost enough to drown out the voice in my head shrieking that it was never going to happen. I wanted to melt into his arms and steal the safety and comfort that only existed when I was with him. I wanted to let him hold me while we talked things out and somehow let him convince me that we were as right as it had felt only minutes before.

But it wasn't. No matter how it had felt wrapped in his arms with his mouth pressed to mine. He wasn't mine to keep. He never had been.

"This is so wrong," I squeaked. "You're… Mia's."

His arms spasmed around me. "Excuse me?"

"I swore this would never happen. No matter how much I wanted to." My anxiety grew with every word spoken. My chest constricted, and my hands began to tremble. "She was my best friend. You…

you were hers."

He rocked back on his heels and glided his hands up to frame my face. Tipping my head back, he rested his forehead on mine and very calmly said, "This has nothing to do with Mia. This is about you and me. And us finally starting something that it sounds like we've both been fighting for a long time." He kissed me again.

But, no matter what he said and no matter how much I wanted to spend a lifetime feeling his lips pressed to mine, it could never happen.

I twisted from him before he even had a chance to react or my body had a chance to change my mind. I only made it halfway through the ropes before he was dragging me back into the ring.

"Where are you going?"

"Nowhere!" I screamed at him. "Nowhere, Quarry. I'm not going any-fucking-where. I can't walk away from you no matter how many times I should have. Which is exactly why I'm still standing here right now, your cum all but dripping down my legs. It's the biggest slap in the face I could have ever issued Mia, alive or dead." I threw my hands out to my sides. "And, worse, I know that and still can't seem to just walk the fuck away!"

"Christ," he mumbled, pinching the bridge of his nose.

Gnawing on my thumbnail, I paced a circle around him and continued. "Honestly, I can't see how you think there could ever be an us. She wanted to kill me when we were sixteen when she even thought I wanted you. God, if she only knew the half of it! Are you insane enough to think she would ever approve of me and you together?"

"What I *think* right now is that you're currently having some kind of orgasm-induced nervous breakdown."

I stopped and glared at him. "You think this is funny?"

"Not at all. But I'm going to let you rant and rave for a little while to get all that shit you're spouting out of your system before I wade into the quicksand in your head and pull you out."

"You can't pull me out! It's the truth."

His body went ridged, and he cracked his neck menacingly. "You done yet?"

"Stop acting like I'm freaking out for no reason. This is wrong and you know it!"

And that's when he moved. Fast.

Charging forward, he forced us both into the corner.

"We are not wrong! We could *never* be wrong," he snarled inches from my face.

"But that doesn't mean we're right, either."

"She's gone, Liv. Mia doesn't get to approve of anything. Stop acting like she's sitting at home while we screw around behind her back."

"But that's just it. If she were at home, we wouldn't be standing here at all. Would we?"

His lips thinned as he closed his mouth. He knew the answer to that question. He just didn't want to say it any more than I wanted to hear it.

"That's what I thought. You're fooling yourself if you think I would ever be anything but a consolation prize. She'd always be in the back of your mind." I attempted to duck under his arm, but he shifted to the side, blocking me.

"How long?" he growled.

"How long what?"

"You said if Mia only knew the half of it. So tell me how long you've wanted me."

My mouth was locked and loaded to fire the scripted answer I had been telling myself for years, but that was when I realized I didn't even have it in me to lie anymore. Quarry had admitted that he wanted something between us. I wouldn't be able to fight him off alone. I needed all the guilt in the world to have my back in this one. Luckily for me, the overwhelming weight I'd been carrying since I was a kid was finally good for something besides threatening to break me.

"Before I met Mia? I had been in love with you every day since we first met," I answered.

He held my stare with gentle eyes and then asked for my deepest, darkest, dirtiest secret. "And for how long after you met Mia?"

My chin quivered as I fought to keep the truth safely trapped in the confines of my mind—where, if I were a stronger woman, it would have stayed for all of eternity.

I wasn't a stronger woman though. I was a woman who was irrevocably in love with the only man her dead friend had ever loved.

"Every single day," I admitted. "Every. Single. Day."

I was vaguely aware of Quarry's mouth landing over mine. I even went willingly into his arms as he lifted me off my feet. It wasn't as frenzied or desperate as it had been before.

It was slow and apologetic.

Comforting and consoling.

Deep and compassionate.

And it only made me feel guiltier—because it made me feel so much better.

Quarry continued to kiss me even as the tears fell from my eyes. His thumbs stroked back and forth across my cheeks, wiping them away as his mouth made unspoken promises I knew he could never keep.

When my eyes dried, he released my mouth long enough to climb from the ring with me still securely held against his chest.

Ten minutes later, the gym had been locked, my car had been moved to the back parking lot, and I was in the passenger's seat of his car on our way back to our apartment.

There was no more discussion.

The radio was blaring on the way home, but with the truth of my deception hanging between us, it was the most frightening silence I would ever experience.

CHAPTER
Eighteen

Quarry

I KEPT MY HAND ANCHORED to her thigh on the drive home. I was afraid that it was the only thing keeping her from disconnecting from me all over again.

"Every. Single. Day."

Her words echoed through my mind.

When she'd made that announcement in the ring, I'd felt like I'd taken the worst beating I could ever experience within those ropes. How had I never seen that she was in love with me? With the exception of our drunken night, she had never been flirty. But, then again, I wasn't sure I would have noticed. We lived together. So it wasn't like she had to go out of her way to spend extra time with me. She didn't have to make up reasons to stay up late bullshitting with me or text me just to say hi twelve times a day. That was expected in our relationship.

She didn't have to think of creative ways to touch me. She had always been a hugger. I didn't count how often her arms found their way around me. I just loved it when they did.

I was a funny motherfucker, so of course she laughed at my jokes.

We spoiled each other with gifts every chance we got. And, well, Liv just spoiled me in general.

There hadn't been a chance to flirt. But maybe that was what our relationship had been all along, and precisely why I'd missed all the signs.

"Every. Single. Day."

Fourteen years.

Fourteen years she had experienced the torture I had been living for the last four months. I couldn't imagine how she had lasted that long.

Maybe there had been subtle clues I should have seen.

The way she dropped her entire life to make sure mine was running smoothly.

The way she took care of me as if the small things like the way I ate or if I was getting enough rest mattered more than anything else.

The way I knew without a shadow of a doubt that she would always be there for me. Unconditionally. Forever.

Okay, so maybe they hadn't been so subtle and I was just a blind dumbass.

"Every. Single. Day."

God. She loved me.

When we arrived at our apartment, I folded her hand in mine and walked up the sidewalk. She didn't try to stop me, but she didn't exactly tuck into my side the way I would have liked, either.

I unlocked and opened the door. Then I paused before walking inside.

"Nothing changes," I whispered, bending to kiss her forehead.

Her eyes closed, but it wasn't in rapture. Her lids were pained, and when they fell, it set off a chain reaction, crumbling her face all the way down to her chin.

"Right," she smarted.

"Stop and listen to me. Everything is absolutely going to change between us. But that's just the details. Me and you. We don't change. Ever. When we walk through this door, we aren't going back to the fucked-up lie of friendship we've been living. We start the real us. We go to bed naked and wake up kissing. But that is the *only* shit that changes." I lifted her hand to my chest, settling it over my heart. "This doesn't change. It's you and me to the core. I'm not going anywhere, and neither are you. If it happens to you, it happens to me, remember? And this is definitely happening to *us*. Please don't fight it."

Her big, brown eyes lifted to mine. "This is weird."

I smiled. "Get used to it. It's going to get a whole lot weirder when we get in the shower."

Her cheeks blushed, but not in a shy way. It was heated, and it said that she didn't think the shower would be all that weird, either. She was struggling, but the way she still sparked for me spoke wonders.

Brushing my nose against hers, I teased her lips. "Nothing comes between us. No matter where this goes. Or how it goes. Or how many times I make you come." I paused to smirk. "We don't change, Rocky."

"Okay."

"Say it."

"We don't change." She didn't sound convinced, but I heard her promise.

And, if Liv knew me at all, she felt mine banging in my chest.

We would *never* change.

I wouldn't accept it any other way.

She was the one woman I'd never be able to survive losing.

I found that out the hard way when I was thirteen years old.

I sure as hell wouldn't allow it to happen again.

Releasing her, I ushered her through our front door for what felt like the first time.

A beginning.

An end.

A brand-new start.

The way it should have been all along.

The door had barely clicked when I pushed her up against the wall and crushed my mouth over hers. Her eyes were wide with surprise, but her hands wrapped around my neck and slid into my hair.

Her moans reverberated in my mouth, and her agile tongue dueled with mine—my cock responding to every twist.

"Welcome home," I mumbled. Taking both of her hands, I tugged them around my hips and then placed them on my ass. "Where ass-grabbing is now a requirement."

A sexy growl rumbled from her throat; a chuckle escaped from my own. I continued our kiss as she explored the curves of my glutes. Liv really was an ass girl, and it was all I could do to keep from laughing. Fortunately, the twitch of my cock staved the humor away.

"Let's take a shower," I suggested.

Her mouth froze, and her hands suddenly disappeared.

Leaning away to catch her gaze, I prompted, "Liv?"

She looked anywhere but at me. "I…uh…need some time."

I was fully aware of what she meant, but I pushed anyway. "Okay, well, just meet me in my bathroom in a few."

"That's not what I mean." She went to work picking invisible fuzz off her dress. "I think…we need to take a step back. A lot has happened tonight. I can't do this with you. I know what I said earlier…but…we've established my body's stance on this whole thing, but my mind is reeling. I think I need some space. I'm sorry. I hear what you're saying—I swear I do. I'm just…not ready."

"Fine, I'll give you some time."

Her gaze shot to mine. "Really?"

"Yeah, really. You're right. A lot did happen tonight. And, shit,

Liv. It was incredible." I fisted my hands in the fabric at her hips. "But, tomorrow night, we're going on a date."

Her eyes flashed with excitement before dimming with dread. "I'm not thinking that's a good idea."

I pecked her unresponsive lips. "Then stop thinking. If you're not ready for alone-and-naked yet, you have to at least give me clothed-and-public. Besides, I have somewhere special I want to take you."

Again with the flash of excitement. "Quarry—"

"Go. Before I'm forced to change my mind about the shower." I nipped at her bottom lip.

The war within showed on her face. She wanted to be in that shower with me. She just wouldn't allow herself to have it.

"Go." I gently pushed her shoulder to get her feet moving.

I stood in the doorway, watching her shuffle down the hall. Just before she disappeared into her bedroom, she peeked over her shoulder.

"Later, Q."

The corner of my mouth hiked. She needed normal. I could give her that.

For now.

"Later, Rocky."

Twenty minutes later, I was standing in our kitchen with the sink running.

While our apartment was relatively nice, it was still an apartment. The water pressure was shit when someone was in the shower, which…up until that moment had been annoying as hell. But, as I waited not so patiently for the signal that Liv's shower had turned off, I definitely considered it a perk.

My hearing aids were in a case on my nightstand, and I was wearing a pair of flannel pajama pants and a gray thermal top Eliza had given me for Christmas the year before. They had never been worn, and I could promise they'd never be worn again. I'd felt like I was wrapping myself in a cotton body condom just pulling the damn shirt on. But, if I wanted my plan to work, sacrifices had to be made.

When the water on the faucet suddenly picked up to full blast, I turned it off and shifted my attention to the clock on the stove. For ten agonizing minutes, I stared at those sluggish, red numbers, nervously waiting until I was sure she was dressed.

Strolling past her door with the casual coolness of a man on fire, I spotted the blue tint of her nightlight.

That was my cue.

She was in bed.

And, in less than a minute, I would be too.

I opted for the element of surprise, pushing her door open without so much as a knock.

She sat straight up as I stepped into her room.

Her mouth moved with words I was able to read as, "Hey, what's up?"

My cocky grin shifted to a grimace when I caught sight of the glistening tracks of her tears.

I wanted to ask if she was okay. But I knew she wasn't. She had probably been in that shower drowning herself in worthless guilt while trying to frantically scrub away whatever had been left of me from between her legs. Not too long ago, the idea of her cleansing me from her body would have wrecked me. Now, with the knowledge that she was not only on the same page I was, but fourteen years' worth of pages ahead of me, I was willing to let it go. After our conversation in the ring, Liv could reject me for the rest of her life and I'd never stop trying.

I didn't say anything as I flipped her covers back and slid into the bed beside her. I faintly heard the bass line of whatever music she was playing, or maybe that was the pounding in my chest when I saw she was wearing those little, pink shorts again.

Her mouth moved, no doubt to scold me, but I gave her arm a tug and pulled her down onto my chest.

"I gave you time."

She pushed away and lifted her hands to translate the accusation her voice was communicating. "*An hour is not time!*"

"It was actually only thirty minutes, but I'm a man who lives life in three-minute increments in the ring. Rest assured, it felt like a lifetime. I'd like to note that I'm not naked. That was all I promised you. Now. Can we get some sleep? I'm exhausted." I fake yawned and stretched my arms.

She shot me the glare I'd expected. "*You're not sleeping in here!*"

"Yes, I am."

"*No.*"

"Yes."

"*No.*"

"Yes." I grabbed her hand to stop her from signing again. "It's late, and we have a date tomorrow night."

Her eyes grew wide as she yanked her hand from my grasp. "*We do not have a date.*"

"Yes, we do."

She huffed and then swung her legs over the side of the bed. True to her word at the gym, she didn't leave. Her hands fisted the edge of the mattress, and her chin fell to her chest in defeat.

Starting to feel guilty, I looped an arm around her waist and dragged her back against me. "Rocky, listen."

Her hands started to respond, but I guided them down.

"Don't talk. Don't sign. Just listen."

She rolled her eyes, but her tense body relaxed a fraction.

"Tonight, you told me that, every single day since we met, you've been in love with me. It's been playing on repeat in my head since you said it. Truthfully, I'm not sure I'll ever forget it. Tomorrow night, on our date"—I shot her a challenging glare and received yet another eye roll—"we'll deal with all the other crap you threw at me, but tonight, you're stuck sleeping with me. I'm sorry, but I think fourteen years has been more than enough time alone."

Her eyes cut to the ceiling. *"This... Being here with you... I'm scared."*

"Don't be. Please, God, don't be scared." I flipped to my stomach, draping an arm over her midsection and gliding my palm under her back, forcing her closer to me. Holding us both up on an elbow, I brushed her dark hair away from her face. "We'll figure this out, I swear. Just give me tonight. Yesterday, I damn near had a nervous breakdown because I could feel you slipping through my fingers. I've survived a lot in my life. But that? Losing you? I wouldn't have recovered." I pressed a gentle kiss to her lips. "Then, tonight, I found out that you've always been mine. *Every. Single. Day.*" I kissed her again, breathing in deeply and refusing to exhale.

She didn't exactly kiss me back, but her hand reassuringly settled on my back. A telling gesture I recognized for the first time. She was uncomfortable as hell—and still comforting me.

That was Liv.

"It's been a hard twenty-four hours. Just give me, like, eight more of sleeping next to you, and then you can have all day tomorrow to twist shit up in your head. I'll untangle it"—I paused to smirk—"on our date."

Her chest rose with a suffering sigh, but she eventually nodded. *"Roll over,"* she said.

I flipped to my back, but she pushed at me until I was on my side, facing away from her.

Not a second later, she buried her face in the back of my shirt and folded her arm over my abs. Her knees nudged mine until I bent them and hers shifted in to spoon me.

I twisted my lips, taking in our apparent sleeping position. Not exactly what I'd had in mind, but it was more than she had originally offered.

When her hand pushed the hem of my shirt up and splayed across my bare stomach, I smiled to myself.

Resting my hand on top of hers, I intertwined our fingers. "For the record, you get this tonight because I'm done pushing my luck. But don't get used to it. This has got to be the most emasculating way possible to sleep. I bet this is how Davenport sleeps with his mommy every night."

With her hand cradled in mine, she couldn't respond, but the shake of her body at least let me know she was going to fall asleep with a smile.

We both were.

CHAPTER
Nineteen

Liv

IT WAS NINE IN THE morning when I pulled into Till and Eliza's driveway. My car was still at the gym, so I'd had to swipe the keys to one of Quarry's sports cars. If he could sleep in my bed without asking, surely I could drive his Porsche. And I didn't give a damn if he wanted to bitch about it later. His cars were his babies. Which made peeling out of the parking lot feel so much better.

I had texted Ash and Eliza for an emergency coffee date this morning. They'd both responded immediately, and since Blakely was home sick from school, we'd agreed to meet at Eliza's.

"Spill it!" Ash ordered as I flopped down on the barstool at the end of the long, granite island.

"Where's Blakely?" I asked.

"Till's watching TV with her in my bedroom. I'm giving them a few minutes together before I have to inform him that his baby girl is not actually sick at all. She started her period."

"She's eleven!" I cried, clutching my heart.

"Yeah. He's going to lose his mind. He nearly had an embolism when he found her training bras a few months ago, so this should push him right on over the edge. But hey, he was the one who wanted a girl so badly. He's gonna have to find a way to cope."

Ash set a cup of coffee in front of me. "Ick! I'm so glad we have boys. That is one conversation I never want to have with Flint."

Eliza slid the cream and sugar my way. "All right. Let's move on. I need to save my strength to wrestle the chains from Till's arms when he tries to lock her in her room for the rest of her life. What's going on with you to warrant an emergency coffee date?"

I would have rather continued to talk about poor Blakely, who was clueless to the terror of adolescence that awaited her.

Eliza and Ash peered at me expectantly.

While I hadn't even been properly caffeinated yet, I guessed there would be no use in trying to delay.

I took a sip of the bitter coffee, not even bothering with the condiments, and then swayed back to check down the hall to make sure Till wasn't anywhere nearby. When the coast was clear, I sucked in a deep breath and then announced, "I slept with Quarry."

I expected gasps of surprise, but I was nowhere near ready for the chaos that exploded around me.

"When?!" they shrieked in unison.

My back went straight as they both snatched their cell phones off the table, their fingers frantically tapping the screens.

"Uhh...who are texting? Don't tell the guys! I don't think anything is going—"

"When?" Ash snapped.

"Keep it down!" I whisper-yelled, checking for Till again.

"When?" she repeated, only half of a decibel lower.

"Jeez. Last night."

"Damn," Eliza groaned. "Not one of my days."

"Mine either," Ash replied. "Shit…looks like Sarah won."

I cocked my head in question. "My mom?"

"Yep," Ash confirmed, dropping her phone back to the island. "The pot has to be at least a grand by now. I'll have to ask Flint to check the books. Not too shabby though."

"What pot? What the hell are you talking about?" I glanced from Ash, who looked proud, to Eliza, who appeared slightly ashamed.

"Well…" Eliza started. "About a year ago, we started a small betting pool for when you and Quarry would finally hook up."

My jaw fell open in horror. "You were *betting* on when we would have sex?"

Eliza knotted her hands uncomfortably. "It was just for fun. Nothing crazy or anything."

"The pot was *a grand* and my *mother* won. How exactly is that not crazy?"

Ash chimed in. "Your mom is actually very competitive. She's going to be pumped to find out she won."

I slapped my hand on the countertop and spat, "You are not allowed to tell my mother I had sex with Quarry. Ever. Never. Ever. Ever."

Ash laughed, throwing her hands up in surrender.

Eliza smiled tightly. "If it makes you feel any better, your dad refused to buy in. Slate too—but only because Erica bought so many days there wasn't any left."

Folding forward, I rested my face on the cool granite. "Oh my God. This is not happening."

Her hand soothingly landed on my back. "Quit freaking. One thing at a time. Okay, so you slept with Quarry. That's good, right?"

"You guys were supposed to be surprised," I told the table.

"The only surprise is that it took this long," Ash said, hopping up on the counter and propping her neon Converse in the chair beside me.

I rolled my eyes and then sat up. "This is officially the worst day of my life."

"The sex was that bad, huh?" Ash asked before looking toward Eliza, who was shooting her a death glare. "What? It's a valid question."

I groaned. "No. The sex was…incredible. I just don't think I can give him what he wants."

Ash nodded in understanding. "Ah…he's kinky? I can see that."

"Don't answer that!" Eliza yelled and plugged her ears. "For God's sake, Ash."

I pulled Eliza's hands away from her ears. "He's not kinky."

"Shame," Ash mumbled.

I ignored her. "I'm scared," I whispered.

Eliza settled on the stool beside me. "Of what? That things will change between you two? Because when Till and I—"

I interrupted her. "I'm scared that I'll never be *her*."

They both sighed, and a pair of arms folded around me in a tight hug.

They weren't Eliza's.

It was Ash.

"Don't say that. When Flint and I—"

But that wasn't even the half of it.

"Mia loved him so much. I can't stop feeling like we're having some sort of torrid affair behind her back."

Ash squeezed tighter.

I kept going. "And then there's the fact that I'm a terrible excuse for a friend. Because I've been in love with him for a really long time." I lifted my gaze to Eliza's, ready for the disgust I deserved when I confessed, "Even when Mia was alive."

Her lips thinned in a sympathetic smile.

Ash squeezed me again.

Tears filled my eyes as I swallowed hard. "And the absolute, most horrifying part of all of it is that there are so many reasons why we shouldn't be together. But I still can't seem to stop hoping that maybe we can." I sniffed back the tears I refused to shed.

"Okay. It's nine a.m. Wine is out. But I'll get the Baileys for your coffee," Eliza announced.

"I'll call Flint to pick up the boys."

"No. It's fine. Don't do that," I insisted.

"Too late. Let me get Blakely and Till moved to her room, and we'll reconvene in Chick Central in ten minutes."

"Eliza, stop! You have enough to deal with with Blakely right now. You don't need me moping and crying all day too. Besides, I have a class at the community center this afternoon and a million things to do for Quarry. I can't be drunk."

"Stop worrying. Blakely will probably dub you as her favorite aunt if she finds out you delayed me telling her dad about her period."

"Hey!" Ash objected.

Eliza lifted a hand to hush her. "And for the rest of it. Fine, no Baileys. But Quarry can answer his own e-mails today. This is more important. And I think he'd agree."

She had a point. He definitely would agree with her. And I desperately needed to talk all of this stuff through with someone who wasn't him.

"Yeah. Okay," I relented.

An hour later, the three of us were sprawled out in Eliza's art room. I had just filled them in on the last month of my life—starting with the night of the Gala and ending this morning, when I'd snuck out from under Quarry's arm draped possessively across my hips.

"Wow," Eliza said then looked at Ash. "Well, do you want to start or should I?"

"I've got this." Ash dramatically cleared her throat then offered me a healthy dose of pity by way of a tight smile. "You're fucked."

I ignored her and turned my attention to Eliza only to find her nodding.

"Well. Awesome. That clears it all up," I smarted, pushing to my feet.

"Sit down!" Ash called. "I was just getting started."

I crossed my arms over my chest and gave her my full attention for what I was positive was going to be a waste of time. "Go on."

"I never understood why he was with Mia."

I flinched. Never would I have expected those to be her first words.

"It's harsh, but true," she continued. "You've heard about when Quarry was fourteen and his mom tried to regain custody, right?"

I nodded, settling back down on the futon.

"Then I'm sure you also know that she was married to my dad and that Quarry lived with me for about a month. Well, every night, we would stay awake until the early morning, talking. I was mostly pumping him for information about Flint, but he filled my ears with you."

"Seriously?" I blinked in shock.

Those were the years Quarry and I hadn't been speaking. The years when I'd had my head low, pretending I hated him for having locked me in the closet when, really, I'd just hated him for having proved me right—I couldn't trust anyone.

"Yep. I knew all about Liv James," Ash assured me. "The little Hispanic angel who used to bury her face in his back. The one he vowed to protect from the silence. The one who he regretted failing more than anyone else in his entire life."

I sucked in a sharp breath. "He...told you about that?"

"He wouldn't tell me why you were afraid or why he was so attached to you, but yeah...he told me all of that. Multiple times."

My eyes flashed between the two of them. We were tight, but I never would have revealed Quarry's secrets to them. Even if he was telling mine.

"Did he tell you why we stopped speaking for those years?"

"No." Eliza jumped in before Ash had a chance. "Your dad told us about the closet. Quarry has never once spoken about it, not even when I cornered him after I'd heard what he'd done."

I glanced at the floor and lied, "It wasn't as bad as it sounds."

"It was to him," Eliza said. "He was a mess. After Vegas, Quarry was never the same. He didn't come out of his room for weeks. He started skipping school and getting into fights. He eventually got kicked out of school, and then he quit boxing."

"What?" I gasped. "He quit boxing?"

"Yep. You have no idea how bad things got with him. Back then, we were so focused on Flint, but what we failed to see was that Quarry was equally as injured. His wounds just weren't on the surface."

I swallowed around the lump in my throat. Mine weren't on the surface, either, and I knew firsthand that that was exactly what made them lethal.

"Neither Till nor Slate could get through to him. We tried counseling, but he refused to go, and the harder we pushed, the harder he fought us. The thing was that we all assumed he was torn up over what had happened with Flint and me, but it wasn't until he talked to your dad one night that things started to turn around."

"My dad?" I breathed. "What…what did he say to him?"

Eliza shrugged. "No clue. Till just said Quarry came out of Slate's office almost in tears and Leo looked murderous."

Well, that wasn't all that shocking. My dad wasn't exactly a teddy bear, especially when it came to me. But one thing stuck out to me.

"And things got better after that? I mean…with Quarry?"

"Yep. He started going to the gym again the very next day. No more fights at school. He started laughing again. Hanging out with his brothers. It was like he just reappeared."

"Wow. I didn't figure my dad for the inspirational-speech kind of guy."

"Flint looked for me for three years," Ash announced randomly. "We had only been together for a month and he ripped up the weeds from his old apartment and planted them at his house just to take a piece of me with him when he moved."

Eliza picked up with more randomness. "Till climbed through windows for eight years. He was so afraid to step out of his fantasy world because he couldn't bear the thought of it changing us. But, when he finally walked through my door, things went from zero to married in a year."

"Okay?" I drawled.

"So you're fucked," Ash repeated.

"Totally," Eliza agreed.

Ash stood and moved beside me on the futon. "Way I see it, Quarry has been sitting on some serious feelings for you since he was a kid, and a few weeks ago, he woke up and realized that those feelings were still there. And, if I had to guess, they're probably stronger than ever. You think a man like him—a Page man—is just going to walk away from that? And, more so, do you think you could handle it if he did?"

My pulse spiked. "I won't lose him. We could stay friends."

"The friend thing doesn't work when you're in love, Liv. It will destroy you faster than anything else. Longing and love turns to bitterness and anger." Eliza smiled. "Trust me. I've been there."

I shook my head adamantly. "No. Quarry and I are…different." Panic began to build in my chest. As sad as it may sound, Quarry was my life. Without him, it would just be me and the silence. "N-nothing changes. He…told me so."

"Simmer down." Ash's hand gently landed on my back. "You look like you're about to pass out or puke."

I was about to do both.

It was all too overwhelming.

The idea of losing him.

The idea of being with him.

The idea of trusting him.

The idea of him leaving me when I couldn't give him that trust.

The idea of just being friends after the way it'd felt to wake up in his arms.

The idea of never having him inside me again.

The idea of…Mia.

Then the idea of *having* him inside me again.

Too much. All of it.

"Hey…you want to breathe?" Ash hit me on the back like I was choking.

A rush of breath I hadn't known I'd been holding flew from my mouth.

"I can't do this." I jumped to my feet and began pacing the room. "Help me think of a way to get out of this date with him tonight."

"You're in love with him. Do you think dodging a date will make that disappear?" Eliza asked.

"No! But I think it will give him more time to realize how fucked up this whole thing is. He wasn't supposed to develop feelings for me. And, now that I know he has, I can't seem to keep mine shut down anymore." I groaned. "No. This isn't happening. He loves Mia. I can't fill those shoes. He needs to get over this…so I can too. End of story."

Ash's eyes lifted to Eliza then back to me. "Love is different. It's not a one-size-fits-all. And it's definitely not universal or transferable. There are no shoes to fill. Whatever you and Quarry have is unique to the two of you. It's not what he had with Mia—and I mean that for better or worse. You can't compare his feelings. If Quarry is risking what you two have to take it to the next level, then you have to assume they are pretty freaking strong."

She drew in a deep breath and lowered her voice as if she were going impart some serious wisdom. "If you hear nothing else I say today, please hear this. It took me a long time to realize this, and

I don't want to see you make the same mistakes. So listen up." She leaned toward me, her eyes imploring. "There are no shoes to fill, Liv. And the way I know this is because, if there were, Mia would have been filling yours for years."

My heart stopped. "You…you don't know what you're talking about. Quarry loved Mia."

Eliza nodded. "He did. Very much. But he loved you first."

I shot to my feet. "You don't know that."

"We all know that! Everyone who has ever seen you two together knows that! It's not a competition between you and Mia, Liv. It's not an affair. It's not some dirty little secret. It's life. So cut yourself some slack. Go on a date with the guy you've always wanted, talk to him, and then figure out how to start the real relationship you both so obviously want." Ash threw her arms out to the sides in frustration and then turned to Eliza. "Christ! Please tell me I wasn't this stubborn."

Eliza giggled. "Worse."

I stood frozen.

Could it be that easy?

I had to admit flighty-and-crazy Ash wasn't too shabby at advice.

While the chat about Mia did make me feel marginally better, the biggest problem I saw with all of this was that, in order to be with Quarry, I was going to have to find a way to trust him.

It was impossible.

"He loved you first."

"I don't know how to do this," I admitted.

"Well, that's better than the 'I can't do this' you were claiming a few minutes ago." Ash smiled and tossed my cell phone into my lap. "Start there."

Me: I'm going to the community center and setting up some stuff for Don so he can handle my tutoring appointments for tonight. What time should I be ready for our date?

Quarry: Actually, I'm busy tonight. Can we do something tomorrow?

Me: That's better for me anyway. The male revue is in town for tonight only.

Quarry: Jesus. I was kidding. You aren't going to a fucking male revue.

Me: I was kidding too…kinda.

Quarry: I'll pick you up at seven. Dress warm.

Me: Are you sure about this? I mean…this is weird.

Quarry: I'll pick you up at seven. Be naked. Better?

Me: Aaaaaaaanddddd…I'll dress warm. K. Thanks.

CHAPTER
Twenty

Quarry

I SPENT THE DAY RUNNING around to get everything ready for my date for Liv. She was going to absolutely hate every single minute of it. Which was precisely why I was so excited. I hadn't been lying—I did have somewhere special to take her, but I had a sneaking suspicion it was only going to be special for me. I could live with that though.

With my hand poised in the air, I stared at the second hand on my watch until it clicked to seven o'clock. After knocking, I nervously shoved my free hand in the pocket of my slacks.

"What are you doing?" she asked when she pulled the door open. "Did you lose your key?"

I smiled wide as I took her in. Liv was beautiful. I was well aware of that. But, that night, knowing she'd gotten dressed just for me, I felt things I hadn't expected.

"What the hell, Liv!" I growled, extending the bouquet of white roses her way.

"Um…thanks?" she replied, hesitantly taking them from my hand.

"I'm offended!" I tugged at the collar of my dress shirt and then straightened the lapels on my suit coat.

She bit her lip to stifle a laugh. "It's the jacket. You know how it cuts off the oxygen to your brain and all." She giggled, but I found not one thing funny.

"You're wearing jeans and a sweater." I made a show of raking my eyes from her head to her toes and back again.

Liv looked undeniably gorgeous. The dark skinny jeans were tight, and the tall, black heels elongated her already-long legs. Her pale-purple sweater hugged her tits perfectly. I was sure it would have given a spectacular show when we walked into the cool October night air. However, the fact still remained that she was wearing jeans and a sweater.

She lifted the roses to her nose, hiding the wide smile she was sporting. "You didn't tell me I needed to dress up. You just said dress warm."

"Douchebag Boatshoes got a dress," I stated simply.

"Douchebag Boatshoes didn't tell me to dress warm." She twisted away from me, her ass swaying seductively as she made her way to the kitchen.

Maybe those jeans hadn't been a bad choice after all.

"I'm in a suit," I announced as if she hadn't noticed.

"Congratulations!" she shouted over the running water as she filled a vase.

I scratched the back of my head. "I'm not sure they'll let you in the restaurant in jeans. I guess I could always call to check."

Her eyes perked. "Really?"

"Yeah, really. I'm worth millions, Liv. You think I'm taking you to a drive-thru?"

"Ah," she replied in understanding. "My best friend once told me about douchebags like you. I'm not particularly interested in money. I siphon enough off my boss to keep me set for years."

"Your boss should fire you. But your best friend sounds brilliant."

"Meh. He's okay," she teased. "So, where are we going?"

With a proud smirk, I joined her in the kitchen.

She stared up at me nervously as I wrapped my arms around her waist and tugged her against me. Her breathing sped when I nuzzled my cheek against hers. Switching to the other side, I nipped playfully at her neck. A breathy moan encouraged me further, so I raked my teeth against her flesh before pulling away.

"It's a surprise," I whispered.

Gripping her hips, I lifted her to sit on the counter.

Her fingers went to the top button of my shirt. It wasn't a nervous gesture. It was heated and sexy as fuck.

"Is this the suit from the Gala?" she asked before licking her lips.

"Mmm," I mumbled while staring at her mouth. "It's my most successful outfit from the Liv James collection."

"Technically, that would be your boxing trunks, but this is a close second." She smiled. Then it disappeared, taking the woman I so desperately wanted with it. Her pink cheeks paled, and her hands fell away. "Give me a minute and I'll change into a dress."

Lifting her legs around my waist, I inched closer, not stopping until her denim met my zipper. "What just went through your mind? You were flirting and then you shut down."

"Nothing," she moaned, shifting away, but I refused her the space.

I cupped the back of her neck and forced her eyes to mine. "What. Happened?"

She tried to shimmy off the counter, but I blocked her.

"Can we just go?" she huffed.

I sighed and closed my eyes, pleading for patience. None was found.

"Are you going to spend the entire night trying to put distance between us?"

Her head snapped back, and attitude filled her masked eyes. "Maybe."

"It doesn't matter what I do, does it? You're going to shut me down, aren't you?"

She disconnected her legs and leaned away. "I am if you don't stop acting like a dick."

"I'll take that as a yes." I shrugged. "Nothing to lose. Fuck it," I mumbled.

"What's that supposed to—"

I crushed my mouth over hers. Swallowing her surprised cry, I went to work coaxing her tongue into a rhythm. It only took seconds for my Liv to reappear.

Folding her arms around my neck, she used it as leverage to take the kiss even deeper. Slowly, her hand slid down my chest and into my jacket before gliding around to my back.

She tugged the back of my shirt up until it untucked.

I chuckled as she slid her hands into my pants. Then I groaned as her nails bit into my ass. Cursing into her mouth, I ground my hard cock between her legs.

She gasped then circled her hips for more.

"This is exactly why you should have worn a dress," I said, finding the seam of her jeans and tracing it up and down.

She threw her head back, and her long, brown hair teased my hand at the small of her back.

"Give me this woman tonight." My fingers continued to play as I spoke against her lips. "We'll talk. Figure this shit out. But don't go into this closed off from me. Give me a chance." I wrapped the length of her hair around my fist and tugged her head back to catch my gaze. I dragged my tongue over her parted lips then finished. "Give *us* a chance."

"Okay," she panted.

I smiled triumphantly before abruptly stepping out of her reach. "Go put on a dress."

She blinked at me through sex-fogged eyes. It took everything I had in me not to rip her jeans and fuck her right there on the kitchen counter.

But, as hard as it was for me to remember, I needed to get her on the same page more than I needed to be balls-deep inside her.

Fucking her then would have only been a short-term answer.

Fucking her for the rest of my life was the long-term goal.

"That was mean," she whined, jumping off the counter and starting out of the room.

I caught her around the waist and pulled her against my chest. "No. Mean would be if I didn't have plans to make you come on my mouth when we get home." I kissed her chastely and gave her ass a squeeze. "Go get dressed. We're gonna be late."

Her lips lifted in a mischievous grin. "I'll be quick."

I watched her saunter away. Concerns that perhaps I was turning into an ass guy passed through my head, and then...

All.

Thoughts.

Were.

Gone.

Liv paused just outside her bedroom door and peeled her sweater over her head. Calling over her shoulder, she said, "I guess this would only be mean if I didn't have plans to show you the front tonight."

Son of a bitch!

But...score for tonight!

I fought the urge to throw my hands in the air in victory.

I failed.

CHAPTER
Twenty-One

Liv

OPEN MIND.

> *No guilt.*
> *It's not a competition.*
> *Of course I can trust him.*
> *We can do this.*

That was my mantra as I walked out of our apartment on Quarry's arm.

I had replaced the jeans with a modern, red dress with half sleeves and a notched hem. It hugged my every curve like a glove, but the high, rounded neckline kept it classy for whatever five-star restaurant Quarry was planning to take me to. My long hair had been pinned into a loose side-bun, and diamond stud earrings kept the whole look simple yet dazzling.

Open mind.

No guilt.

It's not a competition.

Of course I can trust him.

We can do this.

"You look incredible," Quarry told me.

I felt like an imposter.

My clothes. My skin. My heart. Walking out on his arm.

That all fit perfectly.

On a date with him? After having slept with him? After having admitted that I had been in love with him for my entire life? Wrong. So fucking wrong.

I swallowed hard and willed my heart to slow. "Thanks." I peeked up and found him watching me with every step. My cheeks heated when his smile turned to his signature smolder.

"You excited for the best date of your life?"

"I'm on pins and needles," I teased.

He barked a laugh and then stopped in front of...Till's beat-up truck?

"Your brother's here?" I asked looking around the parking lot.

"Nope," he answered, running his hand over the rusted-out hood.

Till's truck was a hunk of shit junkyards probably wouldn't even allow on the premises. He had other cars and more than enough money to restore it to all of its budget luxury of its heyday, but with the exception of keeping it running, Till hadn't fixed anything on it. I suspected that it had sentimental value to him. What I didn't understand was why it was parked in front of our apartment.

Quarry answered my unspoken question when he pulled open the passenger's side door for me. "Hop in." He smiled.

"What's wrong with your cars?" I asked, thoroughly perplexed.

Quarry was a car whore. He paid thousands of dollars each month to rent out four of the small garages our apartment complex offered to store his collection of sports cars. I never knew what was hiding behind those garage doors because it seemed the cars were always different. He rotated through them, trading them in whenever a newer or a nicer one came out.

"Nothing. I borrowed this from Till special for tonight."

I scrunched my nose in displeasure, which only made him laugh.

"Get in, Rocky. We can't be late."

"Valet is going to love this," I smarted, sliding into the open door.

Quarry twirled the keys around his finger as he circled the front of the truck. With an unbelievably loud creak, the driver's side door opened, and he slid behind the wheel.

"Here. Put this on." He lifted a blindfold my way.

I stared at it dangling from the tip of his finger. "Where'd you get a blindfold?"

"Flint said Ash likes to get crazy in bed sometimes," he said nonchalantly.

Curling my lip, I slapped it out of his hand. "Ew!"

He laughed and scooped it off the floor. "I'm kidding. I bought it today." He stretched the strap over my head. "Come on. I want to surprise you."

I glared at him until he finally understood.

"Oh, right." He cranked the noisy truck and flipped the radio on. Then his hand anchored to my exposed thigh. "I'm right here. Nothing to worry about."

He was wrong. That was exactly why I was worried in the first place.

Open mind.

No guilt.

It's not a competition.

Of course I can trust him.

We can do this.

I sighed then pulled the mask over my eyes.

Minutes later, with a blanket thrown over my lap since the heater didn't work, we were roaring down the highway.

"Don't take it off until I tell you," Quarry ordered as the truck slowed to a stop. He put the car in park but didn't cut the engine.

"Okay," I agreed, shedding the blanket and straightening my dress in preparations to exit the vehicle.

Only that didn't happen at all.

"Um…yes, I'd like two chili dogs. No onions. Two large fries…"

"Are you kidding me?" I snapped as he continued to rattle off a mountain of fast food.

I went for my blindfold, but he caught my wrists in one hand and locked them together in my lap.

His voice was filled with humor as he finished ordering. "What's wrong, Liv?" he asked when he was done.

"You made me put on a dress and blindfolded me for chili dogs?"

"Hey, I'm wearing a suit. Imagine my disappointment." He released my hands and glided his fingers up my thigh. "Fine, I'll confess. The dress was for me."

I sucked in a sharp breath when he brushed the bare flesh at my core.

"Oh. My. Fuck," he whispered.

My mind forced me to back up in my seat in order to escape his touch, but my body had other ideas and uncrossed my legs to offer him more access.

"This…dress doesn't exactly look good with panties," I said breathily.

Actually, that might be why I picked it to wear tonight.

After our moment in the kitchen, guilt couldn't even trump my desire for him.

I could feel guilty for the rest of my life.

I only had one date with Quarry. Or so I'd told myself as I'd removed my panties.

His finger deliciously ran up and down my slit, and I felt the blanket fall back over my lap.

"Are...are," I sputtered when he found my clit. "Are we in a drive-thru?"

"Drive-up. But no one's around."

Oh...I was classy.

I was with my friend's man, letting him finger me under a blanket at a drive-up restaurant. How old was I again? My thoughts started to win out over my desires. However, just as I convinced myself that this had to stop, he dipped inside.

Screw my thoughts.

My head fell back and my legs spread wide.

"Fuck," he cursed as his hand disappeared.

He growled loudly. Then his mouth covered mine. The faint flavor of my arousal lingered on his tongue as it snaked into my mouth.

He'd licked his fingers. Dear lord. Why was that so hot?

Slanting my head, I gripped the back of his neck, attempting to pull him impossibly closer.

I felt the blanket pull taut on my lap, but it still covered me. It was as if he had crawled under it with me.

"Shit. I should have ordered more food," he mumbled as he suddenly moved away.

I heard the manual crank of the window, and then a female voice joined us.

"Hey. How's it going tonight?"

I giggled as Quarry bit out a frustrated hello.

The crinkle of plastic bags sounded just before they landed in my lap.

"No change. I'm good. Thanks. Have a good night," he gritted out then promptly rolled up the window. His hand found its way under the blanket again. "I did not need to know you weren't wearing any panties." His fingers brushed between my legs again, but he quickly removed them and pulled my dress down.

It was a good thing he was stopping. We didn't need to be doing that—regardless of how much my body was screaming for more. For a minute there, even my mind had been begging for it.

Which reminded me: I needed to start packing in the morning for my one-way trip to Hell.

"Can I take this off so I can eat?" I pointed to my eyes.

The truck shifted into gear.

"Not yet." He was reversing when I felt his hand start digging through one of the bags. "Open up," he ordered.

My legs immediately obeyed.

He barked a loud laugh and then amended, "Your mouth. For now, at least."

"Shut up." I rolled my closed eyes and followed his instructions. A french fry landed in my mouth before he dug back into the bag—I assumed for his own appetizer.

Moments later, we were once again roaring down the highway.

"Hang tight, and no peeking," Quarry instructed when he cut the engine.

This time, he gathered all the bags of food and then pulled the blanket off my lap before he got out.

I blindly smoothed my hair down and ran my fingers around the outline of my lips to hopefully get rid of any lipstick that may have smeared at the drive-up.

I was so nervous I couldn't even remember my mantra anymore. Something about an open mind and some other bullshit. However, it seemed like it was a lot more like open legs when I was with Quarry.

"What is wrong with me?" I asked myself over the loud music he'd left playing solely for my benefit.

I loved that he knew that about me.

I loved that I hadn't felt awkward when opening my mouth for him to shove french fries in as we had driven.

I loved that, despite how uncomfortable I felt about being on this "date," I was unbelievably comfortably with him.

Really, I just loved *him*.

And I hated myself because of it.

The cool air rushed through the truck as my door swung open.

"Okay. Come on." He unbuckled my seat belt and then helped me to my feet. He held my hand as he guided me down the side of the truck. Then he stopped at the tailgate and used my shoulder to turn me away from it.

When he had me positioned just right, he stepped away. "Now you can take it off," he announced excitedly.

I didn't waste a second before pulling the blindfold from my eyes. Quarry was standing proudly in front of me with his hands shoved in his pockets. Looking every bit as tantalizing as he always was. I smiled shyly as he popped that dimple with a lopsided smile. I was so focused on his mouth that I barely registered the light of the bus station sign glowing behind him.

"I've never brought anyone in the world here before." He rested his hands on my hips and swayed me forward.

I twisted my lips. "I'm not sure I'm excited to find out that the last place in the world you haven't taken anyone else on a date is a bus station."

"No. Smartass. You are the only person I've ever brought *here*."

I arched an eyebrow in question. He shook his head with a smile and slid his hands under my arms, and then he lifted me to sit on the tailgate.

I expected cold metal, but I was met with a plush fleece blanket covering the bed of the truck.

It was cold, but he tugged his jacket off, draped it over the side, then settled beside me.

I bumped him with my shoulder. "Are you this romantic on all your dates? Or am I just that special?" I teased.

"Just you."

"I'm assuming there's a story here?" I motioned a hand to the bus station.

He went to work passing me food, leaving what was left of the fries at the bottom of the bag between us. "Yep."

"You gonna tell me?" I asked before taking a bite of my hot dog.

He lifted a finger and then finished his dinner in three bites. After washing it down with a large soda, he winked and popped a mint in his mouth. "I should have taken you on our first date at sixteen."

My smile fell, and I lost my appetite completely. Dumping my food in the bag, I became fascinated with the concrete parking lot.

He linked his hand with mine and settled them on his thigh. "This is the date I would have taken you on. I was a broke sixteen-year-old back then. But Till would have let me borrow his truck, and Eliza would have snuck me some money for dinner even if I hadn't done my chores at home. I splurged on the roses, so you got chili dogs." He smirked. "Even feeling you up at the drive-up would have happened, and I definitely would have brought you here. Because, if we were going out on a date back then, this place would have been the way I got you back."

He stopped talking and turned to face me. Then he stole a boyish kiss that made me blush.

I nervously fidgeted with my dress as if I really were that fifteen-year-old girl in the back of his truck.

Quarry laughed then continued. "Two days after my sixteenth birthday, Till and I got into a huge fight because he wouldn't let me get my driver's license, seeing that I had a C in Spanish."

"*Y por eso deberías haberme mantenido alrededor*," I mumbled. (And this is why you should have kept me around.)

"Showoff." He bumped me with his shoulder. "Anyway, I took off. Wandered around aimlessly with no place to go. I was on foot, so it wasn't like I could make it far, but I refused to go home. I ended up here." He pointed to a bench just outside the door to the run-down terminal. "I sat there for hours, watching people as buses came in and out. It was crazy, but I started trying to imagine what those people's lives were like. Were they better than mine? Worse? Did they also have to live under the tyranny of an older brother who actually cared about their grades?"

He shook his fist in the air in humorous defiance. Then his face turned serious again, and he squeezed my hand impossibly tight.

"Did they have parents who loved them instead of abandoning them? If not, did they have a woman like Eliza in their life who, at only twenty-one, became the surrogate mother she didn't have to be? No? What about a brother like Flint who spent his childhood making sure they were fed and clothed? Were they happy? Did they have a little brown-eyed girl who'd stolen a piece of their soul at ten years old?" His voice was thick, and he paused to swallow. "And, if they did…did they fail them all too?"

"Stop," I whispered, scooting closer and moving our joined hands to my lap.

He kissed my forehead. "I was a kid. I couldn't stop. Anyway, watching people got me thinking about you. I was positive that you hated me. But I started wondering what you were doing. Had you grown up? What did you look like? Were you still scared of the silence?" He lowered his voice and whispered, "Did you miss me like I missed you?"

My stomach had already been in knots, and my heart was breaking, but it wasn't until he tipped my head back and stared deep into my eyes that I felt the true pain.

"Every. Single. Day," he whispered my confession reverently. "That was the only answer I truly needed."

His lips pressed against mine, and his thumb traced my jawline.

I melted against him. Anxiety and guilt were temporarily banished from my thoughts.

Opening my mouth, I silently requested more of a connection. His tongue obliged my plea and glided against mine. Much to my dismay, he kept it short.

I was still drunk from his kiss when he said, "That was when I got an idea. I decided to buy a bus ticket to come see you." He tucked a stray hair behind my ear and squeezed me with the hand I was clinging to. "I marched into that office, slammed my wallet down on the counter, and demanded a ticket to Chicago."

I blinked up at him expectantly. I knew how this story ended. I'd lived it. He'd never made it to Chicago, but my heart raced with anticipation as if, this time, the story could somehow be different. As if Quarry could magically travel back in time, show up at my door when I was fifteen, and sweep me off my feet exactly the way I'd dreamed of at least a million times.

We could have still been sitting right there years later.

But this time.

It wouldn't be wrong.

It wouldn't be weird.

There wouldn't be guilt.

There wouldn't be pain.

But, if that were the case, there also wouldn't have been Mia.

That was the kind of friend I was. I had gotten so lost in a fantasy where I got the boy that I'd just written her out of my life altogether.

My heart sank all over again.

Quarry must have felt my body tense, because he released my hand and scooped me into his lap, cradling me like a lost and confused little girl.

Maybe he could travel back in time after all.

"The next bus wasn't until the following afternoon, and I was five dollars short," he told the top of my head. "It was just a silly idea. I wasn't even sure what I would have done when I got there, but it crushed me when I couldn't make it happen. I hadn't seen you in three years, but every second after I walked out of that bus station felt like an eternity, and each one broke me a little more. And I'll be honest, Liv. There wasn't a whole lot left of me to break at that point. I'd been trudging along for the sake of everyone around me for years, but it was all a lie. And, in that moment, completely alone at a bus station with memories haunting me with every step, I gave up the fight and called Till. I sobbed like a little bitch when he showed up to get me. Sitting in the cab of this truck, I lost my ever-loving mind, pouring out my heart and soul like I was on death row."

I curled into his chest, offering him comfort when, in reality, I was taking it for myself. The idea of Quarry breaking broke me too.

He continued. "I think Till got his first real glance of how bad off I was. I started counseling the next day. A month later Till moved me to a private school for the hearing impaired. My first day there, I met Mia. And, nine months later, you came back to me. My life went from completely empty to overflowing in a matter of months. I didn't even know how to handle it. But I was determined to hold on to it."

I buried my face in his neck and cursed the gods of bus schedules and five-dollar bills.

And, while I was at it, I threw in closets, silence, and brain tumors too.

His voice became raspy and low. "We aren't wrong."

I looked up at him. "Huh?"

"Last night, you said we were wrong. That's bullshit and you know it."

I sighed. "She *was* my best friend. You *are* my best friend. There are some lines you just shouldn't cross."

He groaned and shook his head. "I seriously don't get you. What do you want me to do? Spend the rest of my life alone because Mia died?"

"Of course not! She never would have wanted that."

A loud laugh escaped his throat. "But, somehow, *we're* wrong?"

I clamped my mouth shut.

"Right," he scoffed, moving me off his lap. He stood off the tailgate and intertwined his fingers, resting them the top of his head. "This is ridiculous, Liv. Why is this about her? She has not one damn thing to do with our relationship."

My head snapped back. Was he insane? She had everything to do with our relationship.

"She was your girlfriend!" I snapped.

"And I loved her! Don't punish me for that!"

"I'm not punishing you for anything. I'm simply stating the facts to explain why this *is* absolutely wrong." I bit my lip, instantly regretting my choice of words.

A stifling rage began radiating off his strong shoulders. He was beyond pissed. His hands clenched at his sides as he paced back and forth from hood to bumper.

Knowing exactly what would follow, I jumped to my feet when he stilled. Then I rushed in front of him and protectively leaned against Till's beater truck as it if were the crown jewels Quarry was about to destroy with his fist.

"Don't you dare!" I seethed. "You break your hand again, Davenport wins. Calm the fuck down."

His jaw ticked as he held my glare. His chest was puffed, filled with breath, but he wasn't breathing. Thankfully, that was a good sign. It meant he was reigning himself in. With the exhale, his temper would fade—or so I thought.

"We are not wrong!" he roared.

I startled at the sudden outburst, but his body closed in on me, flattening me against the side of the truck. He bent down and took my mouth in a punishing kiss. As always, my arms instantly folded around him. His hand dropped to my thigh and lifted it to his hip, leaving me balanced on one heel.

"Tell me this feels wrong," he ordered, fisting a hand into the back of my hair then slamming his mouth back over mine.

My lips ached under the force of his, but my tongue greedily swirled in his mouth.

"Tell me," he gritted out.

I turned my head to answer, but he sucked hard on my neck before biting it. The pain seared through me only to transform into ecstasy as he rolled his cock against my core. A strangled cry tore from my throat.

"Tell me this doesn't feel like everything you've ever wanted. Because that's exactly how it fucking feels to me."

"Quarry," I breathed—my only objection before I thrust my hips forward to find friction.

His mouth continued to assault me, breaking from my skin only long enough to growl, "Tell me you don't want me." Bite. "Don't love me." He soothed the spot with a lave of his tongue. "Tell me this doesn't feel like the rest of your life and I'll fucking let it go right now." Rake of his teeth. "Tell me, Liv." His hands moved to my breasts, kneading before plucking my peaked nipples over the fabric of my dress.

I was about to mount him in the middle of a parking lot, and I cared not one single bit.

I couldn't tell him any of those things.

There was no doubt that I wanted him.

Even when I'd tried not to, I'd always loved him.

It felt exactly like the rest of my life with him.

I couldn't even stop my mind from firing off the random images of diamond rings, white dresses, hazel-eyed babies, my name on his tongue in climax, whispered I-love-yous before falling asleep in his arms. Forever.

And, for that reason alone, I said, "We're not wrong."

His mouth moved to my ear, his breath sending chills down my spine as he spoke. "I refuse to let you fight me on this. I refuse to deny the way I feel about you. And I absolutely refuse to let you deny what you feel for me. You want this. I get that you're scared, but trust me. I *will* make this work for us."

"*Trust me.*"

Right.

Even with that thought ricocheting through my mind, my only response was a nod.

"We deserve to be happy, Rocky. And I'm sorry if you have issues with this, but I dare you to tell me that Mia would have wanted us to be miserable and apart rather than happy and together."

"I don't know what she would have wanted," I mumbled.

He froze. "Then you're lying to yourself. There is nothing in this world, including dying alone, that she wouldn't have done to see us happy."

That's when *I* froze.

"She did that, Liv. And I was mad at her for a lot of years because of it. But the truth is she didn't just want to live the rest her days happy. She wanted us to live the rest of ours happy too."

I swallowed around the emotion lodged in my throat. He was right. Deep down, I knew he was.

Still, it felt impossible to accept.

Dropping my forehead to his chest, I asked, "How are you the rational one here?"

"Because it's you."

I sighed. I knew that half of the reason I'd ended up being Quarry's assistant was because I was the only one who could handle him. Over the last few years, I'd been able to talk him down, no matter how out of hand he got. Up until that moment, I'd always assumed I was just good at crisis management, but I was suddenly realizing that it had nothing to do with me at all—and everything to do with us.

"Did you love me first?" I asked for no other reason than I was curious as hell.

He chuckled. "I was thirteen when you took off. Love back then consisted of who had bigger boobs and was willing to let me touch them." He grazed his hand up the side of my breast.

I slapped his chest, causing him to laugh, but he soon turned serious again.

"But, if you're asking if, even as a kid, I felt an undeniable connection with you that I would never be able to explain, but I still recognized with every cell in my body, every breath in my lungs, and every beat of my heart that I needed to hold on to it no matter the consequences? Then my answer would have to be..." He paused and nuzzled his cheek against mine before whispering, "Every. Single. Day."

CHAPTER
Twenty-Two

Liv

"EVERY. SINGLE. DAY."

Whether he'd loved me or not, I didn't know. But Quarry Page had returned the only three words that could trump any declaration of love he ever had to offer. The war raging within me had come to a stalemate, leaving me to make a decision based solely on the hazel eyes I'd never been able to get over. I was officially going to give in to my innermost desires and, in turn, give Quarry his too. I didn't know how anything was going to work between us. But, with three simple words, I vanquished the guilt and filled my heart with hopes of the future I'd wanted since I was a little girl.

Wrong or right, I'd wanted him for forever.

Wrong or right, I was finally going to follow through.

My head was a jumbled mess, my emotions had been put through the wringer, and my body was on the verge of spontaneous combustion, but one thing had become abundantly clear.

"Stop freaking out. We're doing this," Quarry stated.

My eyes were clamped shut as I signed, "*It appears we are.*"

"Jesus. Don't look so excited."

"*It's weird!*" I whined.

"Was it weird when you were coming on my cock last night?" he asked in a deep voice, skating the fine line between frustration and hilarity.

"*It is now!*" I replied, skating an equally fine line between joining a convent and dropping to my knees in front of him.

"Well, was it weird when I was finger-fucking you not even ten minutes ago?"

No. That had been the furthest thing from weird. The man was incredible with his hands.

I decided not to inflate his ego and lied. "*A little.*"

Water suddenly doused my face, causing my eyes to pop open in surprise.

"*Stop!*" I yelled, doing my best to keep my gaze aimed at his chin or higher.

His laughter was infectious, so as much as I wanted to crawl into a hole and hide, I started laughing too. Unfortunately, this act gave my mind a chance to forget the whole chin-up thing, and my eyes took the opportunity to drop to Quarry's hand gliding over the defined ridges on his stomach.

And they didn't stop there. They continued down until they landed on Quarry's long, hard dick jutting out in front of him.

Did I forget to mention that Quarry was naked?

And hard? So damn long and thick.

And in the shower, waiting for me to join him?

It.

Was.

Agonizing.

After I'd finally given in and agreed to give a relationship a shot, we'd quickly packed up and left the bus station.

However, Quarry hadn't driven us home. He'd taken us to the nicest hotel Indianapolis had to offer. He'd immediately been recognized by the staff, and after he'd posed for a dozen selfies, the valet had eventually rumbled off in Till's clunker.

When we'd arrived in the lavish suite, I'd discovered that this wasn't just the impromptu overnight stay Quarry had made it sound like. My travel bag had been sitting on the sink beside his, and a five-hundred-dollar bottle of champagne had been chilling in a silver bucket next to the bed. Beside it had been a bottle of my favorite ten-dollar wine from the grocery store.

A random collection of snacks had been neatly organized across the long bar. Everything from elegant chocolate-covered strawberries to—my favorite—a bag of Oreos and a half-gallon of one percent milk.

On a chair in the corner, I'd spotted the pair of purple Chucks he'd bought me for my birthday. My jeans and one of my fitted "The Stone Fist" T-shirts had been draped over the arm. One of my simple everyday bra and panty sets had been sitting on top of them.

Huge bouquets of white roses had covered nearly every surface, including both nightstands, and a playlist I'd recognized as my own had been playing from a set of speakers hidden somewhere in the room.

Oh, Quarry Page had been busy.

Looping his arms around my waist from behind, he'd said, "Broke sixteen-year-old me took you on the date. Loaded twenty-four-year-old me is stepping in for the evening."

I'd craned my head back to flash him a huge grin over my shoulder.

He'd stepped away and announced, "Let's shower." He then had gone to work removing his hearing aids and stripping out of his suit.

I had to admit that watching him slowly unbuttoning his shirt with his eyes glued to me had done some seriously tingly things between my legs.

Over the course of the evening, Quarry had stroked, touched, and teased me with his fingers numerous times—including on the way over here, when he'd snuck his hand under my dress while he'd been driving—but never once had it been long enough for me to find a release.

And, as I'd ogled his naked ass sauntering to the bathroom, it had almost been enough.

It hadn't been though, and against my better judgment, I'd followed him to the bathroom, which was where I found myself standing, fighting desperately to keep from watching his hard-on bob in front of him as he washed his gorgeous body.

When he noticed my eyes aimed at his hips, he chuckled softly, drawing my attention back up. The moment we made eye contact, his mouth split into a gorgeous grin, popping that dimple that drove me wild.

"Get in the shower, Liv."

"*It's a little intimidating,*" I replied.

"Getting naked or my cock, which you can't stop staring at?"

Definitely the latter. "*Getting naked while you stand there gawking. What happened to the whole heat-of-the-moment thing?*" I replied rudely only so I could cross my arms over my chest to hide my rock-hard nipples.

He threw his head back in laughter. When he finally sobered, his gaze was no longer filled with amusement. "Fine. You want heated and in the moment?"

"Uhhh…" I mumbled, instantly realizing my mistake as he prowled from the shower.

His tattoo-covered arms, swayed as he made his approach. His pecs flexed, and his abdominals rippled.

And, suddenly, he wasn't the only one dripping wet.

He stopped in front of me and bent his head to capture my mouth. Water dribbled from the ends of his hair, running down my face and my neck and into my dress while he skillfully worked my mouth.

I wasn't actually nervous, per se. I just didn't like the idea that, the first time this perfect specimen of a man saw me naked, I was going to be awkwardly struggling out of a dress in a brightly lit hotel bathroom.

I would have preferred a dimly lit bedroom where he walked in after I was already naked and seductively lounging on the bed, strategically posed with my hair fanning out around me.

I quickly got over the lighting issues when he peeled my dress over my head.

His tongue was again tangling with mine when his large hands proved their dexterity by snapping the clasp of my bra. As my bra fell to the floor, I momentarily lost his mouth only to find it at my breasts a blink later. His shoulders were rolled forward, bowing his tall body awkwardly, but it might have been the sexist sight I had ever seen.

I'd seen Quarry without his shirt on thousands of times. Whether he was at the gym working out, in the ring during a fight, walking around our apartment, or just sitting out on our balcony while shooting the shit, Quarry was never wearing a shirt.

Striking, black tribal tattoos covered nearly every inch of his back. I'd always thought they were attractive, but never once had the sight of them caused my knees to buckle.

But, then again, never once had they been hunched over my naked body while he was devouring my breast.

"Oh, God!" I cried, gripping the back of his head for balance.

He groaned, dropping to his knees and switching his attention to my other breast. "Fucking perfect."

Closing my eyes, I swayed against him. His tongue teased one nipple while his fingers rolled the other.

Pure erotic torture.

My clit pulsed with need.

With his mouth working me toward the edge, it was becoming

too much—or, more accurately, not enough.

I guided his hand down my stomach. His eyes flashed up to mine in question. Stepping to the side, I spread my legs wider as my reply. He didn't delay in dipping between my legs.

My core clenched when he hummed his approval against my breast.

But then it was gone.

His hand disappeared, and then the mouth, and then so did the ground.

With his arms around my thighs, he carried me to the bed. "Fuck the shower," he cursed under his breath.

I landed on the bed, and a split second later, Quarry's mouth landed between my legs. He hooked my calves over his shoulders and gripped the tops of my thighs as he devoured me. It was a frenzied feast that alternated between wild licking from top to bottom and back again, only slowing when he thrust his tongue inside my opening, and sucking at my clit before jolting me with an exquisite flick of his tongue.

It was the most unbelievable combination of sensations.

But it wasn't for me.

This was for Quarry's pleasure, and judging by the loud growls and purred moans, he was enjoying himself immensely.

It was beginning to drive me insane. Each time I would get close, he'd switch up his technique. The edge of climax evaded me only to reappear, taunting me with an unattainable release seconds later. I was on a sexual bungee cord I couldn't seem to break.

My frustration was unmistakable, but either he didn't care or he was too busy ravaging me to notice.

I pulled at his hair—the ache of my clit making the action far rougher than I had intended. Finally, his eyes flipped up, and with one last lick, his mouth disconnected.

"*You're killing me*," I signed, my voice barely able to accompany my hands.

A slow, sexy grin played at his lips. "Oh, I'm sorry. Did you *want* to come?"

I gave him my best death-stare, but it was rendered worthless when I realized I was also smiling.

He dipped his head and trailed his tongue up to my belly button. "I'd apologize, but you have no idea how badly I've wanted to taste you."

My hips lifted off the bed, pleading for him to go back down.

He didn't—at least, not yet.

After sliding his hands up my stomach, he palmed my breasts, squeezing firmly before gently brushing his thumbs over my nipples.

I greedily arched into his hands.

"I've known my entire life that you were beautiful. But this..." He shook his head, at a loss for words. Upon gliding a hand back between my legs, he pushed one finger deep while still rolling my sensitive nipple. His eyes were aimed at my chest when he asked, "You want me to make you come, *Liv*?" He said my name in what could only be explained as awe.

I did want to come. So fucking badly.

But the way in which he'd said my name, as if he had been in shock that I was actually lying there with him, made me want more.

I no longer wanted the release his fingers or his mouth would surely give me. I wanted the connection of him inside me. His eyes on mine. His heavy weight anchoring me to the bed in the present while our bodies made plans and promises for a future together.

For however long it lasted, I wanted to give Quarry Page all of me.

Even the dark and distrustful parts that would eventually ruin us.

Threading my fingers through the top of his hair, I forced his attention back to my face.

"I'm more scared of you than I've ever been of the silence."

His eyes narrowed, and I knew he couldn't make out my words

without his hearing aids.

But, just like the way he'd taken what he'd needed with his mouth between my legs, this was for me. He didn't need to hear it. My confession alone was more than enough to release me.

"A part of me died the day you locked me in the closet."

"Sign," he urged on a gravelly demand.

I kept talking.

"You made me see that friendship is a farce and trusting anyone other than myself is the biggest mistake I could make. It was a lesson I had been learning my whole life up until that point. But you tattooed it on my soul in a way I could never forget."

He crawled up the bed until he was hovered over me. "I don't know what you're saying. Sign."

I didn't. "You are, and always have been, the one person in my life who has the ability to destroy me. For years, I clung to you, knowing that, as long as I kept you close, I didn't have to be scared of anything else. You, Quarry Page, are the embodiment of my greatest fear." My vision swam.

He was notably confused, but his face softened. "Please sign," he begged.

I couldn't. "Getting into a relationship with you—giving you the few guarded pieces of my heart you didn't already own is the scariest thing I can fathom. Losing you is frightening. Trusting you not to break me is petrifying."

His eyes frantically searched my lips for the words I was refusing him. "Damn it, Rocky. What are you talking about? Sign."

A tear escaped my eye, but a smile tipped up the sides of my mouth and the weight of the world lifted off my chest. "I don't trust you. And I don't know that I ever will. I do love you though. So I'm hoping that will be enough...for as long as we last."

"For fuck's sake," he huffed, slapping his hand to the nightstand for the case of his hearing aids.

I tapped on his chest to grab his attention and then finally signed, "*Make love to me.*"

He squinted at me skeptically, his strong jaw clenching as he gritted his teeth. "What were you just saying?"

"*Things every woman thinks in bed. I'm just lucky enough to be able to say them out loud.*" I slid a hand between us and gripped his softening cock.

His breath caught as I began to stroke over his smooth length.

He clearly didn't believe me, but that didn't matter. For the first time in my entire life, I had admitted to him how I truly felt. I'd never even been brave enough to say the words out loud before.

Those words freed me from the solitude of my fears. I'd still get hurt—that was a given. Now, I could at least enjoy the exhilarating thrill of the rise before the fall.

Leaning up, I took his mouth in a kiss.

It wasn't sensual.

It was a step forward.

And that's what made it the most arousing of all.

With a low moan, Quarry gave in to my request and lowered himself over me.

I was forced to release him from my hand, but he was soon positioned between my thighs.

"I brought condoms this time," he said, trailing the head of his dick through my folds.

Wrapping my arms around his shoulder, I held his gaze. "No. Just you." I over pronounced to be sure he read my lips correctly.

A boyish grin hiked the side of his mouth even as his eyes became downright sinister. "Always."

A sharp, euphoric cry flew from my mouth as he filled me. My chin tipped to the ceiling, and my entire body arched into his. His mouth latched on to my neck, nipping and sucking as he worked me with his cock—pushing me higher with every thrust. And, despite how hard I tried to fight it off, my orgasm won out.

As I fell apart around him, Quarry slowed and repeated solemn promises in my ear.

"Every. Single. Day."

And, if the way my heart swelled was any indication, I think I might have even believed him for a second.

But only a second.

Quarry didn't follow me over the edge. He worked my body for hours. By the time he whispered my name in release, there wasn't a part of my body he hadn't branded with his fingerprints.

He made love to me.

He fucked me.

He held me tenderly.

He pulled my hair and bit my shoulders.

He stared deep into my eyes while taking me gently.

He took me hard and rough from behind.

The champagne went untouched.

But we eventually fell asleep, naked and sated, drunk in a different way.

Some hours later, I awoke to Quarry once again guiding himself inside me.

I was sore and exhausted and emotionally spent.

But none of that stopped me from spreading my legs and relishing in everything I had ever wanted with him.

It was my month to pay our water bill, but we were at a hotel.

The shower ran all night.

CHAPTER
Twenty-Three

Liv

IT'D BEEN TWO WEEKS SINCE Quarry and I had officially become an item. It hadn't been a hard transition to make. He had been right. Nothing had changed. Sure, we shared a bed every night, and I had to retrieve a few pair of my panties from under his bed on laundry day. And he'd fucked me on nearly every flat surface in our apartment—and I only say nearly because there were a few I had fucked him on. But, besides that, it was pretty much business as usual for the two of us.

Ash and Eliza had blown up my phone with texts after our date, but I'd downplayed our new full-throttle relationship as much as possible—and then I'd avoided the two of them at all costs. I was still trying to wrap my mind around things between Quarry and me, so the last thing I needed was a barrage of questions I probably couldn't answer, which would spook me even more. Quarry had caught on to my hesitance pretty quickly, and the first week, he'd even made an excuse so we could skip the Page family dinner. I'd repaid him by adding another flat surface to our growing list.

All was good and well until a stupid magazine published a picture of Quarry and me kissing outside an Indianapolis restaurant. The caption read: *Quarry Page and his long-time girlfriend, Liv James, finally caught in action.*

After that, my phone exploded—and not just with calls from Ash and Eliza, who had basically already known but wanted details. Calls came from Mom, Dad, Uncle Slate, Aunt Erica, and Aunt Emma, and even Uncle Caleb shot me a text.

Mom was thrilled. (I should also disturbingly note that she squealed in delight when I told her that she'd won a cool grand from the little Quarry-and-Liv betting pool.) My dad demanded I bring Quarry home for a visit. I promptly penciled that into my schedule for the day after Hell froze over. The rest of my family shared the "it's about damn time" sentiment, but they all seemed genuinely happy to see us together.

Well, except for Ash, who threatened to add murder to her "Newsies List" if I didn't show up for family dinner that week and fill her in completely.

That death threat was exactly why I was trying to rush out of the community center after my last class. It was time to face the Page family head on.

"Are you sure you don't mind?" I asked Don as I shrugged my coat on.

"Quit asking me that. I told you it was fine." He smiled warmly.

"It's just, I know I've been leaning on you a lot recently. And I know my peanut butter brownies are incredible, but I'm not sure they are adequate payment for as much as you've been helping me the last few weeks."

He laughed, patting his belly. "My expanding gut disagrees."

My phone pinged in my purse, and I was relatively sure it was either Quarry wondering why I was late or Ash making more threats on my life. I ignored it long enough to gather the rest of my stuff. "Okay, but you will be getting a sweet Christmas gift, so get your list ready for Santa by next week. I'm an animal on Black Friday."

He laughed again and went back to grading papers.

"Goodnight," I called to him and Gwen as I headed out.

After pulling my phone from my purse, I checked my texts as I walked to my car.

It was Quarry, but I was wrong about his reason for texting.

Quarry: Why are there 50 boxes of Christmas tree cakes in my closet?

Me: I went grocery shopping.

Quarry: Okay. That doesn't help. Let me rephrase. Why are there FIFTY boxes of Christmas tree cakes in MY CLOSET?

Me: Okay... Let me rephrase. I went SHOPPING. Does that help?

Quarry: Nope. But where'd you put the shirts that used to be hanging in my closet?

Me: Top drawer.

Quarry: Cool. We'll discuss the Christmas tree cakes later. I'm running late. Just got out of the shower but I should still beat you to Till's.

Me: Okay sounds good. Oh and btw...it's actually 70 boxes but I'm guessing you haven't seen the ones under your bed yet.

Quarry: Nope. Just found those. However, I'm starved so you're down to 69 boxes.

I was laughing, typing a message to scold him for having eaten my coveted seasonal snack cakes that were only sold for three months every year—hence my need to stock up—when a voice startled me just before I got to my car.

"About time. I was starting to wonder if I had the wrong place."

A chill ran down my spine, and my head shot up.

Garrett fucking Davenport was standing on the sidewalk, smiling at me.

"You have got to be shitting me!" I cursed to myself.

He arrogantly sauntered in my direction, popping the collar of his coat for warmth when the wind picked up. Davenport wasn't a bad-looking guy. He had the tall-dark-and-handsome thing going on; he was just so repulsive on the inside that my stomach churned at the sight of him.

"Liv, it's so good to see you again," he purred, closing the distance between us.

It was all I could do not to gag, and while the idea of puking on his shoes held a fair amount of appeal, I was late for dinner.

"You're wasting your time. Quarry isn't here," I sniped, shoving my phone into my purse before pulling my keys out —including the mace my father had insisted I carry at all times.

"If I'd wanted to see Quarry, I would have gone to On The Ropes. I came to see *you*."

My shoulders shook in disgust. God, he was slimy.

"Oh goodie. Lucky me." I clicked the locks on my car and pulled on the handle, but then his hand suddenly landed firmly on the roof, blocking the door from opening.

His tall body menacingly loomed over me, but I refused to respond with fear.

"Fuck off, Garrett." I tugged on my door again while secretly flipping off the leather strap on the top of my mace.

"I just came to offer my congratulations on your relationship with Page. It's about time you two came out of the closet." His hip shifted to lean against the door, the front of his jacket brushing against my shoulder and causing me to shudder.

"Back up," I ordered, but he didn't budge.

If anything, he leaned in closer. "Trust me. I get it. My whore has been aching for years to weasel her way into my spotlight."

My back shot ramrod straight, but I didn't even have a chance to act before my entire body went on an even higher alert.

Brushing the hair away from my neck, he whispered, "Oh, don't look so upset, Livvie. You know the entire world is thinking the same thing."

I had once read an article that suggested, after spending significant time with a person, you started to develop their personality traits. It said that that was how couples evolved together. It wasn't until that moment that I believed it.

Because, as if I were Dr. Bruce Banner shifting into the Incredible Hulk, a loud roar escaped my mouth and then Quarry fucking Page came out in me.

"You sorry piece of shit!" I yelled, slapping him as hard as I could across the face.

His smile grew ominous as he lifted his palm to his cheek.

"You are a professional athlete. Not a fucking henchman for the mob. You don't get to show up at my job, talking shit you know nothing about."

He chuckled without humor. "Your reaction says otherwise."

"What is wrong with you? You have millions in the bank, women throwing themselves at your feet, fans who think you shit gold, and you are standing here, trying to intimidate your opponent's girlfriend? Really? Who does that shit? I mean, seriously." I threw my hands up in exasperation. "For fuck's sake. Man up. Stop acting like a sociopath and get to the gym. It won't help you win, but it might at least give you a shot at being conscious to see Quarry walk out of the ring with your belt."

His body hit me so fast that I didn't even have a chance to brace. My back slammed into the car, jerking as the door handle bit into my spine. He propped himself on a fist, his other going immediately to my wrist. Gripping tightly, he roughly shook until the mace fell from my hand.

My heart was racing as he pinned me against the car.

"You dumb cunt…" He opened his mouth to continue, but I spit into his face.

"Get off me!" I shrieked, fighting against his painful grip.

His nostrils flared, and his gaze turned positively evil, which sent my courage running for this hills.

My body instinctively shrank under his icy stare.

Sucking in a breath, I turned my head and prepared myself for the physical blow that was surely on its way.

"Hey!" Don called. "Get the fuck off her."

My breath escaped in relief. Don was no match for Davenport, but if I was going to die, at least I'd have a witness.

Much to my surprise, Davenport's stiff posture melted into me. His hard eyes swung to Don, and he very calmly stated, "None of your business, old man."

Don fearlessly stepped toward us, his eyes so angry that my body shrank even lower. "Let her go, Davenport. I swear to God this will not end well for you. If her man doesn't kill you, I can promise you I will."

Whoa! Don could be scary.

Garrett laughed. It wasn't daunting or malicious. It was filled with honest-to-God humor, and it scared the shit out of me.

Garrett Davenport wasn't just a coward—he was mentally unstable.

I closed my gaping mouth as I watched him lose himself in a fit of laughter. His body had slacked, but he still effortlessly kept me pinned to the car.

"It's appears we've been caught, my love."

Caught?

My love?

He dug for something in his pocket. I jerked, preparing myself for whatever weapon he was going to reveal, and I vaguely noticed Don reach to the back of his navy dress pants. We both froze when Davenport produced a hotel keycard and tucked it into the cleavage of my dress.

"Room two forty-seven, love. Don't be late."

Then he kissed me.

Hard.

Painful.

Vile.

Just as quickly, he released me and moseyed away, unfazed.

My knees shook, and my ankle rolled, almost sending me to the ground, but Don caught me around the waist.

I was in shock, and tears started to well in my eyes.

Don was obviously uncomfortable and most of all confused, but he kept his arm anchored around my waist until I was able to get my bearings.

In the distance, I heard a car peel out of the parking lot. I could only pray that it was Davenport.

"I-is…is he gone?" I asked.

He didn't exactly answer me. "I don't mean to sound disrespectful, and I'm only going to ask this once. Do you have something going on with Garrett Davenport?"

My head jerked to the side as if he had physically slapped me.

He pulled me into a hug. "Goddamn it. I'm sorry," he replied, having read my response loud and clear. "Yeah, he's gone, Liv."

And that was when the tears came. Full force.

"Oh my God. I'm going to lose Quarry!" I wailed as the adrenaline fled my system. "He…he kissed me."

"Shhh," Don soothed. "You're not going to lose anyone. He can't be mad that some lunatic held you against a car and kissed you."

I rocked out of his arms. Doubling over, I rested my hands on my knees and attempted to catch my breath. "I am. I'm going to lose him. Quarry is going to kill Davenport and then spend the rest of his life in prison."

Don's mouth hitched in a smile.

"This isn't amusing," I informed him.

He put his hands up in surrender, but his smile grew to full-blown.

"Stop smiling! This is going to be the worst kind of bad. He'll probably go all Mel Gibson in *Braveheart* and paint his face with Garrett's blood."

Don laughed—like an actual laugh. "That doesn't happen in *Braveheart*."

"Right. Well, let's hope Quarry hasn't seen whatever movie that does happen in."

"All kidding aside, are you all right?" he asked, shoving his hands in his pockets.

I sucked in a deep breath and did a quick physical assessment. My back hurt like hell, but everything else seemed to be in working order, so I nodded.

"You want me to get Gwen to drive you home?" he asked.

Swiping my index fingers under my eyes, I fixed my makeup. "No. I think I'm okay. I'm supposed to be meeting Quarry at Till's for dinner."

"Good." He bent down and scooped my keys off the ground before offering them my way.

I reached out to take them, but he didn't let go.

"You have to tell him, Liv. Even if he does go *Braveheart*. You *have* to tell him. That shit Davenport just pulled is not acceptable, and your man has a right to know he had his hands on you."

I closed my eyes in defeat. "Can I leave out the part where he had his lips on me?"

Don chuckled. "No. But I would definitely forget that hotel room number before you tell him. That is…unless you feel like hiding a body tonight."

My eyes popped open. "Oh, God!" I yanked the hotel keycard

out of the top of my dress and then Frisbeed it across the parking lot.

Don grinned his approval then swung my car door open. "Get home safe. Let me know if you need me to cover for you tomorrow."

I returned his smile. "Thanks." I tipped my head in the direction Davenport left and finished with, "For everything."

"Glad I could help."

Don stayed on the sidewalk until I pulled onto the road. At the first stoplight, I retrieved my phone from my purse and texted Quarry to let him know I was finally on the way.

My phone chirped with his reply, but my shaking hands gripped to the steering wheel until my knuckles turned white.

For the first time in my entire life, I was dreading seeing Quarry.

CHAPTER
Twenty-Four

Quarry

I WAS SITTING ON THE couch with Till's son, little Slate, when Liv finally arrived. While she hadn't come right out and said it, I knew she was nervous to tell my family about our relationship. But, to be honest, there wasn't a whole lot left to tell. Every single one of them had cornered me over the last two weeks, even before our picture together had been published. And, while she was hesitant, I was fucking ecstatic.

So, when Liv walked in, her eyes wide, looking like she had just seen a ghost, I couldn't help but laugh.

"Liv!" little Slate called out, hoofing it in her direction to show her the new Lego ship we had built.

"That's great, buddy," she said absently, her eyes flashing to mine before immediately bouncing away.

Even before things had changed with us, Liv would always come straight to me and chat for a minute before tracking down the girls in the kitchen.

This time, she walked straight to the dinner table, where Till was putting out plates with Blakely, and she whispered something in his ear. A plate froze in midair and his body tensed before his eyes dangerously cut to me.

Now that got my feet moving.

"What's wrong?" I asked before I'd even made it over to them.

"Blakely, take Slate and Cole upstairs and put on a movie," Till ordered.

Her eyes lit. "But it's a school night."

"Go," he said in a gentle but firm tone. "Flint! Get in here!" he called into the kitchen.

By this point, my entire body was on alert. When I got within reach, I curled my hand around the back of Liv's neck and forced her eyes to mine.

"What the hell's going on?"

She pressed to her toes and placed a lingering kiss on my lips.

It did nothing to answer my question though.

"Rocky?" I growled.

"Everything's fine." She looped an arm around my hips and tucked into my side. "Let's get the kids upstairs and I'll tell you, okay?"

"Bullshit," I gritted out, studying her eyes, which I now noticed were red-rimmed. "Were you crying?"

Resting a reassuring hand on my chest, she answered, "Stop. I promise I'm okay. Let's just get the kids situated so I can tell everyone at once."

The room fluttered around us as my family caught the angry chill that had begun to fill the room. My imagination was running wild as I paced a hole in the carpet in front of the couch. Ash and Eliza settled next to Flint on the sofa, while Liv sat in the recliner, chewing on her thumbnail.

When Till reappeared from upstairs, he didn't settle next to Eliza. He eerily walked beside me and got all up in my space. Not touching me. Just looming.

Fucking hell. He was bracing for the explosion. Whatever she had whispered in his ear must have been really fucking bad.

"Talk," I demanded.

"Okay, so, ummm, Davenport was waiting for me outside when I left the community center tonight."

The room erupted into a combination of gasps and curses. Five sets of eyes all landed on me, but mine stayed leveled on Liv.

"He was waiting for you?" I asked in a malevolent whisper, my muscles going taut.

"I'm fine," she reiterated.

Which was fantastic. I needed her to be fine because I was as far from fine as a person could get.

I sucked in a deep breath and then held it. Cracking my neck, I motioned for her to continue, hopefully to the part where he had been hit by a truck when he'd left.

"I guess he saw the picture of us together. And...uhhh, well... He came to say congrats. Sorta. But it was fine. He left. All's good. Don kinda saved the day." She was rambling—and lying some kind of serious.

Davenport was a big enough asshole to show up just to piss me off, but with our fight less than two months away, he wouldn't have left without delivering a message.

"What. Happened?" I pushed.

Her eyes jumped to Till's then to Flint's. Then she moved toward me. "Turn around."

I shook my head.

No way I was going to let her to bury her face in my back, hiding the truth in her eyes so she could feed me more glossed-over shit. I wanted the entire motherfucking story, especially the little details she was going to try to leave out.

"It wasn't as bad as it's going to sound," she whined.

Which only meant it was far worse and she was trying to soften the blow for me.

I ground my teeth and prepared myself. "I'm not asking again, Rocky. Tell me *all* of it."

Her shoulders fell, and she rolled her eyes. "He called me a whore. Pinned me against the car and then kissed me." She rested her hands on my chest and rushed out, "But I swear to you, I'm fine. Please don't kill him."

"Son of a bitch."

"He kissed you?"

"Oh my God!"

"What the fuck."

Those all echoed behind me, but I couldn't make out who'd said what around the blood roaring in my ears.

Liv could beg every day for the rest of her life, but I was still going to kill him for so much as breathing her air.

Blinding rage consumed me.

The last thing I remembered was Liv standing in front of me, pleading for his life, before I found myself being physically restrained across the hood of my car.

"Stop!" Till said, wrestling me down.

"Let me the fuck go!" I seethed, rearing back to head-butt him.

He quickly dodged it and forced me back down. "Chill out and get your shit together. Davenport will still be an asshole in ten minutes. Liv is freaking the fuck out right now though."

My senses started to return to me, one by one, and I heard Liv screaming my name from inside the house. Flint was blocking the front door, but his gaze was aimed over his shoulder at me.

"Shit," I breathed, the fight ebbing from my system.

My knuckles ached, and my lungs felt as if I'd just gone ten rounds.

"There you go," Till encouraged. "Now, take a damn breath and calm down."

"Let me go," I replied, my voice jagged.

I was slowly coming down when Liv shrieked my name again.

"Let me go!" I repeated, becoming agitated all over again.

He didn't. He leaned into my ear. "I know how you feel, Q, but I swear to God there is nothing you can do to Davenport right now. And all you are going to do is ruin your own career by trying. Let's call the cops. Let's call the boxing administration. Let's call Slate and get him to throw some weight at this. But you, right now, need to get your ass inside and take care of your girl."

He was right. I needed to take care of Liv. But he was so fucking wrong about the rest. The cops wouldn't do shit. The boxing administration would do even less. Slate could throw all the weight in the world behind this kind of attack, but it wouldn't change the fact that it had still happened.

And I hadn't been there to protect her.

Two weeks into our relationship and I was already treading dangerously close to failing yet another woman.

And, this time, it was Liv.

Not a consequence in the world could sway me from making Davenport pay.

And I knew that that was exactly why Liv was freaking out. She knew me all too well.

It was my turn to lie.

"Okay," I told Till. "Call the cops and fucking let me up so I can get to her."

Liv

I had expected Quarry to lose his shit, and it was precisely why I'd made sure his brothers were there when I'd dropped the bomb. They could at least physically prevent him from going off the deep end until I had a chance to calm him down and talk some sense into him.

However, I never could have expected the scene that played out.

His face turned red, pure madness brewing in his thunderous eyes. I was still clinging to the front of shirt when he spun on a heel. His powerful stomps carried him to the door, Till barely managing to get in front of him before Quarry threw a punch. And it was thrown with such a force I knew that it had been intended for Davenport and not his brother. Quarry had one hell of a temper, but this was something else altogether. Intense anger rolled off him as Till fought to pry the keys from his hand.

I was able to hold it together until Till dodged a punch and Quarry's hand went through the sheet rock. That's when I lost my shit too.

Davenport was once again going to get his way. One way or another, whether Quarry found him and beat him within an inch of his life or Quarry broke his hand in another fit of rage, the fight was going to get canceled.

I gave up on Till handling the situation and attempted to step between the brawling brothers.

Unfortunately, Flint caught me around the waist.

But, on the other hand, it was fortunate Flint caught me around the waist because I almost caught an elbow to the face.

When Till and Quarry had made it out the door, Flint promptly blocked me. I was having a nervous breakdown from not being able to see what was going on.

I was seriously contemplating the ramifications of stealing Flint's cane and beating him with it when Quarry suddenly appeared behind him. Flint gingerly stepped out of the way for his seemingly no-longer-irate brother to pass through.

Raking my eyes over his body, I checked for any type of injury, but his stormy eyes held the only lingering proof of his outburst.

I opened my mouth to ask if he was okay, but his thick arm hooked across my stomach, folding me over and lifting me off my feet.

"What are you doing?" I cried, dangling like a rag doll at his side.

He didn't answer. Nor did his feet slow until we reached his old bedroom.

After kicking the door shut, he deposited me on the bed. Then my arms were yanked up and my dress was stripped over my head. His shirt followed. Then he landed on the bed next to me. Rolling to his back, he tucked me into his side, and only then did he breathe a huge sigh of relief. His heart was still slamming around in his chest, and his body was stiff, but his words were soft.

"What happened...exactly?"

"Uhhhh, is there a reason we have to be almost naked to have this conversation? If you decide to haul ass out of the room again, it's going to be embarrassing when I have to chase you down in my underwear."

"I won't leave again," he replied emotionlessly, but his lips found the top of my head.

"Okay, but if you're planning to have sex with me, you're going to have to be quiet because I'm pretty sure Ash and Eliza are listening at the door."

This time, his voice was terse. "My head is two seconds away from exploding. If I fucked you now, I might kill us both. So, please, just tell me what the fuck happened." His lips once again found my head, easing the sting in his tone.

So I told him.

Every single bit.

Except for the hotel room number.

Thank God for Don Blake! Because, if the way his body went rock solid when I got to the keycard part was any indication, I would have in fact been hiding a body later that night.

After I finished, Quarry remained silent for several minutes. I tried to soothe him by tracing the black tattoos that covered one of his pecs, and his breathing gradually slowed and then evened out. I thought for a moment that he'd fallen asleep. But, when I glanced up, his eyes were wide open, staring at the ceiling in deep contemplation.

"What are you thinking?" I asked quietly.

"Honestly?"

"Yeah."

"Right now, it's how I'm going to keep your dad from killing Davenport before I get the chance."

I giggled, relaxing into him, relieved that he at least had it in him to joke. Ten minutes ago, I would have thought it impossible, but when he shifted his gaze down to me, the tiniest of smiles tipped one side of his mouth.

Then it vanished as his expression turned serious again. "I took your dress off because I wanted to be sure you weren't hiding anything else from me. Downplaying the way he put his hands on you just to keep me reeled in. But I have to be honest with you here: I'm terrified to look at your back. I swear to God, if he left a mark on you—"

"My back is fine." It wasn't totally a lie. It didn't hurt anymore, but I was sure the car door handle had left a bruise.

He closed his eyes and shook his head as if he could erase the thought of it.

"Quarry, listen to me. This is worse than his normal brand of asshole. I'll be the first to admit that, but getting a reaction from you is what he wants. It's what he's praying for. And, if he doesn't get it before the fight, you know he's going to use it in the ring. He's going to talk shit and have you fighting with your heart and not your head. And, when you give him that, he *will* beat you."

Quarry barked a laugh. "Is that your pep talk?"

"No. That's my 'keep your head together and embarrass this guy in front of the entire world' talk." I pressed a kiss to his still-smiling lips. "You're so close, Q. Two months."

He suddenly rolled so I was on my back and his upper body was pressing against me. "And what if he tries something like this shit again? What if it's worse next time? Then what? Because I don't give one single fuck about that fight anymore. Embarrassing him isn't going to give me peace of mind. Eating popcorn and listening to his screams while he burns inside a fiery inferno might be the only possible thing that could give me any kind of satisfaction at this point."

"Okay, and if, in six months, you want to follow through with that, I'll buy the popcorn. But we will watch the inferno on TV in the middle of a public bar so we at least both have an alibi." I smiled. "For now, though, we're going to let everyone else handle Davenport."

"I can't just sit around and let this go. He touched you, Liv." His voice was harsh, but his fingers gently sifted through my hair.

"And I slapped him for it," I answered matter-of-factly.

He groaned. "And that's another thing. What the fuck were you thinking?"

"Oh, shut up. I'm fine." I waved him off.

"I'm serious. If anything like that happens again: You don't speak to him. You don't acknowledge him. You sure as fuck don't challenge him. You walk away. And, if you can't, you scream for help at the top of your lungs."

In hindsight, that would have been the best thing to do. But it had felt amazing to fight back instead of cowering. I didn't tell Q that thought. I could hardly give him a keep-your-head-together lecture if I couldn't do the same.

I opted for a sheepish nod.

He was still staring at me sternly when a pounding on the door made us both jump.

"Liv! Get out here." It was Slate.

Shit, when did he get here?

"The cops are here."

Fantastic.

"Also, your mom and dad are on the way down."

God help me. "I'll be right out!" I let out a long-suffering sigh. "I should probably get dressed. Is your head all sorted now?"

"Not even close." He smiled tightly, shifting off me.

While redressing, I was careful not to let him see my back. We could save the naked inspections for a week from now when my back had healed.

I was finger-combing my hair in the mirror on the door when Quarry's strong chest pressed against my back.

"I don't know what I'd do without you."

It was a sweet thing to say, but the meaning behind his words was transferred with his mouth when he brushed my hair away and kissed my neck.

"You'd be okay."

I wouldn't be though. I knew that to the pits of my soul. I also knew I'd eventually have to face that reality.

"I'm not so sure about that. So let's not test the theory." He kissed my neck again.

No. Let's not test the theory at all.

At least, not yet.

CHAPTER
Twenty-Five

Quarry

"I WANT IT ALL. ARM it like the fucking Pentagon!"

Leo shook his head. "I cannot *arm* a community center, son. I'll make it secure though. I'll get some guys in there in the morning. We'll do it up right."

I crossed my arms over my chest and glanced over at Liv. She was talking to her mom and Erica. Leo and Sarah had rushed down from Chicago, having made it to Till's in record time. They'd arrived just in time for Leo to pull one of the officers aside before they'd left. As a former DEA agent and the owner of one of the biggest security firms in the country, he had a little more pull than I did in gathering information about what the hell was going on. So, as much as it had ticked me off, I had sat back and let him handle it.

Over the last four hours, we'd learned that Davenport had an alibi and claimed he hadn't been in Indianapolis, but rather in Kentucky over three hours away. *Lying piece of shit.* Don Blake had issued a verbal statement, corroborating Liv's story. But, in the end, the case was nothing more than a he-said-she-said. I wasn't surprised in the least.

Davenport was despicable, but he wasn't stupid. He never threw the first punch, but he always had the last word. He was cold, calculated, and, I was quickly learning, demented too. It was almost as if the bullshit outside the ring were more exhilarating for him than the fight itself.

Liv caught my eye and tried to smile, but a yawn overtook her. She wanted to go home, and I couldn't blame her. It had been one long-ass night.

Eliza was flittering around, filling coffee cups, and cleaning up plates from our family dinner that had turned into a buffet line; Ash was upstairs, helping Blakely get the little kids in pajamas; Slate, Flint, and Till were huddled in the corner, discussing what actions needed to be taken with the boxing administration; and Leo and I were arguing over how to prevent this shit from happening again by beefing up security at the community center.

Let's go, I silently signed to Liv before turning my attention back to her father. "Spare no expense, Leo. Cameras inside and out. Also cover every inch of that parking lot. Motion sensors on all the lights. New security system on the entire building, not just the ASL program. And I want a guard at the door twenty-four-seven."

"Quarry. Chill. I said I'd do it up right."

"I swear to Christ, you hire a senior citizen for the door—"

"I said"—he lowered his voice and menacingly tilted his head— "I'd do it up right."

I stoically held his eyes. "Send me a bill."

"She's my daughter. It's on me."

I lowered my voice to match his. "And I said send me a bill." I paused before adding, "Itemized."

His jaw twitched at the hinges. "You think I'm going to cut corners when it comes to her safety?"

I shrugged. "Probably not, but I do know, when it comes to her, I'm not going to wait around to find out."

Leo laughed, and if I wasn't mistaken, it was genuine. "You've been together a few weeks, Q. Slow down."

"No disrespect, Leo. But you of all people know that's a load of shit. Liv and I have been together our entire lives, and despite the fact that I now plan to father your grandchildren, I would have insisted on this being done correctly no matter when it had happened."

Leo's eyes sparked ominously, and his nostrils flared.

I casually quirked an eyebrow.

"You're lucky I like you." He took a step toward me. "You're lucky you come from a good family." He held my stare. "You're lucky she's in love with you."

A flush of adrenaline hit me. I knew that Liv had *loved* me, but it wasn't until that moment that I allowed myself to truly internalize her words.

"Every. Single. Day."

It wasn't past tense.

It included that very moment.

A bold smile grew on my face even as her dad continued with his failed attempt to intimidate me.

"But I swear to God, son. You utter one more fucking word about making babies with my twenty-three-year-old daughter, I'll kill you on the spot. Yeah?"

My grin spread as I arrogantly winked at him. "Right."

Leo flipped his coat back, revealing his gun in a shoulder holster. "Right," he repeated on a challenge, his eyes locked with mine.

Liv suddenly appeared, sliding up against my side. "Well, this looks pleasant."

I draped an arm around her waist and squeezed her hip, never dragging my eyes off her dad.

"Not to spoil this testosterone party or anything, but I'm exhausted and Mom and I decided we're all going to Fleet's for champagne brunch in the morning."

Leo and I both groaned. Fleet's champagne brunch consisted of pussy gourmet food that would no doubt lull my taste buds into a coma. Women loved it though. Eliza had flipped when Till had taken us all there for her birthday one year. It was expensive as fuck, and Flint and I had still had to stop at a burger joint when we'd left to keep from starving.

I tossed Leo a commiserating smirk. "I'll pay for Fleet's—you pay for wings on the way home?"

He extended a hand my way. "Works for me. We'll go over security plans in the morning. Bring your checkbook."

"Can't wait."

After a quick shake, Liv and I set about saying our goodbyes. Ten minutes later, I was following her back to our apartment.

And then to my bed.

"Fuck," I cursed. Reaching down, I brushed back her long, brown hair, which was curtaining off my view of her face. Her mouth was wide and filled with my cock.

I hated not being able to see all of her, but she was wearing one of my T-shirts. Rarely would I complain about such a sight. However, I wanted to see her large breasts swaying every time she glided up to my tip. And I wanted to feel them naked and pressed against my thigh as she took me to the back of her throat.

"Give me your pussy," I ordered.

She hummed her refusal, and my balls tightened from the sensation.

"Not until I'm inside you," I growled only for it to turn into a groan when she raked her nails down my abs, not stopping until she was gripping my nuts.

Staring up at me through her lashes, she silently dared me to come in her mouth.

She'd been playing this torturous game for at least a half hour.

Each time I'd refused, she'd worked me harder.

I'd been gentle when we'd first gotten home. After the shit night we'd had, I'd wanted nothing more than to bury myself inside her and forget the cloud of chaos that had settled over us. However, she'd been attacked while leaving work. I didn't think mounting her from behind in the shower would have been appreciated.

Liv had proved me wrong though. As soon as we'd crawled into bed, she'd shifted directly between my thighs and sucked me until I'd gotten hard.

Now, she was about to suck me empty.

My hand fisted in the back of her hair. "Shit. You win," I gritted out through clenched teeth, holding her head down as my cock fired off in her mouth.

Her hand found the base of my shaft, stroking the length her mouth couldn't accommodate.

Inventing new curse words, I came hard down the back of her throat. She hummed in pleasure as if she were getting off on nothing more than swallowing my release—the idea only made me come harder.

As my body relaxed beneath her, she licked from base to tip, cleaning every inch while I jerked and twitched against her tongue—the sensations becoming too much.

I was still a panting mess when she finally crawled up the bed and rested her head on my shoulder.

"Jesus Christ, woman." Gripping her jaw, I guided her mouth to mine.

She giggled against my lips, purring when I palmed her breast over the cotton.

"*I figured you needed to relax tonight.*"

"You figured right, but there was no reason we couldn't relax together."

She kissed me again, nipping at my bottom lip as she pulled away to sign, "*Are you complaining?*"

I returned the nip. "Not at all."

"*Good. Then go to sleep. You have to be up early to go to the gym before brunch, and I'd like to be thoroughly ravaged before you go.*"

"I could thoroughly ravage you now."

"*You could but then I'd have to take another shower before bed, and you'd feel the need to join me because, for some reason, nothing makes you hornier than running water, and then it would be, like, two in the morning before we got back in bed. And I'd be exhausted at brunch tomorrow, so when my dad asked why, I'd have to tell him that you spent the night fucking me. Then I'd have to add him killing you to my growing list of murders I need to prevent. So, really, it's best if you just go to sleep and do dirty things in the morning.*"

I stared at her for a moment then burst into laughter.

"Golden" Garrett Davenport had ruined my night. I'd spent half of it in a fit of rage, willing to take out my own brother if it meant I got my hands on him for even one minute.

Yet, somehow, I was going to fall asleep sated, with Liv safe in my arms, a smile on my face, and an overwhelming sense of contentment filling my veins.

And, if I had any say over it, this would happen…

Every. Single. Day.

My entire body went stiff, and Eliza's eyes grew impossibly wider as he roughly shoved, sending me scrambling forward. Just as quickly, he

grabbed Eliza and dragged her to the door.

"No!" I jumped to my feet.

He had no fucking business even talking to her, but I'd kill him before I let him hurt her.

"Get your fucking hands off her! You're not taking her anywhere!" I rushed forward.

I heard Eliza screaming with every step, but adrenaline fueled me. She was ours. I wouldn't let him have her.

"Oh, for fuck's sake." He spun Eliza to the side just as I got close, sending her crashing to the ground.

I landed a blow to his side, but his hand folded around my throat and the cold, metal butt of his gun landed hard against my face. Pain exploded as someone dimmed the lights.

I felt my body crash onto the floor, but then everything changed.

I wasn't thirteen.

I wasn't in Vegas.

And it wasn't Frankie dragging out Eliza.

Right before my eyes, Liv appeared in Davenport's arms.

Her long, dark hair cascaded over his shoulder as he tipped a gun to her temple.

Her big, brown eyes were wide and filled with a fear I had never seen before—and would never be able to forget.

Her mouth opened, but it wasn't her voice that came out. Well, at least, not the one I'd come to know. It was the sound of twelve-year-old Liv screaming from behind a closet door.

And it was like a knife to my gut—only worse.

"Get up, Page!" Davenport taunted, pressing the gun deeper into her flesh.

I couldn't move though. I was paralyzed, unable to even blink.

Liv's scream continued in one long continuous cry, and Davenport laughed wildly as I sat immobile on the ground.

A flash of movement caught my attention, drawing my eyes away from Liv. Then a weight so heavy that I thought my chest would break hit me. I saw Mia's body seizing on the floor, her hands flailing wildly until one landed in a pool of blood. My heart lurched as I followed it up to Flint's lifeless body. His cold, dead stare somehow managed to remain filled with quiet disappointment.

My lungs burned, and regardless how hard I fought, I couldn't catch my breath.

Liv's scream suddenly cut off, snapping my attention back to her. She was still being held captive in Davenport's arms, only now the fear was gone and a tender smile covered her beautiful adult face. Her voice was still that of Liv the child as she uttered the familiar words, "I'm safe with you, Quarry."

Davenport pulled the trigger.

Drenched in sweat, I shot up in bed. My stomach rolled, and bile crept up my throat. I scrambled over Liv and into the bathroom, barely making it to the toilet before throwing up.

I was vaguely aware of the light coming on and then a cool, damp washcloth being pressed against the back of my neck.

"I'm safe with you, Quarry," echoed through my deaf ears.

My stomach heaved again. *Oh, God.*

Closing my eyes, I attempted to breathe, but visions of my nightmare projected on the backs of my eyelids made it impossible.

I had a minor success and managed to stop puking. Shifting back against the side of the bathtub, I took the cloth from her hand and used it to wipe my mouth.

Liv squatted in front of me. Just the sight of her opened my airway and breathed me back to life.

"Feeling sick?" she signed.

"I… Fuck." I gave up and grabbed her shoulders, pulling her into a hard hug.

She came willingly, even straddling my lap to allow me more contact. I was naked, and she was only wearing my oversized T-shirt, but I wasn't sure my cock would ever get hard again after a nightmare like that.

She let me hold her for several minutes before she finally leaned away. "*Are you okay?*"

"No," I answered curtly, tucking her face into my neck and ending any further discussion.

Fucking hell. What had just happened inside my head?

I closed my eyes, but the vision of that gun at her temple leveled me and caused my stomach to heave again. She scrambled off my lap, but I didn't move back to the toilet. Nor did I close my eyes again.

Staring blankly up at the ceiling, I felt her dab another cool washcloth across my forehead.

Lifting her hands into my line of sight, she asked, "*You want me to get you something to drink?*"

I *wanted* a lobotomy.

I shook my head at her question.

"*You want to try to get back in bed? I can get a trash can in case you get sick again.*"

No. I never wanted to go get in that bed again for the rest of my life. Insomnia had never been so appealing. That dream…

What time is it? I silently signed, because I didn't trust my voice.

She leaned out of the bathroom door to find the clock. "*Five.*"

Gripping the tub, I pushed myself to my feet. "I think I'm just gonna go ahead in to the gym. Get a head start on things."

She pressed a hand to my chest. "*You just woke up puking. You can't go to the gym. Call in sick.*"

"Nah, I'm good. I just…" I stalled, not willing to tell her that I'd just watched my biggest fears play out in my head.

She looked up at me expectantly.

"I guess I ate something bad last night. I'll survive."

At the sink, I turned the water on, splashing it on my face and then pasting up my toothbrush.

I participated in the rest of the conversation only by watching her hands sign in the mirror.

"*I ate the exact same thing you did last night.*"

I shrugged.

"*Why don't you just lie down and give it an hour or so? You aren't supposed to be at the gym until seven.*"

I shrugged again before rinsing my mouth and then moving to my closet.

When I opened the door, Christmas Tree Cakes rained from the top. "Shit," I mumbled. "Any chance you can move those to your closet?" I bit out, my fears shifting to anger for no other reason than I didn't know how to deal with it.

She was trying to catch my attention as I swirled around the room, but I couldn't slow down.

I was desperate to get out of there.

Away from her.

Away from the memories of failing her.

And, because of that, facing my greatest fear of all—losing her.

Less than a minute later, I'd tugged on a pair of shorts and a T-shirt, grabbed my keys and hearing aids, pecked her on the lips, and swiftly left.

CHAPTER
Twenty-Six

Liv

"WHAT THE HELL WAS THAT?" I whispered to myself as I heard the deadbolt on our front door click from the outside.

Quarry was full of shit. He hadn't eaten something bad the night before. But what I couldn't figure out was why he was acting like I had something to do with his getting sick. At first, he'd clung to me so tight that I could barely breathe. Then, after that, he had been so standoffish that it was as if he'd decided I'd poisoned his food.

I had still been signing to him as he rushed out the door—a brisk kiss on the lips my only acknowledgement.

So freaking weird.

I lay in bed, staring up at the ceiling, stuck in my ponderings of the great mystery known as Quarry Page, when I decided sleep was a lost cause. The sun was still well below the horizon, and only the soft, white rays of a nightlight illuminated the room.

Quarry had purchased it for his room a few weeks earlier. I hadn't asked him to buy it. Nor had I asked him to buy and sync a secondary iPod just to keep on a docking station on his nightstand. He'd done it though. Because he'd worried I might be scared. Of course, he hadn't come right out and told me that. But I knew.

I was a twenty-three-year-old woman who still slept with music and a nightlight. It wasn't exactly my most redeeming quality, but Quarry had never made me feel like it was a flaw, either. He knew all about my past. He'd once used it against me. But, most recently, he'd used his knowledge to make me feel safer than ever before.

An odd feeling slid over me—it wasn't exactly a chill, but it still made me shiver.

If I really thought about it, over the years, Quarry had always taken care of me.

Even while he had been with Mia, he'd still made me a priority in his life. Sure, he had done the mandatory job of taking care of his girlfriend's best friend when the three of us had hung out. But it had always been more than that. He had been my friend just as much as Mia had. I hadn't been the third wheel or the annoying girl who wouldn't give them time alone. He'd gone out of his way to spend time with me. Maybe not alone, out of respect for Mia, but he'd made sure I was never left out. He'd bought me the required birthday and Christmas gifts, but he'd also changed my tire when I got a flat and taken me to the dentist when I had to have my wisdom teeth removed, and as a newly (practically) widowed twenty-year-old, he had opened his spare bedroom to me because I'd been too scared to go home.

He'd been handling me with care my entire life.

As hard as it was to admit, I had to let go of the past with Quarry. His actions the day he'd locked me in the closet had been those of a shattered child.

Unfortunately, it had still changed us though.

But not all change had to be bad.

Maybe we *needed* to change.

Maybe *I* needed to change.

I just didn't know how. I hadn't exactly been born into a life where I could afford to trust blindly. My mother had been a druggy, and her boyfriends, pimps, dealers—whatever they were—had been cruel. None of them had hit me, leaving scars for the world to see. No, their weapons of choice had been much subtler: words.

Eighteen years later, I could still hear the detailed threats of what would happen to me if I came out of my room at night.

Those were the scars my childish body had never had to bear. Yet they had been so deeply etched into my subconscious that my adult mind still couldn't process the fear I'd felt back then.

I'd told everyone that I was afraid of the silence because of the night my mother had died.

It hadn't been a lie.

It hadn't been the complete truth though, either.

I was terrified of being alone.

Scary things had happened while I'd been alone in that bedroom.

Her drug-induced, manic laughter.

Her screams—some in pain, some in pleasure.

The worst had been when the sounds would disappear though.

Was it over or just beginning?

The silence.

The only defense mechanism I'd had at that age was to spend as much time as possible at our neighbor's house. She wasn't particularly a kind old woman, but she adored reading to me from her Bible. Her lessons were usually only good to inform me of the terrible sins my mother committed each day. I could overlook that though. I just liked the company. The interaction. *The safety.*

She quickly took it upon herself to teach me how to read from her Bible. I hated it, but for those hours, I'd sit next to her in a chair, forcing myself to sound out words I didn't understand, just so I didn't have to go home.

After my mother died, my struggle to trust only amplified. So much so that even a relationship with my father was difficult at first. He was so nice to me, but I feared the moment that would change. I did the only thing I could think of: I showed him a little girl who was easy to love, not the troubled tomboy that existed below the surface.

When Quarry entered my life, he wasn't a man. And I immediately opened myself up to him. In hindsight, my heart had been too fragile to give to an equally troubled ten-year-old boy. But maybe that's exactly why I'd given it to him in the first place. The quiet storm brewing in those hazel eyes had been so familiar that I'd instantly felt a connection.

And there I was, lying in *his* bed, staring at *his* ceiling, after he had spent years trying to put me back together, most recently by offering me the few remaining shards of his own heart to fill in the lost pieces of my own.

In many ways, I was still that lost little girl—too scared to trust but too terrified of being alone.

I closed my eyes and allowed the countless memories of our past to filter through me.

All the times he'd been there for me, even when he, himself, had been barely breathing.

All the times the lights had been left on and the music had been left blaring all night long.

And, last but not least, I finally realized that maybe I really had always trusted Quarry Page, no matter what I'd told myself. I'd been hiding my feelings and guarding myself my entire life. I shouldn't have given my heart to Quarry the boy. But, without question, I was ready to give it back to the man.

And then I promptly had a panic attack.

But, when that was over, I threw the covers back, got dressed, and set out to the gym to watch my sexy boxer work out before *officially* introducing him to my father as my boyfriend.

The gym was still dark when I pulled up. I drove around to the back parking lot only to find it vacant. My watch read six a.m. Even if he had stopped to grab some breakfast instead of his usual protein shake at the gym, he should have been there. I snagged my phone off the passenger's seat and sent him a quick text.

Me: Where ya at?

His reply came almost immediately.

Quarry: I'm about to get in the ring… You okay?

I got out of my car and checked up and down the street. His Porsche was pretty hard to miss though, and as suspected, I came up empty.

I racked my brain, trying to remember if there was possibly anywhere else he could have been getting in the ring, but like before, I came up empty again.

Me: I'm fine. Are you at the gym?

Quarry: Yeah, babe. You need something? I need to get my gloves on.

My heart sank, and the backs of my eyes stung.

But my fingers didn't move to type my reply. I could only blink at the screen.

I reread his message a dozen times, and each time I typed a different response. Some were concerned. Some were snarky. And, admittedly, some were even jealous.

I deleted them all.

This was Quarry. He didn't lie to me.

Me: What gym?

Quarry: My gym. Do you NEED something? I have to go.

My nose burned, and my stomach wrenched. I was so confused that I didn't even know what conclusion to jump to. And, God, did I want to jump to some conclusions. My mind raced with a million different scenarios. Some good, like maybe he was planning another over-the-top date for us. Some bad, like he was having an early morning breakfast with one of his random girls he'd sleep with after fights. Some really bad, like maybe he was having second thoughts about us and needed some time alone to figure out a way to let me down easy.

It had to be something big though. Quarry Page was a lot of things, but he wasn't a liar. I decided not to beat around the bush.

Me: Yes. I need to know why the hell you're lying to me.

Quarry: About what?

I laughed, not finding one single solitary thing funny. Quickly losing my patience with the entire exchange, I clicked out of my messages and dialed his number. My anxiety was climbing rapidly in expectation of a straight answer.

Panic hit me like a brick wall when I got his voicemail.

My phone pinged in my hand almost immediately.

Quarry: Text. I don't have my hearing aids in. I'm about to get in the ring!

I was already clinging by a thread to sanity, but that damn exclamation point pushed me right over the edge. Clenching my teeth, I quickly typed another message.

I should have deleted it.

I hit send.

Me: You fucking liar!

Quarry: Excuse me?

Me: You have two seconds to tell me the truth.

Quarry: About what? And for the record, you call me a fucking liar again, I'm turning my goddamn phone off.

Yeah, that just infuriated me even more. He was lying to *me*. He didn't get to make the threats.

Me: Wow! Wouldn't that be convenient for you? You know, FOR THE RECORD, you jump out of bed with me, lie to me about where you are, and then threaten to turn your phone off...a girl can get certain ideas.

Quarry: Oh yeah, Rocky? What the fuck kinda ideas you getting?

Me: Tell me where you are?

Quarry: No, I'd really rather hear about these ideas. Because it sounds a hell of a lot like you're accusing me of something.

Me: Where are you?

Quarry: I was supposed to be getting into the ring, but now I'm standing here fighting with my girl like a pussy-whipped punk.

My hands were shaking, and I was fighting back tears. Quarry and I didn't fight. We bickered. We made fun of each other. I rolled my eyes at him. I made fun of him. He laughed at me. This entire exchange was not how we communicated. It was different, and not in a good way.

Me: Look at us. You promised me we wouldn't change. You PROMISED me.

I was typing another message to tell him that I was at On The Ropes when his incoming FaceTime lit my phone up.

"What's going on?" he asked before the picture came into view.

His voice was stilted, but not angry.

I turned the phone to the On The Ropes sign as my answer.

When I looked back at the screen, he was sporting an endearing grin. "Ah, well, I'm not at that gym, Rocky." He lifted his phone and did a quick spin, showing a small gym barely big enough to hold a ring and a few hanging bags.

"*I can see that,*" I signed with one hand.

He chuckled. "I need you to trust me right now."

I used the corner of my T-shirt to wipe under my eyes. "I'm trying!" I exclaimed.

He read my lips. "Well, try harder."

I rolled my eyes. If he only knew.

"Now, stop freaking out. Hang up. I'm gonna send you an address. Come straight here. And I'm gonna warn you: You're probably going to freak when you get here, but take a deep breath and do it anyway." He smiled teasingly. "Stop crying, crazy. We're good." His dimple danced on the screen, easing my nerves.

I nodded. "*Okay. I'm sorry.*"

"Hurry up. I have an asshole to kill in two months. I actually do need to work out today." He laughed before ending the call.

I was still trying to collect myself when my phone pinged with an address.

I recognized it immediately.

Quarry had been wrong; I didn't even need to arrive before I started freaking out again.

CHAPTER
Twenty-Seven

Quarry

IT WAS COLD AS BALLS, but I was sitting on the front steps when her car pulled through the security gate I'd left open. The last few weeks had been a crazy roller coaster of emotions, and this moment right here was either going to be the highest of highs or yet another terrifying low. Who the hell knew with Liv though? She'd been all over the place recently. I never would have guessed that she would have flipped out the way she had when she'd realized I wasn't at On The Ropes. The jealous bit was usually my thing. And that was the only reason I'd calmed down while we had been texting. I hated the way she'd reacted. But I fucking loved the idea of Liv getting all cavewoman possessive over me. I would have acted way worse if I'd thought she was lying to me, so I had to cut her some slack.

Plus, it'd damn near broken me when she'd called me out on the nothing-changes-between-us promise I'd made her. I refused to fail on the very first test, even if it meant spilling a secret I'd been hiding for several years.

When she cut the engine, I stood up and walked over to her. Pulling her door open, I found her just as I'd expected—scared as fuck. It made me an asshole, but I laughed.

"Oh, come on. Don't look at me like that," I said. Taking her hand, I helped her from the car.

"This isn't the gym," she said, craning her head back to look into my eyes.

Throwing an arm around her shoulders, I curled her into my side and strolled up the front steps. "Nope."

Her shoulders sagged in relief until I pushed the front door open.

Then she got all kinds of stiff.

Her hands flew to her mouth, and she gasped my name.

The house was a fucking mess. My shit was everywhere. Boxes upon boxes of products my sponsors had sent over sat unopened in the massive foyer. One side of the split staircase was lined with my shoes that no longer fit in my closet at our apartment. The other side served as a filing cabinet for all the paperwork, news clippings, and fan mail I didn't know what to do with. I had a cleaning lady who came in every two weeks, but even she didn't know how to organize a virtually empty six-point-four-million-dollar house that was being used as nothing more than a glorified storage unit.

"Soooo." I scratched the back of my neck. "I was kinda hoping to get things cleaned up before showing you this place."

Her face had paled. "Did...did you buy this?"

Pressing a kiss to the top of her hair, I mumbled nervously, "I did. You still like it?"

She quickly stepped out from under my arm, heading directly to the huge living room that ran the length of the house, complete with floor-to-ceiling windows that overlooked the large backyard nestled against a private lagoon. It was the room she couldn't stop talking about when we'd first looked at the place years earlier. I swear she and the realtor had fully decorated that room before we'd even stepped foot into the rest of the place.

When I'd first walked into that house, I'd had zero intentions of buying it. It was nearly twice what I'd wanted to spend and about ten times bigger than I'd ever need. It was a *home* in every sense of the word. The kind you raised a family in. The kind Till had bought for Eliza the minute he'd had the money. The kind Flint had bought for Ash even while she had still been running away from him. The kind a bachelor like me had no business even looking at.

But, for some inexplicable reason, after I'd seen Liv's excitement as she'd raced from one end to the other, sucking the oxygen out of each room as she'd oh'd and ah'd, I'd put in an offer the same night.

I had been confident when I'd bought the place, but now, watching her exploring the room—running her hand over the back of our old couch, which appeared miniscule in the massive space—I wasn't so sure anymore.

"When?" she whispered.

I drew in a sharp breath. "Two years ago."

Her confused eyes immediately lifted to mine. "Why didn't you tell me?"

"I tried. Remember when we came to look at it a second time and I asked you which bedroom you'd pick?"

Her hand slapped over her mouth, and her face turned sad in understanding. "Oh, God. You'd already bought it?"

I nodded. "Yep. I'd signed the contracts not even an hour before you informed me you weren't moving into a house with me." I laughed at the memory. "You said it would be weird for us to continue living together…especially after I'd bought a house. Funny thing is I've only recently realized that 'it's weird' is your go-to phrase when you freak out. If I'd known back then, I would have pushed harder."

"It would've been weird."

I crossed my arms over my chest. "Says the woman who's still freaking out."

She rolled her eyes and then moved to the windows at the far end of the room. "Living in an apartment together was one thing, but buying a house together. Quarry, it was too much."

After following her to the windows, I stopped at her side but shoved my hand in my pocket to keep from looping it around her waist. "It wasn't too much for *us*. It was too much for *you*."

Her voice was thick with regret. "That's probably the truth."

An awkward silence fell between us, and I swiftly pulled my phone out and turned a playlist on. Propping it on the edge of the window, I gave her the time she needed to process it all. But I didn't allow her to do it in silence.

Her face turned soft, and her hand caught my elbow, tugging my hand from my pocket before intertwining our fingers in unspoken gratitude.

We must have stood in front of that window for at least ten minutes. Watching her closely out of the corner of my eye, I squeezed her hand reassuringly when I felt her emotions build.

Finally, she asked the window, "Why didn't you leave? You bought this gorgeous house but spent the last two years in a cheap two-bedroom apartment."

"You," I told the same window.

She shook her head and dropped her chin to her chest. "That's insane."

It wasn't. Not knowing what I knew now. I might not have been fighting the need to strip Liv naked all those years ago, but I'd loved her all the same. And living without her hadn't been an option.

I cleared my throat and sighed. "I couldn't sleep that night. As naïve as it sounds, I'd never actually stopped to consider the possibility that you wouldn't move with me when we started house shopping. You were—are—a huge part of my life. I was still in a bad place back then, and I wasn't sure I could do it on my own."

She swung her head to look at me, but I squeezed her hand and kept talking to the window.

"I paced the hall all night long, eventually waking you up to bullshit about something. I can't even remember what it was, probably boxing or something equally as stupid to be discussing at two a.m. But, as usual, you gave me a grand pep talk and sent me to my room feeling better than ever." I paused to look at her. "After that, I decided to move. You made me realize that, whether you came with me or not, you would always be there for me. Only a phone call away, right?" I smiled painfully.

Liv didn't respond, but she tugged her fingers from mine and sidled closer until her front was pressed into my side. I soothed a hand up her back and sifted it into her long, brown hair.

Kissing the top of her head, I murmured, "I woke up three hours later to find you in my bed."

Her shoulders jerked. "I..." She rocked back a step, but I tightened my grip in her hair and refused her the space.

"It's okay. I've known for years. And, if you want to know my secret, I used to pray every night that I'd find you there. It was the only time I really slept."

She buried her face in my chest and mumbled something I couldn't make out, but I didn't ask for clarification.

"That's when I decided I couldn't leave you. I still have no idea what comfort I offered you by just being there in the middle of the night, but after everything you had done for me, I knew I'd never take that away from you."

With a gentle tug, I tipped her head back and forced her gaze to mine. Her eyes searched my face nervously, looking anywhere but at my eyes.

"If you need it, I want to be the one to give it to you, Liv. I felt that way then, and I feel it even more now. So I stayed."

When her eyes landed on my mouth, I offered her my most charming smile, being sure to pop the dimple I knew she loved so much.

"It wasn't exactly a hardship. I hate that apartment, but I'd have taken up residence on a park bench if that's where you were."

Her eyes fluttered closed, and a single tear rolled from the corner. I brushed my lips against her mouth, letting them linger without actually kissing her. Her body slacked in my arms as our breaths mingled between us. Sucking in deeply, I reveled in the feeling of more than just my lungs being filled. The hollowness I had been carrying my entire life vanished with every inhale.

"I gutted the guesthouse to make a gym. I come here a lot when I need to be alone. I wasn't lying to you about that, but you're right. I am a liar," I admitted on a whisper.

Her eyes popped open.

"I could stay in that apartment with you for the rest of my life, but I started to worry that, one day, you'd want to move out on me."

"What are you talking about?" She pushed on my chest.

I pushed back—with my lips.

She struggled for only a scant second before she melted. Our tongues tangled together. Slanting my head, I took it deeper, forcing a soft moan from her throat. My cock thickened between us, and Liv inched closer to press against it.

I was ready to throw her down and take her on the floor when she suddenly backed away.

"What have you been lying about?"

I groaned at her retreat, rushing forward, not stopping until her tight body was once again flush with mine. Lifting her off her feet, I walked to the couch and confessed, "I pay you shit as my assistant. Seriously, it's near criminal. But, if I'd paid you what you deserved, there's no way you would have stayed in our apartment with me. I couldn't risk you leaving."

A flash of relief hit her face, and then her lips tipped up, brushing against mine as she murmured, "I buy all of my shoes on your credit card."

I nipped at her bottom lip and gently lowered her to the couch.

"I know. Which is why I haven't been eaten alive by guilt over the years."

She giggled then gasped as I settled on top of her, my hard-on landing at the junction between her legs.

"Goddamn it, I hate when you wear jeans. How about you use my card to buy some fucking winter dresses?"

"I can do that," she replied, tugging my shirt off.

Sitting up, I peeled the shirt over her head and made fast work of stripping her jeans and panties down her legs and then removing my workout pants before moving back on top of her.

Her mouth landed on mine as I shifted to my side and squeezed my large frame into the back of the couch, my hand immediately diving between her legs. Her hips writhed as I alternated between gliding through her folds and circling her clit.

"Please," she moaned into my mouth.

She was drenched by the time I gave in and pressed a single digit into her tight heat. Her mouth disengaged from mine as her head flew back on a strangled cry.

Her dark nipples tightened as her hips bucked against my hand. I temporarily quelled her need by adding another finger, but it came with a price.

"Say you'll move in here with me," I ordered.

"Quarry," she breathed, circling her hips off the couch when my hand stilled.

"After that shit last night, I don't feel safe with you in that apartment anymore." I nuzzled her with the stubble on my jaw, feeling her breathy mews breeze across my skin. "I want you here, behind a security system and a gate."

"Please," she whined. "We can talk after you fuck me."

She was right. But that wasn't the way I was playing this. Without a doubt, she was going to fight me, but after my dream, there wasn't a chance in hell I was taking no for an answer. I'd been in a cold sweat all fucking morning, trying to figure out how I could keep from failing her again. I hadn't been planning to tell her about the house yet, but maybe her finding out the way she had was a sign from whichever god I hadn't pissed off yet.

"There's nothing to talk about." I twisted my hand and again found her clit with my thumb. "Say you'll move in here. This is different than the last time. We're together. We're starting a life. I need peace of mind that you're safe."

"It's too soon," she cried, rocking herself against my hand. "Please, Q. I need to feel you inside me."

I rolled on top of her, spreading her legs to accommodate my hips. Poising myself at her entrance I demanded, "Move in here with me."

"Fuck me," she ordered as a reply. Lifting her greedy little hips, she stole an inch of my length.

I watched in awe as she rode the tip of my cock from the bottom, moaning like she could come off that alone.

She was so fucking beautiful.

It was Liv though, so that wasn't exactly a surprise.

She was my undoing.

She was also mine now. And it was my responsibility to take care of her.

The one task I couldn't afford to fail.

Pressure mounted in my chest.

Through a ragged breath, I rasped, "Move in here with me." Even I heard the desperation in my voice as I finished with, "Please, Rocky."

She stilled immediately and, her eyes locked with mine. "Quarry?" she breathed in obvious concern.

With a hard thrust, I filled her in order to keep my overflowing emotions in check.

Her arms folded around my shoulders, clinging to me as I mercilessly drove in again. She moaned, and her pussy clutched my cock, even as she whispered, "What's going on?"

"I can't lose you too," I answered on a grunt when I roughly planted myself at the hilt.

"You'll never lose me," she pledged, rocking into me while I collected myself enough to start moving again.

After another hard thrust, I found myself even more lost. I couldn't get deep enough to experience any kind of pleasure. The anxiety and fear in my head numbed me physically, but I pounded away, desperately seeking comfort and reassurance within her small body.

And she freely gave herself to me as I fucked her harder than ever before. I bit her neck and painfully squeezed her breasts, trying to find anything that would make me feel again.

Her nails scored my back each time I slammed my hips against hers, and her fingers tugged at my hair as I raked my teeth over her neck and her shoulders.

She wasn't exactly in pain, but she wasn't far from it.

Yet she still gave it to me.

Her body was mine to do with as I pleased, and that notion made me take her even more savagely.

We were both going to have bruises when it was over, but I couldn't stop, and before I knew it, my mouth had joined the fuckfest.

"He killed you," I blurted.

Her body turned rock solid beneath me. "What?" she cried as I sucked hard at the soft skin beneath her ear.

One at a time, I guided her long legs around my hips and drove in impossibly hard. "In my dream this morning…when I got sick," I panted, drawing back slowly before slamming back in.

Her face contorted in a way that could never be mistaken for ecstasy. But her muscles pulsed around me when I stilled.

"Davenport." Trailing my mouth up her neck, I whispered the words I never wanted to hear myself say, "He held a gun to your head and pulled the trigger." My voice lodged in my throat, and my stomach knotted at the memory.

With one last powerful thrust, the fight left me in a rush and my body sagged on top of her.

It wasn't in the wake of orgasm.

I was lost in defeat.

"Sit up, baby," she cooed, pushing on my chest.

I sucked in and held it as I followed her order.

Moving onto my lap, she wasn't happy until my cock was once again seated inside her.

I buried my face in her neck and hugged her tight as she started to move over me. Her desperation was far gentler than mine, and it made me realize how severely I had taken her delicate body.

"Christ, Rocky. I'm so fucking sorry."

If she heard my apology at all, she didn't acknowledge it. "No one will take me from you," she vowed. "It's you and me. Forever." Slowly gliding up and down my shaft, she soothed my wounds by saying, "I'll move in, Quarry. Whatever you want. I'll do it. No argument."

I choked on my breath as it rushed from my chest.

God, she had no idea how much I'd needed to hear that.

"Oh, God!" I clung to her even tighter. Taking over, I lifted her up before slamming her down my cock, giving her the only thing I had to offer at the moment.

Her moans grew louder, but she wasn't getting closer to release—and neither was I.

"Quarry, stop," she finally whispered, pushing me back against the couch.

"Damn it. I ruined that." I pinched the bridge of my nose, not willing to look at her in the middle of my meltdown.

"Nothing is going to happen to me," she pressed.

I laughed without humor. "Famous last words." Sighing, I attempted to move her off my lap after having decided that it would be in the best interest of everyone involved if I just finished in the shower. Alone.

She wrapped her arms around me and refused to budge. "Don't push me away. Talk to me."

"What do you want me to say? I had a nightmare, and it fucking destroyed me. I'll be okay."

Her hand glided up the nape of my neck. "Okay, fine. I'll talk. I think you're about to go off the deep end. I said I'd move in. I said I'd do anything you want to make you feel comfortable, and I still feel like you just left me."

"I'm right here, Liv." I made my cock twitch inside her as further proof.

"You're all over the place, Quarry. I know you. This is what you do right before you lose your mind. You can't figure out how to make yourself feel better, and you're going to disappear into your own head, where whatever answer you come up with is going to be *wrong*. And, if it's anything like the one you came up with when we were kids, it's going to ruin us."

My whole body flinched at her honesty, but just as quickly, I felt relief. She knew me better than anyone in the world. There wasn't even any point in lying.

"I love you so fucking much."

Her arms convulsed around me.

"I can't stop preparing myself to lose you. I've not even had you a full month and I'm already obsessing about failing you."

"You can't fail me."

"I can. And I *will*. I always do. Eliza. Flint. You. Mia. The list just keeps on growing. And, last night, Davenport put his fucking hands on you because of me. I don't know what to do with that." I barked a manic laugh. "Clearly my subconscious does though."

I was gearing up for another round of word vomit when she interrupted me.

"You...you love me?" Her voice was so packed with genuine surprise that it almost offended me.

Grabbing her shoulders, I leaned her away and caught her equally disbelieving gaze. "Are you kidding me?"

She shook her head.

"Of course I love you. I always have. I've felt it my entire life, but something just clicked recently. It was like I'd buried it so deep within myself that, when it finally made it to the surface, we went from friends to soul mates in the span of a minute."

She didn't reply, but her breath shuddered. Her eyes filled with unshed tears, and a mixture of hope and fear showed on her face.

She was busy chewing on her lip when she lifted her hands and silently signed, *You think we're soul mates?*

"Without a question," I replied instantly.

"But what about—"

I narrowed my eyes and reminded her, "My cock is still inside you. Don't even say it."

"It's just—"

"Goddamn it. Don't!" I growled. "I love you, *Liv*. Whatever you're thinking right now, get that shit out of your head." I palmed each side of her face and dropped my forehead to hers. "I love *you*. I *love* you. *I* love you."

She swallowed hard and closed her eyes. "I love you too."

"Good to know," I breathed, pressing my lips against hers.

"I always have. Even when I wasn't supposed to."

I smiled a real honest-to-God smile.

"And I trust you, Quarry. So, if you want me to move into this absolutely incredible house, it will be hard, but I'll figure out a way to be happy about it." She giggled, and my veins flooded with relief.

Just that simple.

Just Liv.

Two minutes ago, I'd been on the verge of breaking down, but somehow, she'd flipped the switch. Calmed me in ways no one in the world had ever been able to accomplish—not even me.

"You serious about moving in here with me?" I whispered

against her lips while sporting an impossibly wide grin.

She nodded and opened her mouth, rolling her tongue with mine.

I took it greedily, my cock thickening all over again.

"And I'm talking one bedroom. We share a bed. No more of that roommate shit."

Her hands glided over my shoulders and up the back of my neck. "Okay," she murmured, rising up on my cock. "But I want you to talk to me about your dream. I hated the way you rushed out this morning."

I forced her down quickly, smirking when her throaty groan rumbled against my mouth. "Can I make you come first?"

"I already came."

My eyebrows popped in surprise. "You did?"

She laughed. "You were in the middle of some kind of barbaric mating ritual, but yeah, I came."

"Sorry about that," I lied, dropping my hands to her hips and rocking back and forth.

"Mmm," she purred. "Why don't I believe you?" Her head fell back as she started moving over me again.

I was about to take her hard and see if I could make her come again. But then she whispered, "You love me."

I smiled to myself and decided the fuck would have to wait.

"*Every. Single. Day*," I replied, reclining her down on the couch and then showing her exactly how much.

CHAPTER
Twenty-Eight

Liv

LUCKILY, IT WAS WINTER, BECAUSE when Quarry and I finally made it off the lonely couch in the middle of *our* enormous new living room, I realized I'd have to wear a scarf for at least a week. My neck was black and blue with a combination of hickies and bite marks. And he didn't look any better. He had claw marks covering his entire back. They were so pronounced that they could easily be made out even amongst the dense black tattoos. I made him swear on his life that he'd keep a shirt on at the gym until they healed. He made fun of me but reluctantly agreed.

We went to brunch that morning with my parents, where Quarry bluntly informed my dad about the new house and made it quite apparent to everyone at the table that this wasn't another roommate situation by *repeatedly* mentioning the need for a security panel in "our bedroom." My father didn't miss it. Neither did my mom. Dad's response was to scowl as Quarry possessively draped his arm around my shoulders. Mom's response was to shriek with joy. (I'd like to disturbingly note that she then quietly tugged at my scarf and exaggerated a knowing wink.) I couldn't stop the laugh that bubbled from my throat. My mom was crazy. And, if possible, I loved her even more for it.

After brunch, we made a brief stop at the wings place near the highway, and then my parents headed back to Chicago. Quarry and I went back to the new house, where he changed and went to work out. I spent the first hour taking measurements of each room. Then I made my way out to the gym and watched my man—the one I'd been in love with my entire life and who I now knew loved me too. And it came with the added bonus of him thinking we were soul mates, a fact I'd always thought but never dreamed he would too. And, for the first time, I could admit that I trusted him with not only my life, but my heart as well.

I'd been so wrong before.

It wasn't weird at all.

It was actually perfect.

For the next month, our lives became insanely busy. Don had called off for a family emergency the day after the Davenport incident. He didn't explain, but he assured me he was okay and that he'd be back right after Christmas. It was bad timing for him to be gone with Quarry gearing up for his big fight. Plus, we were trying to get moved into the new house before Christmas, but we did the best we could.

Which meant absolutely nothing got done at the apartment, and it was now the day before Christmas Eve and we were frantically trying to pack—just three hours before the movers got there.

Quarry was stomping around like a maniac, pissed because, while I had remembered to book the movers, I had somehow managed to forget the packers. I'd learned this little detail during the confirmation phone call the night before. Quarry had been none too happy, but after I'd spent over an hour talking to the manager, it had appeared we were on our own for packing. Quarry had rushed out and bought as many boxes as he could find, but it wasn't going to be enough. It was truly amazing how much shit the two of us had been able to cram into that apartment over the years.

"Babe!" Quarry called, suddenly appearing in the kitchen, where I was packing plates. His hands were filled with three boxes of Christmas tree cakes.

I rolled my eyes. "You don't have to show me every time you find more. I have admitted to having a slight hoarding problem when it comes to seasonal snacks, but you can't fault me. They are only available for a few months each year. Just put those with the rest of them."

His lips quirked humorously. "Really? You want me to just add these to the pile?" He opened the box and dumped them on the floor.

"Q! What the hell!"

"They're green," he informed.

"Of course. They're Christmas tree…" I paused when I got a better look at them. "Oh, God, gross!"

He laughed heartily and stepped around a mountain of boxes to link his arms around my waist. "Exactly how long have you been hoarding snack cakes in my room? Those expired three years ago."

"I have too many shoes to keep them in my closet."

He arched an eyebrow. "Those were under my dresser."

"Which is probably why I forgot them," I retorted snottily.

He only grinned then kissed me. Plates crashed to the floor, shattering as he lifted me to sit on the counter.

"Leave the plates and go pack your panties. I started to do it but stopped when I found your vibrator."

My mouth dropped open, causing his eyes to light with humor. "What the hell were you doing packing my panties?"

He ignored my question, pressed my legs open, and wedged his bulky body between them. "Your batteries were dead. Not sure if that means you've been hitting it every day or if you haven't used it in so long they died. Either way, it made my dick so fucking hard thinking about it." He licked up the side of my neck and threaded his fingers into the back of my hair.

My annoyance was trumped by the sudden heat pooling between my legs. "We have to pack," I moaned, angling my head to give him more access.

"I just got off the phone with the moving company. They're sending packers." He raked his teeth across my skin, sending shivers down my spine.

"I thought they didn't have any available?" I asked, not giving one single fuck about the answer as I glided my hand under his shirt and up his muscular chest.

"Being a professional boxer has some perks, Rocky." He took my mouth in a sweltering kiss, brushing his thumbs over my nipples when he pulled away. "Money doesn't hurt either, Cheapo." He suddenly stepped away and leaned his hip against the counter. Crossing his arms over his chest, he fought back a smile. "Guy told me you talked them down three hundred bucks."

"I had a coupon," I stated proudly.

His lips twitched again. "Right. Well, your *coupon* didn't get us packers, so I paid him an extra grand. Now, we have packers. So let's pack the shit you don't want strangers touching, like, say…your panties and whatever other sex toys you have hidden in your room, and head back to the house, where I can fuck you without the panties but maybe with the toys and then wait for your million Christmas tree cakes to be delivered this afternoon." He grinned wolfishly.

His plan was definitely better than mine.

"Sorry I dropped the ball on this moving thing. I've been so busy."

He helped me off the counter, not putting me down until we'd cleared the broken glass. "I know you have, and you need to slow down. What if you stepped down as director at the community center and took a volunteer position?"

"What if you stop suggesting that I quit the job I love?"

He groaned. We'd had that argument at least twelve times over the last month. We both knew that it wasn't going to end well for him.

"Okay, okay," he surrendered. "I'm just saying you don't *have* to work anymore. Well…I mean, you don't have to work for anyone but me anymore." He patronizingly patted my ass.

Swatting his hands away, I made my way into my bedroom, where sure enough, my vibrator was sitting on my dresser. "Well, you should know, if you keep that attitude up, I'm replacing you permanently with this." I lifted the toy at him.

He laughed loudly. "You're so full of shit."

I really was. Not a toy in the world could replace Quarry. Which was exactly why it was no longer in my nightstand but rather untouched in my panty drawer. I'd gone through more batteries than I'd ever admit over the last few years, but now that he was in my bed every night, I had no use for them anymore.

"Whatever," I replied when a witty retort failed me. After nabbing a box off the floor, I threw it in his direction. "Okay, you pack the top shelf in my closet, and I'll handle my unmentionables. Then we can get the hell out of here. The packers can do the rest."

"Oooo, the top shelf! Whatcha got hiding up here?" he teased.

I shrugged, grabbing my own box and going to work on my drawers. "Not much. Just my collection of midget porn. And the dominatrix whip I've not had the chance to use on you yet."

"Shut the fuck up!"

"I believe the correct answer is: Yes, mistress. But I'll give you a free pass for now since I haven't beaten you into submission yet."

He chuckled, and I heard him digging around in my closet.

A few seconds later, he sighed. "I'm not sure what it says about me, but I'm disappointed to find out you were kidding. Maybe we should make a stop before heading back to the house."

I shook my head with a huge smile on my face. "Just pack," I told him, mentally scheduling a stop at the sex shop to pick up a few last-minute Christmas gifts for my guy.

We both went back to packing boxes.

Holiday music was playing through the speakers in my room while I meticulously folded my underwear, matching them with my bras, when a loud curse caught my attention.

I spun and found Quarry reading papers I immediately recognized.

"Are you fucking kidding me?" he boomed, murderous eyes jumping to mine.

My chest tightened, but my pulse spiked in anger. No one got to read my letter from Mia. Not even him.

"What the hell are you doing?" I stomped toward him and tried to snatch it from his hands, but he lifted it over his head, holding it out of my reach.

"Please, God, Liv. Tell me this is a fucking joke," he snapped.

I stared at him in confusion. What was he mad about? *He* was reading *my* letter—not the other way around. I never would have done that to him. Never.

"Did you seriously just read my letter from Mia?" I yanked at his arm, but it was useless. He was too tall and strong for me to do anything about it.

"I damn sure did," he sneered, storming out of the room.

"Give that back to me. You have no right to…" I rushed after him but paused when I reached his room.

The muscles in his neck were straining, and his nose was still buried in my letter, but his other hand was outstretched, offering a hot-pink envelope my way.

"Why the fuck have we never traded letters?" he asked without looking at me.

"Uh, because they're private," I said, lunging forward and trying to snatch my papers from his hands.

He backed out of my reach.

After tossing the envelope on the bed, he started counting something on the paper.

"Damn it, Q. Give that back to me!"

He finally looked up—a mischievous smile softening his irate face.

"Twenty-seven," he stated in an eerie whisper. "Twenty-fucking-seven, Rocky." He took a dangerous step in my direction.

I instinctively backed away. "W-what?"

He passed me by and snatched the envelope off the bed. "Read it."

I shook my head. "She wrote that for you. It's none of my business what it says."

"You aren't even the tiniest bit curious?" He quirked his lips, incredulous.

I glanced at the envelope and lied. "If she'd wanted me to read it, she'd have addressed it to me."

Groaning in frustration, he looked back down. "Right. Loyal to a fucking fault. Okay." He laughed without humor. "Quiet, quick, quilt, quirk, quaint, quizzical, queasy, quality, quill, and quasi." His eyes flashed back up. "And that's only the first paragraph." He dragged a frustrated hand through his hair. "For fuck's sake, Liv. Please tell me you are not this blind."

Clearly, I was, because I had no clue what the hell he was ranting about. I did know he had my letter and was acting like an asshole for no reason. I focused on that.

"Give me my letter!" I shrieked, losing all patience.

Quarry had already lost his though. He picked his letter up off the bed and made a dramatic show of opening it and then reading. "'I love you, Quarry Page. And I know you loved me too. But, if you're reading this, I'm past tense. You can't be afraid to move on. Live, Q! Love. In the present! Go! Like, right now! Put this letter down.' He paused and lifted his eyes to mine before finishing. "'*And live.*'" He dropped his paper back on the bed and then flipped to the back of mine. "'You can't be afraid of the quiet, Liv. The only thing hiding in the silence is the loneliness in your heart. Quell the silence and find a way to move on. Quit living in fear and quench your thirst for life the way you've always wanted to. You deserve it.'" He stopped and looked up, unimpressed. "Please fucking tell me that you realize that bullshit makes no fucking sense."

I reached forward and snatched my letter from his fingers. "What I know is that you had no right to read that. Those were her final words *to me*. They don't need to make sense *to you*."

He crossed his arms over his chest, and I watched his anger disappear right before my eyes. A small humor-filled smile crept across his face.

"So you think it's completely coincidental that she used twenty-seven words that start with the letter Q in your letter? And I'd like to point out, while I didn't go to college, I'm pretty sure she spelled quintessentially wrong and I don't even think qat is a real word."

I opened my mouth to reply then quickly closed it. I'd actually never thought of it before. Mia had been crazy. Her letter might not have been a work of art by Shakespeare, but it had comforted me on many nights over the years. I'd never once questioned her motives when she'd written it. Now...

Quarry slowly approached, pinning me against the wall with his hard body. Tenderly cupping my cheek, he whispered, "I suppose you also think it's a complete coincidence that my letter clearly states that I should 'move on and live.' Again, I'm not nearly as well educated as you are...but after seeing your letter, it's not fucking lost on me that your name happens to be Liv and my nickname is Q."

My breath caught, and my eyes began to sting. I had no idea what to say.

Quarry did.

"We're not wrong, Rocky. I have no idea what the fuck kind of game she was playing. Or why she would have even attempted to play it. But I'm sorry, it says something that, even in her last days, she gave that to us. I know you, and while I can tell you've put that guilt aside and committed to me, I'd bet my fucking bank account that it's still hidden inside that beautiful mind of yours somewhere."

At that, my eyes didn't just burn—they leaked. He knew me well. No matter what the price, I'd decided I was going to be with Quarry. But there was always going to be a tinge of guilt over the fact that a part of me had wanted him even while she'd been alive. I was suddenly realizing that it wasn't nearly the betrayal I'd made it out to be. Mia had obviously recognized it, and better yet, she'd known I'd loved her enough that I never would have made a move on him. She'd *trusted* me. That alone set me free. I should have known she hadn't been stupid. No, Mia March had been an incredible—albeit slightly twisted—person. This stupid letter crap was merely her way of giving me permission to have the one thing I'd always wanted.

Him.

"Why was she so freaking weird?" I asked through tears. "She couldn't just say, 'Hey, it's okay if you two want to hook up.'"

Quarry chuckled, pulling me tight against his chest. "No, because I'm pretty sure she would *not* be okay with us hooking up. She'd find a way to cut my nuts off from the great beyond if she thought I was *just* fucking you."

I laughed through tears. "She totally would."

"She wanted us to be happy, Liv," he whispered, brushing his lips against mine. "And she knew that, after she was gone, you were the only person who would ever be able to give that to me." He released me and crouched down so we were eye to eye. Holding my gaze, he swore, "She was right. No one in the world could have pulled me out of the darkness, time and time again, the way you have. I don't know why you and I had to suffer to get here, but this right here is how it was always supposed to be. I've never been able to find a purpose in her death before, but those letters, the way I feel right now, knowing I can finally have *all* of you… I can't help but feel like maybe this was her purpose. This was the madness we had to overcome in order to finally realize we were meant for each other."

Staring into the hazel eyes that had always owned my heart, I couldn't help but agree with him.

I sniffled and dropped my forehead to his chest. "Qat is a word."

He chuckled. "Learn something new every day."

After gliding my hands up his chest, I circled my arms around his neck, "I love you."

"I love you too, Rocky. Every. Single. Day."

CHAPTER
Twenty-Nine

Quarry

"WHAT WERE YOU THINKING?" I bit out, pacing a path into the manicured grass. Considering I was alone and standing in front of Mia's grave, my question went not surprisingly unanswered.

It had been a while since I'd been out to the cemetery, but after dropping Liv off at the new house, I knew that it was time for a special trip.

"Those letters were the most ridiculous play I have ever seen. Do you have any idea how hard I've had to work to convince her that we weren't having an affair on you? For fuck's sake, Mia. You really could have saved me a lot of trouble if you'd stopped with the mind games." I stilled, glancing down at the small stone that marked her final resting spot. At the sight, the pain still sliced through me, but a smile grew on my face. "Thank you," I whispered into the cold, dark night. My breath formed a puff of white, and as it dissipated, it took a lifetime of pain along with it. "Thank you so fucking much for her."

I stood there for a few minutes longer, trying to find words to express my gratitude for the way Mia March had touched my life.

For keeping me in line as a teen when I'd thought that, at any minute, the world was going to crumble at my feet.

For loving such a broken boy who had been so angry that he couldn't even figure out how to love himself but had somehow found a woman who would love him anyway.

For accepting Liv and healing her timid soul in a way I never would have been capable of doing.

For being so strong in the face of death that she'd still had the foresight to offer Liv and me peace in a world where she no longer existed.

And, most of all, for just being the type of woman who loved with wild abandon even in the middle of utter chaos.

She'd been gone for almost five years, and I could have stood there for five more, trying to find those words of gratitude, but that wouldn't have been living. Right then, the woman Mia had all but given to me was at home, curled up next to a fire, waiting for me to come home, so that's what I did.

With a simple nod, I signed the words *I love you* and then headed back to my car.

"Leo, come on, man!" I complained.

Liv shifted in my lap, passing me her empty wine glass to set on the end table. "Let him talk," she scolded, burrowing into my side.

It was Christmas night, and we were all over at Till's house, relaxing after a huge dinner. Slate and Erica had come over with their kids, and Leo and Sarah had driven down the night before with Liv's little brother, Ty, so we could all be together on Christmas Day. I had personally invited Leo with one thing on my mind, but as he stood in front of my entire family, preparing to tell this story, I knew I'd made a huge mistake.

"Jesus, how old were you, Q?" Leo asked, but I refused to answer.

"Thirteen!" Till called out with a huge smile from the couch, his arms securely anchored to Eliza's thigh. His other was wrapped around a beer.

"Right. Okay, so he was thirteen. You have to remember Quarry didn't look anything like a kid back then. I knew grown men who would have cowered if he'd approached them in a dark alley."

"Damn right!" I yelled, causing the whole group to laugh.

"So there I was, doing some paperwork in Slate's office, when the door swung open, and lo and behold, there stood this mutant teenager. I shit you not, the light flowed in from behind him like he was the grim reaper coming to take my soul."

I groaned, knowing that, if this was the sensationalized spin Leo was giving it, this story was going to get a whole lot worse in a few minutes.

Liv looked back at me and giggled. I found not one thing funny, but her exuberant reaction still made me chuckle.

Leo continued. "When my eyes adjusted, I couldn't believe what I was seeing. The Great 'Stone Fist' Page, king of amateur boxing, was standing in front of me with tears streaming from his eyes." He raked his fingers down his face to exaggerate the tears.

"It was, like, one tear!" I shouted.

"Bullshit! I've seen rivers that contained less water."

I cursed under my breath, and Flint decided to chime in.

"Little baby Q always has been good at the waterworks."

I flipped my brother off before turning my attention back to Leo. "Can you just fucking get on with it?"

"Language!" Sarah yelled with a grin, tossing an empty water bottle at me.

I quickly caught it and then hurled it at Flint. He easily caught it and acted like he was going to retaliate, but I ducked my head behind Liv.

Erica scowled and then confiscated the bottle like we really were the kids we were acting like.

Leo started up again. "You should have seen him. His chin was quivering and everything. I'd heard all the trouble he'd been in since coming home from Till's fight in Vegas. Hell, I think it's safe to say we were all having trouble adjusting to life after that."

A solemn air blanketed the room at the mere mention of that day. We all recognized it, and Liv went stiff in my arms at the memory.

Flint decided to lighten the mood. "Not me," he said. "I had a blast in Vegas. Came home with a set of new wheels and everything."

Ash tapped her foot against the bottom of his cane and shuffled under his arm, tossing him a glowing, white smile that visibly eased him.

A warmth washed over me when my kiss on Liv's temple seemed to have the same effect on her.

"Right. Well, at this point, Quarry had been skipping almost every day at school, and the few days he did attend, he'd somehow managed to get into so many fights that he'd gotten expelled. Oh, and even though he seemed to truly love brawling, he'd decided to quit boxing. He was one step away from being a juvenile delinquent, and there he was, standing in front of me, begging me to let him see my daughter." He laughed, but the humor fell from his voice as he swung his angry gaze to mine. "The same daughter who was never the same after that day in Vegas, either."

"Daddy," Liv warned when Leo's glare lingered for a few uncomfortable beats.

It sucked, but I deserved far worse, so I squared my shoulders, held Liv on my lap, and took the heat.

Still holding my gaze, Leo puffed his lip out in an exaggerated a pout, "'But…but, Leo,'" he mimicked in a baby voice. "'I…I love her. I'm a Page man… We know love.'" His scowl turned into a grin as the room started laughing.

Liv quickly looked at me. Her eyes were wide and downright hopeful. "Did you…" she trailed off.

I didn't want this story to be told at all, but that look on her face made every second of the embarrassment completely worth it.

I confirmed with a nod. "I wasn't wrong." I lifted my chin to Till and Eliza then to Flint and Ash, "We do know love."

She sighed like it was the most romantic thing she'd ever heard.

Leo silenced the room with a hand and pushed further. "You should have seen his face when I wrapped my hand in his shirt, snatched him off the ground, and pinned him against the wall." He scratched his chin and asked, "How'd it go after that, Q?"

I cleared my throat and lied. "I can't remember."

"Luckily for you, I do." He smirked. "I said, 'Well, marry her, then.' You all should have seen his face as it morphed into absolute terror. I swear, right then and there, he developed a stutter." Again with the baby voice. "'L-l-like right now, Leo?'"

I dropped my head and laughed right along with everyone else, including Liv. "Yep. Laugh it up! Hi-larious!" I said, tickling her.

"Poor kid looked at me like I was about to force him to the altar." Leo barely managed to get the words out around his laughter. "After that, 'The Stone Fist' was more than willing to listen to anything I had to say. The first thing I told him was that I would never allow him near her again if he didn't get his shit together. This included, but was not limited to, studying hard, making good grades, being the decent human being I knew he was capable of, treating Till and Eliza with respect, and securing his future by getting back in the ring we all knew he was born for."

The laughter quieted.

"The second thing I told him was that, if he was man enough to know that he was in love with her, he was man enough to realize that she deserved better than him. I stand by that opinion too. But you see, Quarry caught me on a loophole. My daughter was twelve, so, Sarah, you'll have to forgive me here." He looked back at his wife, who was all but glowing. "I told him if and when he accomplished all of that, I would personally walk her down the aisle to him one day."

The women all swooned.

Liv's hand found mine and intertwined our fingers.

Oh, but Leo wasn't done yet. Not even close.

"You know, Liv, I wasn't around when you were born. I've always regretted that. I missed so much of your life in those early years, and your mom can attest to this. But I vowed shortly after you came to live with us that those days were over. So I'm real sorry if I ruin this for you, baby, but you have to realize Quarry has made good on his promises to me."

My entire body went on alert as Leo's face softened while looking at his daughter.

"He's a good man, Liv. He can more than provide for you and whatever family you decide to make in, say…twenty years. While you two haven't been 'officially' together for a long time, I'd have to be blind not to see how much he loves you."

I pushed to my feet with Liv still in my arms. "Leo," I said, attempting to cut him off as Liv slid to her feet.

He kept right on talking. "There is not a doubt in my mind that he would lay down his own life to protect you from even a second of harm. And, for those reasons alone, I gave him my blessing to ask for your hand in marriage not even an hour ago."

Son.

Of.

A.

Bitch!

The room broke into a mixture of gasps and loud laughs. I, however, closed my eyes and cursed under my breath as Liv turned rock solid in my arms.

"Sorry, son. She'll like this better. I promise. That quiet proposal around the Christmas tree wasn't going to cut it for me." Leo chuckled before walking over to grip my shoulder.

"Wow. I was unaware my proposal had to cut it for you *at all*," I growled, pinching the bridge of my nose.

It was Liv's quiet voice that caught my attention.

"Proposal?" she squeaked.

Opening my eyes, I found her staring up at me with tears pooling.

It was not at all how I had planned it.

I had the grand idea of us being alone—together in our new house. Lounging in front of a crackling fire with the twinkling lights of our Christmas tree glowing in the background. Liv's small body tucked into my side—my strong arms protectively wrapped around her. I'd nuzzle into her hair and remind her that, while we had only been together a few months, we had already spent a lifetime together. She'd smile up at me with those big, brown doe eyes. I'd place a gentle kiss on her lips, and when she opened her eyes, I'd be holding the diamond ring I'd had custom-made for her the day after she'd told me that she loved me.

That had been my plan.

This—in the middle of Till's living room with both of our families looking on—was definitely Leo's plan.

However, the *yes* shining bright in her eyes was more than enough to have me abandoning my plan altogether.

"So…funny story," I started nervously. "I asked your dad a little while ago if he'd be okay with me proposing."

"So I've heard," she breathed.

I glanced up to find every eye in the room glued to me. Ash, Eliza, Erica, and Sarah were crying already. Slate was grinning impossibly wide. Flint was wearing a crooked grin I'd long since discovered beamed with pride. And Till and Leo looked every bit of the emotional fathers they were. Every face, no matter the emotion, was covered with a huge smile.

Maybe surrounded by family wasn't the worst way to do this.

I looked back down at Liv, who was staring up at me with rapt attention.

"Hang on. Okay?" I said. Then I released her and jogged from the room.

I could hear the loud chatter of questions as I rushed to my gym bag hidden in my old bedroom and pulled out the ring I'd shown Leo.

Shoving it in my pocket, I made my way back into the living room.

"Sorry," I said, wiping my suddenly clammy palms on my jeans.

Why was proposing so nerve-racking?

I knew that Liv was going to say yes, but my heart still raced as I took her small hand in mine.

Her bright eyes sparkled with unshed tears as she looked up at me. "You don't have to do this just because of my dad."

"You're right. I don't. Technically, I don't ever have to do this." I smirked, pulled the huge, square diamond solitaire out, and lifted it in her direction.

Her hand flew to her mouth, and she reached toward the ring before pulling her hand away. It was as though she were afraid to touch it for fear it would disappear.

"This. Changes nothing, Rocky. Sliding this on your finger won't make me love you any more than I already do. A romantic vow won't change my dedication to you. A marriage license won't make us any more serious. This ridiculously expensive ring changes absolutely nothing but my bank account." I paused as she giggled. "With or without this ring, I'm going to spend a lifetime with you. I'm still going to love you until the day I die. Nothing changes, Liv. Nothing."

I sucked in a deep breath, but I didn't hold it.

Not now. Not with Liv.

Dropping to a knee, I said, "I will love you forever. But that doesn't start when I give you this ring. It started the very first time I laid eyes on you—and it will never end. Marry me, Liv."

She didn't say a word as she flew into my arms and buried her face in my neck. Her shoulders shook, but I had no idea if she was crying or laughing. I figured, either way, it was a positive sign, so I squeezed her impossibly tight. Glancing up at the warm faces of our family surrounding us, I couldn't even be pissed at Leo anymore. The smiles were bright as love illuminated each one of them.

Some minutes later, Liv still hadn't answered.

"I know I said that you don't have to say yes, but it would go a long way in not making me look like a dumbass right now." I whispered.

She barked a laugh and leaned away, replying with a megawatt grin, "Yes."

No sooner had I slid the ring on her finger than she was gone.

Her mother hugged her. Her dad shook my hand, welcoming me into the family. Ash and Eliza squealed over the ring, while Till and Flint each took their turns wrapping me in a painful bear hug.

Eventually, Eliza rushed to the kitchen and made quick work of uncorking the champagne she had on hand for New Years, all the while scolding Till for having bought the cheap stuff. Ash went to work passing glasses to everyone, and Flint made a toast, but I couldn't concentrate long enough to hear what he was saying.

I was in a state of absolute shock while staring down at Liv James tucked under my arm, admiring her engagement ring—*my ring*.

I was right. The ring changed nothing.

That one simple syllable in the word *yes* though?

Changed my entire life.

CHAPTER
Thirty

Liv

"YOU HAVE A GOOD NIGHT," Rich, the night guard, said.

"You too." I smiled warmly and drove out of the parking lot.

At the first stoplight, I dug my phone out of my purse in order to type out a text to Quarry, letting him know I was on my way home. But I realized my phone must have died somewhere over the last three hours, and my charger was connected to the wall in my office.

"Shit." I breathed, debating the merits of circling back around to get it versus just driving all the way to the new house without a phone.

It had just started snowing, and the roads were bound to be icy. Quarry would probably have a shit-fit if he knew I was even considering driving without a phone. I groaned to myself then pulled a U-turn.

The parking lot was empty, and the building was dark. It scared the crap out of me, but I sucked it up and managed to get through the front door, immediately clicking the Christmas music on over the new intercom.

Less than a minute later, I was once again arming the alarm when a sudden pounding on the glass door made me jump.

"Shit!" I screamed at the top of my lungs.

My heart was pounding as I took in the large shadow lurking outside the door. It took me a second, but I smiled when I recognized the bright-blue eyes staring through the glass.

"Sorry," he mouthed, lifting his hands in apology before shoving them into the pockets of his heavy coat.

I twisted the lock and pushed the door wide. "Jesus, Don. You scared me to death."

"I knocked quietly at first, but I guess you didn't hear me." He looked up at the speakers on the ceiling. "I see the intercom system got fixed."

I sighed and locked the door behind him. "Yeah. A lot of things have changed around here." I took a giant step back and dramatically lifted my arms.

The room instantly illuminated with lights.

Don laughed and nodded approvingly. "Motion sensors. Nice."

"Oh, you have no idea. My dad and Quarry got their hands on this place right after you left. New security system. New lights. New intercoms. Guard at the door."

He leaned away and frowned. "Is the guard imaginary?"

"Ha! No. Rich just left. I circled back around to grab my charger." I lifted the cord as evidence when his frowned deepened.

"You shouldn't be here alone, Liv. It's dangerous."

"Well, so is driving in the snow with no cell phone."

He gave me a you-should-know-better glare that made me roll my eyes then smile.

"Okay, Pops. I'll be more careful next time. But I'm glad I came back. What are you doing here?"

He shoved his hands in the pockets of his jeans and rocked onto his toes. "I was on my way home and saw your car. Decided to stop in and see if you'd already replaced me."

"Replace you? Are you kidding me? No way." I playfully slapped his arm.

He immediately grabbed my hand. "Holy shit. Look at that rock."

My cheeks heated. "Quarry proposed last night."

"Uh, yeah. I noticed." He lifted my hand to inspect my ring. "Christ. I bet the astronauts on the space station have probably noticed too."

"Quarry isn't exactly a simple and understated kind of guy."

"I'd say not." He smiled tenderly. "You got a minute? How about you plug in your phone and catch me up on the last month while it charges."

"Well…" I drawled, glancing down at my watch.

My parents and the Page family would already be waiting for me at our house, but if it meant I got Don back, Quarry would happily keep them entertained.

"Only if you being here means you're back."

He patted his stomach. "I don't know. Are there any Christmas cookies left? I've lost five pounds over the last month. I'm borderline emaciated."

"You happen to be in luck. I brought in a batch tonight."

Ten minutes of catching up with Don wouldn't hurt anyone.

It hurt *everyone*.

"We need to talk," Flint said when I opened the front door.

Leo and Slate were stoking the fire, and Sarah and Erica were cooking in the kitchen.

"Hey, Q." Ash pushed to her tiptoes and kissed my cheek.

"Where's Liv?"

I held Flint's troubled gaze as I replied, "She should be here any minute. She had a class to teach tonight."

"Babe, can you go call the babysitter and check on the boys?" Flint asked.

She huffed. "We've been gone ten minutes. I'm sure they are fine."

"Humor me," he ordered dryly.

She rolled her eyes and flittered away.

"What's going on?" I asked as soon as she was out of earshot.

"This is not public yet, but I just heard from my guy at the boxing administration that Davenport is being stripped of his belt."

"What?" I gasped.

"Two fighters have suddenly stepped forward about Davenport pulling the same shit he did on Liv with their women. Loman and White. Loman had a surveillance video, but considering his girl was actually his mistress, he wasn't all that excited about releasing the footage of her being assaulted. Davenport's manager paid off the chick, and then, after White lost the fight, it all disappeared right along with him. However, Loman's footage magically landed on the boxing commissioner's desk last night."

My jaw ticked, but my smile grew. "Apparently, Leo's been really fucking busy over the last month. Good to see my dollar's being well spent."

Flint narrowed his eyes. "You knew about this?"

I crossed my arms over my chest. "No. I knew that Davenport was a piece of shit. There is no way that motherfucker hadn't pulled this shit before. I only funded Leo's efforts to take him down. Liv would have stroked out if I'd ripped his dick off the way I would have liked to, but no fucking way I was letting him get away with the shit he did to her."

He blew out a frustrated sigh. "Fucking hell. I guess this is a good thing, seeing as to how it doesn't end with you in prison, but bad news—fight's off."

I shrugged arrogantly. "Shame. I was looking forward to it."

Flint laughed. "I'll make sure you're in the ring to claim his vacant title."

"Twenty-two percent of sixty million? I bet you will." I playfully jabbed at his shoulder.

"Hey! Feeding all of Ash's stray dogs is expensive as fuck."

I arched an incredulous eyebrow. "Thirteen million dollars' worth of dog food?"

He threw a hand to his heart in mock surprise. "Dear God. The dumbass can do math! I should probably stop padding my fees now."

I laughed and kicked his cane, but he didn't even stumble. "Shit. Between you and Liv skimming off the top, it's a wonder I have any money at all."

He started toward the living room. "Have you spoken to your accountant recently? You might not."

Liv

"So then he dropped to a knee, and obviously, I said yes. I'm thinking a summer wedding. My mom is already chomping at the bit though. We'll see if I can hold her off that long." I lifted my phone to see that Don and I had been chatting for well over twenty minutes. "Shit! I need to get out of here." I pushed to my feet.

Don stood with me. "Well, congrats. I'm glad to see he finally did it."

I smirked. "Finally? We've only been together for a few months. This was fast."

He sheepishly glanced down at the ground. "Right. Well. Since, it's Christmas and all, I have a bit of a confession. When I first came in for my interview, I recognized you. I'm a huge boxing fan, and I'd seen you in pictures with him. Everyone thought you were his girlfriend. I forget sometimes that you two were just friends at first."

My eyes went wide, but a laugh bubbled from my throat. "You rat! I can't believe you didn't tell me."

"Like you would have hired me if I'd spent the entire interview talking about boxing."

"If you were signing, I doubt I would have cared. I was desperate. What else have you lied about? Do my cookies suck too?"

"Uh, no. But I will admit your brownies are better," he teased.

I started collecting my phone and my charger in preparation to leave. "You know, now, I don't feel so bad about basically abusing your volunteer assistant services." I smirked. "Come on. Let's get out of here. I need to get home before Quarry sends in the SWAT team to look for me."

"Smart girl," Don said, turning the lights off.

After flipping the Christmas music off and arming the security alarm, I was digging my keys from my purse when Don clicked the inside lock and pushed the door open. The alarm started beeping our warning that we had sixty seconds to exit the building just as the cold, biting wind rushed in.

I was still focused on my purse when Don's back suddenly collided into me, sending us both to the ground. I was in such shock that I didn't even have time to get my hands under me to break my fall. My head cracked hard against the tile floor, and my vision tunneled.

Then I heard a deep malicious voice roar, "Where the fuck is he?"

Don climbed off me.

I couldn't get my bearings to figure out what the hell was going on, but my questions were soon answered.

"Back the fuck up, Davenport!" Don growled.

My eyes came into focus just as the icy metal edge of a knife landed against my throat. I froze as panic overwhelmed me.

"Where the fuck is Page?"

"I-I don't know," I lied, my eyes filling with tears.

Dropping to his knees over me, he gripped the crown of my hair and pressed the knife even deeper into my throat until I felt the warm trickle of blood slide down to my collarbone.

"Where is he?"

I opened my mouth to answer, but it was too late.

I ran out of time.

Quarry

"Shut the fuck up!" I laughed at Till, who was telling yet another embarrassing story from my youth.

"Dirty shirt and all. You didn't give one single damn. Six years old and you were asking out my girl."

The whole room was laughing when, suddenly, Leo's phone started screaming in his pocket. It was an annoying-as-hell ringtone, but it was the way his face paled that really caught my attention.

He quickly released Sarah and frantically started digging out his phone. His wild gaze lifted to mine from across the room. "Call Liv," he ordered.

My heart lurched, but I followed his direction without question.

"What the hell's going on?" Slate asked, reading the sudden shift in the room.

Leo ignored him and began pacing the room with his phone at his ear.

The drone of an unanswered phone played in my ear as my eyes remained glued to Leo.

"Rich, tell me all is good," he barked. After several agonizing seconds, he growled. "Well, she's not fucking here yet!" Pinching the bridge of his nose, he lifted his distraught eyes to mine in question.

I shook my head and fear sliced through me—the sound of her voicemail iced my veins even further.

"Get your ass back over there. I'm en route." He lowered his phone.

His legs were already moving to the front door when I caught his arm.

"What the fuck?"

He snatched his arm out of my grip, not even sparing me a glance as he raced out the door, yelling, "She supposedly left over a half hour ago, but now, the alarm is going off at the community center."

Terror and fury mingled in a dangerous cocktail within me. Snatching my keys from my pocket, I rushed out of the door after him.

Liv

"Please. Stop," I cried as Davenport used my hair to force my face into the security panel by the door.

"Turn it the fuck off!" he shouted.

"I-I can't think!" I sobbed.

The alarm was blaring, distracting my already-hysterical mind even more.

He yanked my hair so hard that my knees almost buckled from the pain. "Turn it off!" His face shook with exertion, and spit flew from his mouth.

My eyes bounced to Don's body unconscious on the floor. The moment the alarm had sounded, Don had made a move, but Davenport had been quicker. He'd never even let go of me as he'd landed a nasty right to Don's chin. The only positive of this was that the knife he had been holding had gone skittering across the floor.

"Now!" he barked, shoving my face back into the security panel.

I sucked in a deep breath and tried to get myself together. Finally, I came up with the right combination of numbers and the room fell quiet.

"Damn it!" Davenport slung me forward.

I stumbled before slamming into the tile and then skidding to a halt on my knees.

Just as quickly as I'd gone down, I popped back up, scampering to get away. I didn't make it but a few steps before his thick arm hooked me around the waist.

"Where you going, Livvie?" he purred, lifting me off my feet and holding my back to his front.

Bile crept into my throat as he rubbed his scruff into my cheek.

I wanted to fight any way I could. Claw my way out his arms, biting and scratching before jamming my high heel into his balls. I wasn't usually a violent woman, but I had an overwhelming urge to watch him bleed out onto the floor in a slow and agonizing death. I wasn't going to be able to do that to him though. Quarry had told me not to challenge him, and right then, I knew exactly why. Physically, Davenport was superior to me in every way.

"Nowhere," I replied through clenched teeth.

"Good answer," he said, carrying me across the room.

I went willingly until I saw his knife come into view on the floor.

My legs thrashed violently, but his large hand bit into my hip as he bent over to retrieve it.

"Easy there," he soothed. "I'm not going to hurt you."

I sucked in a shuddering breath, fighting back the reemergence of my tears.

"At least, not without Page here to witness it."

Quarry

I don't remember taking a single breath as I sped down those icy roads faster than any mortal should ever drive. My lungs were on fire, and my chest ached with every passing minute. The gas pedal was on the floor as I weaved through traffic like a maniac. I'd even passed Leo on the highway.

I was less than a minute from the community center when Liv's number lit up my cell phone. A huge breath of relief flew from my mouth, and my foot slowly lifted off the pedal.

"Thank fucking God," was my greeting.

"Don't come here!" she screeched into my ear, spiking my pulse all over again.

My lead foot fell back on the accelerator. "Liv!"

I heard the bellow of a maniacal laugh.

"You better hurry." Davenport's voice filtered through the line, solidifying my worst fears. "Before it's too late"

"What the fuck are you—" I started but stopped midsentence when Liv's agonizing screams hit my ear. The pain in her voice was paralyzing, and my already-tense body convulsed. "Liv!"

I helplessly held the phone as her cries continued. It wasn't until her voice disappeared that I realized Liv had always been right.

The silence was fucking terrifying.

Liv

"Please don't do this!" I whispered, cradling my dislocated finger against my chest.

Davenport had left it mangled after forcefully ripping my engagement ring off.

"Please, shut the fuck up," he replied, casually lifting my ring in the air as if he were inspecting the stone.

Tears were streaming from my eyes as I stared at my phone, lying on the floor across the room. The screen was lit with an incoming call, which I knew was Quarry. Davenport had just hung up on him. I was in unbelievable pain, but nothing hurt as much as the agony in his voice as he'd shouted my name just before the call had been ended. It was a sound I could never unhear.

Suddenly, red-and-blue police lights caught my attention as they filled the parking lot. Davenport gripped the back of my neck and hauled me in front of him.

"Looks like your boyfriend brought reinforcements." He laughed, not a care in the world.

He was seriously insane, and as if I hadn't already been scared, the sound of his hollow laugh sent me into the petrified territory.

Movement from the floor caught my attention.

Don was starting to come to.

Lifting my hands, I silently signed, *Help is here. Don't move.*

His confused eyes shifted from me to Davenport before closing again.

I was forced to the double glass doors, where dozens of police cars had joined our party. Tears of relief flooded my eyes as I saw my dad's SUV and Quarry's Porsche parked behind them.

"He took my belt," Davenport whispered ominously.

"N-not yet. You could still win," I replied as a cold chill ran down my spine.

"Dumb bitch," he mumbled.

I saw Quarry's strong body in the crowd long before Davenport did.

But, judging by the terror on Quarry's face, he saw Davenport lift the knife long before I did.

We *all* heard the gun explode before Davenport did.

Quarry

It was unquestionably the scariest moment of *my entire life.*

"No!" I roared as a gun fired from out of nowhere just as Davenport lifted a knife to Liv's throat.

It was a wonder I wasn't sucking the oxygen out of the state of

Indiana for as hard as I had gasped. Blood roared through my veins as my worst nightmare played out in front of me. Dozens of officers were rushing toward the door when another shot was fired, forcing them all to shift to the sides of the building, flanking the door.

"Get down!" an officer at my side ordered, but my legs were already moving—and it wasn't to hide.

Sprinting down the middle of the sidewalk, I ignored every single officer shouting my name.

Fueled by desperation and adrenaline alone, rational thought left me. I would not fucking fail Liv James—no matter the cost to myself.

Yanking on the glass door, I found it locked. My chest heaved as I prepared to bust it down. But I paused when I saw Liv scrambling away with Davenport hot on her heels. Frantically, I banged on the door, trying to catch his attention, but then everything suddenly got worse.

In that moment, I didn't even know that was possible.

But it was my life. It could always get worse.

The only person I could ever hate as much as Garrett Davenport suddenly appeared in front of me with his gun held high, aimed directly at my chest.

The moment his blue eyes met mine, his face softened.

Get back, he mouthed.

I couldn't do anything but blink.

Swinging his gun away, he lifted a single hand and signed, *I'll get her.*

I had been wrong.

That was unquestionably the scariest moment of *my entire life.*

"Dad!" I screamed, pounding my fists on the glass as he disappeared down the hall.

CLAY PAGE

I had been a lot of things in life: thief, con man, gambling addict, drug dealer, bookie, inmate. Most recently, I was the assistant to the director for the American Sign Language program at the local community center.

It was a job I took very seriously.

If you asked my kids, they would probably add a few other names to my laundry list of titles, such as: spineless, slimeball, coward, deadbeat, worthless, loser.

And they'd be right.

Over the years, I had more than earned every single one of those. However, that didn't change the fact that, over ten years later, the only title I truly wanted was father.

And it was the only one they would *never* give back to me.

And they'd be right for that too.

I'd spent years watching my kids grow up and start their own families through the pages of sports magazines. After the shit I'd put them through, I didn't even deserve that. But I was lucky enough to have donated sperm to create some amazing men. I'd followed Till closely as he'd grown up, selflessly giving back to not only the community, but the boys I'd abandoned when I'd lost myself in a life of drugs and gambling. I'd watched my weak and premature baby boy Quarry grow into one of the toughest fighters to ever step through the ropes. Flint had been harder to track, but a life of crime had some benefits. I'd called in some favors, and I had been able to get enough info to find myself in the audience the day he'd crossed the stage to get his college diploma. I hadn't even graduated high school, and there he was, paralyzed, relearning how to walk, and still graduating with honors in only two years.

And Eliza had been right all those years ago when we'd first met in Las Vegas—I had not one thing to do with any of it.

Those boys had forged their own path through life and come out the other end stronger than I could have ever imagined.

I *was* a loser.

I *was* spineless.

I *was* a deadbeat.

But I still missed them more than words could ever express.

So, when I caught wind that Quarry's long-time girlfriend had put an ad in the newspaper looking for an ASL assistant, I jumped at the opportunity. That first meeting, I went in guarded, unsure if she'd recognize me. But I should have known my boys wouldn't have photos of dear old dad lining the walls of their new multimillion-dollar mansions. If they were as smart as I thought they were, any evidence of me had gone up in smoke years earlier.

After I got the job, I fell in love with Liv. It was easy to see why Quarry loved her like he did. I didn't get to see her often, but on the days I did, she'd fill me in on what was happening in the boys' lives. She loved the Page brothers so much that it didn't take but a single question before she'd whip her phone out and show me countless pictures of my grandkids. I never would have gotten that without her. It was well worth the rest of the bullshit of grading papers and tutoring the adults.

And, right then, I was pissed all to Hell and back that Garrett Davenport had just cost me all of it. I'd been gone for the last month to avoid having my identity exposed after his first stunt. Now this? Fucking asshole.

I'd cleaned up my life a good bit, but I still had warrants out for my arrest and a pretty fucking substantial gambling debt, not even to mention the unregistered—and probably stolen—gun I had just fired in front of half of the Indy police force. There was no way I was making it out of that building without a pair of cuffs, but before I went in for my extended stay at the big house, I was finally going to do something right for my boys.

"Garrett!" I yelled, following the path of lights that had been triggered by motion sensors.

The creaks from the soles of my shoes against the tile were the only noise in the building. Even Quarry's shouts from the front door had fallen quiet. I jerked every door open as I slowly made it down the hall. Davenport was nowhere to be found. And, if I could just find Liv, I could let the cops in to clean up the piece of garbage. But I didn't trust that that mental case wouldn't hurt her when a million uniforms rushed into the building.

I'd shot him in the leg when he'd lifted that knife to her throat. He wouldn't find himself lucky again. I was aiming a little higher this time.

"Oh, Davenport!" I singsonged down the hall.

After I'd snatched the door to the supply closet open, I caught sight of Liv. I could barely make out her silhouette through the darkness, but from what I could tell, she was folded into a ball with her head on her knees. She didn't look up as I jerked the door wide. It was for the best though. It meant she didn't see when Davenport appeared out of nowhere and tackled me to the ground.

"Son of a bitch," I groaned.

The guy was huge, so there wasn't much I could do except for kick the door shut so he hopefully didn't see her. The gun vanished during the scuffle; that was probably my only saving grace. Because, as much as I wanted to destroy that piece of shit, I figured killing him might not help my pleas for leniency in court. So, while I couldn't do much to fight against him without a weapon, my only other option was to draw him away.

His fist landed hard against my face just as my foot stomped the bleeding hole in his thigh. He howled in pain, allowing me the opportunity to climb to my feet and haul ass back to the front door. I swear to God it took every ounce of self-restraint I had not to roll my eyes as I heard his grunts as the dumbass limped after me.

After I'd reached the doors, I was fighting with the locks, trying to get them undone, when the insane ogre finally caught up. Steeling my shoulders, I braced for impact. He plowed into me—just seconds *after* I'd twisted the final lock open.

I couldn't even count how many times his fists landed on my face. But, as officers rushed in, I took every single blow with a smile, knowing that, for the first time in my life, I'd finally done right by my kids.

CHAPTER
Thirty-One

Liv

"I'M NOT SCARED," I WHISPERED, sinking even deeper into his arms. The warmth of his strong chest pressed into my back, reminded me of the security that only existed when I was with him. "I knew you'd come." I turned my head to nuzzle against his bicep, his arms tightening around me. "I'm safe with you, Quarry," I mumbled—my words from all those years ago, wholeheartedly believing them all over again.

Even if he was only in my imagination, nothing could hurt me when I was in his arms.

Not Davenport.

Not knives.

Not guns.

Not pain.

Not fear.

Not when I was with him.

"Just a few more minutes," I whispered.

A tear dripped off my chin, joining the growing collection in my lap.

"Just a few more minutes." I repeated.

Not even a second later, a soundless sob tore from my throat as Otis Redding's *White Christmas* filled the silence.

My breath caught on a shudder. "He's coming."

Quarry

The officers had just gotten Davenport in cuffs, and I didn't wait for a sign, nor did I ask for permission before I rushed into the community center in search of Liv.

"She's in the supply closet in the hall," Clay called out as he lay face down in a pair of cuffs.

My heart stopped, and the very idea of her hiding in a dark closet made me want to kill Davenport that much more. And I'd already wanted to watch him burn alive. Now, even that was too kind.

That would have to wait though.

I paused only long enough to press the power button on the speaker system, turning it as loud as it could go before sprinting down the hall.

"Rocky!" I yelled over the Christmas music. I began snatching door after door open, finding each one empty. With only one left at the end of the hall, I sucked in a deep breath, holding it as I slowly opened the door.

There she was.

Still breathing.

Heart still beating.

Scared to fucking death, hiding in a motherfucking closet.

But she was still alive.

Still mine.

Forever.

"Liv," I said softly, dropping to my knees beside her.

Her arms were wrapped around her legs, her forehead resting on her knees. She flinched when I brushed her hair off her shoulder. "Are you okay, baby?"

I could barely hear her when she asked, "Are you really here?"

My voice lodged in my throat. I couldn't be positive of the answer, but if it were a dream, I never wanted to wake up.

"Yeah, Rocky. I'm here. You're safe now."

All at once, she dove into my arms. Burrowing her face in my neck, she clung to my shoulders as sobs ravaged her. "I-I didn't know where else to go."

"Shhh. You did good." I stood up with her in my arms.

Leo was just outside the door, his pale face etched with relief. I was sure it matched my own.

"I knew you'd come."

"Always." I kissed the top of her head. "*Always.*"

I carried her into a breakroom across the hall. Settling in a chair, I held her securely tucked against my chest. Her mom, along with Till and Flint, appeared in the doorway, and Leo paced the length of the room, only stopping to snap his fingers when an officer would try to interrupt us.

The Christmas music had been turned down, but it still softly played in the background as I allowed her the time to collect herself.

"Is...is Don okay?" she finally asked.

"Don?" The proverbial light bulb went off above my head. "Oh, God. Is the old guy your assistant?" If I hadn't been holding her safely in my arms, that would have been the moment my blood began to boil all over again.

She nodded without looking up.

"He's fine," I said shortly, looking to Leo, Till, and Flint, whose angry faces told me they were sharing my little realization.

307

"Can I see him?"

"No," we all snapped entirely too roughly given her current state.

Her head popped up, and she looked at me before nervously flashing her gaze around the room. "Why not?" she asked in a shaky voice.

"Because he's probably on his way to jail right about now."

"No!" She jumped to her feet. "He didn't do anything wrong."

"His name isn't Don, Rocky. It's Clay Page."

Her eyes grew wide in understanding. "No way."

"I have no idea what this was about, but I'm gonna find out. I swear, if he had anything to do with this—"

"He didn't," she whispered sadly. "He tried to save me. He yelled at me to run after he shot Davenport…but I remember what he did to Flint and Eliza." She stopped, and tears once again filled her eyes. "This is too much. Can we just go home now?"

"Yeah, babe… Jesus!" I cursed when I saw her swollen and contorted ring finger.

"I'm fine," she immediately lied as her father closed in on her.

"No, you are not!"

"What the fuck!"

"Shit!"

That had all come from the door.

"Medic!" Leo yelled.

"Oh my God, Daddy. Stop! I'm fine."

"Let me see," Till said, busting into the middle.

"Move!" Sarah exclaimed, pushing him out of the way.

Flint even got in on the action, lifting his iPhone and talking out loud as he started Googling finger injuries.

I didn't move. Not even an inch. I sat in the chair, watching her cop an attitude with her parents while batting off my brothers' concerned hands.

I swallowed hard as the adrenaline started to leave me. My mouth dried, and I folded my hands together, linking them behind my neck to hide the fact that they had begun to shake. My mind went to work terrorizing me with all the possible what-ifs that could have happened. I felt like the biggest pussy to have roamed the Earth, but the intensity of it all was crippling. I must have looked like hell, because Liv's attention snapped to mine, concern and understanding painting her face.

"Everyone out," she demanded. "Now."

Till walked over and squeezed my shoulder. "You're okay. She's okay. We're all okay. Nothing else matters, Q. Not Dad. Not Davenport. Nothing."

"I know," I replied unconvincingly, my impending breakdown only seconds away.

I was still struggling to collect myself when the door clicked behind them. A second later, Liv climbed into my lap.

"You okay?" she asked.

"Nope." I sucked in a deep breath, holding it as I stared up into her dark-brown eyes.

The warmth only she possessed slid through me, soothing me from the inside out. Her tender gaze slowed the vortex in my head, and with a slight reassuring tip of her lips, the world suddenly became manageable again.

"But I will be," I finished.

"We both will be." She brushed her lips across mine. "Every. Single. Day, Q."

It was a promise.

And the only words that could ever quell the anxiety blazing within me.

"Every. Single. Day," I repeated back to her.

CHAPTER
Thirty-Two

Flint

Six months later...

"GET YOUR FUCKING HANDS UP!" I yelled at Quarry after he'd taken a hard right. "What the hell are you doing?" I shouted over the sold-out crowd in the same Vegas arena we had almost been ruined in all those years earlier.

"Give him a minute!" Liv shot back, nervously twirling her wedding ring around her finger.

After the whole Davenport incident, Quarry had thrown one of his testosterone-induced temper tantrums and insisted Liv marry him as soon as possible. She'd reluctantly agreed, and then we'd watched yet another one of his fits when he realized "as soon as possible" wasn't the very next day. As usual, Liv had talked him off the crazy-train, and three months later, they'd said, "I do," in front of over five hundred guests in an insanely over-the-top wedding in Chicago.

"He's not going to have a minute if he doesn't get his head together," I retorted, flinching when he caught another blow.

"He's got this," she assured. "You know Q can't do anything without being dramatic. This is just the buildup."

"He does love the drama," Ash stated in agreement.

"You are entirely too chill right now," I told Ash. "Just so you know, if he wins this fight, we make double on the next one."

Her eyes flashed wide, and then she shot to her feet, shouting, "Get your fucking hands up, Q!"

I laughed without dragging my eyes off the action in the ring.

The bell rang, and Till and Slate climbed into Quarry's corner, forcing him on to the stool and icing his swollen left eye. Till's hands were signing a mile a minute, and Quarry was smiling and shaking his head at everything he said.

Little shit.

Some things never change.

At least they didn't until I caught Liv signing to him, *You're scaring me.*

Quarry's face turned to stone, and he quickly nodded at her.

"You want to sit down?" Ash asked, ducking under my arm.

"No." I smiled.

Tipping her head to the side, she asked, "What are you smiling about? I figured you'd be cranky Flint after that round."

I flashed her a wide grin. "This is the dream, Ash. For all of us. I'm *standing* here, with my wife, in the building where I was shot and paralyzed over a decade ago. Till won his fight. He's no longer deaf. Eliza's safe. My father is in prison. And we all have the opportunity to replace the memories of that God-awful night with this moment right here." I squeezed her tight into my side and kissed the top of her head. "My little brother is about to achieve his lifelong goal of fighting for the world heavyweight championship, where, win or lose, he'll make enough money to support even our great-great-grand-kids. When we were kids, we couldn't even dream of something this big. And look at us now. We have it *all*. Cranky Flint doesn't even exist in this moment."

Till

"*Stop showboating and finish this shit!*" I signed, squirting water in Quarry's mouth.

If his wicked grin was any indication, though, he didn't give a damn what I'd said. He was going to finish the fight the way he wanted. Such was life with Quarry. And it had only gotten worse over the last few months.

When Davenport had been deemed mentally incompetent to stand trial, Quarry had changed. I'd expected him to do what he usually did and get pissed off and show his ass in one of his usual hotheaded ways. He hadn't done any of that though. Quarry had actually chilled out. It was like that wedding ring Liv had slipped on his finger held some sort of magical powers—or, at the very least, tranquilizers. When the judge had issued his verdict, I hadn't been required to wrestle Q to the ground in order to keep court security from tasering him. He hadn't even flinched, actually. He'd just walked out of the courthouse with his arm draped around his new wife and never looked back.

Liv was a saint. I'd spent my entire life up until that point trying to keep Quarry from overflowing, and she could do it with a single glance. Like the one she'd just shot him from outside the ropes. It was exactly why he was smiling. And the only reason I had any faith that this might actually be the final round.

As Q pushed to his feet, I followed Slate out of the ring.

"He gonna stop screwing around?" Slate asked, crossing his

arms over his chest.

I shrugged. "Hell if I know. Ask that one." I pointed over to Liv, who was nervously toying with her ring but doing it while sporting a mischievous smile that matched my brother's.

My eyes drifted to Eliza, who was doodling on a sketchpad, not paying any attention to the fight. She loved boxing. She just hated watching Quarry. I couldn't imagine how she was going to handle it when little Slate got in the ring. He was already chomping at the bit, but she'd made me promise to wait until he was at least eight. Only a few more months.

As if she could sense me watching her, her gaze flipped to mine. "*You did it,*" she mouthed as she signed.

I arched an eyebrow and signed back, "*Did what?*"

"*This.*" She motioned her finger down the front row, where Liv, Ash, and Flint were all sitting. "*That.*" She pointed to Quarry in the ring. "*All of it.*"

I shook my head as the bell rang, starting a new round. "*They did this.*"

She smiled and then tipped her chin to the ring.

I looked back up in time to see Quarry storm forward, dodging a jab before landing a combination ending with a knockout left hook.

The arena exploded in loud cheers as the ref started to issue the count.

My heart exploded when he got to ten.

He did it.

He fucking did it.

Pride soared.

Flint and Liv appeared at the ring before I even had a chance to climb inside. Liv wasn't exactly one to adhere the formalities, so she was in the ring with her legs locked around his waist before his opponent had even made it off the mat.

My mind was reeling as I spun in a circle, listening to the crowd chanting our last name. It made me a bitch, but the emotions of it all were staggering. Photographers clicked away, capturing history. The crowd roared, celebrating right along with us. Every major network on television had a cameraman on the skirting, fighting for the best angle.

I could have been blind and still would have had the best seat in the house just because I was his big brother.

That was how championships were supposed to be won. Quarry didn't have to rush from the ring to find out his brother had been shot. His pregnant wife hadn't been kidnapped. He got to actually enjoy it.

And, because of that, I was wearing an impossibly wide smile and enjoying it too.

Amongst the chaos, I found myself looking for Eliza once again. Ringside was a mess, but I finally located her standing on her chair in the front row, holding her sketchpad up. Scrawled across it, in big letters, were the words: *This is reality.*

I couldn't fight back the emotions any longer.

Reality didn't seem like the right word at all.

That moment felt a whole lot like fantasy to me.

Quarry

Standing in the middle of the ring while thousands of cameras flashed around us, I kissed Liv one last time before lowering her back to the feet.

"*Go. Celebrate,*" she signed, backing into my corner.

The sound of the announcer's voice was so loud that even my weak ears couldn't miss it. "Winner and *new* heavyweight champion of the world, Quarry 'The Stone Fist' Page!"

The ref made a move to grab my glove, but I had other plans. Evading him, I walked to my corner. Tearing at the tape on my gloves with my teeth, I yanked them off without even asking for help.

Slate smiled proudly as I lifted both fists and bowed to him with immeasurable gratitude.

"Thank you," I mouthed.

He continued to grin and simply nodded, wrapping his arm around Liv's shoulders.

"Yo! Come here!" I yelled at Till, who was staring at Eliza in the crowd. Then I turned, snatched Flint's cane out of his hand, and tossed it into the corner. "Come on." I dipped my shoulder under his arm to help him balance.

The three of us walked to the center of the ring together.

I hadn't won that fight alone.

I wouldn't have even made it to the fight without them.

Sure, we all had wives now. They had kids. We owned homes—huge ones. Our bank accounts held more zeros than we could have ever imagined. Yet, somehow, we were still the three broke kids in stained shirts and dirty jeans, eating ramen noodles in our filthy kitchen.

And that was exactly how I knew we had truly made it.

Till, despite the fact that he'd been forced into parenthood at twenty-one years old, still smiled with the crooked grin and mind-blowing confidence I'd spent my entire life trying to mimic.

Flint walked with a cane, yet every single step he took had a purpose. Whether it was digging clothes from the free bins at the local church or negotiating a sixty-million-dollar contract, he'd always been there for me no matter what.

I wasn't the only champion in the ring that night.

So, with Till on my right and Flint on my left, I lifted all of our fists in victory.

EPILOGUE

Liv

"I'M NERVOUS!"

Quarry laughed and shook his head. "Why?"

"What if my voice is annoying?"

He looked at the audiologist. "Any chance this baby comes with a mute button?"

I slapped his leg. *"I'm serious!"*

"So am I!" he teased, brushing my hair over my shoulder.

Rolling my eyes, I crossed my arms and rested them on my swollen belly.

Quarry had been wrong the day he'd proposed. Nothing stays the same forever. Over the years, everything had changed for us. However, it wasn't a bad thing, because we'd changed together.

After the Davenport incident, my life had flipped upside down. The press had launched full force on the community center when the story broke. While I had been insanely proud of everything I had accomplished while working there, it had been clear that it was in everyone's best interest for me to resign. Once Quarry had won the title, he'd been even more famous than before, and as his wife, my life had been slung into the spotlight right along with him. I couldn't teach anymore, but sign language was still my passion. So I became an advocate and spokeswoman for the National Association of the Deaf. With a little help from Q, we were able to raise enough money to fund over twenty new ASL programs across the country.

Three years after Quarry had first won the title belt, his hearing suddenly took a significant turn downward, and within a few months, he was completely deaf. As to be expected, I flipped. He just laughed and held me. I was six months pregnant at the time, and what I had expected to be a meltdown as my husband entered the world of silence turned into a hormone-induced fit of epic proportions. Quarry wasn't concerned in the least though. He was sad that he was going to miss hearing the baby cry for the first time, but he simply stated that holding his son safe in his arms would be more than enough to make up for it. And the day March Leo Page was born, I knew he'd been right. Watching my husband—my soul mate—tough, tattooed fighter, Quarry "The Stone Fist" Page, holding his son was the most beautiful sight I'd ever seen. And that said a lot because Quarry had given me a beautiful life.

Kids were another thing that changed our lives tremendously. March was born with my dark skin and eyes, but he was one hundred percent his father's brand of trouble. And that did not bode well for us. We adored being parents, but we both questioned if we could handle another one. We loved March more than life, but one was enough for us.

Or so we thought.

After Ash and Flint adopted a little girl, baby fever hit me—hard. I feared Quarry's head was going to explode when I told him that I wanted to try for another child. March was starting first grade, and we'd already made several large donations to his private school to ensure he wouldn't get kicked out—again. Things were finally starting to calm down for us, so Quarry put his foot down on the baby thing. Which caused me to put *my* foot down and reject his definitive no. We argued for weeks until he finally shut down all further conversations in order to focus on his next fight. I was pissed, but he swore we could revisit the topic afterwards.

Quarry successfully defended his title eight times over the course of his reign in the ring. And, even after he'd lost it, he remained a substantial competitor in the sport. Proof being that, even at thirty-three years old, he was offered another shot at his old belt. A shot he not only took, but also won. That wasn't all that shocking though. He'd been born to be a champion.

However, it was at the press conference after the fight where he truly surprised everyone—including me—by announcing his retirement. When a reporter asked him what he was planning to do next, his gaze had bounced to mine as he proudly answered, "First, I'm gonna knock up my wife. Second, I'm getting a cochlear implant so I can finally hear my little man screaming at me. And, lastly, I have no fucking clue. But one and two are more than enough to keep me busy for a few years."

Yep. He was still breathtakingly unapologetic. That would never change.

And that was how I ended up eight months pregnant with our daughter, Quinn Eliza Page, and sitting in a doctor's office, anxiously waiting for them to activate my husband's cochlear implant. The entire Page family was not-so-patiently waiting in the hall. Actually, it seemed like Quarry was the only relaxed one. Even March, who was digging through all the doctor's drawers, seemed edgy.

"*You ready?*" the doctor asked from behind his computer.

"*No!*" I exclaimed.

Quarry chuckled and squeezed my leg. "I think he was talking to me, Rocky."

I chewed on my bottom lip. *"Right. Well, my answer remains the same."*

"Look at me," he urged.

I peeked up at him, tears already pooling in my eyes.

"What the hell? Why are you crying?" His face gentled. Tossing an arm around my shoulders, he pulled me into his side.

"I have no idea! It's just a big change." I sniffled.

"Come on. This is nothing. Now, in a few weeks when you give birth to that hellion growing inside you, *that's* going to be a change. This though? It's the easy stuff, Rocky."

It *was* easy. Especially compared to everything we had already overcome together.

Quarry's dad was definitely one of those hard things for the two of us. Actually, he was a tough subject for all the Page brothers. Clay had had quite the rap sheet, including blowing parole, so when it had come time for sentencing, it was clear he'd never walk as a free man again. This bothered me more than I could ever explain. I owed my life to "Don Blake," but the rest of the Page family still wore Clay's scars.

When the truth came out about why Clay had been at the community center with me that night, everyone had seemed relieved. Watching their faces when they'd realized he'd actually done something right for once was the only happy part of the whole ordeal. And, because of that, I never could have fathomed Quarry's reaction when I'd innocently mentioned mailing his dad a letter in prison. He'd been livid. Till had shared his opinion, but Flint, surprisingly enough, had taken my back on the issue. After multiple heated family discussions, Till, Flint, and—yes—even Quarry had eventually given me permission to mail their father monthly pictures. This agreement had come with caveats. The two biggest being: I was never allowed to give him our address, and I wasn't allowed to have any correspondence with him. No notes. No chats. For the love of God, no visits. Only pictures. I'd immediately agreed. All things considered, it was more than fair. And it spoke volumes about the amazing men the Page brothers had become.

"Relax," Quarry urged, brushing his lips across my jaw. "This is a good thing."

I swallowed hard and nodded, not even the least bit relaxed.

March suddenly flopped into the chair beside his father. "*Is she seriously crying again?*" he signed.

Quarry smirked and ruffled our son's dark-brown hair. "If you think this is bad, you should have grown up with Aunt Eliza. She cried about everything, pregnant or not."

"*She still does,*" he mumbled. "*So, you getting new ears or what?*"

Quarry's gaze drifted back to mine, and he arched an eyebrow in question. "I don't know. Am I?"

Drying the tears from under my eyes, I straightened in my chair. "*Yeah. You're right. This is nothing.*"

Tossing his arm around the back of March's chair, Quarry anchored his hand on my thigh. "Okay, Doc. We're ready."

The doctor began rattling off information, going over a few simple instructions and warning us to keep our expectations low. We had been told that sounds were easy, but it sometimes took a while for voices to become clear with the implant. And, over the last few days, I'd been obsessing over the fact that, sometimes, it didn't work at all.

I listened with rapt attention, but Quarry barely paid him any mind and instead snuck his fingers down to tickle March's neck.

I tapped his arm to catch his eyes then snapped, "*Pay attention!*"

He made teasingly wide eyes at March, which made him laugh, before turning back to me. "Okay. What in the ever-loving hell is going on with you right now? You freaked when I lost my hearing. Now, you're freaking when I'm about to get it back?"

I swallowed hard, those damn tears appearing once again.

"Jesus Christ," he mumbled, pulling me back into his side. "Maybe we should come back another day."

"*No!*" I shot up straight. "*I'm sorry.*" I glanced at Quarry, strategically avoiding the doctor, who was impatiently glaring at me. "*I guess… It's just… I don't think I've ever realized how much I want this for you. And, now, I'm scared that it won't work.*" I smiled tightly.

His face warmed in understanding.

"*Mrs. Page,*" the doctor said, interrupting our conversation. "*Can I please reiterate what I told you during our phone call last night?*"

It was my turn to glare at him. That call was supposed to be our little secret.

"You did not call him last night!" Quarry howled with laughter.

"*I was nervous!*"

The doctor didn't wait for us to quiet before continuing. "*The failure rate is less than one percent. Mr. Page is an excellent candidate, so I don't anticipate any problems today whatsoever.*"

"*Well…what if—*"

Quarry cut me off. "So what. So what if it fails? So what if I can never hear again? Is that a bad thing?" he asked me.

"*No. Of, course not. It's just—*"

"You hate the silence. After all these years, I know that better than anyone. But I'm not scared. I'm not nervous. I'm not upset. I'm not anything. I want to hear my kids. And you. And my brothers. And their kids. I want to watch a movie. And listen to music. But, if I don't get that, so fucking what?"

March slapped his arm to scold his father for cussing, but Quarry ignored it.

Taking my hand, he leaned even closer and implored, "Nothing changes, Liv. Whether I hear it or not, our lives are still going to happen. We're still going to be happy. We're still going to be together. You're still going to pop out my daughter in a few days. March is still going to grow up—God help us all. We're still a family, Rocky. We go home together and keep living, no matter what the outcome is. It's what we do. Together. Always together."

Even I couldn't argue with that logic.

I did hate the silence. I even still slept with music on, but with Quarry sound asleep at my side each night, the volume was significantly lower—and, truth be told, sometimes it was virtually inaudible.

But I was no longer living in fear.

We had both vowed the day we'd gotten married that fear and insecurity were no longer a part of our lives. Our love was dense—filled with the solitude of our past but empowered because we'd made it through together. Nothing could take that from us.

We had each other.

Every. Single. Day.

Forever.

So, staring into his hazel gaze, I dried the tears from under my eyes and squared my shoulders. "*Let's do this.*"

A smile spread across his face. "We're ready, Doctor."

Moments later, Quarry's eyes lit.

Moments after that, they filled with tears.

"Hey, Daddy." March smiled, popping the dimple that matched his father's.

"Oh, God," Quarry choked, covering his mouth with a hand. Turning to me, he admitted, "I think you were right. This was a bad idea. I'm never gonna be able to ground him again if he calls me Daddy like that. We're screwed." He then smiled, scooped March into his lap, and tickled him.

I let out a loud laugh, and Quarry immediately froze.

His gaze snapped to mine, and his lips twisted in pain.

"Quarry?" I asked, concerned.

He lifted a finger, asking for a second, and then shifted March back to his chair.

Cautiously, I rubbed his back, waiting for him to collect himself.

"I just…" he started in a gravelly voice before clearing his throat to finish. "I didn't realize how much I missed your laugh." He gripped the back of my neck and pulled my face against his chest.

His strong heart beat a staccato rhythm in my ear, melting the anxiety away.

Purring, I curled in closer. "I love you."

He squeezed me tight. "I love you too, Rocky."

March interrupted our quiet embrace by announcing, "I'm telling Uncle Flint that Daddy cried."

"Don't you dare!" Quarry laughed.

In that moment, my smile was unrivaled.

That was one thing that would *never* change.

Every. Single. Day.

Forever.

FIGHTING
Solitude

ON THE ROPES SERIES

THE END

ACKNOWLEDGEMENTS

And here we are again. Ten books later and I'm pretty sure I have thanked everyone in every possible way. Why? Because I'm one of the few who has been lucky enough to collect an amazing team. I didn't write this book alone. It took a village.

Allow me to break this down for you.

Poor Mr. Martinez spent countless hours being Mr. Mom for our kids so I could write. (I'm a lucky lady.)

Mo Mabie, Meghan March, Erin Noelle, and Jessica Prince were the lucky four who got to listen to be bitch and complain every step of the way when Quarry wouldn't do what I told him to. (Trust me, I totally understand how Till feels now.)

Ashley Teague spent many of nights talking to me about Liv's obsession with Christmas tree cakes. (We may or may not have been dieting and hungry at the time.)

Natasha Gentile spent hours upon hours searching for the perfect gifs to adequately explain how mean I was. (She's right.)

Amie Knight and Miranda Arnold spent long nights scouring the Internet in hopes of finding just the right hot guy inspiration to keep my words flowing. (It's a tough job.)

Bianca Smith and Bianca Janakievski read every dreadfully unedited word and pretended that they knew what I was trying to say. (Not even kidding when I say, that *is* a tough job.)

Megan Cooke slaved over beta notes that were roughly the same length as this book. (She's awesome like that.)

Mara De Guzman kept me thoroughly entertained by sending me the play-by-play as she read. (And unlike Natasha, she didn't tell me I was a terrible person once. HA!)

Elle Jefferson sent me the most amazing emails yelling at me for making her cry in public. (It's a skill of mine.)

Stephanie Rose almost missed her train stop twelve times while beta-ing this. (Now if that is not dedication, I don't know what is.)

Danielle Buol saved you *all* from having to meet Mrs. Marched. (She's kin to Flinted in Fighting Shadows.)

MJ Fryer and Gina Barrett were my lifesavers. They proofread the hell out of this book. (Unfortunately they didn't proofread these acknowledgements. You have been warned. HAHA!)

Mickey Reed sacrificed the keys H, A, and D on her laptop. (After adding the word "had" approximately 467897363567 times while editing.)

Stacey Blake has already started filtering her emails waiting for me to send her a million emails to fix a typo in her beautifully formatted book. (I mean seriously. Look at that header!)

TRSOR Promotions has more than likely blocked me on Facebook at this point after my one hundredth message that asked, "How many ARCs are we sending out again?"

The Vegetarians have held my hand for ten books now. Encouraging me with the likes of "Eggplant Friday" and "Vegetable porn." (Don't ask. I love them so hard! Pun intended.)

Then there are all the bloggers and readers who have left amazing reviews. (There would be no Page brothers without them.)

So to make a long story even longer...Yes, it took a village to publish this book. And I can't imagine what I would do without them!

Thank you all from the bottom of my heart.

ABOUT THE AUTHOR

Born and raised in Savannah, Georgia, Aly Martinez is a stay-at-home mom to four crazy kids under the age of five, including a set of twins. Currently living in South Carolina, she passes what little free time she has reading anything and everything she can get her hands on, preferably with a glass of wine at her side.

After some encouragement from her friends, Aly decided to add "Author" to her ever-growing list of job titles. So grab a glass of Chardonnay, or a bottle if you're hanging out with Aly, and join her aboard the crazy train she calls life.

Facebook: https://www.facebook.com/AuthorAlyMartinez
Twitter: https://twitter.com/AlyMartinezAuth
Goodreads: https://www.goodreads.com/AlyMartinez

62127665R00183

Made in the USA
Charleston, SC
11 October 2016